I0561211

THE GUARDIAN

BLOOD IN THE SNOW

MJ Kobernus

NORDLAND

www.nordlandpublishing.com

Copyright

The Guardian – Blood in the Sand
Copyright © MJ Kobernus 2016

This is a work of creative fiction. Names, characters, places, events and incidents are either the products of the author's imagination or used in a fictitious manner.

Any resemblance to real persons, living, dead or immortal is purely coincidental.

MJ Kobernus asserts his moral right to be identified as the author of this book.

All rights reserved. This book, or any portion thereof may not be reproduced or used in any manner whatsoever without the express written permission of the author, except for the use of brief quotations in a book review.

Any copyrighted material is reproduced here under the fair use doctrine.

Published by Nordland Publishing 2015

ISBN Print: 978-82-8331-011-5
ISBN E-book: 978-82-8331-012-2

The Guardian Series

Blood in the Snow is the second volume of the Guardian series. The complete series comprises the following titles:

Vol.I   Blood in the Sand
Vol.II Blood in the Snow
Vol.III Blood in the Fire
Vol.IV Blood in the Heavens

Another book, *Dark Path*, is planned. It is a prequel to the Guardian series and follows Elizabeth Sandwell as she grows in power to become the most powerful witch in England.

Find out more about these, and other at
http://metaphysicalgeometry.blogspot.no/
or at www.nordlandpublishing.com

Dedicated to the men and women who live their lives in service to others...

CONTENTS

ACKNOWLEDGMENTS

For the continued support of my wife and family, I would like to say a huge thank you. Without question, they are my inspiration. To my writing community, I also offer my thanks for their encouragement, support and unflagging enthusiasm for the Guardian.

A big debt of gratitude to my editor, C.H. who has shown, time and time again, that less is more, details matter and one can never be too harsh.

And finally, to the many volunteer, and occasionally pressganged, beta readers that have helped along the way. The check is in the mail. Honest.

Prologue

AD 998
Central Norway

They had called him Bjorn the Mighty, but no longer. The sickness that took him was swift, eating him alive. In less than a week he had gone from being the first amongst the Northmen to less than a thrall.

If it had not happened before his own eyes, Egill Thrandsson would not have believed it. When they laid him in the ground, Bjorn was like a feather. An old man made of sticks and dry skin. He was twenty-nine.

Egill added another stone to the elongated ellipse ringing the shallow grave, a dragon ship for the departed. Bjorn would be missed. He had been a good warrior, a good man. Open-handed and generous, dutiful to the gods too.

Egill had fought shoulder to shoulder with Bjorn, and that was when you learned the true worth of a man. Against Blámenn, against Persian, it mattered not to him. After they slew the trollman in the great desert, no blade could touch him. He seemed blessed, favored of the gods. Yet now, in the time of his triumphant homecoming, something, some sorcery, had laid him low. Worse still, it may have robbed him of his place in Valhalla.

Egill straightened up and stared at the fresh dirt at his feet. Bjorn had been a tall man, like him. Thick armed and bearded, with long hair woven into a braid. They were as alike as brothers and as shield brothers they had lived. But dying in a field with a blade pressed into your hand was not a warrior's death. It was not going to impress the father of men, old One Eye.

Before the sickness, Bjorn had been cunning and fearless, the craft of war his greatest joy. Now he was buried in the mud like one of the fish men, the followers of the White Christ.

Egill's face twisted in a grimace of hatred and contempt for the weakling followers of the nailed god. With their obscene beliefs and stories, they were like sick-minded village idiots. They were barely men, not even fit for thralldom.

The wind picked up and the brown cloak of rough wool flapped about his legs. A glance east confirmed his worry. Dark clouds, moving fast.

He spat to one side, hand brushing aside his cloak, automatically going to the hilt of his sword. Red Asgeir passed him a skin and he put it to his mouth, swallowing rank water, wishing it were wine or even beer. Wiping his face with his forearm, he passed the skin back to his kinsman.

"This is no way to send a man like Bjorn to the beyond," he said, bitterly. He did not say Valhalla.

They stood atop a small hill rising like an unexpected blemish on the land. An ancient haug, a burial mound from the time when the gods still walked in the world of men. Bjorn deserved a real ship, but this was the best they could do.

The haug had been raised on a flat plain, the floor of a deep, steep-sided valley. To the west, the forest edged in close. New saplings of spruce and birch were visible; in time the forest would swallow the haug and with it all that remained of his friend. A little to the east stood a turf-thatched hut, a twist of smoke rising through a hole in the grass covered roof. The land workers. Probably thralls, thought Egill. He considered taking shelter there for the night but they still had a long way to go and many hours before nightfall. Best to press on.

Now it fell to him, Egill son of Thrand, leader of men. Not a name that was known or sung with praise in the halls, but a doughty warrior and a good man nonetheless. He did not fear death, unless it came slinking like a thief in the night, taking his strength as it had taken Bjorn's. Egill shivered, turning to look at his men. Of the nine that had set out against the trollman, there were four left.

Only his cousin Asgeir, and the two brothers from west of Bjørkedalen, remained. And Mannuki of course. He was a strange one, wild, with tangled black hair and eyes like blue ice frozen in a deeply tanned face. An old, weathered scar traced the cut that had almost taken his left eye. He and the brothers stood off to one side, the former desert man holding the reins of the six shaggy horses, three to a hand.

Mannuki was not a slave now but no one knew his tongue and their attempts to talk to him were largely ignored, although it was clear he understood them well enough.

He had joined them after they slew the trollman and plundered his tower. Even though they had bested the sorcerer, Egill doubted they could have done it were it not for Mannuki.

And it was Mannuki that had revealed the tower's secrets, the gold and jewels that had been paid as tribute to the trollman for more years than a man could count.

It was more wealth than they could carry, and now they were each as rich as a king. Of course, the Empress had taken her share. She had been especially delighted in the jewels. But they had enough gold, and to spare.

As a pledged man, a captain in the Varangian

guard, it had been his duty to ward the Empress of the world and the task had not always been easy. The ruler of Miklagard was a beautiful woman and, some said, a sorceress herself. New arrivals to the guard would scoff, but Egill knew better. He had seen her curse a man and that man dead within the hour, writhing in agony, foaming at the mouth like a berserker. He shook his head, clearing it of memories and the keening sense of loss.

Mannuki grunted and gestured to one of the brothers to take the horses' reins. Handing them over, he climbed to the top of the small mound and knelt in the mud. He began to speak then, words meaningless to the others but sending a shiver through their veins. Egill and Asgeir took a step back as he pulled a small square of folded gray metal from a pouch at his waist.

Egill had seen it before. Mannuki had made them walk three days to a cave in the desert where he had dug the odd thing out of the sand.

And now the little man buried it again, covering it with wet earth. He continued to speak in a singsong tone, the words growing more forceful until, with a final word, almost a cry, he bowed low, pressing his forehead to the ground. A strange smell filled the air, like when lightning strikes the earth. Standing, he turned to the other men, his eyes a brilliant, unnatural blue that seemed to radiate cold like winter wind off fields of ice. Then, in words as fluent as if he had been born in the valleys of the North, he spoke.

"Come, Egill. It grows late. We should keep moving."

Crossing to the horses he took his, leaping into the saddle with practiced ease, driving his mount forward with a kick of his heels. Without a backward look, he struck off at a trot for the mountains in the distance.

Egill stood gaping as the outlander rode away.

Then, with a shake of his head, he sighed. After all he had seen, should anything still surprise him? Yet he wondered what the little man had gifted to Bjorn. Whatever it was, he had earned it. There had been so many adventures with Bjorn the Mighty, each wilder than the one before. Always Bjorn came out of the thick of battle covered in blood, but never his own. His name was legend and towns gave tribute when they knew who was at their gates. Now here he lay, with no grave goods, save Mannuki's gift and the gold he took from the trollman.

But no ship to carry him, no slaves to serve him. Nothing to take into the afterlife but a sword and shield. It was not fitting.

The trollman who had enslaved Mannuki had been fierce. Egill could not remember a harder and more desperate fight. Nine of the guard it took, against one man with neither armor nor shield.

They prevailed, in the end. Egill had severed the trollman's arm with the creature's own blade. He shuddered at the memory of the hand, still grasping, even as the limb lay in the dirt. He had never seen anything like that, not even in Miklagard which knew every wonder.

After the arm was taken, cold iron worked well enough on the creature and they took its life. He had tossed the severed arm onto a brazier where it sizzled like a spit boar, filling the room with the smell of pork. All the while Asgeir was hacking off the creature's other hand and Bjorn was taking its head. Trollman or not, the creature had tasted their iron and few lived that ate from that dish.

Egill chuckled and Red Asgeir questioned him with a look.

"If ever there was a man that could take what he wanted, it was Bjorn," he said.

"So long as he could swing his axe," replied Asgeir, nodding.

The kinsmen descended the small hill and mounted their horses. With one of the brothers leading the spare they headed home, following Mannuki towards the mountains—for Jotunheim.

I will raise a stone, thought Egill. For Bjorn, telling his story in runes as they did in the days of the gods. It will be a great tale, and men will know the name of Bjorn the Mighty for a thousand years to come.

These ancient tales of sorrow

1

Those songs I know, which neither sons of men
nor queen in a king's court know;
the first is Help, which will bring thee help
in all woes and in sorrow and strife.
—*Hávamál*

Present day,
South London

The thirty-something, sandy-haired Philip Entwhistle started as the huge, meaty hand of Detective Topley came slamming down onto the steel tabletop with a retort like a gunshot.

"Nervous, are you, Entwhistle?" said Topley, his massive bulk and perspiring face looming over the younger man.

The windowless office they had used for his last interview had reeked of disinfectant. This one, identical in size and layout, stank of sweat and old gym shoes but detectives Hanlon and Topley seemed to almost relish the oppressive, cramped box of a room.

Entwhistle looked up into the detective's rotund face and smiled. "Nervous? Only for you, Topley. You look like you're about to have a heart attack."

Topley reared up with a snarl but a smaller hand on the big detective's arm cautioned him. Topley's partner, the much younger Detective Rachel Hanlon, sat back in her chair, gazing at Entwhistle as if contemplating a difficult puzzle, one she did not particularly enjoy. Although petite, she carried herself with an air of authority and keen intelligence. The brute Entwhistle could handle, but Hanlon was a worry. She was like a dog with a bone and clearly in no hurry to close this particular file.

Just over a month ago Philip Entwhistle's life had changed in the most fundamental way possible. He had become the guardian of a djinn. He had believed himself well prepared from his time with his predecessor but from the very first things had gone badly wrong. He had failed to protect the elemental, at the cost of its life and nearly his own. Not a day, scarcely an hour went by without a tortuous, compulsive recapitulation of that terrible sequence of events. What should he have done differently? What could he have changed that would have prevented that blade slicing through his throat and the djinn's sacrifice of its own life force for his sake?

As if that wasn't enough, now the police were trying to pin the death—the presumed death—of Elizabeth Sandwell on him. Sandwell had been performing a spell requiring the djinn's energy. He had tried to stop her. That he had succeeded, after a fashion, was down to Sandwell's own bloodlust rather than any clever move on his part. Cutting his throat had released a fountain of blood that had derailed the spell. As it failed Entwhistle had sensed someone—or more accurately something—dragging Sandwell into a raging vortex that closed behind her. Then he had died, bleeding out on her attic floor.

Miraculously, he had regained consciousness, lying in a pool of his own blood, yet perfectly hale. Grabbing the djinn's meta-anchor, a small clay bowl, he had fled, knocking over a candle and setting fire to a threadbare curtain. The police had found no trace of Sandwell in the burnt ruins of her house. She was gone; Entwhistle sincerely hoped to some lower region of hell.

Without evidence of a body, the police needed a confession. They would not get one from Entwhistle.

In Interview Room Three of Headley Police station the stalemate was causing intense and rising frustration for the two detectives and their suspect. Entwhistle sighed, concentrating on maintaining an air of bored detachment, well aware that it would provoke his interrogators. In a tweed jacket, leather elbow patches and slightly frayed shirt, he looked much like any other teacher. But in the face of the good cop, bad cop routine, he was keeping his cool in a way that suggested to the officers that there was more to him than met the eye.

Philip Entwhistle glanced warily at Hanlon. Smarter and more observant than her partner, she was the one to watch. Entwhistle strongly suspected Topley's aggressive posturing was an act put up by Hanlon while she assessed him, watched him, waiting for him to give something away.

But they had nothing. He knew it and they knew it. Around the time of the fire and Sandwell's disappearance, Entwhistle had been pulled over by a highway cop miles from the scene, an alibi all the accusations and suppositions in the world could not dent. Yet they were not giving up.

"We have a witness," Hanlon said, "who puts you at the scene of the fire on Woodhall Drive, on the afternoon of the twenty-third. A heavily bloodstained man was seen leaving the house minutes before the blaze and being driven away, at speed, by a woman. That man has been positively identified as you. It *was* you." She glared at Entwhistle, picked up her notes and read aloud. "The driver was a female, middle-aged, small in stature, perhaps five feet two inches, short brown hair, slim build, driving an old Morris Mini, registration unknown."

Hanlon put down her notes by the open case file, partially obscuring a photograph showing the burnt shell of Sandwell's house.

"It appears you had an accomplice, Dr. Entwhistle. And don't kid yourself; we are going to find that car and its driver. And when we do, we'll have another little chat. But then you'll be wearing these."

She dangled a pair of handcuffs in front of his face then dropped them onto the table with a metallic clang. Entwhistle looked at the rings of shiny steel, then up into Hanlon's unwavering stare.

"I don't think so, detective."

He had had enough of the badgering. Time to apply some pressure of his own. He leaned forward, steepling his fingers on the desk, his green eyes boring into the petite detective's gray.

"Detective Hanlon. You explain how I could be in two places at once and I'll concede you might, just might, have a case. Or produce my identical twin and charge him. We both know Kendrick stopped me at that time. Explain that!"

Hanlon frowned and looked away. Entwhistle smiled. It was the only thing keeping him out of prison but it was plenty. Around the time of the fire he had lost control of his car and skidded off the road just outside of Shoreham, a good hour's drive from Sandwell's house in Epping. The pursuing patrol car had caught up with him and taken his details. Then he had disappeared, vanished right in front of officer Kendrick, whisked by the djinn to Sandwell's attic. Entwhistle had no doubt that the hapless policeman would take that piece of information to his grave.

Against that, one eye-witness, no matter how certain, was worthless. Short of a confession, they were dead in the water.

"Now listen," he said. "I came here today voluntarily, happy to co-operate. Again. But I've had quite enough of banging on tables, sweaty faces and baseless threats. This is harassment. It stops here."

Topley bristled and exclaimed, "Now you listen here, you little . . ."

"Sorry. I'm leaving." Entwhistle stood up and, ignoring Topley, addressed himself to the still seated Hanlon. "If you want to stop me, charge me and take the consequences, and consequences there will be. If you wish to talk to me again, and I can't see why you would, call my lawyer." He took a card from his wallet and tossed it onto the table. Emblazoned on the card in gold leaf was the name *Rappaport and Associates*.

"I know you have a job to do but it's time you found someone else to pin this on. Get yourself another suspect. Perhaps the real arsonist?"

He strode to the door. As he reached for the handle, Hanlon spoke. Entwhistle stopped, as much in surprise at the soft tone of her voice as the words themselves.

"A woman is missing, Mr. Entwhistle. We don't just let that go."

Once outside, Entwhistle's bravado evaporated. Leaning against the door he let out a long, slow breath. Of course she was right, but it could not be helped. Sandwell had been a dangerous woman who had to be stopped, by any means necessary. Had he not acted it would have fallen to Fern's coven to deal with her, although he suspected they might have stopped short of burning her house down.

He followed the now familiar route to the front desk where the duty officer buzzed him through.

11

Outside the station, the gray afternoon light reflected his mood. He made quickly for the car park, eager to get out of there. Fern, waiting in the Land Rover, smiled as he climbed in beside her.

"So," she said, "You're still a free man then?"

A nod and a wry smile. "Yes. That's the end of it, I think. Let's go home, please."

Fern gave his arm a squeeze, then turned the key and the old diesel engine burst into life, its familiar shaking and thumping soothing Entwhistle's rattled nerves.

"Glad to hear it," she shouted. Shoving the vehicle into gear she pulled out of the station car park. "I would hate to have to visit you in prison."

As the Land Rover passed through the gates and onto the street, a figure emerged from the far side of the car park. A large man, he threw a cigarette butt to the floor and ground it down with a heavy black boot. A freshly shaven face and head did nothing to improve his thickset, ugly appearance, with a nose set crooked after a fight.

Paul Sumpter flipped up the collar of his denim jacket and swaggered out of the car park, through the heavy metal gates and onto the still busy sidewalk, shouldering his way through crowds of people heading home after work. He was going back to the pub. He would need a drink to wash away the bile in his mouth.

The sight of Entwhistle leaving the police station had made him angrier than he had ever been in his life, which was saying something.

Earlier, a mate had walked into the bar with the news that he had seen Entwhistle being led into an interview room at the pig shop. Sumpter had rushed over. Any chance Entwhistle might go down for burning Sandwell's house was too good to be true and he had left a perfectly good pint untouched to see for himself. But he lost his nerve and would not go inside the station. Besides, he had spotted that good looking hippy chick from his old apartment waiting outside. This galled Sumpter. Was Entwhistle *doing* her? Why else would she be hanging around outside the station, while the high and mighty professor was inside?

Sumpter had not seen her since the day he had burgled Entwhistle's apartment and he was reluctant to be recognized. So he found himself an out-of-the-way corner where he could keep an eye on the station door. He did not have long to wait. He was only on his third fag when Entwhistle came out, free as a bird.

It was only right that Entwhistle got nailed. There was no question he had done it. Sumpter had seen the bastard with his own eyes. He'd come out of Lizzie's house, covered in blood, just as it started to burn. Then some woman showed up in an old beater and drove him away.

Why had the pigs released him? But he already knew–they did not have enough evidence. So then what? Sumpter frowned, his lips curling back as he tried to work things out. How in hell had the smarmy bastard managed to talk his way out of it? People had seen him!

Sumpter was not a man overly concerned with the rights and wrongs of things, but he burned with rage seeing Entwhistle free as a bird while he was stuck with hundreds of hours of community service for one little breaking and entering bust. It was out of order. Entwhistle gets away with arson, while he has to clean graffiti off the fucking underpasses.

The pigs were useless. Entwhistle was going to get what he was owed, one way or another. Sumpter smiled in anticipation as he exited the car park.

The horn of a taxi blared out, and Sumpter turned to see an old woman hurrying to get out of its way. The taxi driver leaned on his horn a second time. Sumpter frowned. That was not right. The old dear was going as fast as she could.

He strode into the street, standing directly before the vehicle which had to brake to avoid running him over. He leaned onto the hood, staring down the driver. The old woman made it across the road and gave him a grateful look. Sumpter glared at the driver a moment more, then casually crossed the road.

"Ignore 'im, love. Ignorant fucker," he said, as he continued on his way. He had hoped the driver would get out. He would have welcomed a fight right then.

If the pigs didn't have enough to hold Entwhistle, he was going to give things a nudge, maybe point them in the right direction. He knew something they didn't and much as he hated them, he hated that prick Entwhistle more.

He needed to think this through carefully. First he had to find out who was in charge of the investigation. Then he would sort out Entwhistle, good and proper.

Inside the interview room, Detective Topley sat heavily in the chair recently vacated by their only suspect. Hanlon could feel his gaze as she stared thoughtfully into space.

"You still think Entwhistle did it," he said quietly, all bluster gone.

Sucking her teeth, Hanlon shook her head. "Killed Sandwell? No, not that. I don't think he's got it in him. He's not a sociopath."

Topley grunted in reply. Hanlon looked at her partner. He would be retiring soon. Time for the gold watch, a few drinks with the boys, and knowing him, a stripper. This would be his last major case. She was fond of Topley, even if he was a complete asshole most of the time. But he was a good detective, in his way. Old school, that's what he was. Smack them first, ask questions later. But the police force was not like that anymore. Now it was all about profiling and getting inside the head of the perp, something she had a particular knack for and he simply didn't.

Her gut told her Entwhistle was involved and knew more than he was saying. It would be a shame if they had to let him walk. An unsolved murder did not look good on the books. Even though no remains had been recovered, Hanlon was sure Sandwell had met her death in the fire on Woodhall Drive. But now the chief was putting pressure on her to either close the case or move on. The problem was, she couldn't do either.

"He's lying about something," she said. "I can tell you that much. My guess is he knows what happened to Sandwell. That, or he's covering for someone else. Maybe his girlfriend?"

Topley picked up the case file and flipped to a color picture of an attractive redhead. A note at the bottom stated, *Elizabeth Sandwell, University ID.*

"Shame about the victim. She was quite the looker."

Hanlon gave him a withering look. "Like that makes a difference to anything?"

"I was just saying . . ."

"Well, don't."

Topley dropped the file back on the desk.

"The problem is his alibi," he said.

"Yeah."

Entwhistle had been caught on camera driving over ninety in a sixty zone. He had received heavy fines, of course, but it had provided him with the perfect alibi, while supporting the patrolman's report. Officer Kendrick, had caught up with Entwhistle near Shoreham, on the M1. That was about as solid as any alibi could be.

Hanlon shook her head. So what did that leave them with? She gnawed on a fingernail, then pulled it from her mouth, frowning at her lapse. She mentally cringed when she thought what her mother would say about the state of her nails. Not to mention the rest of her life.

"There was something Entwhistle said. About being in two places at the same time."

"What about it?" Topley replied.

"I don't know. But the witness was so sure it was him. She picked out his picture immediately. She said he was covered in blood and looked panicked. Well, he would, wouldn't he? The house was on fire and he'd just killed someone, or perhaps seen her killed. Then a car pulls into the drive, somebody gets out and pushes him in. He was there, dammit. But how?"

"So maybe there's two of him. Twins, or something, like he said. I saw an episode of Columbo once . . ."

She quelled any further reminiscence with a sour look. "Forget twins. I checked that. He's an only child. Parents dead. Not even any cousins."

"Then all you got left is either time travel or, what's that thing they do in Star Trek."

"Matter transportation," she said.

"Yeah. Maybe someone beamed him up?"

She could not help laughing. "I'll beam you up."

But for just a moment, she wondered. Science moved fast. Was it possible someone had invented some kind of new technology? Something to do with wormholes maybe? They were always being discussed on science shows. She shook her head. She would start believing in fairies next. No. If there was an explanation that would put Entwhistle at the scene of the crime, it was not science fiction. It would be much simpler. Occam's razor. The simplest explanation was probably the truth. So what was the simplest explanation? She sighed. That was the problem. There just wasn't one. Yet.

Entwhistle was relieved to be finished with the police. The knot of tension in his stomach was dissolving and he smiled more on the drive home than he had in the last month.

Since that day at Sandwell's house, he was a different man. The former cheerful optimist had become withdrawn and morose. Entwhistle was not given to self-analysis but even he could see he was wallowing in a combination of self-pity, guilt and depression. It did not take a genius to figure out why, either. Sir James Francis, former guardian of the djinn, had entrusted him with an extraordinary responsibility. Philip had greatly liked and admired the old man, and had leapt at what was practically a sacred trust.

Only a few months ago he had not even known such a thing as an elemental existed. Being a guardian to one would never have occurred to him as part of his future but when it happened he had embraced it, swearing to protect the surprisingly fragile creature from harm, keeping its secret and providing it with the stable companionship it craved.

He had failed. Spectacularly.

Since then, Entwhistle had been in a funk. He did not need telling that his emotional state was straining his newfound relationship, but Fern bore his bouts of accusatory self-pity with an equanimity bordering on heroic. Nothing seemed to faze her.

He glanced at the Norwegian woman as they pulled into the country lane that led to his house—their house—Little Flower Cottage. It was named after his benefactor's wife, a Tuareg girl, named Tajeddigt.

Literally translated it meant 'Little Flower' and old
Mr. Francis had spent the last hundred years of his
life creating a shrine to her memory in the beautiful
cottage gardens.

It occurred to Entwhistle that there was a
surprising synchronicity between him and Francis.
His girlfriend was also a wild spirit, named after a
plant. Fern too was breathtakingly beautiful. Her pale
skin, contrasting so vividly with her black hair gave
her an ethereal look. But there was nothing delicate
about her. She was stronger by far than she looked.
Slender, like a reed of willow, only wrought from
spring steel.

Entwhistle prayed that this was where the
similarities ended. The old man had lost his wife in
the most horrendous way, forced to watch her throat
being cut, before he was stoned and dragged into the
desert to die.

Entwhistle felt bad about the depression that had
swallowed him in the last month. He wanted to make
it up to Fern. She was the best thing that had ever
happened to him and he was blowing it.

Fern shut off the engine and as the deep rumble
died away, Entwhistle reached out and took her hand
in his own.

"I'm sorry," he said.

The words hung in the air. Philip did not know if
Fern understood what they meant, what they meant to
him at that exact moment. But she squeezed his hand
in return.

"You know it will all work out, don't you?" she
replied.

He smiled. Fern believed in fate, believed in it the
same way he believed in gravity.

"Things are getting messed up," he said. "And I
know it's my fault, only there's nothing I can do. It's

like I've been set on a path and can't get off, no matter how hard I struggle."

Fern nodded, her expression serious. "I'm sure it seems like that now. But in time you'll learn to forgive yourself. Frankly I'm amazed you feel so bad about that woman. She was a wicked person, doing evil things and doesn't deserve your sympathy."

He hated letting Fern go on thinking that was the reason for his misery. His silence was like a lie. But he could not tell her the truth. She still knew nothing of the djinn. He had guarded the secret. The one thing that he had managed to do right, so far.

"I don't want to lose you, Fern. You mean more to me than I can say. I'm just afraid that you'll get . . . I don't know, exhausted or something."

Fern dazzled him with a smile, showing dimples and a flash of white teeth in the dark. "It was in the cards, Philip. Our paths are entwined. For whatever reason, the Universe wants us together. So don't worry. You're stuck with me."

Now Philip smiled. "I have to say, that pretty much gives me carte blanche to do whatever I want, doesn't it? I mean, you've just said that no matter what I do, we're destined to be together."

Fern pulled her hand away from his. "Yes, I suppose. But that doesn't mean I'll be nice to you, or sleep with you. Being together and *being together* are different things. So you just watch it, mister!"

They both laughed, and Fern leaned in to kiss him. It would be alright, he thought. So long as he had her, he would be fine. He would put the business with Sandwell behind him, and perhaps even learn to forgive himself for what had happened to Jinny.

"Come on," he said, pushing open the passenger door, "let's grab a bite then get to bed. This day's been long enough already."

He put his arm around her waist as they walked down the narrow stone path to the back door of the cottage. They passed one of the many rose bushes. The light from the back window of the kitchen illuminated it, showing flowers that seemed to hang their head in shame.

"There's something wrong with this one," Fern said, gently running her fingers over the petals. "I've tried everything short of magic."

She went to her knees before the plant, placing her hands on the ground at its stem. With eyes closed, she whispered quickly, too fast for Philip to catch anything. He was not sure if he imagined it or not, but there seemed to be a blue nimbus around her hands. After another moment, she got up, brushing grass and dirt from her jeans.

She shrugged. "Well, that'll have to do. Now it's up to the plant."

The dream was torment. The same dream that had plagued Philip Entwhistle almost every night since he had lost the djinn.

In a dimly lit attic in a suburban house at the edge of London, he stood helplessly as a knife pressed against his throat, his hands hanging impotently by his sides, in anguish over the immortal entity he had failed to keep safe.

Elizabeth Sandwell stood behind him, one hand gripping his hair, the other holding the blade. She was naked, her lustrous copper-red hair falling about her shoulders and down her back. Naked, but far from defenseless. Philip had interrupted her spell just as she was about to sacrifice the djinn and complete the rite that would make her more powerful than any human in history. All she had to do was kill Philip Entwhistle, slay the djinn, and she would win forever.

"Please Elizabeth," he pleaded, his voice held steady by strength of will alone, "you don't need to do this."

"No, but I want to." She smiled, and in one sharp motion, drew the blade across his throat. He could feel in exquisite detail his flesh parting, the nerves and tendons cut, the main artery severed and his blood fountaining. He spun around, eyes wide in fear, shock and sheer disbelief. His knees buckled and he fell to the rough planking of the floor. His blood jetted across her bare belly and breasts, sparking a wild delight as she inhaled the smell of hot copper, the smell of his life draining away.

Philip's blood spouted in time with his wildly beating heart. His life was now measured in seconds, his only salvation the djinn. He began to crawl towards the pentacle where Jinny's meta-anchor lay. It was close. He had time. But each inch became a mile and the pentacle always remained just out of reach. He grew desperate, every fiber of his being willing him to reach his goal, and as always, he failed, the strength in his trembling limbs deserting him.

He collapsed, one hand extending in a futile grasp for help that would not come. As the blackness descended, Sandwell's mocking laughter still echoed in his head.

It always ended the same. Sometimes the words she spoke varied. Sometimes she would tease him, letting him think he would live, but always the knife would find his throat and he would wake with his heart pounding, drenched in sweat.

Entwhistle's eyes snapped open in the dark, his breath coming in quick, shallow gasps. The terror of the nightmare began to recede. Every night he suffered the same reminder of his failure, re-living the moment when he had died, forced to acknowledge what he had allowed to be lost.

Fern's hand fumbled its way across the bed and found him. She mumbled something, then turned towards him, sliding closer, one leg interlocking with his, her hand on his chest as she nestled in closer.

"Bad dream again?" she said sleepily, her quiet voice almost masking the odd lilt that reminded him she was not English. "Why won't you tell me what's wrong?"

Philip did not answer. She would not understand. No one could. He turned to her and pulled her into his arms, holding her fiercely, taking comfort in her warmth. She exclaimed with a drowsy moan, and began to kiss his neck. Her hand slid lower, caressing him. The memory of the dream soon melted into desire and they made love. She moaned at his passion, his rough, desperate lovemaking, and as she came fully awake, she returned his ardor, kissing him harder, raking his back with her nails, letting him work out his fear and anger on her body. When they were done, they lay in a tangle of limbs, both breathing fast. He slid one hand over Fern's smooth skin, stopping at her breast, which he gently cupped. She chuckled in response.

"Not quite satisfied, Philip?"

He smiled in the dark. "Yes, I am. I just can't stop touching you."

"I don't mind," she said, turning to him. He rolled onto his side and looked at her. She was shadows and darkness, but even so he fancied he could see her beauty, her smile. He pulled her close, breathing her in. She murmured something in her native Norwegian he did not understand. Her breathing slowed, became regular, and in a moment she was asleep.

He felt relieved. She was not going to press him to talk about the dream. As if analyzing it would help him understand what was plaguing him. He did not need Freud to know it was guilt that made him experience his failure, again and again, night after night. Guilt and shame. But not for Sandwell. Never for her.

He longed to tell Fern everything, but something would not let him. He had fallen into a pit and was simply not equipped to dig himself out. He sighed. She had always been honest with him, and how was he repaying her?

Right from the start she had made it clear she liked him. They had met in the university library where she worked part-time. There had been something, a spark. She was quite unlike anyone he had ever met before.

Philip had been delighted when circumstances led her to move into his apartment building. Invited to dinner, Fern had opened up completely about herself. At least, about everything that mattered. That she was wiccan, that she was Norwegian and that she had been placed in the university to hunt a powerful and highly dangerous rogue witch, probably someone on the faculty. Fern had still to identify her target but could feel her presence. Philip knew. He knew only too well: *Sandwell.*

Things had gone from casual acquaintance, to friends and then lovers so fast his head was still spinning. Perhaps she sensed there was something broken in him and like many women, felt she could fix it. But there was no way to fix this. He had caused the death of an elemental creature. How do you fix that?

He rolled onto his back and closed his eyes. Using the technique Fern had taught him he slowed his breathing and let his mind relax. Letting go of the worry and guilt, focusing on a single thought, he let it lead him to sleep. He would tell Fern. He would tell her everything. About Sir James Francis, about the djinn, about his promise and his failure. No more secrets. Tomorrow. He would tell her everything tomorrow.

Our lives together tie

2

They shall say: Glory be to Thee!
Thou art our Guardian, not they; nay!
They worshipped the djinn;
most of them were believers.
—*sūrat Saba, Qur'an*

Norway, 20 kms north of Lillehammer
Aasheim Farm

Arnulf Aasheim sat at his desk in the living room of the farmhouse he shared with his wife and son, Jens. A warm room, with wooden paneling on walls and ceiling and an open fireplace, decorated in typical Scandinavian style— many lamps, pine furniture and a wall of floor-to-ceiling bookshelves, crammed full.

Liv was in the kitchen, Jens having already left. At twenty-six, Jens was still in college, which was quite strange as far as Arnulf was concerned. Not like in his day. At that age, he was already married with two children. Still, things changed. And that was the problem.

He stared at the computer screen and made a few desultory clicks with the mouse. No matter how he figured it, the numbers came back pretty much the same. The way things were going, by this time next year they would be bankrupt. The farm was simply not paying its way.

If they could just make it through to spring and the lambing season they would probably cover costs and maybe a little more. Provided they didn't lose too many newborn lambs to frost or wolves. The latter was a new threat, or a very old one, depending on how you looked at it. Wolves were becoming a feature again and now he had to work harder than ever to safeguard the stock. Plus, thanks to climate change, a disastrous late winter was always on the cards. He would just have to try his best to keep the ewes in good shape and hope for an early spring.

It was a big hope, with too many variables beyond his control. The winters *were* starting later and lasting longer, leading to later springs. He could put the rams to the ewes later, but the top prices, the prices he needed to stay afloat, were for the first lambs on the market. No, it was simply not going to work out. He sighed and rubbed his temple with his right hand, pulling his glasses off with his left. There just had to be some other way they could make ends meet.

He stared at the flickering glow of the fireplace, basking in its warmth. Funny how a real fire always felt better than any other kind of heating, no matter if it was less efficient. There was something that touched a man's soul in the naked flames, he thought.

The cut logs stacked next to the fireplace came from trees on his land, like most of the food on the table. But much as they tried, and they came close, they could not live off the farm alone. The fire gave off the distinctive smell of burning birch. Nothing better.

The sound of his wife in the kitchen roused him from his reverie and his mind snapped back to the worry over finances. He had a decision to make, one he did not like. When his father was alive he had been full of little aphorisms. He had one for every occasion, including this. He would have said *never make a major decision before breakfast*. Well, that was one rule he was going to break.

Arnulf got up from the desk and made his way into the kitchen. Liv was pouring golden batter into an electric waffle iron. It was not their typical breakfast, but Liv rightly gauged that Arnulf would need something to perk him up. The batter sizzled on the hot plate as she closed the lid, squeezing the thick fluid it into every nook and cranny. Arnulf spied the pile of cooling waffles and reached for one. Liv smiled indulgently.

"Håper det smaker," she said.

Arnulf and Liv went about their routines as they had for almost thirty years. Arnulf was a big man, stout and strong, with a ruddy complexion from a life in the sun and wind. Life outside could be harsh, especially winter in Norway, and farming was tough. A man had to be tougher still to get the job done.

Coming from a long line of farmers, he had grown up in the outdoors, hunting, fishing and caring for his stock. Liv was also a country girl, from a farm just a few kilometers away. They had been childhood sweethearts. At least that hadn't changed.

He looked with satisfaction at his wife as he prepared the morning coffee. Liv was still a handsome woman, with clear skin, hair so blonde it was almost white and a figure that was buxom without being fat. She still stirred in him the same desire as when they were teenagers. Well, perhaps not quite as often, he thought. But then, he was pushing fifty after all. Allowances had to be made.

"I've been doing the figures," said Arnulf, munching on the still warm waffle. "It's not good."

"What's wrong with it?" Liv demanded, one eyebrow imperiously raised at the assumed slur on her cooking.

"The finances, I mean. They're not good. We lost too many lambs this year and if next year's the same we're in serious danger of going under."

"Oh. For a moment, I thought it was something serious."

They both smiled. But a joke would not be enough to get them over this bump in the road.

"If we don't make at least another two hundred, maybe

two hundred and fifty thousand kroner, then we're done here. No more farm."

"Honey, are you serious?" Liv bit her bottom lip. She put her hand on her husband's arm, eyes searching his. "What are we going to do?"

"Take that waffle out for a start!" said Arnulf, pointing.

The little light on the side of the hotplate glowed green. Liv opened the iron, picked up the steaming waffle with a fork and put it on the nearly full rack.

"We'll have to take some of the trees," Arnulf continued. "The old growth. It's about the only thing of value we have left. I'll call Halldorsen Timber and ask for someone to come out and give us a quote."

"Are you sure? I know how much you love those woods. It would be a terrible shame to cut the trees down. And the kids will be very unhappy. Especially Fern."

The woods on their land were thick and old. A haven for a wide variety of animal and bird life. Arnulf had hunted in them since he was a boy. His kids had grown up playing in them and many was the time he had to go searching for them after dark, often finding them in their tree fort, or enchanted castle as they insisted on calling it.

"Yes, I know. But I don't see that I have a choice. Pernilla and Jens will just have to accept that not everything can stay the same."

"Fern, dear. She prefers that we call her Fern."

He snorted. He knew his daughter preferred the name she had chosen for herself. Why she did not like the name they'd christened her with he would never understand. Fern was in England now, wasting her time over that silly nonsense. Wicca. He snorted again. What was that? An invention of some lecherous Englishman who liked to prance about naked.

Jens was studying to be a police officer. Now that was not a bad career, Arnulf thought. Provided he could find a job when he graduated. His main concern for Jens was that he would be forced to move away from the valley and the farm. Of course, that would be that. No-one left to take care of the place. If neither Jens nor Fern wanted it after he retired that would be the end. The farm had been in his family forever, and the thought of losing it while under his stewardship galled him.

He gazed out the window but saw only his own reflection. A north wind was blowing, but inside the warmth of the kitchen the howling cold did not bother them. The days were getting shorter and soon enough winter would set in. Arnulf had a feeling this was going to be a hard one. They would have to take the trees, there was simply no other way. It would buy them another year, at least. He reached for the phone hanging on the wall near the door.

"I'm calling Halldorsen. There's simply nothing else we can do."

It was seven-thirty in the morning and Entwhistle exhaled slowly as he stretched into the position known as downward facing dog. He tried to emulate Fern but where she was smooth and graceful, he was odd angles and jerks.

He preferred to run in the morning, but Fern insisted he join her. He breathed heavily at the effort of holding the highly unnatural position. Once again he questioned if yoga was ever meant for university professors. Sweatpants and a T-shirt he could handle. Yoga, not so much. Resting his head on the soft blue foam of the mat, he tried to make his body do what it was told.

The early morning light in the cottage library was ideal for their morning sessions. The library. A grand name for the front parlor, with almost wall-to-wall shelves crammed with books. After giving up his lease on his London apartment Entwhistle had moved his own extensive book collection to the cottage, now mostly piled neatly in a corner. But space remained for more shelves and most would find a home eventually.

Fern had kept up her London apartment. Not as a lifeboat in case things didn't work out but because she could not break the lease. However, since moving in with Entwhistle she had been back only a handful of times, and then only to get clothes or something she needed. They were now living together, unofficially. Neither spoke of long term commitment but Entwhistle harbored no doubts. He had fallen for the beautiful, if eccentric, Norwegian. Maybe it was time to have that talk? Put things on an official basis?

He turned to look at her. Her hair hung down over her face, a black waterfall cascading to the mat. Her back was arrow straight, in perfect alignment with her out-stretched arms as she raised herself onto her toes. Philip smiled, appreciating her grace. He tried again to follow, grunting at the difficulty of the pose.

They both liked this room, its peaceful atmosphere. Reading was a historian's raison d'être and Entwhistle felt most at home surrounded by books. Fern, too.

His thoughts went to Sandwell. She would go to war over even the smallest slight. So when they were both up for a promotion, Entwhistle should have know what to expect. Sandwell had concocted an allegation of sexual assault to take him out of the running, leading to his first brush with Hanlon. The diminutive detective had wanted to charge him then and was still trying.

He had to tell Fern. Everything. Why he had turned up at her apartment covered in blood, the deal he'd made with Sir James, about the djinn. He quailed to think of the questions he would face, feeling his stomach churn.

Fern's eyes snapped open, looking directly at him. She always knew when he was watching her. She smiled encouragement.

Fern had told him that she had been sensing his inner turmoil for weeks, hence the reason for the yoga.

"It cleanses the spirit, while helping the body," she had said.

Philip tried his best to emulate her. Why not give it a go, he thought. It certainly couldn't make things worse. He watched her body move into the cobra, or bhujangasana, and tried to follow suit. She held it for a few beats, then, on a deep exhalation, moved into the bow pose, the dhanurasana. He could not quite manage to grip his ankles and pull himself back but gave it his best shot, grunting from the effort.

"That's okay, Philip. Just go into child's pose. You're doing well for a beginner."

"I don't feel that I'm doing anything."

"Just practice breathing. *Will* your heart to slow, calm your mind. It will help, I promise."

"Okay." Focusing on his heartbeat, he consciously tried to slow it down. Taking shallow, even breaths, eyes closed, he cleared all thought. Then the memory of the abject terror on Sandwell's face as she stared into the black void invaded his consciousness. He gave an involuntary grunt; perhaps, he thought, at some level I do feel guilty for her.

As they finished the final stretch, Entwhistle tried to summon the words to explain things to Fern. And failed. Tonight, he thought. After her meeting.

Paul Sumpter swaggered through the automatic glass doors of the police station. He paused, drawing heavily on his cigarette. The duty sergeant looked up from his desk and scowled, pointing to a conspicuous sign. No Smoking.

With a smirk Sumpter studiously dropped his cigarette on the floor, grinding it underfoot. Crossing the few steps to the duty sergeant's desk he blew a last breath of smoke into the officer's face.

"I have some information," he said.

The officer looked at Sumpter as if he were something scraped off the bottom of his shoe. With an exaggerated sigh, he picked up a pen and looked expectantly at his visitor.

"Name?"

Sumpter hesitated. He almost lied. It went against the grain to actually cooperate with the pigs. But it was for her, for Sandwell.

"Sumpter. Paul Sumpter."

"Right, Mr. Sumpter," the sergeant replied, writing it in the visitor log. "What can I help you with?"

"I reckon I knows who did that arson job up in Epping. Woodhall Drive. I got some information that might be," he paused, searching for the right adjective, face screwed up in concentration. "Pertinent.

The sergeant warmed slightly. That sort of information was welcome from anybody. His expression moderated itself to mere contempt; perhaps, if push came to shove, he might *not* scrape him off his shoe.

"Well? I don't have all day." The irritation in his voice matched the scowl on this face. Sumpter scarcely noticed.

"I ain't just gonna blurt it out, am I. This information is valuable. I reckon there's gotta be something in it for me."

"You want a reward? Withholding information about a crime is an offence. Now how about you do your civic duty and stay out of trouble?"

Sumpter's snort of derision made it clear what he thought of civic duty. And empty threats from the pigs.

"Nah. I got the goods and I want something in return. You set up an interview with that investigating officer. That bit o' totty what's running the show."

The duty officer had had enough. "I beg your pardon," he said, biting off each word. "That is Detective Hanlon to you."

"Right, yeah. Get me a meeting with her, and I'll do my civic duty." Sumpter smirked.

The officer held his gaze for a moment. "I'll see what I can do. Why don't you take a seat." He pointed to the row of uncomfortable plastic chairs lining the wall, then lifted a phone and talked quietly into it while Sumpter threw himself down. After a moment, the duty officer replaced the handset.

"Sorry, sir. Detective Hanlon is indisposed at the moment. You'll need to either wait or come back another time. Or you could just make a statement to me now."

Sumpter stood, indecision crawling slowly over his face. He didn't want to hang around, in case someone saw him. But he wouldn't be able to return for at least a couple of days. He had a lot on, at the moment. There were collections to make for the Gracz brothers, he had to sign-on for his benefits, and Traci's mother was bitching about redecorating the house.

He sighed. "I'll be back."

Entwhistle enjoyed the drive to the campus in spite of the butterflies in his stomach. It had been a while since he had shown his face in the History Department. Fern had an afternoon shift at the library so it was as good a time as any to return to the fold. Also, since her coven was meeting in the evening, he would not see her until late. It was worth facing his colleagues if it gave him another hour with her.

Entwhistle wanted to resume his duties at the University and for the last week had been building up the nerve to come back. It had been over two months since he had held a lecture or taught a class. He was not quite ready to jump back in with both feet, but he did not want anyone to think he planned to leave. Or worse, that there was something wrong with him. The closed world of the University was awash with rumor and speculation and he was in no doubt that the gossip mill was already at work.

He pulled into the faculty car park, shut off the engine and handed Fern the keys. She raised a quizzical eyebrow.

"Here, you take the car. I'd rather you drive back later. I'll take the train."

Entwhistle could scarcely believe he still held a driver's license. He had run up the maximum number of points from running a number of red lights and speed cameras the day he lost Jinny. One more offence and he would be off the road for a year. He was grateful to still be able to drive, but it would still be light when he left the campus, while Fern would be coming home long after dark.

"Alright," Fern replied. "That would be great, thanks."

They kissed quickly and he set off across the square. The university was built around a large garden crisscrossed by paths snaking through bushes and flower beds, the work of a full-time staff of gardeners. Before taking over the cottage, Entwhistle had thought them excessive. Now he knew better. Pruning, trimming and weeding to keep Little Flower Cottage's meticulous garden in good order swallowed all his spare time these days, not that he minded. He looked around in appreciation. Yes. A good crew doing fine work.

Entwhistle began to smile, his stride growing longer. By the time he reached the old, red-brick building housing his office he was practically running in his eagerness.

No-one stopped him to ask how he was or when he would be back, and he was grateful for the reprieve. He unlocked his office door and stepped inside, looking around as if seeing the place for the first time. It was tiny, cramped and a mess, indeed the chaos seemed to have worsened in his absence. How was that possible?

Entwhistle made a resolution to tidy the place. Maybe pick up the stacks of books from the floor and shelve them. And sort out all the notes littering the desk. He picked up one of the sticky yellow pieces of paper and tried to read the writing. Sanjay's spider scrawl. Not for the first time, Philip thought his T.A. should have been a doctor. He clearly had the handwriting for it.

The door opened and Sanjay entered carrying a stack of papers and a Styrofoam cup of steaming coffee.

"Professor Entwhistle! So, the jungle drums were right. You're back."

Sanjay put the cup down on the desk and held out his hand, the other still clutching the stack of papers to his chest. Entwhistle shook his hand, smiling at his protégé. Sanjay, a slim, dapper young native of Delhi, had been at the University for five years and was fast becoming a permanent fixture. His recent engagement to another PhD strengthened his ties, both to the UK and the university. Entwhistle hoped he would get a permanent teaching post. He was certainly good enough.

"No, not back. At least, not just yet. I wanted to come in and see how the land lies, so to speak."

Sanjay nodded. "Ah, just putting a toe in? Well, this is probably the right time, if you know what I mean. There have been rumblings about your absence."

Entwhistle chuckled. "What? Are people of the opinion that my head has swollen to new dimensions, previously uncharted?" There was always rivalry between academics, and there was nothing some of them liked more than to stick the knife in.

"You could say that. I don't want to mention any names, but I heard one fellow, who may or may not be head of Oriental studies, say that you had become a prima donna thanks to your new book."

"My absence has been related to that, though it's not the cause. But I can't talk about it. Anyway, how have you been managing without me?"

Sanjay beamed. "Oh, I'm doing very well. Very well indeed! I have been offered a job, part time. No need to worry about my visa status anymore."

Entwhistle clapped him on the back, genuinely delighted. "That's great. I couldn't be happier for you, Sanjay." He paused, took a deep breath then let it out in a whoosh. "Well, I suppose I had better go beard the lion."

"Ah, well. Dr. Evans is not here. He's . . . gone out for a

short while. Something came up."

From the tone, it was clear that Sanjay was torn about saying more. Entwhistle immediately suspected the cause. Either intuition, or simple logic kicked in.

"I see. He's being interviewed by the police. No doubt being asked questions about me. Is that it?"

Sanjay nodded, his previous smile turned firmly upside down. "I had to talk to them too. They want to talk to anyone that's ever worked closely with you."

"Oh? What did they want to know?"

Sanjay shrugged. "Mostly about your relationship with Dr. Sandwell. You know, if you had been fighting, that sort of thing."

"Alright, thanks Sanjay."

Sanjay dropped the stack of papers on the desk, and brushed a lock of hair from his eyes.

"I hope that you don't mind, but I've been using your office."

Entwhistle smiled ruefully. "No, that's okay. I'm starting to wonder if I'm going to get it back though."

Sanjay had a hangdog look of misery. "I didn't tell them anything, Professor. Really."

"Don't worry about it. I have nothing to hide, so you really don't have to try to cover for me."

Sanjay looked relieved. "I thought they were from immigration when they came to my house. I nearly had a heart attack."

He stared at Entwhistle, dark brown eyes regarding him closely. "Why do they think you killed Dr. Sandwell?"

"They have an eyewitness that places me at the scene."

Sanjay's eyes opened wide. "So you *were* there."

"No. It's an old lady. At the time, I was in my car, an hour away, being pulled over by a traffic cop."

Now Sanjay's look of surprise turned to puzzlement. "Then why do they think you did it?"

"I think," said Entwhistle thoughtfully, "that they simply

have no one else."

"Well, I hope it all works out."

"I'm sure it will. I'm going to let Sam know that I want to start work again. I'd like to start with tomorrow's lecture. That okay with you?"

"Of course, Professor!"

Entwhistle nodded. "Alright. I'll give him a call later. But I'll see you tomorrow."

Sanjay nodded. He looked around the office and sighed theatrically. "I guess I'll make do with the library again."

Entwhistle chuckled. "I'll ask Sam to find you an office. Who knows, maybe you'll get lucky."

Sanjay beamed. "I would appreciate that most awfully. Thanks, Professor."

"Think nothing of it."

Philip made to leave, pausing at the door. He turned back to his former student as Sanjay sat himself behind the desk and began gathering his papers. He wanted to say something. Thanks for having my back? Thanks for worrying?

He shook his head, pulling the door closed and, more slowly than he had arrived, made his way outside into the sunlight and the bright laughter of students.

The call had come as a surprise to Sumpter. A woman from Human Resources at the university had rung the night before, enquiring if he knew Elizabeth Sandwell. It seemed that she had named him as a contact in case of emergency, and since they had no one else, they had rung him about her personal effects.

"We've boxed all her things. Books, papers, and such. But we don't have a forwarding address. So, either you take them, or we put them into storage."

Sumpter swallowed the anger he felt at the idea of strangers touching Lizzie's things. If they had to put away her stuff, it should have been him that done it. But the momentary flare of rage was quickly gone as he understood the implications of what the woman, Mrs. Richards, had said. Lizzie had named *him* as her emergency contact.

He felt a glow of pride and smiled. "Yeah, I'll come get them. She was like, my girlfriend, you know." This last was said almost in a whisper. He did not want Traci overhearing that! He looked around to check, but she was still busy in the kitchen.

"Well, we've got everything boxed, but there's a fair bit," the woman continued. "You'll need a van, I think."

"No problem. I'll come by tomorrow and get them."

"Good. Just contact the porter at the main gate, he'll sort you out. And Mr. Sumpter, my condolences."

That had puzzled him. Condolences? Wasn't that for dead people? She could not be dead. That would be . . . he had struggled to finish the thought. Bad. Awful. With a shake of his stubbled head, he ended the call.

And now, as he parked outside the main gate and met with the porter, he felt a sense of righteous anger. Lizzie's boxes were dumped outside the porter's cabin like so much garbage. He snarled and started to stack them in the back of his van. There were almost a dozen boxes, some of them quite heavy, obviously full of books.

He was almost done when he saw them, Entwhistle and the hippy chick. She gave Entwhistle a lingering kiss then made her way towards the library, while Entwhistle headed off in the opposite direction. Sumpter watched them through narrowed eyes.

That girl was a bit tasty. Dark thoughts began to cloud his mind. What he could do to her. Things that would make Entwhistle regret ever crossing him.

He would follow her. Yeah, he would make Entwhistle pay for what he done to Lizzie. No mistake. What was it they said? An eye for an eye?

Fern held the chalice above her head. Not too high though, since both she and Tessa were tall, while Alicia was on the short side of petite. Fern was the Maiden. The Crone and the Mother, the sacred three of the inner circle, stood by her, all supporting the chalice of sanctified water. The chalice was the conduit, a focus for the combined energies of the coven.

There were three circles. Three was the number of perfection; the number of nature. The chalice was the first circle at the center, then the three senior witches made another circle, and around them was the coven; adepts whose linked hands formed the outer circle. Three in one, a trinity of witches.

A hundred years ago, a French witch had insisted to her lover, a flying ace in the newly-invented airplanes, that he paint the French tricolor in concentric rings on the wings of his plane. She said it would bring him luck. The British aviators followed suit soon after. Neither the French nor British authorities were aware that they were flying an ancient pagan symbol and a powerful representation of the natural order of the universe.

Tessa, a striking woman of perhaps fifty-five years, her once black hair now mostly gray, lowered her hands. Alicia, Fern's mentor, wore her chestnut hair cut boyishly short. She too lowered her hands. Fern smiled at the others, the sneer caused by the scar on her upper lip disappearing as her eyes crinkled in the joy of the moment.

As she lowered the chalice the men and women standing in the rough circle let go their neighbors' hands, finishing the ritual. The coveners broke up into small groups, some talking, while some prepared private rituals of their own, as others went on to personal study with a mentor or teacher. Amid smiles and hugs the phrase, 'blessed be' echoed around the room.

Fern was eager to be back at the cottage where Philip was waiting for her. There were things to be said and she had the feeling that he was on the verge of letting her in, of sharing the source of his nightly torment.

She waved goodbye to the group, stopping for a hug from a friend. She took a last look around the drab, spiritless Women's Institute hall. One day, please Goddess, she would found a coven in her own sacred grove, among the trees and wild nature on her family's farm. But fate did not seem to be bending her path that way. She knew Philip loved England far too much to move to her sub-Arctic homeland and they were bound together, she was certain of that.

In the coatroom she slipped into her old khaki army jacket, perfect for the little charms, herbs and plants she gathered in the woods around the cottage and kept in her pockets.

Tessa joined her, slipping on her own overcoat, a very much more expensive item of the finest wool.

"Can we talk for a moment?" she asked.

Fern nodded. "Of course."

Emerging from the hall the pair took in deep draughts of the crisp, cold autumn air, stopping to admire the brilliant canopy of stars in the cloudless sky. As head of the Human Resources Department at the University, Tessa had been able to hire the talented young Fern, ostensibly as a librarian. However, she was really there to track down a practitioner of the dark arts. She had succeeded, more or less, but it was Philip who had confronted Sandwell. It seemed the quiet, well-mannered professor harbored dark secrets of his own.

Tessa tucked a loose strand of gray behind her ear. "You seemed a little distracted in there. Is everything okay?"

Fern sighed, turning to face the older woman. "I know. I'm sorry. It's just that I've been trying to get Philip to open up about things. There is a deep sadness in him, and I'm sure it has something to do with Sandwell."

At the mention of their vanished foe, Tessa cast Fern a

sharp glance. "Any luck?" she said.

Fern shook her head. "He has nightmares. I swear sometimes I can almost see them myself, they are so powerful. The Mara rides him hard. I'm sure they're about her."

"I see," said Tessa. "What about the other thing? You said there was a power in him. Do you still feel it?"

Fern had been worried that Philip might be involved in matters he did not properly understand. A great many of the books in the cottage were on occult subjects. Of course, they had belonged to his benefactor, but who was to say what the old man had taught him before passing away?

A powerful magical force around the man who was now her lover had vanished after the fire at the Sandwell house. The only thing about him of occult significance was the silver talisman hanging from his neck. But if imbued with power it was not from him. It was old, a thing of the desert and a people long gone.

"No, not any longer. But I have no doubt he's keeping something from me."

"You don't think he's a practitioner, do you? Maybe there are still some secrets left at the University?"

Fern shook her head, mouth twisting into a rueful smile. "Who knows? But not Philip. I don't think he knows anything about magic."

They walked companionably together, Fern's feet scuffing the fallen leaves. She stooped to pick up a broad, golden-brown maple leaf. It was still supple in her delicate hands, and she could feel its life force as the tiniest of energies. She willed it to live, pouring some of herself into it. For a few seconds the leaf turned green, then just as quickly it faded to its previous russet tones.

Tessa watched her. "Everything has its time, Fern. It's all a circle."

Fern nodded. She dropped the leaf and turned to face the her friend. "I'm worried about him, Tess. It drives me crazy. The tarot was very clear about my future, but how can I fully commit myself to Philip when there are secrets between us? He has the same nightmare almost every night and he won't let me help him."

"He knows you're a witch?"

"Yes. I told him the day I moved into his building. He was . . . cagey at the time. But then there was this thing with Sandwell, so it's no wonder. But we've been together long enough now for him to . . . well, confide in me, trust me, I suppose."

Tessa nodded, placing a hand on the young woman's arm, smiling slightly. "We'll get to the bottom of it. He owes us. Without Alicia's help he would be in prison right now."

This was true. When Entwhistle identified the rogue witch, Fern had immediately alerted Alicia and Tessa. They agreed not to let Sandwell out of their sight and Alicia was on the job at the time of the fire. Somehow Entwhistle had entered Sandwell's house without Alicia seeing him. It was an incredibly stupid thing to do, with practically no chance that he would survive the encounter. Yet he did. Alicia saw him stagger out through the front door, covered in blood. He did not seem to be hurt, merely dazed. She had rushed to help him, bundling him into her car and driving them both away. Not a difficult decision with the house going up in flames.

Tessa continued. "I won't use threats, but a reminder that we are keeping his secret might get him to open up."

Fern smiled. "I hope so. Thanks, Tess. Maybe you and Alicia can visit? It would be nice to show you the cottage. It's a lovely place. Full of energy and life."

"Absolutely. I would love to see it. After that tiny apartment you used to live in, it must be something of a shock, having more than one room."

They both laughed, hugged and parted ways, Tessa going to her own car. Fern pulled out her keys. Before she could open the door, she spun around, staring into the far side of the car park. Something had pricked her senses. She stared for a moment, but there was nothing there. She opened the truck and climbed into the battered old Land Rover.

They would talk to him together. The circle would support her. They could help Philip, if only he would let them. Decision made, Fern started the truck, put it into gear and slowly pulled out, heading for the cottage and home.

The bright glow of a cigarette flared briefly as Sumpter took a last pull on it, before grinding it out under heel. He had followed Entwhistle's girlfriend from the University to a Women's Institute hall, of all places.

He had even managed to get a look inside, in spite of the fact that heavy drapes had been drawn across the windows. The tiniest of gaps had allowed him to glimpse the hall and what he had seen was instantly recognizable.

They were witches. Or at least, they thought they were. He seriously doubted they were like his Lizzie. She was a wonder. She had shown him things that were, well, magic. But this lot just seemed to prance around and chant. They didn't even take their clothes off!

But his plan to grab Entwhistle's girlfriend and give her a good sorting was not going to work. There were far too many people. He would have to bide his time.

Knowing the so called Wiccans were all busy in the main hall, he had slipped inside and checked out the bulletin board. Just as he hoped, there was a schedule tacked up. He snatched it down, giving it a once over. Yep. The roster contained the times and dates when the Spirit Seekers met. He almost laughed at that. Pretentious fuckwits.

He folded the paper and slipped it into his pocket then made his way out. Now he knew exactly where the hippy chick was going to be and when. All he had to do was wait for her and the right moment was sure to present itself.

He hid himself in the darkest recess of the car park and watched the main entrance. Soon enough she emerged, talking briefly with an older, posh looking woman.

He almost shit himself when she turned and looked in his direction. He froze, not daring to move. But then she got in her truck and drove away. Sumpter smiled, lighting another cigarette. Now he knew where she would be and when. He would come back. He just needed to get a few things.

Little Flower Cottage stood in a remote area, the narrow country roads winding between high hedgerows with no street lamps to guide outsiders. Surrounded by fields on three sides, and a forest on the fourth, the cottage was the sole human dwelling for several miles and the only building at all save the odd machinery shed, pigsty or barn.

Looking into the darkness outside the kitchen window Entwhistle saw only his own worried reflection. He suppressed the urge to pace. He need not worry, he told himself. Fern was a better driver than he was.

He took a seat in the same chair he always used. The chair he had taken the first day he met the old man. He stared vacantly at the half empty cup of tea in front of him, then glancing at the window saw a forlorn man slumped over the table. Well, how should he feel? Certainly not deserving of the cottage and all that came with it, a bitter reward for letting down his friend.

Discovering the full extent of his new wealth had shocked and shamed him. A year ago it would have been a dream to have enough money to do anything he wanted. Now it felt like a penance, a rebuke. He shifted slightly in his chair, staring into the black October night, one hand idly tapping the side of his cup.

Mr. Francis had needed someone to take over as guardian for the djinn that he had brought back from the

Sahara so long ago and Entwhistle had seemed like the perfect candidate. Only he never got the chance to find out. He wanted to scream. It was not fair! How was he to know that Sandwell would take the djinn and kill it?

He glanced at his watch again. She was late. He had been expecting her for the better part of an hour. Perhaps the meeting ran on? Meeting. Hah! It was a coven of witches, not an evening class. *When shall we three meet again?* Ludicrous. But ludicrous or not, she was a witch. Just like Sandwell.

Finally he heard the Land Rover pulling into the lane. The engine cut off with a shudder and a minute later Fern came through the back door, bringing the cold air with her. She always went in and out by the back, even though the front door was closer to where she parked. She was averse to the door, although she could not say why. Of course, Entwhistle knew. But how do you tell your girlfriend that there are spirits *permanently inconvenienced*, as the old Mr. Francis had once said, embedded in the fabric of the cottage?

They were defensive wards now, the souls of men who had come to claim the djinn for themselves. Mr. Francis had not explained how they had been *inconvenienced*, only that the djinn had done it.

Fern gave him a smile as she shrugged her jacket off, hanging it from the back of one of the plain pine chairs, the one Mr. Francis had favored. Now it was Fern's.

"Hello, dear," she said, with a smile. "Miss me?"

"Always. How was it?" Entwhistle rose and went to her.

"It was lovely. So nice to see everyone."

Her hair flowed around her shoulders, straight and dark. She dazzled him with a wide smile. Entwhistle hugged her and she gave him a quick kiss, returning his hug, then extricated herself. She turned to the stove and picked up the old copper kettle, hefting it in her hand, judging how much water it contained.

"It's still hot," said Entwhistle, sitting. Fern nodded, took a cup from a shelf and started to make her usual infusion of herbs and spices. She did not care for Entwhistle's special brand of strong black tea, or as she called it, paint stripper. She spooned the loose leaves into her cup, poured the water and then let it sit, the aroma already filling the kitchen with the smell of Christmas.

She sat and stretched out, grabbing his hands. Hers were ice cold. "I think the heater in the Land Rover is broken. I froze coming home."

The old vehicle had belonged to Mr. Francis. One of many stored in the large barn, a mile from the cottage. Entwhistle's car was still in the police pound in Essex, with a blown engine.

The other cars in the barn were much more ostentatious and Philip felt too self-conscious even to think about using them, especially the vintage Rolls Royce. The old Land Rover was more his style. The barn contained an astonishing collection of old cars and motorcycles. One of the local farmers received an annual stipend in exchange for maintaining the collection. Philip made a mental note to ask Rappaport about that. What else was going on behind the scenes that he had not discovered yet? He was aware that there were some charitable aspects to the estate but did not know the details.

"I'll see if I can get something done about it," he said. He could talk to the farmer. What was his name? No matter. Rappaport would know.

Entwhistle gave her hand a squeeze and reached for his tea. Fern smiled and sipped her concoction carefully, warming her fingers around the cup.

Seeing her there, across his table, his heart swelled at the thought that she was with him. She chose him! He could hardly believe it most days. But grateful as he was for her presence, there was still that nagging doubt. Maybe he shouldn't tell her. What if she didn't understand? What if she left? He took a deep breath, as if about to say something and Fern looked up expectantly. But he remained silent, staring down at the table, silently suffering a now familiar bout of shame over his failure with the djinn. Knowing that she was being patient with him was pressure enough, and the longer he delayed telling her the harder it was to begin.

Shaking it off, he looked up and smiled, calmed by her patience. She was his complete opposite in every way. Yet they complemented each other surprisingly well. They even looked a little similar now. His nose was slightly crooked, thanks to Paul Sumpter's fist. The thug had also punched Fern when she found him robbing Philip's apartment. Fern liked to joke that they were twins: they had identically broken noses.

"I thought I might invite some friends over for breakfast tomorrow. From my circle."

"Sure, that's fine. I'm going to the university, so I won't be in your way."

"Oh. In that case, they can come the day after. I want them to meet you. That okay?"

"I see. Well, alright, I guess."

She nodded. "So, you're going back to work?"

"Yes." He nodded decisively. "Sanjay has done well, but I really need to get back in the saddle."

Fern reached out, patting his hand. "I think it's a great idea. Stop you moping around the house."

Fern looked thoughtful for a moment as she gazed out into the darkness of the garden. "I think the soil needs a little nitrogen. If you can drop me off in the village in the morning, I'll pick up some pellets."

"Alright."

Just then Entwhistle caught a glimpse of something odd near the window, a shimmering like the air over tarmac on a hot day. Was the stove still that hot? He stared, puzzled.

Fern started and put her cup down so quickly she spilled

her tea. She peered at him closely, a worried frown creasing her face.

"Philip?"

"Hmm?" Philip was distracted, still staring at the odd shimmer. He looked back towards her, noting the spilled tea.

"Are you okay?" Fern pressed.

"What? Yes, I'm fine. Why?"

"There's definitely something you're not telling me."

A surge of adrenaline shot through his veins. Did she suspect something? He swallowed. "Why do you say that?"

"Well, you . . . There's something weird."

Philip raised an eyebrow, wondering what she was talking about. Fern leaned in closer, peering at his eyes. He looked away, disconcerted.

"You have green eyes, right?"

"Yes. Of course. What are you …?"

"They're blue Philip. Suddenly they are very . . . *blue*."

Philip snapped his head around, staring back at her. The beginnings of a hopeful smile spread slowly across his face. He reached for the silver amulet under his shirt. He took it out, and his eyes, now bluer than blue, flared from the talisman's touch. An uncontrollable grin split his face and the guilt and shame eating away at him evaporated in a single, joyous instant.

Jinny! She was *back*.

But when duty calls tomorrow

3

Cattle die, kinsmen die
But I know of only one thing that does not:
The fame of the dead.
—*Hávamál*

Norway, Jotunheim

The snow-covered mountain was jagged, deadly even to a skilled climber. But there was a path. It was narrow and rough and not easy to find, even for those who knew of its existence. It wound from the valley floor to a shallow ledge on the mountainside, an hour's hard walking. The path was hidden, but not the vehicles belonging to those who used it. Ten cars stood parked in a neat row at the base of the mountain, guarded by an armed police officer carrying a long, heavy flashlight.

Far above, the ledge on the mountainside gave access to a narrow crevice opening into a cave. Widely-spaced candles, some standing on the rough floor, others lodged in small niches carved into the rock walls created islands of illumination in a sea of darkness.

This outer cave led to another of many such, and not all mapped. Known only to a select few, the closely-guarded secret of the cave system had been kept for over a thousand years. From a vast inner chamber a low drone echoed off ancient stone. Chanting. They had begun.

Svein Eikenes had been inducted into the Cult of Odin in his early twenties. A tall man, blond and blue-eyed, he was everything a scion of the true Nordic people should be. At forty-five, he was still young and had decades of service ahead but was already grooming his eldest daughter to take his place. When that might be, he did not know. The Master chose new members of the council as he needed them. It might even be that she would serve alongside him, although new blood usually replaced old.

And that was how it should be, he thought. He stood in the ante-chamber, removing his clothes, not minding the chill, dank air. He was alone in the outer cave, the others having arrived on time and already joined the Master. As Chief of Police, he had been delayed by an inter-denominational congress he could not avoid. Ministers from many faiths, priests, even nuns were in attendance; he had been forced to attend to represent the secular authorities. In a silent fury he had endured hours of their blathering about their one God, and how He loved everyone. It could not be too soon that the true nature of the universe was revealed to those fools, and the world. They would learn, and when the real gods were restored in all their glory there would be a reckoning.

Now naked he reached into a wooden box at the cave's edge, one of nine identical boxes. He piled his clothes in and retrieved a rough woolen robe which he donned quickly. He slipped his feet into leather sandals, and tied the straps.

Once ready, he started to make his way into the main chamber then stopped with a curse and doubled back. He unstrapped his wristwatch and dropped it into the box.

By the power of Odin, he thought. *That* would be less likely to be forgiven than his lateness. Now devoid of any iron he navigated the narrow passage. Soon it widened, the sound of chanting growing louder.

The low murmur of voices reverberated from the rock

walls of the huge cave, echo playing upon echo in an almost infinite loop fed by the black-robed men and women kneeling before a similarly clad figure; the Master. His face hidden, only the Master's hands showed as he placed them upon the great slab of shining white-blue ice of the altar.

The Master did not move. The voices changed, the tone became darker, slower, the cadence irregular. The Master pressed down on the altar and his hands slid deep into the ice. A glow began to form, deep within the heart of the great block of ancient frozen water, a blue nimbus appeared, thin lines tracing outwards, forming glyphs and symbols. Soon, there were a dozen glowing sigils deep within the ice.

The Master, High Priest of Odin and keeper of the true faith, slowly pulled his hands free. No hole or fissure in the ice showed where his hands had entered, passing through the solid surface as easily as if it were water. The sigils deep within the great slab continued to glow, pulsing slowly.

The Master gestured in benediction and the figures ringed around him fell silent. The echo of their chanting took a minute to fade away but when silence came it was heavy, as if carrying the weight of ages. Svein joined the kneeling acolytes, pulling his hood forward to cover his face. He looked up at the Master, as always a mixture of fear and awe suffusing him.

The Master was not a tall man. There were many present bigger than he, women included. But he exuded strength and power, as was fitting for Odin's chosen. He raised his hands and pulled back his cowl. Though partly shadowed, it was easy to see the ragged scar crossing his face. The arresting blue of his eyes seemed to shine with an inner light. He stepped forward with a pronounced limp.

Svein knew the Master had fought many battles, and not all had been victories. But he had endured, safeguarding the knowledge that would resurrect the gods and return the world to its former glory. In the heavy silence the Master fixed his azure gaze on his acolytes.

"For over a thousand years our order has served the High One," he said. "We have kept his vigil. To us has fallen the task of safeguarding the gods in their slumber."

His voice rang out clear and strong but there was a hint of something archaic in the way he spoke, how he enunciated, with stresses in odd places. "But now the time of their awakening is close, and to those who serve in this time falls the honor of awaking them."

There was a muttering of excited approval from the nine present. Eikenes felt a thrill course through him. That it would happen in his lifetime! He had always hoped, always dreamed. But no one knew when the time would come. To be alive when the gods returned! He lowered his hood, baring his face. The others did the same, revealing a group of men and women of varied age.

The Master placed his hand on the slab of solid ice, caressing its glassy surface. The glyphs deep within flared, as if drawing power from his touch. One, a circle, shone brighter than the others. The symbol of everlasting life. It represented the spirit, the gods, the universe itself. It burned brighter than it had ever done before; visual testimony to the Master's words.

"The barrier between worlds is weakening. Not for tens of thousands of years has it been so fragile. Soon I will release our gods, fulfilling our destiny. On this day let us renew our pledge to the great task. We, who have guarded the true path, here give an oath of life, and promise of death."

The Master held out his hand, and one by one the assembled men and women stood and bowed before him, kissing the black ring on his middle finger, their lips gently brushing the sigil emblazoned there; a snake swallowing its own tail. The circle again, thought Svein. He too wore a ring like this. It was the mark of their order, the serpent that spanned the world. They all had one, but made from silver, not the obsidian of the Master. Only true silver was allowed within the chamber. The fool who brought any other metal would feel the Master's wrath.

"Bring forth the dedication. Let us give life's blood to honor the High One."

One of the robed acolytes led a small goat by a tether. He lifted it up, placing it on the altar. It looked about itself in curiosity, bleating. The priest pulled a blade from within his sleeve. It was black, made of the same stone as his ring, the polished obsidian showing a series of tiny, flaked indentations, each one terminating in an edge as sharp as any razor. Almost gently he caressed the small animal's throat with the blade.

"We give this life to the All Father."

The goat bleated again, its eyes staring about in confusion as its legs collapsed. The blood jetting from its neck stained the blue ice as rivulets of red flowed along the finely carved lines of its surface. The blue glow of the glyphs darkened, turning scarlet. The circle deep within the ice glowed brightest of all, taking on a deep, crimson hue. The sacrifice was accepted.

"To you, Odin, we dedicate this life. Long have we waited, but now the time of the Aesir is at hand. We give ourselves to your purpose, Odin. We are your spear, guide us."

Eikenes repeated the words of his priest, as did all the acolytes, in chanted unison: *we give ourselves.* Then the Master turned to face them, eyes shining brightly in the darkness.

"The time of the fourth moon comes. The gods will be with us soon. I feel their presence, their stirring. We shall need another sacrifice. This time something worthy. You know what you must do."

He made a gesture of dismissal, then turned and limped away towards the back of the cave where his chambers lay.

Eikenes had been there once and seen the austerity in which his master lived. He felt a swelling of righteous fury. Their time of hiding and skulking in shadows was coming to an end. Soon enough they would rise up and cast down the false religions and once again the world would feel the might of the true gods and those who served them. A new Viking age was coming.

He smiled widely, his grin mirrored by the dozens of human skulls that lined the walls behind him, their polished bone shining like alabaster.

Liv Aasheim finished emptying the dishwasher, stacking plates and hanging mugs on hooks. She closed the machine with a thump that coincided with a knock at the door. Wiping her damp hands on a cloth as she crossed the kitchen, she peeked around the back door curtain. It was already dark outside but she had no problem seeing the tall man in the orange hard hat and hi-viz vest over a heavy fleece-lined coat. Even so he hunched his shoulders and clenched his hands against the biting cold.

She opened the door and he gave her a grateful smile. Liv ushered him inside immediately.

"Hello Mr. Hansen," she said. "Everything ok?"

Hansen brought in a bracing wave of cold air and she quickly shut the door behind him.

"Hello Mrs. Aasheim. I need to speak with Arnulf. Is he about?"

"No, sorry. He's out on his rounds. There's no problem with the trees is there?"

"No, not at all. The quality is good. So good they'll probably be worth more than we thought. But we've come across something in the middle section of quadrant two."

"Well, Arnulf's in the south field with the sheep. I'll give him a call. How about a coffee?"

Hansen nodded and Liv went to the kitchen table, picked up a small walkie-talkie from a brightly-painted wooden bowl and thumbed the button. The farm had a half dozen of them, cheap and, unlike mobile phones, free to use. Although only useful for short distances they covered most of the farm reliably enough. The radio crackled and she spoke slowly into it.

"Arnulf. Can you hear me, Arnulf?"

After a momentary silence an answering crackle preceded the thin distant voice of her husband.

"Yes. What is it, Liv?"

"Mr. Hansen from the logging company is here at the house. He says they found something. Can you come back?"

"Yeah. I'm about done here anyway. I'll be back in a couple of minutes."

"Good. Dinner will be ready soon."

She put the walkie-talkie back in the bowl on the table and proceeded to make the hot drink. "Well, Mr. Hansen, looks like you have time for that coffee."

"Yes, definitely. Much appreciated."

Hansen happily sipped the scalding coffee, the mug so hot it almost burned his fingers, red with cold.

"So everything's okay?" asked Liv. "With the trees, I mean?" She was one of those people who found silence awkward. Arnulf called her a chatterbox. He was not exactly taciturn but he did like his quiet moments. Still, she knew he would not have her any other way.

"Oh yes, very good. To be honest, they are even better caliber than we initially thought. We'll be through with the first section by tomorrow, then we'll start on the marked trees in the main area. We should be done by the weekend, no problem."

"Good, good. I suppose it will be nice to have the extra cash."

Hansen nodded and gave Liv a look of compassion. They were not the first farmers to sacrifice natural resources to make it through another year.

Some minutes later the rumble of Arnulf's old Land Rover announced his arrival. A door slammed, and they heard the crunch of footsteps. The back door opened and Arnulf hurried inside, stamping his feet on the mat.

"Hell, that's getting bitter," he said with a nod over his shoulder that was clearly meant to encompass the entirety of the outdoors. Hansen laid his cup on the table and stood up.

"Arnulf, there's something you need to see."

"What's the matter?"

"We've found a small haug."

Liv frowned, puzzled. There were no hills on their land, small or otherwise. From the look on his face, Arnulf thought the same.

"No, that can't be. I've been over every inch of that land."

"Well, it's there. I think you have an old burial mound on your land. Could be real old."

"Alright, let's take a look at it."

They left, Arnulf pausing at the door to give Liv an apologetic shrug and a longing look at the dinner table.

The following morning Entwhistle's eyes were still a startling blue. Fern was not just puzzled—she was astounded. She asked if he had learned to do a simple charm, perhaps one that had gone wrong? Why would he want blue eyes?

He desperately wanted to give her some answers. But the djinn had clearly survived and now that it . . . *she* was back, he was still honor bound by his promise to Mr. Francis. He would keep the secret and he would protect her. That had not stopped even when he thought the elemental was dead, and it certainly held now he knew she was alive.

The djinn's voice entered his mind, a thing Entwhistle had never imagined he would miss.

Thank you, little man. We did well when we chose you.

The reminder that it was both the djinn and Sir James Francis who had chosen him simply firmed his resolve. He was still the guardian, after all, and his first duty was to his vow, even if there was a cost.

Fern stared at him over the breakfast table, her gray-blue eyes boring into his now icy blue. "Philip, there is obviously something you failed to mention when we first got together."

What could he say to that? She was right. He nodded miserably. "Yes."

"Something you've been keeping from me."

"Yes." He ached to tell her, but he could not, whatever the consequences. This was the end for them, without a doubt. As a couple, as lovers, even as friends. She would see it as a betrayal and that would be that.

"Well?" She crossed her arms and, like a school teacher waiting for an apology from a truculent child, stared at him expectantly. He buttered some toast, adding a spoon of jam. He was not hungry but it gave him a moment, a brief reprieve. He put the toast on his plate.

"I'm sorry Fern, but I can't talk about it." He looked away, as if to hide the eyes that would finish them.

"Well, it's not the sort of thing you can ignore is it?" Fern said. "If you're okay with it, I could ask the circle to look into this. Make sure nothing's wrong?"

Entwhistle almost choked. "No, no. Don't bother yourself. There's nothing to be concerned about. I'm sorry Fern. I know how this must look, but you have to trust me. Nothing is wrong."

She regarded him with narrowed eyes. Clearly she disagreed but mercifully, for the moment, she left it at that. Entwhistle claimed he was needed at the University early and had to get ready for work. He hurried to the bedroom, away from Fern's searching gaze.

Once back on campus he realized he was happy. The familiar sights and sounds of the hallways thronging with students, some of whom actually wanted to learn, made him smile. This was his domain, his home, where he belonged. Books, history, classrooms. Not magic, and spells and . . . Well, there was still Jinny. Like it or not, he was part of that other world now too.

But perhaps he could keep them separate? Why not? No one would ever know about Jinny, so why not two lives?

After a brief talk with his boss, Sam Evans, he was on his way to the auditorium and his first lecture. Sam had successfully pressed Entwhistle for a promise that he was back to stay. Rather oddly, he had not mentioned the eyes. Perhaps he had not noticed. He was getting on, after all. Entwhistle suggested letting Sanjay take one of his classes, starting the following term. Evans agreed. He had been considering how better to use the Indian's inexhaustible energy.

Professor Philip Entwhistle turned to face the hundred and fifty or so students arrayed randomly in the auditorium. He had never seen so many at one of his lectures. Some of them must be here to audit the class, he thought. Or just to get a good look at him. After the success of his biography on Sir James Francis, and the business with the police, he had gone from total obscurity to notoriety in one step.

Sanjay had already set up the presentation slides and passed Entwhistle the computer's clicker. Entwhistle cleared his throat.

"Good afternoon everyone. As you may know, I've been on sabbatical. Well, I'm back again. I would like to say a word of thanks to Mr. Patel, who has done an outstanding job in my absence. Thank you, Sanjay."

Sanjay grinned, nodding enthusiastically. He sat down in the front row and resumed his work. He was not there to take notes. He had a stack of papers that needed grading and he got on with the task.

"Not only that," he continued, "but Mr. Patel will be taking over this class next term."

Sanjay looked up sharply, gaping. He made to stand, but Philip waved him back. There would be time for thanks later. Sanjay was a good T.A. and Entwhistle did not doubt he would make a fine teacher.

Like him, Sanjay wanted to write. Not just the dry papers that most academics produced, but popular history books attracting mainstream attention. A tall order, but Philip had proved it was possible. His biography of Sir James Francis was selling in quantities that one outraged critic had claimed was 'simply stupid.' The incorporation of unsourced details and opinions had earned him some harsh criticism, but the book was not just a history text. It told a compelling tale, a real adventure—a one-time spy for His Majesty, George V, a linguist of astonishing ability, had passed himself off as a member of the merchant class in the Arabic world, married a simple Tuareg girl and then lost her in a tragic confrontation in the deep desert. The compassion and sensitivity in the writing resonated with readers. But Entwhistle had told only a part of the truth. Some things were too fantastical and far too precious to reveal. There was no mention of the djinn that Sir James had brought back with him, for one, or the fact that he actually lived, hale and healthy, for well over a hundred years after the events in the book. A fact known only to Philip Entwhistle.

"Alright, let's begin with steam engines," he said as a picture showing a colossus of a machine, easily two stories high, appeared on the screen. "Why should a smaller, more powerful engine be a linchpin technology in the early nineteenth century? Or, to put it another way, what makes these steam engines an enabler for radical change in society?"

He clicked again, and the image changed to a considerably smaller machine. Entwhistle could have delivered this lecture in his sleep. He knew the subject matter inside out and had no need to think ahead. As he talked, his mind wandered back to the events that had started it all—a Bedouin dying in the Sahara.

That old man had given Sir James the djinn. From what Philip had learned from his time with the old man, the djinn would surely have engineered the encounter between his Arabic guardian and the eccentric Englishman at the critical moment. And then, almost a century later, Entwhistle had made a phone call, asking for an interview with the man that he believed at the time to be Sir James Francis' great-nephew. Had Jinny engineered that too? So began the chain of events leading to his being tested for the role of guardian.

Unlike his unfortunate predecessors, who had sought the role and the power it would bring, Entwhistle, seeking only knowledge had unwittingly passed the tests. When the offer of becoming the guardian had been made, he had agreed without really understanding what it meant. Then, through his carelessness with the meta-anchor, he had made a mess of it all. But not, it seems, as big a mess as he had thought and Entwhistle was thrilled. He could not wait to talk with Jinny, learn her secrets and experience past events as if they were his own memories.

He literally could have jumped for joy. Best not, he thought, as he gazed out at the students. He brought his mind back to the lecture.

"So, better engines meant deeper coal mines, which meant more coal was available to power the Industrial Revolution. And this led to the development of another new technology. The system of locks and canals built to transport the coal . . ."

Now that Jinny was back, Entwhistle knew he was going to have to be a lot more careful. She was still very weak, but at least he could now feel her presence. And in time, she would be strong enough to manifest again physically, perhaps taking on the form of a cat again. What could be more appropriate than that? After all, Fern was a witch. It was . . . traditional. He stopped himself. What was he thinking? He couldn't tell her. And the moment Fern understood that he was never going to share his secret, then surely it would all be over.

Philip looked out to the auditorium and clicked the remote, changing the onscreen slide again. He would have to tell Fern something. But what? His stomach churned in frustration, desperation even.

"Professor?" Sanjay said.

Philip realized that he had stopped in mid flow. There were titters from the students.

"Sorry. I got distracted. Right, where was I?" He clicked the remote and moved onto the next topic. "Railways . . ."

Arnulf took the most direct route, the Land Rover bumping over rutted fields, bouncing the men around inside and rattling them vigorously. He gripped the steering wheel tightly, reminding himself, once again, to put a leather cover over it. One winter he had gone out and had actually gotten stuck to it, frozen by the damned arctic cold.

The logging supervisor, Hansen, held onto a grab rail set in the vehicle's roof, barely managing to keep his seat.

"Over there," he shouted above the noise of the engine, pointing west of their current direction. Arnulf adjusted course and before long they came upon the devastation wrought by the logging. What had once been a grand forest, thick with old growth, was now a wasteland of stumps, limbs of trees and large piles of neatly stacked, trimmed logs. Arnulf had not had time to prepare for the sight and his heart almost broke to see it. He brought the truck to a standstill and cut the engine. In the sudden silence the devastation felt even worse.

The two men clambered down from the truck and Hansen pointed to where the huge multi-purpose logging machine stood. It could cut down a tree, strip its limbs and load it onto a transport in a matter of minutes. Not that

Arnulf was looking. Next to the large, yellow John Deere harvester stood a prominent bump in the field covered in scraggly brush. Odd that he had never noticed, but the surrounding trees had been thick. He must have passed it a hundred times without spotting it.

They crossed the field. For Arnulf it was like marching across a bloody and devastated battlefield, each stump a fallen comrade. He shook his head in dismay at the consequences of his decision.

Then he saw the painted planks that lay scattered about and with a shock Arnulf realized that this was where the kids had made their tree house. Now it was just debris in a field. Somehow this was almost worse than taking the trees.

As they approached the haug, Arnulf could clearly see that it was too steep, too symmetrical to be natural. A single tree remained upon it, a great chestnut growing from the top. Some of its roots were plainly visible, cutting through the soil and exposed on the surface.

"Well, I'll be . . ." he said, trailing into silence.

"I've come across things like this before," said Hansen. "Could be Bronze Age. I'd say it goes back to pre-Viking times."

"Well, if it's that old, what're the chances there's something in it? Should we call the university? Maybe they should come out and take a look?"

"Yeah, I think you should. You never know. If there is anything and you don't report it, you could get a pretty hefty fine."

Arnulf nodded. He had heard of similar instances. In one, a farmer had come across a small hoard of coins and bits of twisted gold and silver. He had tried to sell them privately and ended up with everything confiscated, plus a fine. He snorted and shook his head. With his luck, what were the chances that there would be anything to report?

"Anyway," Hansen continued, "if they don't want to come out and look, at least you tried."

"I suppose so."

Both men climbed the hill, Arnulf taking care to avoid tripping on the exposed roots. In watching his step he caught a glimpse of something out of place. He stooped over, peering at an object lying at his feet. Although covered in mud, enough was visible to detect the distinctive sheen of gold. More puzzled than excited he went down one knee and started to scrape away the dirt. Whatever it was, it was still partially buried, having only been half lifted from the ground by the tree's roots. As he scraped away the earth it became obvious that it was gold, large and obviously of great value.

Hansen, looking over his shoulder, gasped. "Oh my . . . would you look at that?"

And for the first time in over a thousand years, the great torc was brought into the light.

Norway, AD 998
3 days travel from Jotunheim

Egill Thrandsson and his followers led their horses along a muddy track. Riding the small horses all day would wear them out and lead to other problems, such as their going lame. Not a risk they could afford to take with no likelihood of trading them between here and Egill's family homestead. So they walked an hour and rode an hour, fair on both beast and man.

It was still raining and they were soaked through, woolen cloaks unable to cope with the constant drizzle. As Egill had feared, his chainmail was beginning to take on the telltale smell of rust. He would need to find some fine sand and scrub the links thoroughly. He cast a glance at the sky. Taking proper care of his gear was important but not something he could do soon, it would appear. The gray clouds did not look like they were going anywhere.

The road winding through the valley had obviously been

in heavy use, and recently. Passing wagons had left deep ruts and churned the mud, and on more than one occasion Egill had to pull hard to free his foot from its sucking embrace.

Red Asgeir quickened his pace, and came alongside him. He looked sourly at his kinsman.

"Never going to stop pissing on us, is it?"

Egill laughed. "You want to complain to the gods, Asgeir?"

At that moment the heavens opened up harder and a peal of thunder echoed through the valley. As one, they reached for the pendants around their necks; silver hammers, in honor of their god, Thor.

"Anyway," Egill continued, "chances are it will snow tomorrow. The ground will harden and we'll make better progress."

Asgeir nodded, his shaggy red hair plastered to his face. "Yeah, that'll be much better. Then we'll just freeze to death." He wiped away an errant strand of hair and tilted his head back, mouth open, as if to catch the rain. Mannuki trotted up beside them. Although a native of desert lands the weather did not seem to trouble the little man. His hair was plastered to his head and the vicious scar across his face was a livid white, in stark contrast to his dark skin.

"The rain will stop soon," he said. "We can shelter in the church of the White Christ, ahead." He pointed along the valley but Egill could see nothing through the misty rain.

"There's no church there," said Egill, with an emphatic shake of his head. He had travelled this road many times in years past, and knew every farm and dwelling. "And Asgeir's right. It's not gonna stop raining."

Mannuki gave him a sly smile. He slowed his pace, and soon fell behind again. In spite of his assurances regarding the weather, Egill looked to the sky. Mannuki was odd, but he was never wrong. The clouds did look less threatening. It was not long before the rain had stopped entirely.

Asgeir threw him a look as the last drops fell. No words were needed. They both knew there was something strange about the man with the bluer than blue eyes. How could he know that there was a Christian presence in this valley? But if Mannuki said there was a church . . .

The low wall surrounding the church of the White Christ was grass-covered; clearly old. But the wooden building had the look of freshly cut timber. They could still smell the pine resin from the boards. Evidently, they had not been properly dried and the place had been built in a hurry. That, or the workmen did not care whether the structure lasted.

Nevertheless Egill could see the place was favored, which was shocking enough; like finding an adder in the bed of your child. The church stood in a prime location, at the confluence of two roads. Egill shook his head and approached the entrance with more than a little trepidation.

A wiry man with the tonsured hair of a monk came out of the wooden building. He stood with hands tucked into the sleeves of his simple brown robe, remaining motionless as if waiting to see what Egill would do. A wooden cross hung from a leather thong around his neck. In other circumstances, Egill might have killed this man and burnt his dwelling. The White Christ was an offence to him as to all right-thinking men and women. And yet here was a church, just three days from his home.

He passed the reins of his horse to Asgeir and while the others waited he approached the priest. Egill towered over the little man yet he sensed the priest was not frightened. This was different. Most men were afraid of him, or at least wary. More fool them if they were not. But he gave the priest a grudging nod of respect.

"My men and I have travelled far. We are wet, tired and hungry. If you would give us a place to sleep and warm food to eat we would be grateful."

The priest stared up into the grizzled face of the warrior. He nodded slowly and gestured to the open door.

"You are welcome here, my son. All are welcome in Christ's house."

Egill's hand went to his throat, fingers feeling for his pendant. Perhaps it would be better to kill the priest, and just take what they needed? The priest stared up at him, brown eyes unflinching. No. There is no dishonor in accepting what is generously offered. He nodded.

Egill made a gesture to his men and stooping slightly, entered the church, one hand on the pommel of his sword. He looked about cautiously, as if expecting Christ to step out and assault him. Inside it was dark, the few candles tiny pools of light. He shrugged off his outer cloak and let it fall across one of three rough-hewn wooden benches. At one end of the small chapel there was a raised area. The altar, he recalled. Upon it stood a wooden cross with a carved effigy of the nailed god. He had seen its like many times in the lands around Miklagard, but never once had he thought to see it in Norway.

The others followed him inside, Red Asgeir looking about with thinly veiled interest, eyes wide. The two brothers showed less concern, simply finding a corner and collapsing.

"Where is Mannuki?" Egill asked.

"Taking care of the horses," replied Asgeir. Egill nodded. Mannuki always put the others before himself, a reason to tolerate the little man in spite of his strangeness.

The priest entered and gestured at the humble furniture. "You are welcome to what little I have. I shall prepare food. It will take a little while. In the meantime, why not take your rest."

Egill nodded. He spied a lectern in a corner. There was parchment and quill. Clearly this little priest was more than he appeared. Few men knew the art of writing. Egill did not. He could carve runes, good as any man, but he could not write in the new fashion. However, he had seen the great scriptoriums of Miklagard and had been amazed when one of the scribes had read from the parchments, ancient words once again living.

He pointed to the lectern. "You can write?"

The priest seemed surprised. "Yes. Forgive me, but few people know of this. How do you?"

Egill shrugged. "I gave service in Miklagard. There are many there who know how to write and read. I do not, but I have seen such before."

The priest nodded, his eyes shining. "Miklagard! I have heard such stories."

Egill laughed. In spite of himself, he was starting to like the little priest. "I could tell you tales you would not believe."

The priest grinned. "If you would honor me with a tale or two, I would be *most* grateful."

"Tell him about Bjorn," said Asgeir from across the room.

"A hero?" asked the priest.

"Bjorn the Strong was just a man," Egill replied. "But he was blessed by the gods. I saw such things that I would not believe had I not been there myself. Come, priest. Prepare the food. When you are done, I will tell you his story."

The priest glanced at his lectern and writing tools. He nodded and went into a small side room. Egill collapsed onto a bench and stretched out, his mind filled with memories of his friend.

England, Southern University

The university campus was much like any other institute of learning. Young kids talking earnestly about things that would not matter once they had graduated, couples kissing in the corners and harried tutors rushing from class to class. Detectives Hanlon and Topley made their way through the throngs towards the Administration block. A young man with straggly hair and beard saw them approaching and did an immediate U-turn, walking at speed in the opposite direction. Topley stared into the back of his head, obviously itching to make an arrest. This was not the first kid to see them and instantly remember pressing business elsewhere.

Hanlon nodded at the speedily disappearing back. "If only it were that easy to tell the villains on the street."

Topley chuckled, holding the door to the Administration Department open for his partner. They knew their way from previous visits. They followed a corridor, marching past the collected portraits of the university presidents, until they came to a door marked T. Richards.

"Thank you for seeing us again," said Detective Hanlon as she and Topley entered the office. Mrs. Richards motioned them in, waving to a pair of chairs.

"Not at all, officers. Come in. Do sit down. Shall I call for tea?"

Topley lowered his bulk into one of the evidently too small chairs, and shook his head.

"No thanks," he said. "This really isn't a social visit."

"I did not for one second think it was," Richards replied, voice tinged with a hint of frost.

Hanlon gave Topley a look that clearly said 'mind your manners' and turned a nervous smile on the head of Human Resources. Hanlon sat on the edge of her chair, back straight, legs and feet carefully arranged. For some reason she found questioning the older woman difficult. She felt like a little girl, called to the principal's office. With an effort she reminded herself that she was the one with the power here, an officer of the law while Richards was just a university administrator.

So why did she feel so nervous?

Detective Hanlon glanced around the large office, taking in the framed certificates on the wall, a new laptop on the desk, and a group of family photos. Richards' children, she presumed and, it would seem, grandchildren. Next to the photographs was a glass containing a twig with some twine tied around it. A coin rested at the bottom of the glass. Curious. Probably a keepsake from a family outing, or some such, she thought.

"Now then, what I can do for you?" the Mrs. Richards asked. "I already told you everything the last time you were here."

They had talked to Tessa Richards a week after the fire at Woodhall Drive, before they had run out of leads. Now, faced with the strong possibility that the miscreant who had torched the house, and possibly committed murder, would get away with it, they wanted to go over every single possible avenue, leaving no stone unturned.

"Yes," said Hanlon, "but since then, perhaps something else might have come to mind? You never know when it comes to one's memory."

Hanlon carefully did not say, *for a woman of your age*. Advanced in years Richards might be, but the glare in her eye signaled a sharp mind and equally sharp tongue.

"I really don't think there's anything I can add," Richards insisted. "But feel free to ask."

Hanlon opened her notebook, flipping to the notes from her previous interview.

"You told us that Entwhistle and Sandwell had been involved in some kind of dispute. Relating to a promotion?"

"Yes, that's right. *Dr.* Entwhistle and Dr. Sandwell were both in consideration for an Associate Professorship. As it transpired, Dr. Entwhistle was awarded the post."

Topley stirred, a large hand raising a finger. "And why was that?"

Richards regarded him for a moment before replying. "Because Dr. Sandwell was forced to withdraw due to inappropriate behavior."

Topley frowned. "You didn't mention that before. And what precisely, does *inappropriate behavior* mean?"

"It means," she replied, "that Dr. Sandwell was caught in flagrante delicto. She had somewhat unorthodox views as to the meaning of a locked door and private email."

Hanlon's brow furrowed as she tried to read between the lines. "Are you saying that you caught her breaking into locked offices?"

"Not exactly caught, but the evidence that she did exactly that was beyond circumstantial. Indeed she admitted as much when I relieved her of a master key that would allow her access to any door in the entire university. Further, there was also clear evidence that she had accessed certain staff members' private email correspondence. As a result, she was suspended, awaiting the results of an internal review. I did not tell you the last time we spoke as it was a confidential university matter. But in the light of her disappearance I cannot see that it can harm her. So, there you have it."

"Do you think that Dr. Entwhistle could have had anything to do with her disappearance?" Hanlon asked. She watched Richards carefully, looking for any sign of avoidance, lowering the eyes, or looking away, or changes in skin color. But the older woman was not to be read so easily.

"No, good Lord! Why on earth would you suggest such a thing?"

"Because we have an eyewitness that places him on scene, at precisely the time when a fire broke out at Dr. Sandwell's home."

Richards shook her head. "Well, I cannot speak to that. But I can say that the disagreements between them were professional in nature. Not the kind of thing that would lead to whatever you are suggesting. I mean, if every fight between the lecturers got out of hand in this way, we would be up to our ears in arson and murder."

Hanlon opened her mouth to reply but Topley beat her to it with a derisive snort. "This was a bit more than just a disagreement about parking privileges," he said.

Hanlon nodded. "Yes. Dr. Sandwell's allegation of a criminal nature against Dr. Entwhistle requires us to consider him a possible suspect in her disappearance."

Richards sniffed. "An allegation that was withdrawn."

"Quite," said Hanlon. "But perhaps under duress? Perhaps Dr. Entwhistle was threatening her?"

Richards shook her head. "Oh no. I don't think so. I asked her the same question myself." She opened her laptop, and searched for a moment. "I suppose it couldn't hurt now."

She clicked on a file. Immediately a gentle hiss and knocking sound emerged from her computer, as if the laptop was being moved. Richards' voice, slightly tinny, but clearly recognizable emerged.

"Dr. Sandwell, you have made an allegation of a serious nature against a colleague. You may not know this, but we began an investigation. However, earlier today I received an email from you stating your intent to withdraw the allegation. I have to ask, were you pressured into withdrawing it?"

"No, there was no pressure. I think I just over-reacted. I had had some wine and we were talking. I guess I'm so used to people hitting on me that I see it everywhere. Dr. Entwhistle did nothing wrong. It was simply a misunderstanding. I have already apologized to him and I hope that the whole affair can be put behind us."

"Well, that's very good, Dr. Sandwell. I am pleased to hear it. So you will sign a statement to that effect?"

"Yes, of course."

"And you have withdrawn the report you made to the police?"

"Well, my understanding is that they cannot proceed with it anyway, as there is no material evidence. But for what it's worth, yes. I did withdraw it."

Richards pressed a button on the laptop, and the

recording stopped.

"There, I think that settles it. Elizabeth Sandwell, in my opinion, made up the accusation in order to take Dr. Entwhistle out the running for the Associate Professorship. The fact that she would stoop to such tactics is somewhat shocking, but given what we discovered regarding her possession of a master key, and her clear violation of university policies . . ."

"You think she was capable of lying to the police?" Topley asked.

Richards laughed. "Oh my. Yes, she was perfectly capable of lying to the police. I believe that she had been lying about a great many things for a very long time. Elizabeth Sandwell was a sociopath of the first order."

Hanlon eyed the framed certificates on the wall behind Richards' head. Several were related to her role in Human Resources, but there, the one with fancy embossing, that would be her degree. It was slightly faded, and the writing small, but she could just make out the words *Doctor Philosophiae* and *Psychology*. Perhaps the old woman does know what she is talking about. Still, that did not mean that Sandwell was not murdered. No one just vanishes. Even sociopaths leave a trail. And since the day of the fire there had been no indication that Sandwell was still alive.

Perhaps this was a dead end. But if Entwhistle was involved, and every fiber of Hanlon's being told her that he was up to his neck in it, then there had to be something that would connect him to the missing parapsychologist.

A thought struck her and she stood suddenly, catching Topley by surprise. He questioned her with a look but she ignored it. She closed her notepad and put it in her jacket pocket.

"Alright, Mrs. Richards. Thank you for your time. If we have any more questions we'll be in touch."

She walked out without waiting for her partner. Hurrying after her Topley pulled the door closed behind him.

"What's the rush?"

"I just had a thought," Hanlon replied

"Care to share?"

"Entwhistle moved into a cottage recently, in the south somewhere, right?"

"Yeah, that's what I heard."

"Where'd he get that kind of money from, on an academic salary?" Hanlon crossed her arms, one eyebrow arched. "Hmm?"

"He inherited it, apparently."

"Exactly. And have you ever known an inheritance that did not lead to some kind of wrangling? Arguments over the will, that sort of thing?"

At first it had seemed to be an academic rivalry, but what if it was more? Always follow the money, that was the first rule. It galled her that it had taken her this long to remember.

"You're thinking that maybe Sandwell was a beneficiary, and that Entwhistle did for her, so he would get the lot?"

"I'd say it's worth looking into."

"What was his lawyer called?"

Hanlon pulled the card out of her pocket. It was expensively made, the embossed words of Rappaport and Associates clearly picked out in gold leaf.

"Time we paid Entwhistle's lawyer a visit, I think," Hanlon replied.

It was still light when the archeologists arrived at the Aasheim's farm. There were two of them, both paunchy and middle-aged but with an excitable energy they did nothing to hide. Far from being the dry, dusty academics that Arnulf had expected they were colorful characters who smiled and laughed often, teasing each other like schoolboys.

Arnulf found himself grinning along with them, their excitement rubbing off. They stood before the haug, the potential burial mound. The trees were gone now, and the stumps and churned-up mud gave the place a desolate air.

Dr. Roger Farrell, from the University of Oslo, and Jens Eriksen, an archaeologist from the local municipality, stood a few steps from the base of the mound, pointing out features to each other. Eriksen made a few notes in his notebook. The Englishman from Oslo with the flamboyant bow tie pulled a large tape measure from his jacket and the two men paced off the length of the mound, Eriksen noting the results.

Farrell slipped the tape back into his coat pocket with a nod to the mound. "Shall we ascend?"

"Don't mind if I do," replied Eriksen with a grin, and they both marched up the small hill. With the chestnut tree gone, only its stump remaining, it was easier to gauge the full scale of the mound. Arnulf climbed up after them. The top of the haug was a little over three meters long, the base nearly half as long again.

"Like I said, the logging company found it when they were felling the trees." Arnulf pointed to the mass of roots where he had found the torc. "That's where I saw something yellow. When I had a closer look at it, I was . . . well, see for yourself."

He pulled a cotton handkerchief wrapped around something large from his pocket. He unfolded the cloth, and the now clean torc was revealed. Farrell exclaimed with delight and Eriksen's wide smile lit his face like a child's before a Christmas tree.

"Well I never," said Farrell.

"Now that is something," said Eriksen.

Farrell peered at it closely. "And it was just lying there on the surface, you say?"

Arnulf nodded. "Yes. Well, half. I think the tree's roots probably pushed it up over the years."

Both academics nodded. "Oh yes, that's entirely possible," said Eriksen.

"But it can't have been buried very deep originally," replied Farrell.

"Quite," said Eriksen. "I wouldn't be surprised if this was not a Viking mound at all. And that,"—pointing to the gold torc—"is quite unusual. We'll need to put in a trench here and see what we're dealing with."

"Is it possible that this was just lost here, I wonder," said Farrell, indicating the torc in Arnulf's hand. "May I?"

Arnulf passed it over, slightly reluctantly. He had already begun to think of it as his, regardless of what the law said.

Farrell felt its weight in his hand. "Solid gold, or I miss my mark," he said. "But it's not Scandinavian. Nor Celtic. Not anything I recognize, to be honest. Torc is from Latin, you know. Torquere, to twist." He turned the object over in his hand, examining it from all angles.

"But look, it has a fused buffer," said Eriksen, pointing with his pen to the ends of the ring of gold where the snake's tail fed into its open mouth.

"A muffer!" said Farrell. They both laughed. Muff was the correct term for the joined ends of a torc designed to be a single seamless circle, but both men seemed delighted with the English archeologist's wit.

Farrell passed it to Eriksen, who frowned at the golden serpent. "It's a snake . . ."

"Now, Jens, don't go jumping to conclusions," replied Farrell.

"Yes, but it's a snake. Eating its own tail. That's the Midgard Serpent. You remember your sagas?"

"Of course I do!" replied Farrell, testily. Suddenly both men had gone from childlike excitement to dour seriousness at the sight of the arm band.

"What?" Arnulf said. "What about the sagas?" He had read pieces from them in school. Everyone in Norway did.

But he heard no bells the way they were clearly ringing for the two academics.

"Well," said Eriksen. "There's this one saga . . ."

"Bjorn the Mighty's saga," interjected Farrell.

"Sagan um Björn hinn mikla," corrected Eriksen.

"It talks about a group of Vikings," continued Farrell, "and their adventures as Varangians. In particular, Bjorn the Mighty, or Bjorn the Strong. There's some confusion as to how he was known. Anyway, he and his blood brother Egill Thrandsson performed mighty deeds, then returned to Norway. But on the way, Bjorn dies. They bury him and Egill places his golden armband in the grave with him. The torc was booty from one of their raids. Taken from a sorcerer, would you believe? It was well described in the saga."

Eriksen nodded. "The torc was described as a snake eating itself. And that," he said pointing to the gold armband, "definitely fits the description. This may be Bjorn's burial. If so, it's the first time anyone has ever identified a Viking age burial with attribution from a saga!"

"Yes, but we still don't actually know if he is in there," Farrell replied. "Or anyone for that matter."

"We must get permission to dig. We probably won't be allowed to touch it until next year, though," said Eriksen. "In the meantime, no one must know about this." He turned to look at Arnulf. "No one. I mean it."

Arnulf nodded. "You're concerned about thieves?"

"Damn right," Eriksen replied emphatically.

"You should probably talk to Hansen, then. The logger. His team found the haug. And he was here when I found the armband. You don't need to worry about me talking to the press or anything, but I can't vouch for him."

"I'll do that," said Eriksen. "Meantime, try and keep an eye on the place. Any lights, or noise, call the police immediately."

With a sigh, Farrell passed the heavy armband back to

Arnulf.

"Here," he said. "You look after that for now. We'll register the find. You just sit tight."

The three men made their way down the steep-sided mound back to Arnulf's vehicle. They climbed inside and the engine started with a deep rumble. Farrell leaned over to Arnulf, so he did not have to shout.

"We're pretty sure this is an important site. Please make sure no one goes near it."

"Fine. You have my number?"

Both academics nodded in assent. "Good," said Arnulf. "You should probably have my son's too, in case you can't reach me."

He passed his phone to Farrell, who took out his own and copied in Jens's number. Eriksen did the same.

"We'll go back to the house. You can stay for dinner, if you like."

"Splendid idea," said Farrell with a smile.

Arnulf gunned the engine and the old Land Rover shot forward. "And you can tell me all about this Bjorn character."

Truth will serve in place of lies
4

Keep not the mead cup but drink thy measure;
speak needful words or none:
none shall upbraid thee for lack of breeding
if soon thou seek'st thy rest.
—Hávamál

Entwhistle had taken the Land Rover to the nearest village to pick up groceries. He had been gone less than an hour but as he pulled into the narrow lane leading to the cottage he was surprised to see another car, a beat-up vehicle he recognized instantly as belonging to Fern's mentor, Alicia. The last time he had seen that car was the day he had died.

He felt a twinge of nerves at the thought of seeing Alicia again. Since learning that Jinny was alive, Entwhistle could scarcely control his excitement but had remained steadfast in his refusal to explain to Fern why his eyes were now blue and what it meant. How could he tell her that it was the mark of the djinn? But sooner or later he would have to say something.

He had no fears that Fern would try to exploit the entity in some fashion but he was still getting used to the mere fact of its existence himself. And how do you tell your girlfriend that there is, in fact, someone else? But it's okay, since she's mostly in your head, except when she wants to manifest, usually as a cat. He smiled grimly and shook his head as he parked the Land Rover. In any case, he was bound to absolute secrecy. The guilt and shame of the last month still fresh, he was staunch, determined; he would not let the djinn and Sir James down a second time.

Now that Alicia was here there would be a confrontation. He would refuse to explain, Fern would leave, and that would be that.

With a heavy heart he grabbed the shopping from the passenger seat and approached the house cautiously, half expecting an ambush. He walked up the path to the front door with its dark red paint, stopping to stare at the heavy bronze door-knocker. Even before he knew anything of the djinn, or magic, he had felt there was something simply not right about the highly detailed and intricately cast bronze piece. Of course, now he knew why. It was one of the poor souls Mr. Francis had once alluded to. *Permanently inconvenienced* he had said. Another secret. He knew perfectly well why Fern instinctively avoided the front door. Looking at it now, he shuddered. Who could blame her?

The knocker was green and black with age, but under the grime and verdigris was the face of a fiercely bearded man with a turban and a hooked nose. The whiskers of the moustache and beard flowed down on either side of the face, joining in a loop under the chin, creating a handle. The thing had an ill-favored air.

Entwhistle knew none of the details but the old man had told him that they were now part of the fabric of the cottage. Something like a defense against intruders, both physical and psychic. These were people who had tried to take the djinn from Sir James through force and were now bound to protect it. Just as he was.

Entwhistle had left the door unlocked. He twisted the wrought iron handle and pushed the heavy oak portal wide, spilling light into the normally gloomy corridor. Out of habit he stopped to look at the portrait of Sir James hanging next to the study door. An unusual painting, to say the least.

The first time Entwhistle had visited he had examined it closely. All he had seen then was Sir James standing next to a fine-looking horse, wearing a costume that could only be described as Byronesque. He even had an old flintlock tucked into the scarlet sash around his waist. But soon the painting would change to reveal a secret. Once linked with the djinn he discovered Tajeddigt in the picture, standing slightly behind her husband, looking out at the world in amusement, a challenge in her tawny eyes.

The old man had never mentioned the painting's secret, and why she was hidden, but it made sense to Entwhistle. Sir James loved her. For over a century he had loved a woman who was violently taken from him. Those few scant months of memories were precious to him and Sir James, Entwhistle believed, had wanted to preserve what was there for himself alone. So the canvas was charmed. A small magic to prevent anyone from seeing the real subject of the painting, his beautiful Tuareg wife.

But then, following the Sandwell incident and the loss of the djinn, she disappeared from the painting again. Further proof that the djinn was dead. But as he stood before it now, he was thrilled to see her back in her rightful place at Sir James' side. The privilege of the painting's secret had returned; once again he was the djinn's guardian.

Someone laughed, breaking Entwhistle's reverie. Voices in the kitchen. He braced himself. The moment of truth, or rather, the lack of it. He shut the front door and made his way to the end of the corridor. In the kitchen he found Fern and two women sitting at the scarred pine table around cups and a scattering of biscuits on plates. He recognized both Fern's guests, much to his surprise. One was Alicia, the woman he had 'met' outside Sandwell's house, the other someone he knew well: Mrs. Richards, the head of HR. The last time he had seen her she had been investigating him for alleged sexual assault. Worlds collide, he thought. He laid the groceries on the counter by the sink.

"Hello," he said cheerfully, shucking off his jacket. "This is an unexpected pleasure."

The three women looked up at him. Three serious faces. Fern came over and gave him a quick hug but there was no smile and the scar on her lip was a livid white, a sure sign she was worried.

"Come and sit down, Philip," she said. "I'll pour you a cup of tea."

The tension in the room was palpable. Entwhistle eyed the trio suspiciously. "Okay. So what's going on? This looks like, what do they call it, an intervention? Hello Mrs. Richards. You too . . . Alicia."

True to her reputation Mrs. Richards wasted no time on small talk.

"It might well be an intervention, Philip. There are some things that are best left alone and we are concerned that perhaps you have been careless?"

Entwhistle held her in a level stare. "I see. So you're a witch too." It was a statement, not a question. "What makes you think I'm doing anything that might need your . . . involvement? "

Fern placed his tea on the table at the only spare place. Entwhistle took a seat, ignoring the cup. Fern took his hand and squeezed.

"Honey, your eyes tell a story, and it frightens me. I asked the circle to come. To talk to you about it. Please, don't be upset. We don't mean you any harm."

"Indeed not," said Alicia. "If you recall, it was I who pulled you from Sandwell's house and, to be frank, saved your ass. Without my help, you'd probably be in prison now. If not for her murder then at the very least for arson."

Philip's face went gray. He nodded slowly. "I didn't kill her. Quite the contrary, in fact. What do you want?"

Fern leaned in close and looked him directly in the eyes. "We just want to understand, Philip. That's all. Tell us what's going on with you. I'm worried."

"I'm not sure you would believe me if I did."

Mrs. Richards laughed. It was the first time he had heard her laugh and the sound was surprisingly youthful.

"My dear boy," she said. "We are probably the only people you know that would believe you!"

Norway, 980 AD
3 days travel from Jotunheim

Inside the church of the White Christ, Egill Thrandsson finished the thin stew with regret. He sucked on the wooden spoon for the last shreds and put down the rough-hewn bowl with a sigh of satisfaction.

"That hit the spot," he said.

"It did that," said Asgeir, finishing at the same time.

The two brothers were still eating, while Mannuki did not appear to have even touched his meal. He sat on the reed-covered dirt floor, legs crossed in that peculiar way of his, and he appeared to have fallen asleep. His eyes were closed and he was not moving.

Everyone else sat on the various benches while the priest occupied a little stool, facing them. The priest gnawed at the last of the rock hard bread. He was as hungry as the rest of them, but he stopped, and with head slightly tilted to one side, regarded Egill. A mischievous smile lit up his face.

"I have something," he said. "You might like it." He jumped to his feet and scurried to the tiny room off the main chancel. He emerged a second later carrying a small wooden barrel and a couple of drinking horns.

"Something to get the storytelling started! What say you to a bit of ale?"

Everybody laughed and cheered, eyes shining, hands outstretched. Egill knocked aside Asgeir's hands grasping at the barrel.

"There's not enough to fill the cave of your belly, Asgeir." More laughter. Asgeir had an insatiable thirst for ale, and could drink any man under the table and still fight in the shield wall. Asgeir shook his head ruefully at the size of the little barrel.

The priest had trouble tapping the barrel so Egill stepped forward, pulled the Trollman's black blade from his belt and levered the cork out. Mannuki stirred, gazing with obvious unease at the edged darkness in Egill's hand. Only when the blade was sheathed did his eyes close again.

The priest poured a generous amount into the first horn and passed it to Egill, then filled the second and gave it to one of the brothers. Egill took a deep drink, shook his head and smacked his lips. He passed the horn to Asgeir, who drained it and handed it back to the priest who promptly refilled it.

"Is there anything better?" asked Egill.

"Only the gods know," said Asgeir. "But for us mortals, this'll do!" and he laughed.

The priest filled the horn again. Raising it he said, "To fallen heroes," before passing it back to Asgeir. The redheaded Northman quaffed deeply and passed it on to Egill.

"Come, Egill Thrandsson," said the priest. "You have eaten of my food. You have drunk of my ale. It is time for you to earn your keep. Let us now hear the tale of Bjorn the Mighty."

Egill nodded. "Alright. Just remember, we were there. This is not the tall tale of a drunk in a tavern."

Asgeir nodded in agreement, draining the horn for a second time. Egill began.

"Bjorn was the son of Rolf and Svanhild, daughter of Eirik the Dane. He was a mighty fighter and never injured in battle. We were like brothers and we became leaders of men. We were closer than brothers. Most of my own close kin died while I was still a boy. I grew up with my uncle on my mother's side. He was a good enough man, if given over to a desire for soft living."

"Whose story is this," Asgeir said. "Yours or Bjorn's?"

Egill ignored him. "All I ever desired had been to go a'viking, like in my grandfather's time, but those ways were dying. Yet I had heard that there was still adventure for a brave man, if he was willing to travel to the end of the world, to the greatest of all cities."

"Miklagard," whispered the priest, eyes fixed hard on Egill's.

"Yes, Miklagard. And so I went, along with my wasteful cousin, Asgeir here. We enlisted in the Varangian guard and we took the queen's gold. They called us the *pelekyphoroi barbaroi,* the axe-wielding barbarians. We could fight as well with spear or sword, but a Northman loves the axe more than any other weapon."

Egill paused to take another pull from the drinking horn, then beetled his brows as he tried to remember where he was.

"Ah, yes. I did not know Bjorn then. We did not meet until a year into my service. Our unit was on patrol. We had taken one of the queen's younger brothers with us. He wanted to know what it meant to be a barbarian. He was an impetuous young fool, but the unit loved him to a man. A drinker, fighter and gambler, he was already like one of us, not like the soft-bellied fools in the court. But he wanted to see how we fought. So for a month we took him out on our patrols. Then one day, we got lucky."

He took another deep draught, and his eyes took on a glassy aspect as he remembered. "We came across a great fight; a massacre. A caravan from the east beset with raiders. They must have outnumbered the guards by three or four to one. The guards were slain by the time we arrived. All except one."

"Bjorn," said the priest, his eyes shining.

"Bjorn," confirmed Egill with a nod. "When the last of his companions had fallen, he just shrugged and raised his shield ready to fight and die. He was impossibly outnumbered, yet he roared his challenge, standing before a small wagon, the last protection for the merchant who cowered within like the dog he was."

Asgeir helped himself to another libation from the barrel and one of the brothers did the same. Mannuki continued to sit, stone still, but he watched Egill with interest.

"When Bjorn saw us, he laughed. He promised to leave us one raider each, and he would kill the rest. We rode down on them and the battle turned to a rout as the raiders tried to flee. But they could not. They had boxed themselves in. The trap they had set for the caravan now became their doom. They must either make their way past Bjorn with his great axe, or turn and fight a half dozen riders with spears."

Egill smiled then, lost in the memories. "It was glorious! They rushed Bjorn, who was only one man, after all. He hacked about himself furiously. The guard rode down the rest. The prince too did his share. He took heads that day. We escorted the merchant back to the city, and the prince offered Bjorn a commission in his personal guard. That was the start. After that, well . . . things started to get crazy."

The priest leapt to his feet. "Wonderful. I need to write this down." He scurried to the corner of the chapel where his writing implements lay and started to mix his ink. Asgeir upended the barrel to get the last dregs of ale out and one of the brothers began to snore.

Egill continued with his tale, occasionally stopping to allow the priest to catch up or ask questions. The warrior talked most of the night, the only sound his voice and the scratching of a quill on parchment as the priest copied down his words.

Lillehammer, Norway
Regional Police HQ

It was a busy, typical working day. People bustled, there

was a constant chatter, either into phones or between the officers and support staff at police central head quarters.

In the small kitchen adjoining the break room, an officer in black leather—a motorcycle cop—sighed and tossed his paper cup into the waste bin.

"Damned coffee maker's on the fritz again," he said to nobody in particular.

In his office, Sven Eikenes, Regional Chief of Police, sipped a cup of black tea, grimacing at the bitter taste. A tea-bag floated inside the cup, a small yellow label attached by a string. He pressed the intercom button on his desk phone.

"Nina, please ask one of the constables to go out and get me a decent coffee. I don't care where they get it from."

"Yes, sir. I'll take care of that right away."

"And Nina?"

"Yes, sir?"

"Go into the kitchen and toss out this garbage tea, would you? No one should have to drink this."

"But, sir . . ."

He cut her off, not interested in her protestations. He closed his eyes and took a deep, calming breath. Eikenes was young for his position. Several other candidates, men and women, were more qualified—and experienced—yet somehow he had won the promotion and now controlled the region's one hundred sixty officers and support personnel. This was one of the smallest of Norway's twenty-seven districts but with a population of only seventy thousand, and most of those located in one central area, it was enough and he made do with the limited manpower.

Naturally, Eikenes wanted more, but he served the Master best by limiting his ambition, a sacrifice he made willingly. Any sacrifice was worth it, for what they were soon to achieve. A jolt, like electricity, ran through him at the thought of the gods finally awaking and the thrill that he would be alive to see it. It would be like the time of legends, when Norsemen bestrode the world like colossi.

But the time was still not right. The Master needed a certain artifact he had hidden long ago. He did not say much about it. Eikenes got the impression that the Master had hidden it in haste. Although he had never said as much, Eikenes got the impression from little clues over the years that the Master had been hunted by powerful enemies.

However it seemed that it may have been discovered by a local farmer. That would not do. It was up to him to make sure that things happened in a particular way.

Eikenes leaned forward in his high-backed leather chair, hunching over his laptop, finger light on the touchpad. He clicked and opened an email, quickly scanning it. Just another report on juvenile delinquency, nothing important. He deleted it and opened the next. As he read, he fingered the silver ring he wore on his right hand. He toyed with it as he read, one finger tracing the outline of the stylized snake eating its own tail. He clicked the mouse again, deleting another email. And there it was. A report about a farmer who had found something of potential historical interest on his farm. People were always digging up stuff from the Viking period in Norway. Eikenes read the report intently, a slight smile tugging at his lips when he read the name Aasheim. He knew that family. Oh yes.

When he was done, his finger stabbed the intercom. "Nina, where the hell is my coffee?"

"It's on its way, sir. I sent Pedersen out to get . . ."

He snarled something offensive, cutting her off in mid-sentence. He leaned forward again, elbows on the desk. He read the email again. A possible Viking age burial. Although it was not clear from the details in the report, the farmer may have found the hiding place where his Master had hidden the seal, the means to awaken the gods. If this was the site, then the Master would expect fast results. He would have to talk to his contacts in the municipality, make sure the dig was authorized quickly and get someone he could trust onto it.

He sat back, pulling his mobile phone from his inside jacket pocket. He scrolled through the contacts until he found the name he wanted. Jens Eriksen. He punched the dial button and waited for the call, a wolfish smile forming. Leverage. You had to have leverage. And with Eriksen, he had all the leverage he would ever need.

The sun had yet to rise and darkness clung to the valley. Winter comes, Arnulf thought. But that was fine, he liked the long evenings. Pretty soon the ground would be iron, too hard to dig. But luckily for the university people, not just yet. Eriksen had called, informing him that a small group would come to put in a test trench. They were in a rush to get started. Eriksen explained that they would put in a narrow cut across the center of the haug but before that happened, Arnulf was determined to have a poke about himself. He felt a little guilty, but it was his land, so why shouldn't he have a look?

He climbed the steep sided hill and stood looking out over the devastated land that had once been a proud forest, his greatest pleasure. He liked nothing more than to walk amongst the trees, taking in their stillness and majesty. The money from the sale had not made the loss any more bearable. He prayed that Fern would understand the sheer necessity. Arnulf clung to the hope his daughter would return and carry on the family tradition. Aasheims had farmed here since pagan times. With the money from the timber already in the bank they had at least another year, maybe two.

Arnulf felt a small thrill at the prospect of a possible treasure trove. Who knew what they might find when they started digging the following day? One thing was certain; as land owner, he was sure to get something from it. The laws granted reasonable compensation to property owners, but it would not bring back his forest.

The irony of the situation did not escape him. The value of the torc alone was more than enough to keep them afloat for years to come. But he would never have found it if the forest was not cut down first.

Arnulf sat on the stump of the chestnut tree, staring at the ground and twisted roots that had broken through. He shook his head. What were the odds of finding something else? Still, it couldn't hurt to look.

On his knees he started to scrape away the hard surface soil. It was tough going, so he took a small work knife from his belt and probed around. The knife slid in easily, encountering little resistance. Again and again he plunged the blade into the earth, levering chunks of dirt aside as he explored around the roots.

He was about to give up when the blade hit something hard. Probing carefully he found an edge. There was something there. Poking with a finger he could feel it. A straight edge. So there *was* more to be found.

More curious than excited, Arnulf scraped the earth away, slowly revealing a gray corner. He could not tell what it was, exactly, except it was not stone. Another ten minutes and he had it exposed. A plate of what looked like lead, covered with dirt. It must have been put there at the same time as the torc. He slipped the flat of the blade under the metal plate and lifted it out. It was small, about the size of his hand and roughly square. He rubbed the object on his trousers, removing enough dirt to make out what appeared to be writing, although not in any alphabet he knew.

He shook his head in wonder. Gold he understood. The torc, still in his pocket was treasure trove. This little piece of lead was probably worthless. He peered closely at the writing. It was tiny, and dense. Row after row of strange symbols. Perhaps not quite so worthless after all. He had a bottle of water in the cab of his Land Rover. He would give it a quick wash, and see what he could see.

Decision made, he ran down the steep sided hill and

yanked open the door to his vehicle. He screwed the plastic top off a water bottle and trickled a little onto the surface of the metal plate, rubbing with a corner of his jacket. This only seemed to make it dirtier, smearing mud over the surface. Arnulf frowned. The odd script was still visible but he could not make out everything.

It was definitely not an alphabet he had ever seen before. Not Greek, or Russian, and certainly not Runic. But Farrell or Eriksen would probably know what it was. He climbed into the cab, settling himself behind the wheel.

His eyes kept going back to the plate. He looked deliberately away, turning on the ignition, ready to go. But he could not resist another peek. If it was buried with gold, surely it had to mean something? With a slight frown, he picked it up, trying to make sense the dense writing. He fumbled in his pocket for the handkerchief wrapped around the torc. He would give the plate a little clean. That would make easier to see, if nothing else.

He could not help touching the torc, feeling its rugged warmth. Suddenly, his vision blurred and the writing on the plate seemed to writhe, as if rearranging itself. He dropped it on the passenger seat in sudden fear.

What the hell was that? Was he going crazy? But the plate was the same as before. The chicken scratches of the unknown script were still just that. Cautiously, he reached over and picked it up again, peering closely at the odd writing. Nothing happened.

He must have imagined it. Arnulf pulled the handkerchief from his pocket, once again his fingers brushing the torc. Then it happened again, his vision blurring as the letters re-ordered themselves. Suddenly Arnulf could read them, and they burned like fire in his mind. He gasped, his body rigid as his mouth formed words he could not possibly understand, a grimace of pain stretching across his face.

At the final words his eyes closed and he dropped the

plate onto the seat beside him. Then Arnulf slumped forward over the steering wheel, head pressing down on the horn, which ceaselessly blared out a warning.

Detectives Hanlon and Topley left their drab, unmarked police cruiser outside the offices of Rappaport and Associates, Attorneys at Law. Benjamin Rappaport was clearly part of a well-to-do outfit. Situated in a modern office building constructed of steel and glass, it was sleek and expensive.

Topley appraised the grounds around the building. "Very la-di-da," he said.

Hanlon pursed her lips. It did not look as if Entwhistle's lawyers were hurting for money. There might be a recession, but you would not know it from the cars parked here. Two new Bentleys, and a car that neither of the detectives had ever seen before: a Maybach.

Entering the automatic glass doors, Hanlon noted the metal casing of a mezuzah mounted on the right side of the frame tilted towards the spacious lobby. She touched it out of habit. Inside would be a scroll, or parchment with verses from the Torah. Rappaport and at least some of his associates were clearly Ashkenazim. News to her.

The reception area was even more impressive than the outside. Expensive leather sofas and chairs were clustered around a glass coffee table. A very tall plant or tree stood in one corner. It was an odd looking thing. Narrow, with budding green leaves growing close to the trunk. It was over two stories tall, reaching up to the offices that were located on the mezzanine floor.

The detectives approached the front desk. A mature woman with bottle-blonde hair watched them with a professional smile on her face.

"Can I help you, officers?"

Topley did a double take. "How'd you know?"

The receptionist smiled. "Because I can see in the

register that there is an appointment, first thing, with Mr. Rappaport. Since there is no one else here, you would most likely be the two officers that are in my book. Detectives Hanlon and Topley."

Topley smiled. "You should be a detective yourself."

The receptionist laughed, clearly delighted with the compliment. "You're expected. You can take the stairs or the elevator to the third floor."

They turned to leave, when Topley turned back. Anything strange or new drew him irresistibly. "What is that?" he asked, pointing to the peculiar tree.

"It's a coffee plant. Every year we roast and grind the beans from it."

"Ahh," replied Topley. "Interesting."

The receptionist leaned forward and whispered conspiratorially. "It tastes awful, but it's a tradition."

They both laughed while Hanlon tapped her foot, casting a very obvious glance at her watch. Topley shot her an apologetic look as they strode away from the reception desk. Hanlon headed for the stairs, while Topley made a beeline for the elevator. They stopped, glared at each other, then with a sigh, Hanlon joined her partner.

"So," she said, "that resolution you made to exercise was just what? A threat?"

Topley frowned. "One does not a mountain climb in a day."

"Pfff. Not if you're already a mountain you don't."

"Oi! I'll have you know I lost six pounds this month. Let's see how good you look when you get to my age."

Hanlon eyed his impressive bulk, but did not comment. It was inconceivable to her that she would ever let herself go the way Topley had. They took the elevator to the third floor and exited, their bickering behind them. Now they were all business.

Outside the elevator, a tall middle-aged gentleman in an impeccable Savile Row suit waited for them.

"Good morning. I am Benjamin Rappaport. What can I do for you, officers?"

They each shook the proffered hand. Hanlon spoke. "Mr. Rappaport, we understand that you represent a Mr. Philip Entwhistle. Is that correct?"

Rappaport smiled the thinnest of smiles. "Yes, as you well know."

"We would like to ask you a few questions concern . . ."

Rappaport interrupted her. "This is most improper. You come to my office expecting me to discuss a client, a client whom I understand you have subjected to repeated questioning without the benefit of counsel. As a good citizen he has, probably unwisely, submitted to this harassment, and now you turn up wishing to question *me* about him. I regret that without specific instructions from my client . . ." He shrugged.

Hanlon, suppressing a surge of anger, kept her cool. "I understand. We don't expect you to disclose anything prejudicial to your client. But you may be able to give us information that will reduce the suspicion under which, I assure you, he currently stands."

It was a clever ploy. Rappaport considered for a moment, then nodded.

"Perhaps you should step into my office. Let's not dance about the issues. I'm a busy man, and I'm sure you have better things to do as well. Come, let's see what it is you're after."

Hanlon nodded. She recognized the attitude. She had grown up in a Jewish household and her father had brooked no nonsense. The lawyer had the same straightforward air about him. She caught Topley's eye and pointed to herself. He nodded. She would ask the questions.

Rappaport showed them into a pleasant but austere room. No expensive furniture or ostentatious oil paintings, just a simple office for doing business. Hanlon approved. With the detectives seated, Rappaport settled into an old fashioned oak swivel chair behind his desk. He examined them both, first Topley, then Hanlon.

"Alright. I'll answer only questions that I do not feel contravene my client's rights or interests. What do you want to know exactly?"

Hanlon leaned forward. "Mr. Rappaport, we understand that Philip Entwhistle came into some money recently."

Rappaport's mouth twitched in what might almost have been a smile. "Yes, Mr. Entwhistle did indeed receive an inheritance. A matter of public record."

"Yes, we checked. Were there other named beneficiaries in the will? Specifically a person who, for any reason, failed to claim their inheritance?"

Rappaport considered the question. He shook his head. "No. Philip Entwhistle was the only named individual, other than myself. He inherited everything, except of course that which we had to render unto Caesar."

Topley frowned in puzzlement. "What's that?"

Hanlon leaned over to him. "Taxes and such."

"Quite right," said Rappaport. "It wouldn't do to leave a prospective client with a big mess of paperwork and forms. We handled the transition of the estate. We continue to have the honor of representing Mr. Entwhistle's interests."

"How much money was it, Mr. Rappaport?" Hanlon asked.

"I am not at liberty to say."

Hanlon could see that this was a waste of time. The man was not going to reveal anything that might conceivably contravene Entwhistle's interests. What it must be like to have money, she thought.

"Okay. Thank you for your time." Hanlon stood and motioned for Topley to do the same. She headed for the door, then paused.

"Just one more thing, Mr. Rappaport. Does the name Elizabeth Sandwell mean anything to you?"

The attorney frowned as he considered the question,

then shook his head. "No, sorry. Should it?"

"I don't know," Hanlon replied. "It was just a thought." She gave the attorney an appreciative nod. "We'll see ourselves out, sir. Ah shae-nehm dahnk."

Rappaport smiled and responded in kind. "Zol es zayn dir voyl bakumen."

As they walked back to the elevator, Topley spoke. "Seems to be pretty straight, for a lawyer."

"Yes. And I'm sure the name Sandwell really did mean nothing to him. So she was never a beneficiary. Pity."

"So, what's next?"

"Can you find out how much Entwhistle got? Exactly?"

"Sure," Topley replied. "The probates office have it all on file. I can make a call."

"Fine. And one other thing, let's see what we can dig up on the old fellow he inherited it from."

Topley pulled his notebook from his jacket pocket and flicked through the pages. The elevator arrived at that moment and they got in.

"Here it is. Some old duffer called James Francis."

"Right. Supposed to be a bit of a recluse. Find out what you can about him too. There's something fishy going on, I know it."

The elevator doors closed with a ping.

Entwhistle had not been this nervous since he had defended his dissertation before a panel of experts, and that was five years ago. Feeling cornered, he instinctively looked about the kitchen for a bolt-hole, but there was nothing he could do to avoid the three women's questions. If he wanted to continue his relationship with Fern, then this had to happen. He would have to come up with something plausible. But what? Some medication, perhaps? Wracking his brain, he drew a blank.

He cleared his throat, took a sip of tea, then coughed and spluttered as it went down the wrong way. This was not helping. He sipped again, slightly more cautiously as he eyed the three witches. They were giving him their fullest attention, their eyes boring into his. It was most disconcerting. He took a deep breath.

"I can't tell you anything. It's that simple. I made a promise." Then Jinny was there. Her voice, soft and distant, but clearly heard, entered his mind.

Little Man, Hearken. Your mate you can trust. I see her. These others are her people. They seek nothing for themselves. You may trust them too. Explain to them. Tell them of the witch. Your blood made her spell fail. Your blood saved me, as my life force saved you.

Entwhistle cocked his head to one side, as if listening. He frowned slightly. Did Jinny really mean to give him permission to disclose the secret? The answer came at once.

It is well, Little Man. They must know. There is no danger.

Entwhistle slumped in his seat, relief flooding through him. Mrs. Richards frowned slightly and looked about the kitchen as if searching for something. Philip wondered if she could sense Jinny's presence.

"Okay. Here it is. I have permission."

"I beg your pardon . . ." started Alicia.

"Please, wait." He drew a long breath and began. "I know that you are all more experienced in certain aspects of the world than I. That being said, you may not know everything, and what I am going to tell you might sound crazy."

Fern reached out, placing her hand on his arm. In her eyes Entwhistle could see warmth and comfort. He smiled. In the faces of Alicia and Mrs. Richards there was no hostility but neither was there any warmth. Clearly, they were reserving their emotions—and their judgment—until he had spoken. His smile slipped a little and he swallowed.

"But before I say anything, you have to agree that this goes no further. As I hope you will understand when I'm through, it is very important that this stays among us. No-one else. Do you agree?"

Mrs. Richards narrowed her eyes. "If you have done something wrong, something criminal . . ."

He smiled. "Crazy, perhaps. But in spite of all the police attention, nothing criminal. Absolutely not. So, do I have your agreement?"

The trio looked at each other and slowly nodded, first at each other and then at him.

"About six weeks ago I made a promise to a very old man to look after his companion. They had been together for almost a century. When he died I became its . . . protector."

Fern stirred. "But what has this to do with your eyes, Philip?"

A knowing look passed between Alicia and Mrs. Richards. Entwhistle continued.

"I have a djinn. A genie, if you prefer. Well, when I say that I have one, that is not quite true. You don't really own a djinn. I am its protector. Its guardian."

Fern's face changed instantly from compassionate support to incredulity, mouth hanging open in surprise. But the older women shot each other a quick look, Alicia raising an eyebrow and making the tiniest of nods, as if her suspicions were confirmed. Then she and Mrs. Richards returned to staring at Entwhistle, their faces neutral. Or not quite. He sensed a slight hint of amusement from the older woman. Was Mrs. Richards finding this funny? Or perhaps it was watching him squirm that amused her?

"I was chosen by the djinn. I did not seek it. I did not dabble in mystic powers or some such. The djinn needed someone, and it chose me."

There was a silence. It seemed to stretch on forever. Then Mrs. Richards smiled and suddenly the tension in the room was gone. She leaned back in her chair, which creaked in protest.

"Well, I'm glad to hear that," she said. "So, chosen by a djinn, eh? How exciting!"

Fern looked at her, and then with a conscious effort, closed her mouth. "You're kidding, right? Genies aren't real . . ."

It was now Fern who felt sympathetic eyes turn to her. Alicia nodded slowly, her mouth twisting in wry amusement. Mrs. Richards merely shrugged.

"You may as well just tell her," she said.

"Alright," Alicia replied. "Fern, you're a wonder. You're stronger than any of us, and have come further, faster than almost anyone we've ever heard of."

Fern smiled briefly. "The women in my family were famous for their sight," she said. "I always believed our valley was enchanted."

Alicia nodded, indulgently. "That may be. However, we have not shared all our secrets with you. Not yet. There are certain things one should learn when the time is right, when the student is ready. Well, it looks like that time is now. Yes, genies are real. And more. Your boyfriend is proof of that. When a creature of the other world possesses a mortal, their eyes always reflect their changed nature."

"Now hold on," Entwhistle interjected. "I am not possessed. Far from it. The djinn manifests when it wants. It is entirely separate from me. I am me, not some . . . some kind of puppet."

"I'm sure you're not, dear," said Mrs. Richards. "Alicia was merely commenting with what little we know. The lore suggests that the djinn possess a human host. Whether it was with or without the host's consent, we don't know. But our information may not be quite accurate. To my understanding, the lore is based on hearsay rather than first-hand knowledge. You, my boy, might be able to rectify one or two misconceptions about genies."

"Well, for one, they don't like to be called genies. They are djinn. Genies are something else altogether."

Alicia nodded eagerly. "Excellent. We should really be writing this down."

Fern still looked dazed. She alternated between staring at Philip, Alicia and Mrs. Richards.

"Why don't you tell us more about the djinn, Philip," said Alicia. "It would be wonderful to have a first-hand account."

Entwhistle was far from thrilled at the prospect of relating his tale. Not because of the fantastic nature of it, but for the poor job he had made of the role he was given. He considered briefly trying to hedge around certain facts, but he suspected, rightly, that all three women would see through that tactic. He let out a sigh that contained more than a little resignation.

"Alright. I'll tell you what I learned from Mr. Francis, the previous guardian. According to the Qu'ran, in the seventy second sura, djinn are part of the order of life. Man, djinn, angels. From what I have gathered, djinn are a formless entity. They *can* manifest physically, but this is only relatively small animals or birds. For Mr. Francis, she usually appeared as a cat."

Once again, Alicia and Mrs. Richards exchanged a knowing glance. Evidently, there was something about cats and djinn they were already privy too.

"What form did the djinn take when it manifested for you, Philip?" Alicia asked.

Entwhistle shook his head. "It never did. The day I took over as guardian, she was taken from me. Sandwell saw to that. I really don't want to discuss it. Things happened that I find difficult to . . . put into words."

Mrs. Richards leaned forward and patted his hand. "Go on, Philip. This is most likely the cause of your nightmares. It will help you to share, I am sure."

Entwhistle shot an accusatory glance at Fern, which she ignored. He pursed his lips, suppressing the anger over her talking about him with these other women.

"Well, djinn exist within some of the same dimensions as we do, only more of them. They come from a place that," here he paused as he struggled to find something that might adequately explain the djinn's world, "that exists on top of, or alongside our own world, but is separate. Jinny had powers that appeared to be magical . . ."

"Jinny?" said Alicia and Mrs. Richards in unison.

"Uhm . . . that's what Mr. Francis called her. I don't know if they actually have names of their own. It never came up."

"Sorry for interrupting," said Alicia. "You were saying about her powers?"

"Yes. She could do things. Mr. Francis always maintained that it was merely physics. Everything was physics. I won't say that I understand. But all matter is energy, and energy can be matter. Change one and you change the other. I have no idea how *that* works. But I have noticed how magic creates a smell, like ozone from a lightning strike. The djinn also does that, so I assume that means that it uses the same . . . *mechanism* as witches use in their spells."

"How do you know about the ozone, Philip?" asked Fern. "I've never performed any spell around you like that."

"It was Sandwell," he replied with a shudder. "She was doing something particularly nasty when I . . . stopped her. The attic in her house reeked of it."

Both the older witches nodded. This was part of the metaphysics of witchcraft and was something little understood, but they were both intimately familiar with the smell of a working spell.

"Before Mr. Francis died, we made a deal. I would accept the djinn and he would help me write my book. I agreed to be both the djinn's guardian and companion. The process where it . . . transferred from Mr. Francis to me, weakened her. It was at that point that Sandwell took the meta-anchor. That's something, in this case a clay bowl, which holds the djinn to this sphere. Sandwell could control Jinny so long as she had it. And she planned to sacrifice Jinny . . . kill her."

At the mention of the meta-anchor, Fern looked at him sharply, one hand going to her nose. "That was what Sumpter took from your apartment, wasn't it?"

Sandwell's *familiar*, the slow-witted skinhead and Entwhistle's former neighbor, had broken into his apartment in order to take the meta-anchor. He then wrecked the place, destroying furniture, glassware, and making as big a mess as he could. Petty revenge for Philip having given as good as he got the last time they tangled.

Fern had gone to the apartment to investigate the noise and Sumpter had punched her in the face as he left. Fern called Entwhistle, thus starting the chain of events that led to Sandwell's death and the burning of her house.

"Yes," he confirmed. "That was the meta-anchor. Sandwell needed it in order to control Jinny. I was on my way back to the city, driving like a lunatic, when the engine blew. I thought it was all over, but I touched my medallion and suddenly I could hear Jinny in my mind. Then I was no longer in my car. Jinny brought me to her. Unfortunately, Sandwell was also there. And she had a knife."

Without being aware, Entwhistle rubbed his throat. He could still feel the sharp blade parting the skin, his blood pumping from him in great, jetting arcs.

"Why didn't you say anything?" said Fern, her face twisted in horror. "You could have told me. All this time and you never said!" Her eyes glistened. Was it compassion or anger? Philip was not sure.

"How? How could I tell you? What could I say? By the way, I killed a witch the other day, but it's okay, she deserved it."

His flippant reply did not satisfy Fern, or the other women who scowled, fixing him with their unwavering and uncompromising gaze.

"Perhaps she did deserve it, perhaps she didn't," said Mrs. Richards. "You are not best suited to judge, I think."

"Well, it was not my doing anyway," Entwhistle replied hotly. "She cut my throat and left me for dead. The blood went everywhere. I think it dissolved the salt in her pentagram, breaking the circle."

Alicia snorted in derision. "Typical. No matter how smart some people think they are, they forget the basics."

Mrs. Richards kept Philip locked within her gaze for a moment more, then she looked to Alicia. "Hoist by her own athame."

Alicia laughed out loud, and Fern looked blankly at them both. Entwhistle could not even raise a smile. He was suddenly, chillingly reminded that these were powerful women who would kill, should the need arise.

Alicia looked at Philip with narrowed eyes, an accusatory finger leveled at him. "You appear to be in remarkably good health for one who has recently had his throat cut, Mr. Entwhistle."

Mrs. Richards too stared at him with a particular focus. Only Fern seemed to show any compassion. She reached out, grasping his hand fiercely.

Entwhistle sighed. "I died. I was dead and Jinny brought me back. She used every bit of her own life force. At least, that's what I thought."

"But you were wrong," said Fern.

"Yes."

"And now she's back?"

"So it appears. I can feel her now. She's getting stronger. She just told me I could tell you about her."

Fern pulled her hand back. "Wonderful."

Richards looked out to the garden, then at Fern. The older woman seemed to come to a decision as she suddenly stood and nodded to the door, a brief tug on Alicia's sleeve pulling her up too.

"Well, my boy," Richards said, "this was most interesting. We must have another little chat sometime. Come Alicia. It's time we were going."

"What?" said Fern, alarmed. "You can't leave now."

Richards gave her a brief hug. "Clearly you have some things to discuss. You don't need us getting in the way. Goodbye, Philip."

"Stay well, Mr. Entwhistle," said Alicia. Then to Fern, "Blessed be."

They left by the back door, and a minute later the sound of Alicia's old car came to them as it pulled into the lane, before speeding off. Entwhistle looked at Fern who seemed to still be reeling from the morning's revelations.

"I'm sorry Fern," he said. "I've wanted to tell to you since the beginning. Really."

Fern stared at him, but her eyes were unfocused. Entwhistle could tell she was reciting a mantra in her head. Calming herself.

"So, this Jinny creature," she said. "She'll live here, with us?"

"Yes. She wants, or needs, companionship just as much as you and I."

"And you are linked to her. Psychically?

"Yes."

"So she sees what you see, knows what you know?"

He scrunched up his face at the question. The memories or visions that the djinn had made him experience as part of his testing were taken from Sir James' mind. Presumably, Jinny remembered everything, like a databank. Nothing got lost, it was all stored away.

"I believe so. I don't really know all that much."

"Great." Fern chewed her bottom lip. "I need to think."

She stood and walked out, heading to the library. Entwhistle stared after her miserably. This was exactly what he had been afraid of. Far from bridging a divide, his revelation had pushed them apart.

He had to be at work by ten, and it was already eight-thirty. Somehow he did not think they were going to patch things up before he had to leave. He did not even want to contemplate the possibility that they would not be able to resolve their differences at all. He sighed. To hell with work then. He would stay a while longer. He had to make her understand.

So the treasures of the mighty

5

And those who planted the Golden Grain,
Flinging it to the winds like so much rain,
As one to the Earth they are turned
That which is buried, Men want dug up again.
—*The Rubaiyat of Omar Khayyam*

Dr. Farrell had spent the night in a Lillehammer hotel. He had intended to go back to Oslo the same day but changed his mind at the last minute, deciding that the torc was too valuable to be left in the hands of a farmer. On the phone, Arnulf had tried to assure Farrell that the torc was perfectly safe. The farmer's tone of voice convinced Farrell he had made the right choice—the longer he held on to the torc the less inclined Arnulf would be to surrender it. He could not really blame him. The thing did seem to exert an uncanny grip on anyone who held it; he had felt it himself.

He took a taxi from the hotel, arriving at the farm to find an ambulance pulling away from the house. It sped off down the gravel and dirt road at high speed, narrowly missing the front bumper of his taxi. The driver swore, as he pulled up in front of the house. Farrell jumped out, then reached back in for his leather briefcase.

"I won't be a minute," he said to the driver. "Just wait here please."

He ran to the house and as he raised a hand to knock the door swung open to reveal Jens. He frowned at Farrell.

"What's happened?" Farrell asked, alarmed.

"It's my father. He's taken a bad turn. I don't know what it is. Maybe a stroke. We're on our way to the hospital."

"Oh, my. I'm so sorry." Farrell said, with genuine feeling, standing aside as the younger man pushed past. Jens went to his car, which stood to one side of the house, started the engine but came back at a brisk walk. Jens was obviously unhappy to see him.

"Look, I don't mean to be rude," he said, "but what are you doing here?"

"Ah, well. I had an appointment with your father. I'm supposed to be picking up the torc; the arm band. Now it's officially registered, it needs to go somewhere secure."

"Sorry, I guess he still has it. You can always come to the hospital. Maybe it's in his jacket?"

"In that case, yes, I think I had better. It would not do to lose it, after all. Can I get a ride with you?"

"Of course." Jens ran back into the house and yelled up the stairs. "Mama, come on. He just needs pajamas and a tooth brush."

The sound of hurried steps followed, and Liv Aasheim came flying down the stairs, a small overnight case in her hand.

"Mr. Farrell is here," Jens said unnecessarily. His mother nodded, clearly distracted.

"Perhaps I should come back another time?" said Farrell.

"No need," said Jens. "Why waste a trip? It's no problem. Papa's as strong as an ox. He'll be fine, I'm sure."

Both men went out and Liv followed a moment later. Jens paused to lock the door. Farrell hurried over to the waiting taxi and paid him off, then returned to Jens's car. Jens was behind the wheel, with his mother in the front passenger seat. The rear door gaped open. Before Farrell could climb inside, Jens nodded towards Arnulf's Land Rover.

"You may as well take that other thing as well," he said.

"What other thing?"

"On the passenger seat. A weird bit of metal."

Puzzled, Farrell went to the land rover and peered through the window. There, lying on the passenger seat was an arresting sight. A square of gray metal, streaked with dirt. He opened the door and peered closer at the object. It looked old. He took out a pair of woolen gloves, put them on, then picked up the plate, turning it over in his hands. Extraordinary.

Farrell hurried back to the others and climbed in the car. Jens immediately let the clutch out and they shot after the ambulance. Farrell leaned forward between the two front seats. He held the metal object in his hand.

"He found this on the haug?"

"Looks like, yeah. What is it?" Jens replied.

"I have absolutely no idea," Farrell replied as he dropped it into his briefcase. "But I know someone that might. I'll take it back to the University. We have some experts there in ancient languages that should be able to figure this out."

Jens Eriksen unfolded a large map until it covered most of his desk. It was covered in shaded areas that marked forested land, the swirling lines of topographic contours showing the elevation of the mountains. Except in one area. The central valley was quite flat, created by glacial erosion long ago in Earth's history. Now it was home to a number of farms, including the Aasheim's. He looked around for something to put on the map to mark the spot where the haug was situated, finally pulling his mobile phone from his jacket pocket and laying it in roughly the right area. The terrain there was bordered by the rising valley walls at a distance of many kilometers.

He reached for his coffee and took a deep, satisfying sip, smacking his lips in appreciation. His phone rang at that moment, vibrating manically on the table. He snatched it up and checked the caller ID. Blocked number. He almost rejected the call, but curiosity got the better of him.

"Hello?"

"Eriksen?"

"Yes. Who is this?"

"What you need to understand, is that I can make your life very difficult. Your recent DUI is sufficient grounds for jail time. You will certainly lose your license for three years and after you are released, I would be very surprised if you still had a job. Trust me when I say that I can make sure you don't. Do you believe me?"

Eriksen froze, the coffee halfway to his mouth. He put it down and sat heavily in his chair.

"Who are you?"

"Who I am is not important. What is important, is that you acknowledge that I have the power to do what I claim. Do you believe me?"

Eriksen's face blanched, his throat suddenly dry. He took a gulp of coffee, holding his cup with a shaking hand. This time there was no appreciation of flavor.

"Yes. I believe you."

"Good."

The voice on the other end of the line was friendly, even jovial. Like two buddies making plans for the weekend.

"You will be given the job of digging the mound on that farm. Say yes, if you understand."

Eriksen's eyes flicked to the spot where his phone had lain just moments before. "Yes."

"Good. You will also make sure that the girl who comes to your office later today is on the team that performs the dig. Say yes, if you understand."

"Yes. But I don't choose. It's the Department of Conservation and Heritage that does that."

"You will find a way to ensure that this person is on the team, Eriksen. Or it may as well be your own grave you are digging."

"Look, I'll do my best, but I cannot guarantee anything. What's this all about?"

There was a pause, then the voice spoke again, all hint of humor gone. "There is something buried in the haug, Eriksen. It must be returned to me. Give the girl the object that, shall we say, does not belong."

There was a click. The conversation ended as abruptly as it had begun. Eriksen stared at the phone in his hand as if it were suddenly poisonous. Whoever it was knew about his arrest, and how it had been hushed up. Which probably meant the caller was police. Someone had wanted to make sure they had something on him, just in case they needed a favor.

Eriksen drained his coffee. He really had no choice in the matter. Not if he wanted to keep his job. He just hoped that whoever this girl was, she would not be a liability. What the *object that does not belong* means, he could not imagine. But he had a feeling he was going to find out.

Philip was still in the kitchen, slumped at the table, the tea Fern had made him now cold. He drank it anyway. His boyish face usually wore a smile, but now he was grim, his mouth a hard line. He felt miserable at the turn of events, but things were going pretty much as he had expected. He heard footsteps and Fern entered. The set of her shoulders spoke volumes. Philip could see the tension. He tried a wan smile, but she did not respond. She did not speak at all, but proceeded to make breakfast as if here were not there.

If Philip did not already know she was angry, he would have guessed from the manner in which she handled the eggs. She picked them up, two in each hand, whereupon they spontaneously cracked, the shells splitting asunder. She poured the eggs into the frying pan, then crushed the shells in her fist, tossing them onto the countertop. She always said you should never leave the eggshell whole. It was a superstition on her part that Philip accepted with tolerant amusement. But today the action was not cute or amusing. He wondered if perhaps she imagined it was his skull she was crushing. Angry? No. She seemed to have gone beyond anything so petty. Philip hardly dared speak. She stirred the eggs with sharp, almost savage jerks of her hand. Breakfast this morning was not going to be the usually pleasant and relaxing event that Philip had come to love.

Since he was expected for a lecture at ten, there was now only thirty minutes before he had to leave. Unfortunately, with Fern in the mood she was in, that was likely to be thirty minutes of uncomfortable silence. If something did not change, he would call Sanjay to take his lecture; he could not leave matters as they stood.

During the night, he had tried to connect with the djinn, surreptitiously touching the silver amulet. It had been a gift from Mr. Francis, and had once belonged to his long dead wife, Tajeddigt. It was a powerful totem against evil, but it was also a conduit. A link, almost like a hotline. However, instead of the expected connection with the elemental, there was a distinct absence, as if Jinny knew better than to come near him with Fern so close at hand.

Evidently the djinn had more sense. Ah well, nothing ventured. "Fern, I understand you're not happy, but I ask you, what should I have done?"

She did not reply, but the stirring increased in intensity. Philip decided to press on. "I made a solemn promise to protect the djinn. That did not mean that I should immediately tell everyone about her. Anyway, forgive me for stating the obvious, but I didn't exactly have the best experience when it came to witches. Sandwell was evil personified, and I had no real reason to trust you then. We'd only just met."

The stirring stopped, but the tension in her shoulders increased as she stared down at the pan. When she looked up, eyes meeting his, he was shocked. It was not anger as he had expected, but rather sadness in her. He was misunderstanding something.

"You could have told me about the djinn at any time in the last month," she said. "And you didn't say anything. You kept it secret from me. How do you think I feel, knowing that you've been dishonest all this time?"

Entwhistle's brow came together in puzzlement. How was it dishonest not to mention the djinn? She had not shared all her secrets with him, he was sure. How did it matter? Except, the djinn was not a thing of the past, but a very real part of their present. And their future.

Then it came to him. A slight smile tugged at his lips and he almost laughed at the ludicrous thought. The realization that Fern, the most beautiful woman he had ever known, was actually jealous of his relationship with the djinn hit him like a thunderbolt. With sudden clarity, he understood that she was threatened by the relationship she imagined that he had once had, and would clearly have again. A closeness that she and Philip would never share. The djinn could enter his mind, his thoughts, know what he knew, and feel what he felt. It would become closer to him than she ever could. He took a deep breath. Well, this was it. Make or break.

"You're right. I shouldn't have kept it secret from you. I simply didn't know how to tell you. And after the . . . incident with Sandwell, I did not think that it would ever need to come up. I thought the djinn was gone. Dead! Can you imagine how that made me feel? Knowing it was my fault? I'd made a vow, which I immediately failed to uphold. Hardly something to boast about."

She sniffed, the sound conveying multiple meanings, mostly relating to her doubts about his honesty and character. But she continued stirring, her hand movement considerably more gentle than before.

"I was trusted with Jinny's care. All this," and he waved

vaguely around the kitchen, "was meant to be a thank you for taking on the job. A job that I bungled. It was not my proudest moment, I can tell you. Anyway, until this morning," he said, his voice the very essence of reasonable, "you would probably have dismissed the very notion of a djinn even if I had told you. "

This last was certainly true. Fern's shoulders slumped suddenly, as if defeated, then started to shake gently as she cried. Entwhistle went to her, wrapping her in his embrace. She turned to him, burying her face in his shoulder.

"You don't need to worry, Fern. I love you. The djinn won't come between us. Trust me, she wants me to have a family."

"I don't know, Philip. I'm sorry, but I am not sure what I should be feeling. I am very confused. And still angry at you." She shrugged his arms away, and proceeded to dish out the eggs onto two plates.

"Look, why don't we talk about it when I come home later?" Philip said, stepping back. He took the plate she offered. A peace offering, a promise of a truce, or just breakfast, it did not matter. She was talking with him and things would be okay.

She sniffed, slightly mollified and nodded. "Alright. I'm working the late shift though, so I won't be back until a little after nine."

They both sat at the table and began to eat. Neither spoke. But where the silence between them had been oppressive earlier, now it was almost comforting.

Entwhistle was about to thank Fern for the eggs, when she cocked her head to one side, as it listening to a faint sound. Slowly she turned in her seat to stare at the clay bowl on the ledge before the kitchen window. Philip followed her gaze. There was a faint shimmer over the bowl, like a haze of heat.

Fern's head snapped back to look at him accusingly. Jinny was getting stronger, trying to manifest. Philip tried to hide his excitement, but the smile that leaked out was like a slap in the face for Fern. She got up and left the kitchen without a word for the second time that morning.

Norway, Oslo University
Department of Inorganic Chemistry

Dr. Roger Farrell pushed through the swing doors into the Inorganic Chemistry Department. He'd taken the mid-morning train to Oslo and arrived a little before one in the afternoon. After going with the Aasheims to the hospital and collecting the torc, he felt unhappy about just leaving. It looked like Arnulf was in a bad way. Very bad indeed.

Farrell was concerned about the situation with the farmer. It was one thing to be taken ill, but what he had seen had shaken him to the core. It had shaken Liv and Jens too. From when he was found, to the time of their arrival in the hospital, Arnulf seemed to have lost twenty pounds and aged ten years. It was not possible, and yet . . .

Farrell approached the department's lab section. There was a steel door, with a small glass window. Beside it was a keypad. He knocked on the window. There was no response, so he knocked again. Then continued knocking until someone in a white lab coat noticed him. The first called over to another similarly clad figure. This one hurried over, and buzzed Farrell in. The door swung open, and Farrell was met by a small, gray haired man.

"You know there's a bell?"

"What?"

"Right there. You just ring the bell. No need to pound on the door."

Next to the keypad, there was, in fact, a button labeled *bell*.

"Oh, sorry. Are you Dr. Selvig?"

"That's me. And you are Dr. Farrell, I presume?"

At his nod, the smaller man beamed widely. "You do

have it, don't you?"

"Indeed I do, Doctor," Farrell replied, tapping his breast pocket.

Selvig's eyes widened in alarm. "You've been walking around with that thing in your pocket the whole time?"

"No, just today. I picked it up at the Aasheim's. Well, actually at the hospital."

Selvig led the way into the lab. Farrell looked about with interest. There were many nooks and crannies where specialists were doing things he did not understand.

"Hospital?" Selvig queried.

"Yes. The farmer that found it was taken ill. He had it with him when he was rushed to the E.R."

"I see. You also said something about a lead plate?"

"Yes. I left it with the linguists. Ancient languages, don't you know."

Selvig looked angry. "But I'm going to get a shot at analyzing its chemical composition, right?"

"Oh yes. The gamle språk people will deliver it, once they've had a look, made some copies, that sort of thing."

Selvig nodded, relieved, and ushered Farrell into his lab. It had more in common with the control room for a space launch than what Farrell imagined a chemistry lab should look like. There were no bottles of mysterious liquids, or test tubes with bubbling anything. Just computers and a machine that looked like a marriage between a photocopier and a microwave oven.

"So how is the farmer doing? Is it serious?"

Farrell nodded. "Seems so. He looked in pretty bad shape. He looked . . . old."

"I thought he was old."

"No, not really. Fifty, or so. I've not heard anything of his status since, or what's wrong with him. Touch wood, it's nothing bad. Still, it's . . . strange."

Selvig eyed him impatiently, one bushy brow rising. He cleared his throat noisily.

Farrell removed the torc from his inner jacket pocket, where it bulged conspicuously. Selvig snatched it, turning it over and over in his hands, suddenly all business.

"Oh, very nice. Very nice indeed," said Selvig, peering intently at the object. "High gold content, I can tell you that. Very pure. Still, we shall know for sure in a short while."

Selvig marched over to a countertop and placed the torc in a plastic container. "You're welcome to stay, Dr. Farrell. But it will take a couple of hours to get the data."

"No, it's okay. I have some things to take care of."

"How about I call you when I have something."

Farrell nodded and proceeded to jot his office extension down for the scientist. "That's fine. Good luck with the analysis. I'll be in my office," he said.

"Sure. No problem. Talk to you later." Selvig turned his back on Farrell who left with a last lingering look at the golden armband. He returned the way he had come, winding his way between benches and machines. Once out of the Chemistry Department, he hurried back to his own office, a nagging thought pressing on his mind. Arnulf's condition. It was not strange, so much as almost familiar, as if he had heard about something like it before. Or maybe it was something he had once read?

He screwed his face in concentration, trying to make the connection in his mind, but gave up with a shake of his head.

England
Southern University

The day was sunnier than expected, a last gasp of warmth before winter set in. Entwhistle squinted his way into the campus. He crossed the open green, passing clusters of students who talked and smoked and in a couple of cases made out with each other. He smiled indulgently. He had never done that when he was their age, but it was not for lack of trying.

Entwhistle got a few nods from some of the students that had taken his classes and another professor waved in friendly greeting as their paths intersected. Entwhistle smiled and waved in return, as he made for the Humanities building. Inside, he took the stairs to the third floor.

He was late for a meeting with Sam. He could not even call to let him know as he had forgotten to charge his phone and it had died while he was driving in. The old Land Rover did not have anything so modern as a USB port. It did not even have a radio. Sam would be sure to understand. At least, Philip hoped he would.

He stopped in front of a door with no name or title stenciled on the frosted glass. Sam's office. For the head of a Department, Sam was surprisingly reclusive. Entwhistle knocked and went in without waiting for an answer.

Sam Evans looked up from his computer where he had been pecking at the keyboard with single digits. "Ah, Philip. What the hell time do you call this?"

He looked angry, which took Entwhistle aback somewhat. He had never known Sam Evans to actually get angry.

"I'm sorry Sam. I had some personal business to take care of this morning, and it took longer than expected."

"Well, it's a bit rum, isn't it?" Evans exclaimed. "You don't have phones in the countryside?"

"Flat battery."

"Hmm. Well, you're here now. So what kept you?"

If it had been anyone but Sam, Entwhistle would have declined to comment. But they were friends as well as colleagues. It was Sam who had given Entwhistle his first teaching position, and Sam who had recommended him to the Associate Professor selection Committee and who had stood by him when Sandwell had made allegations against him. Entwhistle did not need to be reminded that he owed his boss and mentor.

"It was Fern. We had a bit of a fight."

"Ah, girl trouble." Evans smiled, mollified, and for a moment looked lost in a memory. "I cannot tell you how delighted I am that you found someone that can put up with you, Philip."

He swiveled in his chair, and reached for the decanter of sherry behind him. "Drink?"

This was a ritual for them both. Sam always asked, and Entwhistle always politely refused. Then Sam drank enough for them both.

"No thanks, Sam. Still a bit early for me."

"Never too early if you ask me," replied Sam with a chuckle. He poured himself a generous helping of sherry, which he knocked back in two quick swallows. "Just what the doctor ordered."

Entwhistle laughed. "I seriously doubt it, Sam."

With his mid-morning drink now a rosy glow on his face, Evans became all business.

"Look, here Philip. These last two months have been a bit of a strain on all of us here. Sandwell disappearing, you disappearing to your country estate and poor Sanjay having to cope with your classes. I even had to teach one. Most improper."

"I know Sam. Don't worry, things will be back to normal now. I promise."

"Good! It's time you buckled down and put your shoulder to the wheel, otherwise, we will not be able to keep you on. No more shenanigans."

"I understand, Sam. I can assure you that I will be a model employee. No more shenanigans."

"Well, alright. We need to get things back onto an even keel here and I don't need to tell you that you're disappearing act did not help."

"Absolutely," said Entwhistle with conviction. "I want things to get back to normal as quickly as possible."

"Fine. You can start by getting rid of those ridiculous contact lenses you're wearing."

Entwhistle shifted uneasily in his chair. How much could he tell him? "They're not contacts, Sam. My eyes are like this now. For real."

"Really? How?"

"I cannot really say."

"Of course you can. How about trying the truth?"

"The truth?" Entwhistle laughed. "I don't know, Sam. Sometimes the truth is far stranger than fiction."

"Yes, I am sure it is. But why not let me be the judge of that. We've been friends for almost five years, Philip, and in that time I have kept your confidences as closely as my own. Why not trust me?"

Sam regarded him, one eyebrow rising in query. Entwhistle sat quietly for a moment. He licked his lips, wishing he had said yes to that drink. Suddenly his throat and mouth felt very dry. He looked around the room, avoiding Sam's eye, taking in the rows of old books that lined the shelves. Finally he sighed.

"Okay," he said slowly. "The truth." He leaned forward, locking eyes with Evans. "Would you believe . . . magic?"

Sam nodded. "Well, why didn't you say so before?"

Entwhistle stared at his boss in wide eyed astonishment. Evans had not even batted an eyelid at his declaration.

"This may seem like an odd question, Sam. But how come you believe me?"

"Actually, I am not so sure that I do believe you. But you don't get to my age without seeing a thing or two."

"So, you are saying that you believe that magic is real?"

"Did you ever *read* Bombastus von Hohenheim?"

"Paracelsus? Certainly. I mean, not to the extent that you did, but I covered the basics."

"Well, let me tell you. Some of his observations on nature come perilously close to modern physics with regards to an underlying energy which connects all matter.

He also claimed that knowing how to realign energies was the key to immortality. He believed that matter could be altered by thought, if one simply knew the mechanics of it."

Entwhistle shook his head in wonder. In the library he had inherited from Mr. Francis, there were several books about Paracelsus as well as several volumes without titles that he now suspected may have been *by* him. But what Sam was describing was very much what Mr. Francis had told him. Magic was simply a method of controlling the universe's energy.

"Not all his works were published," continued Sam merrily, "and there are several that are attributed to him, which are not his, while there are others which are, but remain in comfortable obscurity. I would not say that I know magic, but I think I know it when I see it."

But this was too much! All this time he had worried about how to explain the events that had been happening to him. And here was Sam, considerably more knowledgeable than he could possibly have imagined. Entwhistle laughed. Sam raised an ironic eyebrow, but this only made Entwhistle laugh harder.

Roger Farrell closed the door to his office. In the time-honored manner of academics everywhere, his office was a mess of papers, books and old coffee cups. He went straight to the shelves behind his desk and started scanning the spines of the books. He found what he wanted, pulling down an old cloth bound volume. The words *Sagas of the Norse* were written on the spine in faded gilt lettering.

Farrell plumped himself down in his antique, oak swivel chair and flipped open the book to the contents page. He drew his finger down the list of stories. There it was, the Saga of Bjorn the Mighty.

He flipped forward through the book until he came to the correct page, then sat back, the chair creaking in mild protest. There was a short preface, summarizing what was known about the saga's history. He skipped it, jumping straight into the story.

There was a man named Bjorn, son of Rolf and Svanhild, daughter of Eirik the Wicked. Bjorn was a man so tall and strong that none could match him, and he gave service in Miklagard. In fellowship with him was one Egill Thrandsson, a man renowned for strength and daring. Bjorn and he shared everything and were as brothers.

Farrell had read the saga before, although not for many years. That nagging thought had finally connected. There was something in the saga that reminded him of Arnulf. Not just the mention of the torc, but something about sorcery, he was sure. He skipped ahead. Here it was, the part with the burial.

And so it came to be that Egill Thrandsson buried his friend and brother in the ground. They performed the rites as best they knew, and Bjorn was buried with the golden dragon, the cunningly wrought armband that was booty from the sorcerer in the land of the Blámenn. And Bjorn the Mighty was sent to Valhalla with such treasures as they had. And Egill declared that his life had been great, and his deeds many, so that his death, not in battle, but by a slinking thief which wasted him to nothing, mattered not.

There it was, thought Farrell. He tapped the page, thoughtfully. Death by a slinking thief that *wasted him to nothing.* The previous line, with the mention of booty from a sorcerer in the land of the *Blámenn,* was probably not relevant. The *Blámenn* were in Africa, and likely Nubians. The Vikings did not call them black, but rather blue. What was pricking at his conscience was the fact that the saga mentioned how the mighty Bjorn had died. Farrell had seen with his own eyes how wasted to nothing Arnulf had become. How could that be? Now that he had found the report of Bjorn's death, he was at a loss to know what to do with it. Should he contact the hospital? What would he tell them? There were some diseases that could survive, dormant, then infect those who were exposed to them, even years later. But centuries later? Possibly. When the plague graves had been dug up at Spitalfields, in England, they had had to take precautions against Yersinia Pestis, *the Black Death*. Perhaps this dreadful business with Arnulf was the same?

Reluctantly, Farrell had to admit to himself that no one was likely to take him seriously on this matter. A thousand year old burial could not contain deadly pathogens. And the other possibility was so ridiculous he could barely bring himself to consider it. And yet . . . perhaps the reference to the sorcerer was not irrelevant after all?

England
Shoreham Police Station

Detective Rachel Hanlon pushed open the door to the station's canteen. She looked about, eyes scanning the faces of the half dozen men and women, mostly in uniform, scattered around the small room. Some were reading papers, others were locked in conversation over the latest football game or catching up on gossip. But sitting alone in a corner, slumped over his coffee, was an officer wearing a reflective Day-Glo jacket over his uniform. Kendrick, the motorway patrolman who had stopped Entwhistle on the M25.

Hanlon approached his table.

"Mind if I sit down?" she asked in a tone that suggested that it did not matter whether he minded or not.

Kendrick glanced up. "What's CID want with me then?"

"Just a quick word."

He eyed her warily, but grudgingly sat up straighter. "Sure, of course."

Hanlon pulled out the chair opposite and sat. "I've been going over a report you submitted last month, and there's something of an issue," she said.

Kendrick did not answer. His eyes were focused on his hands, which were clasped together on the table.

"The report in question relates to your pulling over a 1974 Vauxhall Viva. Do you remember the incident?"

Kendrick did not reply but stared fixedly at his hands. Was there a tremor there? Hanlon pressed on.

"You see, the report clearly states that you were following the car at speeds of up to 90 miles per hour, and that you pulled said vehicle over near mile marker 16, on the M25."

Officer Kendrick looked up then. "Yeah, that's right. I checked his license and had the car towed. What of it?"

"Well, the thing is," Hanlon said, leaning in closer, "the report does not mention what you did with Entwhistle after you stopped him. He was not arrested. He was not charged, and you did not even write him up for speeding. You seem to have simply arranged to have his car removed. What happened to Entwhistle, after you pulled him over?"

Kendrick looked away and swallowed. His hands gripped each other tightly, knuckles showing white.

"If you don't want to talk to me here," Hanlon said, "I can see if one of the interview rooms is free."

"What? No, that isn't necessary."

"So tell me what happened when you pulled him over."

"You'll think me mad," he said.

"I think you'll be on a charge, if you don't tell me."

Kendrick tried to take a sip from his coffee, but the shaking in his hands caused him to spill it. He put the cup down with a bang and hid both hands under the table.

"I stopped him, at mile marker 16. I got out and approached the vehicle. I asked for his license. The driver gave it to me and I examined the details. I could see right away that there was something fishy with it. The man in the car had blue eyes, while his license said they were green. I asked him about that, and then . . ."

"Then what?" Hanlon demanded, her eyes boring into

the patrolman's.

When he finally answered, Kendrick's voice was barely more than a whisper. "He wasn't there."

"Pardon?"

"He wasn't there. He'd just gone. Vanished."

"You mean he ran away? Got out the car and made off on foot?"

"No. I mean, one second he was in the driver's seat, cool as you like, the next he wasn't. It was like a magic trick, or something."

Hanlon leaned back in her chair. She looked at the officer for a moment. "You don't really expect me to take that seriously, do you?"

"I told you. But I'm not crazy. The guy disappeared, right in front of my eyes."

"So, you're saying that Philip Entwhistle did not leave the car. You did not, for example, see him running for it across the fields, or thumb a lift from a passing truck?"

"No."

"He was in the car one second," she said, "and the next, he was gone?"

Kendrick turned red with embarrassment, but he nodded. "Yeah. I figured that I must have missed him somehow. Like, he slipped off when I wasn't looking. Thing is, there wasn't time. I looked away for maybe a second. And then he was gone."

"I'm going to need you to make a statement. You understand that this is important, right?"

Officer Kendrick nodded morosely. "I'll say that he left the vehicle. I ain't gonna say how."

"That's okay. That'll be enough. Can you remember anything else of interest?"

"He was holding onto this necklace or something. Funny thing it were. Weird shape. Silver I guess. He took it out from his shirt, and then he wasn't there. Vanished."

Hanlon stared at Kendrick's coffee, slowly swirling

round and round in the chipped mug, her eyes narrowing. Something about the pendant he had around his neck. She would need to look into that. But for now, it was enough. Kendrick had confirmed that Philip had left the scene, and regardless of the distance to Sandwell's residence, he could theoretically have gotten there somehow. Maybe a helicopter picked him up. Maybe Topley was right, and he was beamed up. It didn't matter. Not one bit.

All Hanlon cared about was that Entwhistle's alibi was suddenly up in smoke and there was just a chance they could actually make the charges stick. It was time to talk to the Crown Prosecution Service.

She grinned. This was it. Her hunch was right. She was going to get him.

Fern let herself in at the back door to the cottage. The lights were on, Philip's chair was pulled out from under the table, but she could not feel his presence. He had not been in the kitchen for hours. Everyone gave off a faint psychic energy and if you were sensitive enough you could detect it. Fern was sensitive to the point that not only could she say who had been in the room, but also when.

She went to the stove and put her hand on the copper kettle. Its coldness only confirmed what she already knew. She dropped her bag, draped her coat over the back of a chair, then went into the hallway.

"Philip? "

A feeling of unease stole over her and she cast a glance back at the clay bowl by the kitchen window. Perhaps it was the fight they'd been having, or perhaps it was the thought of the djinn being present, but something was making her restless, tense.

She cautiously made her way down the dark corridor, what Philip liked to call the gallery. She stopped outside the door to his office. Philip often worked there, late into the night. She opened the door, but it was dark, empty of life.

She stepped back, then noticed a narrow thread of light under the door to the library. She opened it slowly.

Philip was in his reading chair. A book hung from his hand, his head at an awkward looking angle. He was deep in sleep. For a moment, Fern smiled. Then the smile was replaced with a thin line of reproach and a sigh. But she stole forward, took a folded blanket from the arm of the nearby sofa, and shook it out before laying it over him. She took the book from his fingers, closing it and placing it on the table next to the chair. It was a strange looking book, vellum bound and obviously very old. There was no title or printing of any kind on the cover, but she was not curious enough to read the contents.

With a last look at Philip, she went back to the kitchen and filled the dented copper kettle with water. She would have some chamomile tea, then go to bed. This had not been the best of days, and she was eager for it to be over. The business with Philip had put a strain on her that she was at a loss to understand. She really wanted to meditate and explore her feelings. She was sure that they would reach an accommodation. But not until Philip understood *why* she was unhappy.

The chirping of her mobile distracted her from her melancholy. She fished it out of a coat pocket, the caller ID indicating that it was her brother.

"What is it, Jens?" The feeling of unease she had experienced when she first arrived home was back now and stronger. Something was wrong.

"Fern, it's Papa. He's sick. The doctors don't know what's wrong with him."

"Is it serious?" she asked, already knowing the answer. Jens did not reply. His silence said everything.

"Jens . . . how long?"

"They don't know, Fern. They have no idea what it is, but he's dying. Days, maybe."

Fern sat down heavily. Her eyes wide, the phone almost

falling from loose fingers. Her father was such a strong man. No one was tougher. He should live forever. But her brother's voice, stressed, upset, emotional, clearly told her she was wrong. Days? Just days left? How could that be?

"I'll come home Jens. I'll take the first flight in the morning. I'll be there by lunchtime. Can you meet me at the train station?"

"Yes, of course. Please hurry, Fern. Whatever it takes."

"Whatever it takes," she replied.

She ended the call. She would have to pack a bag and take a taxi to the airport. But she did not have nearly enough money to pay for the flight. For sure, only first class tickets would be available, and they were far beyond her budget. She sighed. She would have to ask Philip for a loan.

She went back to the library where Philip was still sleeping. Gently she shook him awake. She knelt on the floor beside the chair, and as he opened his eyes they crinkled in tandem with his smile.

"Fern, you're home. I must have fallen asleep." He sat up, then caught site of her face. Instantly he was alert, the smile dissipating. "What is it?"

"It's my father, Philip. He's sick. I need to go home."

"I'm so sorry, Fern. Of course you must. What's wrong with him?"

"They don't know. But the doctors have given him only days to live." She suppressed a sob as she said it. "I need to fly back tomorrow but I don't have the money. Can you let me borrow what I need?"

He nodded. "Of course. You don't need to ask. Just use one of my credit cards to book the flight, and anything else you need."

He reached inside his jacket and retrieved his wallet. He extracted a card and handed it to Fern.

"Thank you, Philip."

"Should I come with you?" his face expressed deep

concern. She could feel his emotions almost as easily as her own. He *did* love her. She almost agreed, then she looked into his eyes. They were blue, cold. They were not his eyes and they chilled her. She shook her head.

"No, I don't want you to come. But thank you for helping with the flight."

"I'm sorry, Fern."

About what, she thought? He put his hand out and caressed her face. She loved it when he did that. She pulled away.

"I have to pack a bag," she said. "I'm leaving first thing in the morning."

Our hearts desire reveal

6

It belongs to the imperfection of everything
human that man can only attain his
desire by passing through its opposite.
—*Soren Kierkegaard*

London
Crown Prosecution Service

Detective Hanlon waited impatiently in the office of an old college friend; a friend who just happened to work for the Crown Prosecution Service. It was a nice office. Not big, but tasteful. A large rubber plant filled one corner. Behind a glass desk she spied a row of leather-bound law books and a series of framed degrees and certificates. Hanlon had put her own degree in a cheap frame from Ikea. Funny how Celine's looked so much better than hers, even though they'd taken many of the same courses. Yet her degree certificate looked positively impressive hanging there. Well, that's a proper frame-up, she thought with a smile at the pun.

Hanlon was not a vindictive person but she had a particular desire to punish violent men. Especially men who hurt women. In her book, they were deserving of the harshest punishment the law could throw at them.

While it was true that Sandwell had withdrawn the allegation of aggravated assault against Entwhistle, something told Hanlon that it was done under duress, regardless of the recording that Tessa Richards had made. This would certainly fit with the known facts.

From talking to the people that Entwhistle worked with, she had started to build up a picture of what he was like. It seemed that Entwhistle had held a grudge against Elizabeth Sandwell for over a year, because she had beaten him to the punch when she published a paper. Professional jealousy could be a powerful motive. Then, when they were both being considered for the position of Associate Professor, he had attempted to intimidate his colleague. Inviting her to his place and plying her with drink. Hanlon did not quite think the term *attempted rape*, but it was not far from her mind.

Then, according to his boss, when it looked like the position would go to Sandwell, Entwhistle had spun a tale about her breaking into his office. That she was later caught with a master key in her possession was a problem. But then, maybe Entwhistle had planted it? To get her removed from the running on an ethics violation? Hanlon made a mental note. She would need to find out who had access to those keys.

As far was Hanlon was concerned, Entwhistle was a vicious man. He looked innocent enough. Like a little lamb, with his herringbone jacket and leather elbow patches. But that was a cover. A disguise. He was a wolf and no mistake. But in her heart she knew the case against him was tenuous. That was why she was at the offices of the CPS, waiting to hear back from her friend; Celine Aspinal, LLB, HONS. Before Hanlon made anything official, she wanted to be sure that what she had would stick.

Celine was a barrister now and it was her job to review cases received from the police to determine if a prosecution was possible, or even warranted. As a personal favor for an old classmate, she was reviewing the case file against Entwhistle. It was clearly a bit tricky, since she had stepped out to consult with another barrister, leaving Rachel to her own devices. Celine had been gone for over ten minutes and Hanlon was getting impatient and more than a little irritated.

One hand found its way to her mouth and she started to chew on a nail. She never bothered with nail polish. There was no point. Her nails were always ragged. When she became conscious of what she was doing, she pulled the hand away, fiddling instead with a class ring on her finger. The exact same ring adorned Celine's hand. Except in Celine's case, there was a diamond ring next to it.

Celine returned then, managing to look elegant in spite of the fact she was heavily pregnant. She carried a fat manila file in one hand, the other resting on the small of her back in an attempt to ease the strain of her enormous belly.

"There you are, Rachel. Well, I have to say," and before she did, she lowered herself carefully into the chair behind her desk, "that the case is interesting. However, it will not fly. The issue is the eye witness. She's an old lady. Then there's the discrepancy over the time frame."

Hanlon nodded, but she was not quite willing to give up. "Yes, but what if the times were slightly off. What if the fire happened a little later?"

"Look, I can see that this is important to you. But you don't have enough. Not yet. Any decent lawyer would get this thrown out. Goodness knows, it could drag on so long that your witness might even die before it gets to court. Things are really backed up here." She waved vaguely, indicating the office as a whole.

Hanlon rose, face red. "So that's it, is it? There's nothing you can do?"

Celine shook her head indicating the file on her desk. "Not with this. You're going to need more. To get past the issue with the timing, you'll need a smoking gun."

"Shit. I don't even have a body."

"Well, maybe that's where you should start. Habeas

corpus, Rachel. Habeas corpus."

Rachel Hanlon nodded. She suppressed an urge to rip her nail right off. If she could not get a confession from Entwhistle, then all was lost. She would have to let it go. She bit her lip hard enough that it hurt, cutting through her despondency.

"Thanks," she said. "I'll just have to keep digging."

For the entire train ride to Lillehammer, Fern worried. To help pass the time, she made simple charms, twisting together buttons with a lock of her hair and some plants that would help provide protection or good luck. She prayed to the Goddess to give her father strength and she prayed that the train would not break down midway between the airport and home. Not that this was likely. It was a sleek, fast train and quite modern.

The ride that morning to Gatwick airport with Philip had been difficult. The divide between them strained her nerves. He seemed like an eager puppy, wanting to please, but not knowing how. This only made her want to scream her frustration and anger but instead she sought her inner peace.

Still, it was not easy. For the thirty kilometers to the airport they sat in almost total silence. Neither of them seemed to know how to talk to the other. She had wanted to say something, but every time she tried, she felt anger and resentment rise up and it swallowed her voice.

She sighed. He was not a bad man, she knew that. He was just a typical man. And she did not want typical. That he had instantly agreed to give her whatever she needed did not surprise her. Yes, he was generous and compassionate. That was one of the things she loved about him. It was just his dedication to this thing, or person, or whatever it was, she could not fathom. Okay, so she was jealous, but for good reason. He had kept a relationship secret from her. One that he was now planning to resume. A relationship so intimate that it would be like inviting another person into their lives, into their bed! Didn't he understand that?

She could not feel more betrayed if he was having an affair with a flesh and blood woman, not a faceless entity. Or would she? With a sigh, she admitted that perhaps it was not quite the same thing. But it *was* something.

She tried to put it from her mind. There were more important things to be concerned about right now. Her father's life was hanging by a thread. And she could help him, she was sure. Her strength, her willingness to give of herself, these would save him. She just needed to get there before it was too late.

She had left the house at five in the morning, and it was now a little after eleven. She would be there by lunchtime, as planned. She looked about with admiration at the modernity of the train. It was clearly much faster than the one she had taken to the airport when she left Norway. She would be in Lillehammer soon, then Jens would meet her. She had not seen her brother for over two years. Nor any of her family. But it was not going to be the reunion she might have wished for. They would go straight to the hospital.

Her hands were shaking. From fear? No. She willed herself to a calm state, staying the shaking, slowing her heart, her breathing.

She hoped there would be time. Time to either save him, or say goodbye. She shook her head in denial. No use in thinking like that. Anyway, death was not the end, she knew that. Death was transformation, not termination. That did not make it any easier though.

Outside the fast-moving train were fields, trees, a few with the bright gold leaves of autumn. Mostly it was fir trees, or silver birch. The evergreens, true to their name, showed dark against the lighter green of the fields. But she hardly paid it any mind. She ignored the scenery, showing no interest when the train line ran parallel to the main north road, before veering off into the countryside.

Only one thing was within her focus: Arnulf Aasheim, her father. She checked her phone. A message from Jens. *Waiting in the car park.* Good. There was just enough time, so she pulled her tarot pack from her rucksack, quickly unfolding the silken scarf that protected the hand painted cards. She cleared her mind, spreading the cards on the table before gathering them back together and cutting the pack. She laid four cards face down, then slowly turned them over, one by one, staring at them with a mixture of dread and confusion. The reading was not easy. Or perhaps she simply did not want to understand. She lightly caressed the cards, one after another, as if they would reveal their secrets to her touch. The Fool, Lovers, The Hanged Man and finally Death. Her instincts told her that the Fool and Lovers indicated there was something to be optimistic about, that she should rely on someone close to her, but the Hanged Man suggested letting go, that fighting the inevitable was pointless. And Death meant change. *Profound* change. She dared not think what this might be alluding to, but in her heart of hearts she already knew.

The speaker system on the train squawked into life, the announcer stating that Lillehammer station was the next stop, in two minutes. She packed away the cards, carefully wrapping them, then gathered the various charms she had crafted, slipping them into the back pocket of her jeans. Then she maneuvered her way past the other passengers, stopping by the doors. She would not waste any time. As soon as the train stopped she would hit the platform running. She hoisted the backpack over her shoulder and waited for the doors to hiss open. But she could not shake the image of the fourth card from her mind.

The sun broke through the heavy cloud for a brief moment, illuminating the two almost identically dressed men as they crossed the University green, heading for the refectory. Entwhistle was deep in conversation with Sam, and he hardly noticed the brief flash of direct light. The portly Dr. Evans, however, turned his face up to the sun, basking in its warm embrace. Entwhistle, realizing that Sam had stopped, turned back, watching his old friend with amusement.

"They don't let you out much?" he said, jokingly.

Sam smiled, but continued to enjoy the sun. Then a cloud passed before it, closing the gap that had allowed the golden light to break through. He chuckled. "I think that when you get to my age, you take more pleasure in the simple things."

Sam had promised Philip a good lunch, so long as he was willing to listen to a proposition. They continued on their way, walking slowly, neither in a hurry. Philip had already asked Sanjay to take the day's lecture. After the fight with Fern, he was simply not yet ready to face the crowds. Especially since the rumor mills had kicked into high gear over his suddenly blue eyes. The current favorite theory was that he was having a mid-life crisis and had bought colored contacts. At least this particular theory was something he could live with. He made a mental note to buy some saline solution and keep it in his office.

But Sam knew the truth, or at least part of it. The fact that he had taken it in his stride continued to amaze Entwhistle. There was obviously more to Sam than he ever knew or suspected.

"Philip, my boy. You have clearly been involved in things of an occult nature, shall we say."

It was stated as a fact but Entwhistle did not nod or agree. He kept his silence. He wanted to see where Sam was taking it. Just how much *did* he know? The answer was not long in coming.

"You may not be aware, but I have long had a deep and abiding interest in medieval alchemy, thaumaturgy and such. I have made something of a study of it, on the quiet. So much so, that about twenty or so years ago, I was recruited into an organization that exists solely for the protection and benefit of wider society. You can think of it as somewhat like the Rosicrucians."

Entwhistle looked closely at his friend and mentor. Was this an elaborate joke? Sam continued, and from the tone of his voice it was clear he was serious.

"We study esoteric truths of the ancient past," said Sam, "that provide insight into nature, the physical universe and the spiritual realm."

He stopped and gripped Philip's arm. "When I first met you, five years ago, I thought that you might make a good candidate for the Brotherhood. That you might one day join us, and continue in the research and the work we are doing. Recent events have demonstrated that my faith in you was not misplaced. You are clearly meant for more than just teaching. But Philip, I have to ask, are you involved in any kind of dark arts?"

Sam let his arm go and Entwhistle took a step back. He was stunned. A few months ago, and he would have dismissed such talk as lunacy. And yet he had gone from being utterly convinced of the conventional, mechanistic view of the world to accepting that there was a vast spiritual and mystical world that permeated the fabric of life. It was a grand deception—most people were completely ignorant of the true nature of the universe.

He shook his head. "No, I am not involved in anything relating to the dark arts. What happened to me was not by my design."

"I see. Well, that is good to know. But I must warn you, the Brotherhood takes misuse of the more esoteric studies very seriously. I shall need to know everything, if I am to sponsor your application into our circle."

The word circle triggered something in Entwhistle's head. It was the same word Fern used to describe her coven. At least, the close unity of the three women at the core. They were her circle. Were the Brotherhood witches? Or would that be warlocks then?

"To be honest, Sam. I'm not sure I want to be a member. I'm not all that keen on getting involved with magic."

Sam looked at him almost sadly. "You don't really have a choice, my boy. You've seen the other side of the mirror, have you not? You have become aware of the mystical elements around you. Once that happens, well, there's really no going back."

As they continued their walk. Entwhistle thought, morosely, that Sam was right. Once you knew, there was no unknowing. That did not mean he would join the first occult organization to come along though, even if he did admire his friend.

"Why do you study that stuff?" Entwhistle asked.

"Well, there are all sorts of reasons, but you can say it is simply for the common good."

"So, this Brotherhood of yours? It's a philanthropic organization?"

Sam laughed. "You could say that. We do good, where we can. We prevent evil when we can. During the last war, our members were very active in the defense of the realm. Of course, we are not a national group anymore. Members exist in most countries these days. But the Brotherhood began here, in England, in the time of King James."

Sam stopped and looked into Entwhistle's eyes. For the first time Entwhistle noted that Sam's eyes were hazel, flecked with green. He had never really noticed before. But recent events had made him quite conscious of a person's eyes. After all, they were the window to the soul, as the saying goes. They continued walking.

"So you practice magic?" Entwhistle asked.

Sam smiled. "Good Lord, no. I am more of a library rat. There are others that actually do the heavy lifting. I prefer a life of contemplation and research. I let others mess about with incantations and such. Come, Philip. I think it would be a good idea if you consider joining our order. We have a noble history, we do valuable and important work, and we have jolly nice dinners a couple of times a year." This last was said with a wink. Sam always did like to tease.

"You make it sound like Hogwarts."

"Ah well . . . not quite. There is no Ministry of Magic, for one thing. But we do what we can. Now, you will be tested, of course, but I'm sure you'll pass."

Entwhistle shook his head. "I've been tested enough, thank you. But I'll think about what you've said."

They continued on in silence while Entwhistle considered this latest turn of events. There was no way this mysterious Brotherhood would overlook his being the guardian of a djinn. Having come to their attention, he was once again endangering the secret he had sworn to protect. Philip was beginning to understand just why Mr. Francis had chosen to live the life of a recluse, tending his garden and keeping to himself. Would they want to take Jinny away from him? One thing was for certain, he was not going to let that happen.

"I believe it's roast beef today," said Sam, with a merry smile. "And this little piggy is going to have some."

Entwhistle laughed, the nursery rhyme reminding him of his mother. Was that Sam's intent? Disarm him with fond memories? He shot his friend and mentor a glance. No, he was just being himself. Sam was smiling and waving to a couple of young women, who giggled at the outrageous wink he gave them. But they both smiled back. Sam was incorrigible. But he was also the most ethical man Philip had ever known. That did not mean that the Brotherhood were ethical though. A sudden thought occurred. Did he know Sandwell was a witch? Does he know Tessa Richards and Fern are too? For a moment he felt dizzy. It seemed that there were connections he had not imagined possible. He resisted the urge to pull out the amulet and talk to Jinny. But he was damned sure going to look into this secret organization that Sam was a part of.

Library rat? Researcher then. Occult researcher. To be

honest, Entwhistle had to admit that it had a certain appeal. But he would have to tread carefully. He could not afford another incident.

"You know, roast beef does sound pretty good," Philip said, and clapped Sam on the back as they entered the refectory reserved for the senior staff members.

Norway, AD 980
Three days south of Jotunheim

The morning came. Egill sat up slowly, working his jaw, which felt as if it had been on the receiving end of a couple of good punches. He did not have the brain-splitting pain that often accompanied a night of drinking, so perhaps that was proof of the White Christ's power after all. What the fish men called a miracle. He snorted, amused at his own joke. He looked around to tell Asgeir, but the redheaded warrior was still snoring, lying against a bench with one leg hooked over it. The brothers were sleeping where they had thrown themselves down the night before, while Mannuki was sitting in the curious way of his people, eyes closed. Somehow Egill did not think he was really asleep and if he were to stealthily creep up on the little man, Mannuki would spring up, fully awake. At that moment Mannuki opened his eyes, turning his head slightly to look at him. Egill shivered.

His neck was stiff, so he tilted his head sharply to one side, cracking neck bones. He repeated the process on the other side, and gave a sigh of relief. Egill never felt right if he did not have a good neck-crack in the morning. He swiveled around slightly, taking in the rest of the small room. There was the priest, slumped over his lectern. Once the ale was gone, the priest had up and disappeared. When he came back, he was carrying another little barrel. This one containing mead. To say that Asgeir's face lit up would be like saying it was cold in the mountains. Egill liked a drink. A little was good, too much bad, he thought. But it was clear the priest was cut from the same cloth as his redheaded cousin.

Egill levered himself up, stiff and sore from sleeping on the rough ground. At least it was warm though. The hall was small enough, and the candles, such as they were, provided enough heat along with their own bodies. He made his way outside, unbolting the door and slipping through as quietly as he could. He fumbled with his leggings, and sighed in deep satisfaction as he pissed against the low stone wall that surrounded the church. Before he was finished, someone approached from behind: Asgeir.

"Egill. I think it's a mortal sin to piss on their holy land."

Egill snorted in derision. "This was the land of the gods, long before the White Christ. I will piss where I choose."

"I'm just saying."

"Well, don't."

Asgeir meandered through the opening in the wall, taking himself a little further, across the narrow trackway. Egill went back inside.

The priest was sleeping, sprawled across his lectern. Egill kicked one of the brothers, and he mumbled an obscenity before slowly dragging himself awake. Egill shook the other brother and received a colorful recommendation on what he could do with the horses, next time he was alone.

"Get up, you two. We have a long travel ahead. Sunna shines her ass for us, so we should be moving." Egill turned to the priest. Odd that he would have killed him without even thinking twice had circumstances been just a little different. Now, incredible as it seemed, he saw him almost as a friend. The priest stirred, waking.

"Thank you for your generosity." Egill held out his arm, and the priest grasped it in the fashion of the north, then he stood.

"I need no thanks. It is I who should thank you. You gave me a great gift."

The story; Bjorn's saga. It was a good tale. He was pleased the priest had written it down. Now it would be preserved for the ages. Men would speak of Bjorn for a hundred years or more. It was fitting.

"Still, I want to thank you. Take this." Egill passed him a gold coin. Payment for the food and lodging. The priest held up his hand in refusal.

"The story was gift enough, my son. You owe nothing. This is Christ's house and all are welcome here."

Egill would have given all the gold in the world, if only the White Christ could have saved Bjorn, or raised him from the dead. But that was not to be. Whatever had taken Bjorn was beyond the prayer of his own gods, and the little priest's too.

He was sure Bjorn was in Valhalla, feasting, fighting and fucking, no matter the manner of his death. Egill laughed. In spite of his feelings for the followers of the White Christ, this little priest was a kindred spirit. Much to his own surprise Egill took his purse, heavy with gold.

"Then here," he said. "Use this to build yourself a proper house for your damned god. This place is little better than a pigsty."

The priest looked shocked, partly at the blasphemy, partly at Egill's generosity, then he laughed. "You are truly an open-handed man, Egill son of Thrand. Perhaps one day you will have your own saga?" He took the purse, weighing it in his hand. It was a fortune. A worthy offering indeed.

"Egill the Pisser's saga," said Asgeir with glee as he came back inside. Egill cuffed him across the head, not too hard, then smiled and started to chuckle at his cousin's jest.

"Aye, maybe that is fitting after all," he said.

Mannuki stood then, flowing up from the ground effortlessly. Egill watched him curiously. He was clearly capable of looking after himself and yet he chose to travel with them. Somehow, Mannuki needed them. Egill did not understand that. The desert man could have gone anywhere he wanted, yet he chose to come with them, to the furthest place possible from his homeland.

With a sudden insight, Egill wondered if that was, in fact, Mannuki's purpose. He needed to be far away from the place where they had found him. From the people who had subjugated him? Or something else?

The priest put the purse on his lectern. He stared in consternation at the parchments lying there. On the last page, in the margins, was a dense series of marks. They looked like something a small bird would leave, if first it wet its feet in ink.

"What is this?" he said, in consternation.

"I did it," said Mannuki, with a smirk. "I finished his tale."

Lillehammer Hospital
Contagious diseases Unit

The hospital was bright, nurses and doctors moving with busy efficiency. Jens knew the way and he traversed the myriad corridors confidently, Fern easily matching his stride. In minutes they reached the isolation ward and Jens held a door open for her.

Immediately Fern was assaulted with the strong smell of disinfectant. She wrinkled her nose in distaste. Fern's mother, older than she remembered, was staring at the floor as they entered the small room. The strain of the last few days had added years to her face. Her eyes were unfocused and it took a second before she recognized her daughter, then they flew into each other's arms.

"Oh Fern, thank God," she said. They embraced fiercely, clinging to each other.

"I came as quickly as I could, mama."

Liv nodded, blinking back tears. "The doctors don't know what to do, Fern. They say we should prepare ourselves . . . that he'll die."

"Shh, mama. It'll be okay. It's papa. He can't die. He's like an oak in the forest."

Instead of providing comfort, Liv sobbed at this, her face ashen. She gulped air, trying to talk. "But Fern . . . the trees . . . are gone. We cut down the forest."

Fern's brows creased together in puzzlement, and as the meaning of her mother's words filtered through, her eyes opened wide. Jens had said that they had money troubles. The trees were worth a small fortune. She swallowed her disappointment. It was not important. Not compared to her father's life.

"Where is he, mama?"

The room they were in contained shelves with disposable gowns, masks and plastic socks to covers shoes. A door with an electronic lock was the only other feature. Liv nodded to the door, and Fern hurried over to peer through its small window. In the other room, sheets of plastic and the blinking lights from unknown machines drew her eye, then she saw the bed. Her father, emaciated, motionless, mask covering his mouth, tubes in his wrist. She gasped.

A nurse bustled in, her practical no-nonsense air immediately changing the atmosphere in the anteroom.

"Do you wish to visit?"

"Yes," Fern replied. "Of course."

"Alright. You'll need to dress in some protective garments then. I'll help you get prepared."

Fern looked to her mother, who nodded. She evidently knew what this meant. The nurse selected various items from the shelves and showed Fern how to put them on. The Aasheims donned masks and protective clothing over their own clothes, the garments covering everything, including hands and hair. Fern felt slightly ridiculous, but at the same time it scared her deeply. This was obviously serious.

The nurse keyed in a number on the control panel by the door. It flashed green and the door clicked open. This scared Fern even more. Clearly, the doctors were taking no chances. What could her father possibly have that required such precautions?

Arnulf lay supine, the plastic sheet around his bed cutting him off from the rest of the room, from the rest of the world. The mask on his face provided oxygen. A needle taped to one hand dripped fluid into his veins. His heart rate and blood pressure were displayed on monitors on one side of the bed.

Fern was appalled. He was so old! So gray. She could feel tears threatening and she swallowed. No one spoke. There were no words to express the hopelessness of the situation. The nurse stayed with them as they formed a half circle around the bed. Fern felt awkward, and what was worse, useless. Her father had lost weight. His face was gaunt, the withered hands belonging to a much older man.

Fern edged closer to the bed. She could see her father's lips were moving, in spite of the mask. She turned to look at her brother. He nodded in recognition of her unspoken question.

"The doctors say he's delirious, Fern. He keeps talking about things that make no sense. No one can understand him."

Fern stepped closer, leaning over the bed, turning her head to catch the sound of her father's mumbles. It was no language she had ever heard before. Odd syllables, strange words. If they were words at all.

She cocked her head suddenly to one side. Something was wrong. Something more than mere sickness. She frowned, reaching out with her senses. She could feel a palpable wrongness. It lay across her father, smothering him. Her hands touched the plastic sheeting. She closed her eyes, straining to understand. The wrongness was stronger.

She visualized the room in her mind. Her father lying in the bed, the tubes and wires connecting him to the machines. But unbidden came something more; a sheen of red surrounding Arnulf; the manifestation of whatever evil was upon him. Fern opened her eyes. Her face flushed as she felt anger rising. There was no doubt in her mind. Someone had cursed him.

Detective Hanlon eyed the stack of files in her inbox balefully, then reluctantly pulled one from the bottom of the pile. She would have to start looking into other cases. The business with Entwhistle was taking too much of her time, and she had nothing much to show for it. Plus, Superintendent Willis had made it clear that if there was no progress, it would have to be filed in the freezer with the rest of the cold cases.

Before she could look at the new report there was a knock on the door. It opened and a woman police constable poked her head around.

"Ah, you're still here, guv," she said. "There's some bloke at the front desk asking for you. Says he has information on the Sandwell case."

Detective Hanlon regarded the WPC coolly. A break in the case? Could she hope for so much? She nodded, face neutral but inside she felt a surge of excitement.

"Well, don't keep him waiting, constable. Go get him."

"Yes, ma'am," the WPC replied and hurried to her task.

Hanlon tossed the unopened file back to the inbox where it landed on top of the pile. Despite years of experience urging caution, she felt a rising sense of anticipation. She hoped to God that this would be a break. Whatever the information was, it had to be enough. It had to!

The door opened again and the WPC ushered a swaggering, heavyset man into the small room. His bald head shone in the institutional florescent lighting like a billiard ball.

"Right," he said without preamble. "Are you Detective Hanlon, then?"

"Yes, come in." Hanlon rose and offered her hand. The skinhead ignored it with a sneer, and walked over to the empty chair in front of the desk. He fell heavily into it, leaning back, stretching out his legs. One hand slipped into his jeans' pocket, the other rubbed at his bald head, feeling for stubble.

"So I got some information, right?" he began, "about Sandwell. I know who done it."

Detective Hanlon reached for a pen and her notepad.

"I'm all ears, mister . . ?"

"Sumpter," he replied with a smug look. "Yeah, Mr. Sumpter."

"Okay, Mr. Sumpter. What do you have to tell me?"

"First you gotta do something for me. You scratch my back, and, well . . . you know the rest."

"Alright. Tell me what you want."

"What I don't want. No more fucking community service."

"I see. Well, depending on what information you have, that could be arranged. Anything else?"

"Yeah. I want to see that fucker Entwhistle banged up."

Hanlon looked up in surprise. So, Entwhistle had a knack for making enemies. She smiled encouragingly at Sumpter.

"You're not the only one. What can you tell me about him and Sandwell?"

Sumpter pulled his hand out of his pocket, pushed on the arms of the chair, sitting straighter. Then he leaned in closer over the desk, eyes meeting Hanlon's.

"Everything. I know everything."

"You have evidence that he was involved in her death?"

"I dunno about her dying. I don't reckon she is dead. But he burned her house down, that's for sure."

"Why don't you think she's dead?"

"I just don't feel it, is all."

"Alright, but can you prove that he torched her house?"

"Yeah. I was there. I saw him come out. He was covered in blood."

Hanlon nodded, writing studiously. Another witness! This would strengthen her case. But at the back of her mind was the knowledge that this man, Sumpter, was almost certainly not going to stand up well in court. Entwhistle's slick lawyer would chew him up and spit him out. She needed more.

"You were there, you say?"

"Yeah, what of it?"

She watched him, her eyes never leaving his. "So you saw him exit the property, covered in blood. Then what happened?"

Sumpter shrugged. "Some woman turned up in a mini and drove off with him."

Hanlon nodded. This corroborated the old woman's story. Sandwell's neighbor had said the same thing. "Would you recognize the woman again if you saw her? Or her car?"

"I reckon," Sumpter replied. "But that ain't all. See, I took something of his. He had to get it back. If he did, he took it from her house that day. Proves he was there, right?"

Detective Hanlon smiled, her hand making quick notes. "Yes, perhaps it would. What was it that you took?"

"It were an old bowl. Like, antique. You find that, you got your proof it was him."

"If you saw this bowl again, would you be able to identify it?"

"Yeah, no worries. I can describe it even."

As he spoke, Hanlon wrote. In her mind there was a growing conviction that this ill-mannered thug might just be the answer to her prayers. But still, the business about the bowl would not be enough. It would just be his word against Entwhistle's. She could imagine how that would turn out. No, she needed more.

A lopsided smile graced her lips, giving her a cunning, almost feral look. "If you want out of that community service, I can help you. You just need to do something for me."

Sumpter's eyes widened slightly and a hopeful smile curved his lips as his gaze travelled up and down Hanlon's body. She scowled in response.

"You find that car, the green mini. Or the driver. You get either of them for me, and I'll see to it that you don't have to do another hour of community service."

Sumpter licked his lips, then sighed. "Fair enough."

He'd only seen the driver for less than a minute, but it was enough. There was something vaguely familiar about her. She looked like an old hippy, and he knew someone else who fit that bill. He stood, taking the business card that Hanlon offered. With a last lingering look at Hanlon's petite form, he turned to the door.

"I'll be in touch."

Jotunheim

They arrived by ones and twos. Six men and three women. Mostly they were late middle aged, but a few were young, in their twenties. One woman was gray-haired and walked slowly and with care, but the reverence with which she was greeted by the others demonstrated respect and affection. They had ascended the side of the mountain in the fading light of day, without ropes, each of them navigating the narrow path that was only a couple of hands width in some places. But they were familiar with the risk. It was rare for one of their number to fall from the path.

The fact that the way was difficult and dangerous was not lost on them. A metaphor for their belief, it was a challenge that had to be mastered again and again. Just as their beliefs were challenged again and again in the world beyond the mountain.

When all were assembled in the ante-chamber before the Great Hall, they talked and laughed. Friends greeted each other with smiles and handshakes. The council of nine met only a dozen times a year, usually, but recently the call had become more frequent. Three times in this month alone. Whatever difficulties this created for the dedicants was nothing compared to what they hoped to achieve. There was a palpable excitement amongst the nine. Things were at last beginning to happen.

Two of the council pushed a third person before them. He was a hiker and had been caught in the valley below trying to get onto the path that led to the cave. This happened from time to time, and when it did the response was always the same. Bring the interloper to the cave and the Master would absolve him.

As one, the nine began to remove their clothes, stripping naked. No one was ashamed, or embarrassed. If any sought to look at another no one cared. They had seen each other often over the years and it had become routine. Two men roughly stripped the hiker, pulling at his clothes, ripping his shirt, cutting the laces on his boots. Before long, he too was naked. They tossed his clothes in a dark corner.

Each of the nine placed their own shoes and clothes in their assigned spaces, the boxes lined up against one rough wall. Then they donned their robes, pulling up the cowls to cover their heads. No one spoke now. Once the robes were on, it was as if a switch had been thrown. It was not fitting to bring thoughts of the outside world into the sacred chamber. They slipped on their leather sandals. All except the hiker. There was no robe for those who wandered too close to their sacred place. He stood, shivering with cold or fear, mouth still bound by cloth, hands tied behind his back with rope.

When all were ready they followed each other into the

Great Hall, the last two pushing the naked man before them. The candles were lit. They were always lit, illuminating the path from the outside world to the inner, to the sacred chamber where their Master waited, the high priest of Odin, last priest to the true gods.

Mannuki watched as they filed in, the sight of the naked man bringing a smile to his face. Four men surrounded their naked victim. They propelled him forward, pushing him, crowding him. He had no choice but to move. His eyes were wide, but he seemed to have gone into shock. This disappointed Mannuki and he frowned at the sight. He preferred to see the light of intelligence in their eyes. And he particularly liked to watch it fade.

Two of the four chosen men grabbed their victim by his arms, and forced him onto the slab of ice, bending him over backwards. He struggled, the sudden cold of the solid blue-white altar bringing him out of his fugue state to full and very sharply aware attention. He thrashed, and now all four men fought to hold him down.

Mannuki smiled in anticipation. He stepped forward and looked down upon the naked man, seeking his eyes, locking onto them. The remaining dedicants arrayed themselves in a half circle around the altar, watching, waiting.

"This is a fitting sacrifice," Mannuki said, satisfaction evident in his voice. "The gods will be pleased."

At his words the hiker began to fight desperately, fear giving him prodigious strength. The four men holding him struggled to keep him pinned down, but eventually the interloper weakened, his struggles ceasing, as if he had finally accepted his fate.

"Good. Know that you are part of something greater than a single life. Your blood will replenish us, strengthen us and give us the purpose to achieve our great goal. You do not die in vain."

Tears ran from the young man's eyes, trickling down the

side of his face, falling to the altar where they froze, adding their substance to the ancient ice. His bladder let go, hot urine flowing down the sides of the block, freezing as it reached the bottom.

Mannuki smiled. He slipped a shining black blade from inside his sleeve, holding it out before him, letting the light reflect from its smooth sides. He stepped towards the young man but at that moment he stumbled, almost falling to his knees, a grunt forced from his lungs.

Svein Eikenes reached out, grabbing one of Mannuki's arms to steady him. For a moment the Master's bluer than blue eyes faded, turning almost brown. A look of wild relief flooded his face, then in an instant was gone.

Mannuki closed his eyes, and struggled to regain his balance. He straightened. After a moment he opened his eyes. They were blue again and blazing with anger.

"Are you alright, Master?" Eikenes said. The look of pure malevolence Mannuki gave him made Eikenes step back, and he quickly averted his gaze.

Too angry to say the words of dedication, Mannuki flourished the ancient blade. He placed it against the hiker's throat and with a gentle pressure made a shallow incision. Then he slid the blade into the parted skin, and with the skill of a surgeon, punctured the carotid artery. Instantly blood jetted, flooding over the pristine altar of ice. It spread. And as it spread, thin lines appeared, suddenly illuminated. The blood filled the intricately carved altar with a red so dark it was almost black. Patterns appeared, symbols of power, and in the heart of the ice, a complex geometric pattern. A mandala of blood.

Once the sacrifice had stopped bleeding he was dragged from the altar, his body dumped in a dark corner. Another trophy to add to the already towering pile of skulls. Mannuki slipped the knife into his sleeve where it disappeared.

"Soon is the time. I feel it nearing. We reach our goal,

after so long."

He placed his hands, palm down on the ice altar. Instantly the dark lines in the ice blazed, shining out, the crimson becoming bright, turning to a rich gold.

He sighed in pleasure from the power flowing into his arms. The hiker's blood was rich. After a moment, the glowing sigils began to fade. He lifted his hands. Once again the thin lines and patterns became dark. He turned to address the dedicants.

"Much has happened these last days. That which was hidden long ago has been found. You must bring me the seal. There will be those that oppose us. They must be destroyed."

His eyes glowed blue as he turned his gaze to look at Eikenes. He hissed fiercely. "Take back what is mine."

Philip paced in the library, the book in his hand unread for the last ten minutes. Fern had gone home to Norway and a part of him suspected she was not coming back. He would never understand women. She was treating him as if he'd had an affair.

The house felt empty, Fern's energy palpably absent. He had not realized how much he needed her presence. Just like Mr. Francis before him, the kitchen had become his favorite room in the house. The heart of the home, he thought. But without Fern, it did not beat. He went there now, book still in hand. The last light through the window illuminated Jinny's meta-anchor.

He stared at the clay bowl. It was still stained with his blood. He should really do something about that. Putting down his book, Philip took the bowl and placed it in the sink. He filled it with water. The dried blood inside dissolved quickly and he scrubbed it with a sponge. Soon it was as clean as the chipped and weathered clay pot could be. He put it back on the window ledge, and dried his hands on a towel.

Mr. Francis had shared his tea with the djinn, when it had manifested as a cat. That was how Philip first saw the elemental, even though he did not understand what it was he was seeing. But a cat that liked tea? He should have known. It had come as quite a shock when he understood what the cat really was.

And what was she? A fitting companion for an old man? Yes, that, for sure. They had kept up a telepathic conversation for over a hundred years and they were about as close as any two people could be. With a frown, Philip suddenly started to understand that Fern had good reason to be upset.

But he had made a vow to the old man, and to Jinny. He was not going to turn his back on them. He'd already died trying to live up to it and nothing had changed since. Except it had. Fern was important to him now as well. He had made a promise to her too, even if he had not spoken the words. He would just have to try to accommodate both. Assuming she came back.

The night before had been nightmare free. The first time in a month. No guilt-ridden dreams of Sandwell or the day she had killed him. Was that Jinny's influence or just relief over finally knowing she was not dead?

He reached to his throat and tugged at the silver chain, pulling it out from under his shirt, freeing the talisman. It was an Abalak cross. An ensemble of small triangles, each joined to the next to create a shape reminiscent of a misshapen ankh. Already a powerful ward against the evil eye, Sir James had contrived to make it more powerful still. Jinny had evidently done something so that it became a conduit, connecting the djinn to the old man in a very direct way. Now that it was Philip's, it connected him to the djinn too. It allowed him to feel her emotions, even see her thoughts. He had only experienced that a couple of times. The last being on his very first day as guardian. After that, there had been nothing.

With the medallion grasped firmly in his hand, Philip closed his eyes and focused. Using the memory of how it had felt to communicate with the otherworld entity, awkwardly he tried to reach out to her.

"Jinny, can you hear me?"

I hear you, little Man. It is good.

"I'm sorry. I thought I'd lost you forever, Jinny."

So it may have been. But I survived.

"I tried to stop her."

You gave your life to save me.

"But I didn't. You saved me!"

You are mistaken. You freed me with your last strength. The witch was gone, but by then so were you. I could not allow that.

"I felt so ashamed. I failed. I was your guardian for one day, and I almost got you killed."

He could sense amusement from the Djinn, as if she found his shame funny.

No, you did not fail. You gave your life for me. You are the first of your kind to do so for one of us in a great age.

"I made you a promise, and I meant it. I still do. That is, if you still want me to be your guardian."

Nothing has changed. I was weak, now I grow strong.

"So you will be able to manifest again?"

If it does not cause your mate distress, then yes. Otherwise, I will keep myself hidden.

"I'm not entirely sure she will still be my mate." He had fallen into the habit of talking out loud, finding it more natural to hold a conversation where he voiced the words. He sighed. "Fern is not happy about the relationship that you and I have."

I have seen many guardians, little Man. You are not the first, nor will you be the last. All found ways to live with their mates. You will do the same.

"I hope so. She means a lot to me."

I can see your feelings for her. She is shining in your

mind.

Shining in my mind? Yes, he thought. She was. He smiled. It was a strange way to say he loved her, but he liked it.

Philip's eyes blazed, bluer than blue. He seemed taller, as if a heavy weight had been lifted from his shoulders.

But don't hold your love too tightly

7

Of these songs I know, which sons of men
nor queen in a king's court understand;
the first is Help which will bring thee help
in all woes and in sorrow and strife.
                                        —*Hávamál*

Fern took a deep breath then turned to her mother. For a moment she wondered what she should say. The truth, or something her mother might believe? In the end, she had no choice.

"It's a curse," she said. "And this is not helping," waving her hand at the machines and plastic that surrounded the bed. "It's doing more harm than good."

The nurse saw her intent and moved to stop her, a shout escaping her throat. "No!"

Fern ripped away the plastic sheeting. She took her father's hand in both of her own. The nurse fled from the room.

"I'm going to get the doctor," she said over her shoulder, as if it were a threat. The door sealed behind her with a heavy click.

"What are you doing, Fern?" Her mother said, anguished, but with a trace of hope.

"There is a geas upon him. A powerful curse. I'm going to try to remove it."

Jens had observed the events of the last few seconds silently. He removed his mask, watching his sister keenly. She ignored him, but followed suit, removing her own face mask.

"I hope you know what you're doing, Pernilla."

Fern raised her eyes and met his gaze. "I believe that I am the only one who does. No one else seems to know what's going on here. I just hope I'm strong enough."

Jens did not believe in magic, trusting only in things he could touch and see. Fern used to delight in teasing him about that. How could he believe in television then, she would say. Could he see the radio waves? Could he touch them? She had never convinced him, but like their mother, Fern suspected that there was a tiny part of him that hoped.

Many women in her family were rumored to have been gifted, her great grandmother for one. As long as Aasheims had been farming their land, the women in the family were known to be special. And if she was the last with the talent, then it would have to do.

Still holding her father's hand, she closed her eyes, gathering her strength. Then she focused on her father, willing him to live, to resist, to fight. She poured her love into him, her strength. At first, nothing happened. Then a little color came back into his face and his breathing seemed to ease. The machine monitoring his heart blipped faster. Then Arnulf opened his eyes.

"Pernilla?"

The voice was hoarse, old.

"Yes, Papa. I'm here."

She concentrated, the lines on her forehead deepening, crow's feet appearing at the corners of her eyes. But her strength gave out and she staggered in near exhaustion. It was not enough. She was unable to give him anything close to the life force he needed to recover, and as quickly as the color had returned to her father's cheeks, it drained away and he became pallid again, his breathing ragged.

Undeterred, Fern pulled a plastic chair close to the bed, collapsing into it, her fingers wrapped around the bony parchment of her father's hand. Tears welled up, running down her face. Liv stood behind her, one hand resting lightly on her daughter's shoulder. She had seen the change, what Fern had done.

Fern knew her mother felt some empathy for her beliefs, and that secretly she hoped that Fern could cure him. Fern had hoped so too, but there was nothing she could do. She did not have anything close to the strength needed to save him. She hissed in frustration.

"He was cursed! Who would do such a thing?"

Her father's lips moved, and he began to mutter. Fern moved closer. His voice was barely audible, but Fern could hear the same incomprehensible nonsense as before. About to sit up, she froze. What was that word? Something stood out amongst the nonsense. Her eyes widened as she heard it again. Quite clearly spoken, a word that chilled her soul; djinn.

She stood, hand flying to her mouth, the chair tipping over with a clatter, her face ashen. How could it be? Only days ago she had not suspected they even existed and now her father was speaking in a strange language, saying the word *djinn* over and over.

She shook her head. Jens said he had found their father in his Land Rover. On the seat next to him was a lead plate. Was it possible that it was a curse tablet? A defixio? But Jens had said that it was covered in writing no one could understand. If it was a curse tablet, then how had her father managed to read it?

There was only one option here. Her father's life was more important than her bruised feelings. She ripped away the green protective gown covering her clothes. Once free, she pulled her mobile from her back pocket and dialed a number. He answered right away.

"Philip," she said, her voice raw with emotion.

"Fern. How is your father?"

"Philip." It was all she could do not to break down. She needed him, more than she was willing to admit. "He's very sick. He's been cursed. I believe that he may have found a defixio."

"Oh my . . . are you sure?"

"There is a geas on him, Philip. It is powerful and I cannot break it. I don't believe my circle could break it, were they all here. But there's something else. He's been speaking in a language I don't know, but he said a word I recognized."

There was silence as Philip waited. "What word, Fern?"

"Djinn."

Again silence. "Send me the address. I'm coming."

Sumpter was ready now. He had some rope, duct tape and a packet of condoms. You couldn't take any chances these days. You never knew what diseases people might have, not to mention leaving DNA evidence. He was no fool. If he was going to put Entwhistle's girlfriend through the ringer, he was not going to be found out.

He had checked the schedule for the Women's Institute meeting hall and there was another meeting of the Spirit Seekers in the afternoon. He almost laughed again as he read the name of the wannabe witches.

And now, in the same corner of the car park, he waited for her to arrive. He would have to be quick, but he knew he could knock her out and get her in the van before anyone was the wiser. His heart raced and he was almost bouncing with excitement. She was one tasty bit of crumpet, and he was going to have some real fun with her.

He checked his watch, a slight frown pulling his eyebrows together. She was late. The class, session, or whatever the hell they called it must have already started. But no sign of the hippy chick. He cursed and spat onto the ground. Just his luck. The bitch wasn't coming.

But the sound of a car arriving made him look up. Was it her? No, just a green mini. It drove in fast, stopping with a squeal of brakes. A slight woman with short hair jumped out, running quickly for the hall entrance. She hadn't even bothered to lock the car.

Sumpter stared dumbly for a moment. Then realization dawned. He had seen her before. It was the woman that had rescued Entwhistle from outside Lizzie's house.

Sumpter almost laughed. Here was his golden ticket out of all that fucking community service! He pulled his phone from his pocket then strolled over to the car, taking a picture of the license plate. He sent the picture along with a short message to a number stored on his phone.

He smirked as he resumed his former place in the shadowed corner of the car park. Okay, not quite the afternoon he had planned, but it was still pretty sweet.

Philip was in the kitchen, making tea, his standard response in the face of emotional distress. He had taken Fern's call while pouring boiling water into a cup. But as soon as the call with Fern ended he forgot his beverage and immediately dialed again. The phone rang a few times.

"Rappaport and associates. How can I help you?"

"This is Philip Entwhistle. I need to speak to Mr. Rappaport immediately."

"Certainly, sir. Hold just one second."

There was no muzak, for which Philip was momentarily grateful. It was not long before another voice spoke, this one soft and cultured.

"Hello Mr. Entwhistle. I am glad you rang. I was just about to call you myself. Now then, what can I do for you?"

"Look, I know that this is probably not the sort of thing that you did for Mr. Francis, but I need to get to Norway, right away. I wonder if you could organize this for me? I simply don't have time to deal with it and I have no one else to ask and it's urgent."

"You are quite correct sir, that Mr. Francis never requested such a service. But we are pleased to help in any way we can. Rest assured, we can organize your travels. There is, however, something I believe you should know. The police have been pushing a case with the Crown Prosecution Service. The subject of the aforementioned case appears to be you. I am not aware of any warrant for your apprehension, but it is my view that for us to book you on a commercial flight may be a mistake."

"Bloody hell."

"Quite, sir."

"How did you hear about that"

"I had a visit from a couple of police officers. They asked a lot of questions about you. Naturally, I told them nothing. Not even what is in the public record. However, I made sure to put in place some safeguards, should their interest be more than idle curiosity. As it turns out, this was a good move, since I have learned that the CPS is confident that there are sufficient grounds to prosecute you for arson. Now, about your travel arrangements, if I may make a suggestion?"

Philip was stunned. Then he realized that Rappaport was waiting for a response. "Yes, please do. I'm all ears."

"Private jet sir. It will not be cheap, but it will be much faster and less fuss than a commercial airline."

"Yes, that sounds fine. Doesn't matter about the cost. I need to be in Norway right now."

"Indeed sir. I will make arrangements. In the meantime, I suggest you obtain your passport and pack a bag. I will have transport at your location to pick you up within approximately twenty minutes."

Philip nodded, wondering where his passport was. He had a box of papers in the library. It was probably in amongst them. It had better be. Fern had messaged him with the location of the hospital and he read off the address.

Mr. Rappaport assured him that he would be there in two hours.

"Fine. I'll be waiting outside the house."

"Understood, sir."

The call ended, and Philip went to the library. Behind his reading chair, hidden away because he did not know where to put it yet, was a cardboard box full of miscellaneous papers. He yanked the chair aside, grabbed the box, and dumped the contents onto the floor. There, in plain sight, was his passport. Oh, miracle of miracles. He snatched it up and immediately headed back to the kitchen, slipping the passport into his jacket pocket.

There was only one other thing he needed. He grabbed his satchel, which had been hanging on the back of a chair. The old leather was worn thin from its many years of service. He dumped its contents on the kitchen table, spilling books, pens, a wireless mouse and power supply for his laptop.

Then he went to a drawer and pulled out a tea towel. He took the djinn's meta-anchor from its place on the window sill and wrapped it in the towel, then placed it inside the satchel. He was not going to leave it behind. He swung the bag over his shoulder, locked the back door, and headed to the front of the house. He paused momentarily to look at the picture of Sir James and Tajeddigt. Then he left, locking the heavy red door behind him. He strode to the end of the garden path and tried to be patient. All he had to do now was wait for the taxi and he would be on his way.

Detective Hanlon finished signing the report that she had spent the morning writing. She added it to the very small pile of papers in her out tray before reaching for a folder from the much taller stack next to it.

Just then her mobile phone buzzed. She put the file back and snatched the phone up. New Message. One click later and a large smile spread across her face, an image of a small green car displayed on the screen along with a single worded message. 'Bingo.'

He had done it. The idiot skinhead had actually done it. Sumpter had found Entwhistle's accomplice. She dialed the number and Sumpter answered at once.

"I see congratulations are in order," she said. "But you're sure this is the car?"

"Yeah. I saw the woman what drove it. Same biddy that grabbed Entwhistle outside Lizzie's house. This is the one you want."

Hanlon got up and swung her door open. She covered the phone with one hand. "Topley!" She grabbed her jacket from the back of the door then put the phone back to her ear.

"What's the address?"

Topley appeared from his office, a half eaten bacon sandwich in his hand. He looked at her quizzically but she ignored him, nodding as Sumpter relayed the location of the car.

"We'll be there in ten minutes."

She put her phone away and donned her jacket all the while grinning up at her partner. Her enthusiasm was contagious and Topley could not help grinning back.

"So, who was that then?" he asked.

"Fate, kismet. Take your pick," she replied, pulling him towards the stairs. "We're going for a drive."

It was more like seven minutes by the time she pulled into the car park. Sumpter waved them over. And there was the car. Battered, old, green, exactly as described. Hanlon felt a surge of excitement.

She jumped out. "Grab that kit off the back seat, please," she said to Topley. Sumpter nodded as she approached, clearly pleased with himself. He looked like the cat that got the cream.

"Has anyone been back to it, since you've been here?"

she asked, a smile tugging at her lips.

"Nope. The woman what owns it is in there." He pointed to the hall.

"Good." She tried the door. It was open. More luck. "Topley, the bottle?"

The huge detective opened an aluminum equipment case and removed a plastic bottle containing a clear liquid, the word *Luminol* on the side. Hanlon took the bottle, then sprayed its contents over the backseat.

"Now the UV, quick!" She was breathing fast. Please, she thought. Please! She flicked the switch on the black tube. Although there was no visible light from the device, immediately, a splatter of faint but clear blobs appeared. Blood, and lots of it!

It was enough. More than enough. This was the smoking gun. She grinned up at her partner as he returned the Luminol kit to its case.

"We're going to need to get this car towed. Call for an assist. Someone needs to take the owner into custody."

She dived back into the mini, opening the glove compartment. Forensics were going to have a field day. Inside the glove box was a mess of papers. Hanlon grabbed one. An electricity bill in the name of Alicia Milton, and her address. Entwhistle's accomplice!

It was all coming together. She pocketed the document, turning to look at Sumpter.

"You did good. I'll have a word about that community service. Now piss off."

Topley chuckled at Sumpter's scowl as he was dismissed.

"Time we paid Mr. Entwhistle a visit," he said, unaware that his fingers had closed into a fist.

The powerful engine roared as Topley shifted gear, hammering the accelerator coming out of the turn. They were driving fast, pushing the limit of the car's ability.

Hanlon did not want to let another minute more than necessary go by before having Philip Entwhistle in custody.

It was Hanlon's car, but, she had to admit, Topley was the better driver and making the collar was more important than her ego. He had smiled when she tossed him the keys. It was an admission on her part, but she didn't care.

Two uniformed officers followed in a car of their own, barely keeping up. She looked behind. They were still there, a hundred meters back. She checked her watch. At the speed they were going, they would be at Entwhistle's house in less than fifteen minutes.

"Can't you go any faster?"

"Sure," Topley replied. "So long as you don't mind me crashing your car."

"Alright. I'm just . . . you know."

"I know. Don't worry. We've got him now."

They were nearing the turn that the GPS indicated would lead to his cottage. Then the system announced, in its oddly mechanical feminine voice, that they should turn left in two-hundred meters.

An odd sound intruded as they slowed to make the turn. It was rhythmic, and though faint, naggingly familiar. It was almost like . . . a helicopter.

Hanlon strained to see out of the window. The distinctive shape of a small helicopter was just visible before it disappeared behind some trees, presumably landing in a nearby field.

"What the hell?"

Some instinct told her she was out of time. She flipped a switch on the dashboard and the siren blared, to be joined a moment later by the car behind. Topley glanced briefly at her, eyebrows raised.

"Go faster, Topley," Hanlon cried out. "Fuck the car."

The dig proceeded with remarkable speed. The stones that marked the outline of the grave were revealed, and the topsoil in a meter wide trench through the middle was gone. At a depth of less than half a meter, they found metal. A twisted sword, clearly made from a relatively low degree of carbon. It was severely tarnished, but unlike many weapons found, it was not eaten through by rust. Soon came other artifacts. The remains of a shield, the severely corroded spherical iron cone of the central boss, as well as a little of the binding for the shield edge. There were no remains of a body. They had half expected to find something. Teeth, a skull, but there was nothing in the grave. If anyone had been there, he had been absorbed into the soil so long ago that nothing remained but the iron of his weapons.

Soil analysis would reveal something. There was discoloring to the earth, indicative of iron oxide. Possibly due to the great mass of chainmail that had probably been there. But no remnants of leather, or woolen garments. That was exceedingly rare, but Eriksen had hoped.

The awning of the command center flapped in the breeze, snapping like firecrackers. Eriksen stood below, examining the finds on the trestle table. So much had been brought to the surface in only a single day. An astonishing gold ring, the shield boss, the sword. Together with the torc and the metal plate, this was a site of national importance. Further work was warranted, but the weather report stated a blizzard was coming. Work on the site would have to be suspended. He would seal the dig. There was still the likely Bronze Age burial to be found, deeper under the mound. But their objective had been principally to investigate the Viking age burial, and this had been achieved. The only thing remaining was to cover the dig with topsoil, send the team home and write up the report.

No, that was not all. *The thing that did not belong.* He had not seen it himself, Farrell having spirited it away, but the metal plate must surely be the object that he was instructed to give to Silvi. He wondered, morosely, if the English archaeologist had screwed him deliberately. The plate should have been left with him, instead, Farrell had taken it to Oslo.

He looked up to see the young woman who had been foisted on him. Silvi. She was standing over at the far side of the field, one foot on a stump, her back to the dig. She was talking on her mobile. She should not have that, really. They did not like the team members to have phones on site. Too much temptation to take unauthorized pictures. That could lead to problems, especially if they put them up on the Web. You might as well invite thieves to your dig, if you did that. But he had to admit, for someone that had been pushed on him, she had worked well. Doing everything she was told without complaint. More than could be said for one of the graduate students, Frank, who seemed to think that the dig was an excuse for flirting and generally wasting time.

Silvi started her way back to the mound, putting away the phone. She ignored Eriksen, going straight to her back pack that was stacked along with the others' and pulling out a thermos.

Eriksen looked at his watch. There was an hour of daylight left. He had to get on with the report. He sat at the only chair behind the trestle table and started again on his notes.

Philip did not have long to wait. After only fifteen minutes he could distinctly hear the thwack thwack of a low flying helicopter. Seconds later he saw it, lights blinking, heading straight for the cottage and moving fast. Philip shook his head in astonishment. Rappaport did not mess around. He had expected a taxi, or maybe even a chauffeur-driven limousine, but this was something else.

He dashed across the lane and jumped the gate into the

field opposite, waving his arms frantically above his head. The pilot spotted him, made a slight adjustment and brought it in gently, square in the middle of the field.

Entwhistle began a cautious approach, wary of the giant spinning blades, but then heard something that sent him bounding across the field, satchel flapping—police sirens, more than one, approaching at speed. The cockpit door opened and the pilot leaned out.

"You Entwhistle?" he shouted.

"That's me," Entwhistle yelled back, scrambling aboard, chest heaving.

"Okay, shut the door, strap in, and put these on," said the pilot, passing him a pair of heavy headphones.

As the pilot flipped a switch and gunned the engine Entwhistle saw flashing lights speeding down the lane. He turned to the pilot, half expecting him to kill the power. But the burly young man just looked casually round and, seeing them himself, broke into a wicked grin.

"Anything for Mr. Rappaport," he laughed and yanked on the joystick, sending the heli-taxi lurching into the air. As they accelerated up and away Entwhistle craned his neck back towards the cottage. From a hundred feet in the air he could clearly make out the familiar figures of Detectives Hanlon and Topley, bathed in flashing blue light, looking up at him.

He heard a voice in his ears. "Your first chopper flight?"

Entwhistle looked around and nodded.

"How do you like it?"

In spite of his current worries, Entwhistle grinned.

"I love it!"

The pilot had obviously been told about the rush and the fifteen mile journey to the private air field was over in short order. The pilot bickered with the tower as they landed right next to a small, gleaming white jet aircraft of the kind favored by rock stars and arms dealers. The pilot killed the engine with a flourish and Entwhistle heard the whistling thunder of the plane already warming up. One thing was for sure—Rappaport took his work seriously. Entwhistle pulled a couple of twenties from his wallet, handed them to the still grinning pilot and scampered up the mobile staircase. The only passenger, he sank with relief into one of the eight luxurious leather seats. Thirty seconds later they were in the air, heading for Norway at a cruising speed just short of the speed of sound.

Dr. Selvig balanced a pair of tiny spectacles on his nose and leaned in to peer at the data columns tabulated on his computer screen. He frowned, pressed a button on the keyboard, and the screen changed to display curves graphed from the data. On the left of the screen were the standard curves—the level each detected element would be compared against. On the right, jagged lines showed the wavelength of each element, the density of the line proportional to its concentration. Comparing the right hand graph with the left would show the concentration of the elements. More exhaustive tests could be done later. Right now, he simply wanted to know what was in the metal and some clue as to its origin.

He cursed. Something was wrong. There was a graph on the right hand side, with no corresponding standard curve on the left. Not to mention there were only two graphs! It had to be an error of some sort. He would have to run it again.

He reset the equipment and spent an impatient hour waiting for the results. Once again, the same result. Although it should have not been possible, the minute sample from the torc clearly showed an alloy containing a previously unknown element.

He suppressed an urge to call everyone he knew. He had a reputation to consider and without proof others would scoff. He would have scoffed himself if he had not been the one to do the test. But better safe than sorry. He would take another sample, process it, and test it a third time. He pressed a button on his keyboard and a moment later a laser printer stirred into life. The pages piled up neatly in the tray attached to its side. Images of the graphs, and their corresponding frequencies.

He picked up the phone on his desk, pressing a four digit number. It rang a couple of times.

"Farrell here."

"This is Selvig. I have the metallurgy results. Most . . . interesting. I think you should come by and take a look."

"Absolutely! I'll be right there."

Selvig hung up the phone and picked up the half dozen pages from the printer. He examined the results. It was not pure gold. But then, pure gold was rarely pure. There were always trace elements of something. But this was different. It was a gold alloy, unlike anything he had ever seen before. And the strangest part . . . He could barely articulate the thought.

Focus on what you know, he thought. The presence of certain isotopes showed the gold to be from Africa. But it could not be old, as Farrell claimed. But the other? What could explain that?

Hearing a gentle knocking, Selvig looked up from the report to see Farrell's cheerful grin through the small tempered glass window in the door. Selvig hit the switch with the flat of his palm. The door clicked and Farrell pushed his way in.

"Right, Dr. Selvig. Lead off. I have to say, I'm rather excited to hear what you've got."

Selvig sighed deeply and pulled a wry face. "Excited? You should be scared witless, more like it."

"Pardon? What are you talking about?"

The two men made their way back to Selvig's desk.

Selvig looked at the slightly older man with his silly bow tie and tweed jacket. To his eyes Farrell looked foolish but Selvig knew he was anything but. He was a well-known chess demon and word had it that he had bested the university's resident genius, a young physicist, at scrabble. But still, this was something else. He did not know if he could explain this in a way that the archeologist would understand.

"Okay, first off, let me tell you that this is not pure gold. It is close, but there is something else in it."

"Alright."

"Second, the gold was mined in Africa, I believe. But that is not the big question."

"Oh? What is?"

Selvig sat down in his swivel chair, and leaned back, one hand going to his chin, a finger tapping on his lip. Farrell pulled up a chair, and sat.

"The big question is, if this is not pure gold, then what else is there? This is actually a gold alloy, which most gold is. You will usually find silver, copper, and other elements within gold, even of the purest standard, the so-called three nines. But this is not the same. There are zero, absolutely zero, traces of any other elements, except one. That in itself is extraordinary, and unheard of in ancient metal. How did they do it? It doesn't stop there. There are two even more astonishing findings to be considered. I've checked—they're real. The first is the ratio of the two elements."

Farrell did not speak. He stared at the smaller man, hardly breathing. Selvig leaned forward.

"The percentage," he said drawing an imaginary number in the air, "is one point six percent."

He let that sink in but Farrell looked blank. Selvig made an expression intended to say *think*.

He listed a series of numbers. One point six, followed by another ten digits. "This is the golden mean. The divine proportion. Tau, or Phi, depending upon which school of thought you follow as to who first discovered it."

"I say, isn't that rather difficult to achieve?"

"No. I would say it's impossible. But that is not even the

most incredible thing."

"Then what is?"

"The other element, the one that comprises one point six percent of the alloy. It does not exist in the periodic table."

Entwhistle stared out the window of a second helicopter, the leather satchel clutched firmly on his lap. A local Norwegian tourist chopper had been waiting at a small private airport not far from Lillehammer. The pilot circled once then landed on the almost empty concrete expanse that was the spillover car park for the hospital. He shrugged apologetically.

"Sorry, but I can't use the helipad on the hospital roof. Not allowed. They'd take my license for that."

"I understand, it's fine. This is close enough."

"Thanks for hiring me, Mr. Entwhistle. You need me again, just call."

The pilot passed a business card to Philip which he pocketed with a nod. Familiar now with the routine he removed his headphones and unbuckled before levering the door open. He jumped down, automatically ducking to avoid the still spinning blades. Then he leaned back into the cockpit.

"Any chance you can stand by? I might need you again on short notice."

The pilot nodded, and Philip slammed the door shut. He was at the back of the hospital. There was no public entrance, but he spotted a hospital orderly leaning against a wall smoking a cigarette. The man was shivering with cold, hopping up and down to keep warm. The orderly watched with interest as the helicopter took off. Entwhistle hurried over to the tall, blond man.

"Hello. I am Dr. Entwhistle." He had to shout above the noise as the helicopter rose into the air behind him.

"Yes?"

"I'm needed on the Isolation ward immediately."

The orderly flicked away the remnants of his smoke and shrugged. He turned and swiped his ID card through an entry control. The door behind him clicked open, and he pulled it wide, motioning for Philip to enter.

"Thanks. Can you show me the way?"

The orderly's expression said he had better things to do but he nodded, setting off at a brisk pace that had Entwhistle jogging to keep up. He led him to an elevator and from there to a floor where nurses worked with quiet efficiency.

"This is Infectious Diseases. Or at least, if you follow the red line, there, you'll come to it." The orderly pointed to an array of lines painted on the floor.

"Thanks, I appreciate it."

The red line led Entwhistle to a wing apparently devoid of staff, but a man in faded jeans and a knitted sweater in a typical Norwegian folk pattern stood at a window staring into the night. Hearing Entwhistle approach he turned.

His eyes narrowed. "Are you Fern's boyfriend?"

"Uhm, what? Yes."

"She's through here." Entwhistle was surprised by the apparent recognition and even more by the taller man's edge of hostility, but he held the door for Entwhistle and followed him into a room filled with hospital gowns. Another door, this one open. Entwhistle entered.

Fern was there, worry lining her face. With her was an older woman standing by a bed. Although blonde and buxom she looked like a good deal like Fern, with the same tall stature and pixie nose. An old man lay in the bed, seemingly unconscious, old enough to be Fern's grandfather or even great-grandfather.

Both women turned as he entered. Fern took a step towards him, hesitated, then ran to him. Clutching him in a fierce embrace she buried her face in his neck. Finally she took a step back.

"How did you get here so quickly? I only called you

what, two hours ago?" She brushed an errant lock of hair form her face, then looked directly into his eyes, before glancing down. "Did you use the djinn?" She whispered it, like a shameful secret.

He shook his head. "No magic. I'll tell you later."

She gave him a tight smile. "I can't do anything for him. It's not a natural illness, Philip, I can say that much for certain."

"What do the doctors say?"

"They have no idea. But I do. It's sorcery, Philip."

Entwhistle nodded, accepting it without question. This was the new world he had been drawn into.

"He's been speaking. It's a language, alright, one I don't understand or even recognize. But I caught one word. *Djinn*. He keeps saying it."

Entwhistle frowned. If there was a djinn involved he was probably the closest thing there was to an expert. And now that Jinny was back he could ask her.

He moved to the bedside and reached for the silver chain around his neck. He closed his hand around it, took a breath, then directed his mind to the djinn.

Jinny, I need you, he thought. There was no reply. He felt a surge of panic. Where was she?

I hear you, little Man. This one is gravely stricken. He will pass through the veil soon.

Is there anything we can do? Anything *you* can do?

No.

The answer shocked Entwhistle. The djinn was capable of healing flesh and bone. She had restored him to life after his throat was cut. But this was beyond her?

I don't understand. How is it that you cannot help him?

His sickness is not of the body, but that which you call the soul. He is being drained of his life-force.

Fern was looking at him with pleading eyes. She went to her mother and put an arm around her shoulder, but her eyes never left his face. Entwhistle looked down, afraid she could somehow sense the conversation in his head.

The man he had met in the corridor, Fern's brother, he assumed, stood to one side, his face stone. Entwhistle could see at a glance that he did not believe in hocus-pocus and that he probably thought that Entwhistle was a charlatan. This endeared him to Entwhistle. He could sympathize. He had been the same just a few short months ago. He grasped the talisman tighter in his hand.

We have to save him, Jinny. What is causing this?

At that moment, Arnulf began to speak. Philip leaned in, listening. He did not understand anything. But he sensed that Jinny could.

"What's he saying?" he said, not realizing that he spoke aloud.

"No one knows," Fern replied.

He is speaking of the seal of Atln. It does not exist any longer. It was destroyed in the schism. And yet he speaks of it, as if he knew such a thing. I do not understand how this can be. I must see his mind.

"How?"

You will have to trust me, little Man. I have need of your body. Do not fight me, or resist me. I promise to leave your form as soon as we have accomplished what must be done.

Sorry, I don't understand. You want to take my body?

Yes, little Man. It is vital I understand what he has seen. You must allow me to take your body as my own.

Entwhistle swallowed. The djinn wanted to possess him. It was exactly what Fern's witches had warned him of. Jinny would wear him like a glove and he would be powerless, unable to command his own body. He swallowed, his heart racing.

Is this the only way?

I know of no other, little Man.

Fern stepped forward. She seemed impatient. "What does it . . . she say, Philip?"

Entwhistle took his hand from the talisman. "Jinny

wants to read his mind."

At this Jens barked a savage laugh and left the room. Fern closed her eyes and took a deep breath. Opening them, she held Entwhistle in her gaze. He could sense the power of her will but also her desperation.

"Can she do that?" she said.

He nodded. "I believe so."

"So, why don't you let her?"

"She needs to use my body to do it."

Fern gasped.

Entwhistle shrugged. "Jinny promises to leave me as soon as it's done."

Fern's face clouded. She bit her bottom lip, conflicting doubt and fear showing in her eyes.

"It is forbidden, Philip. We are taught that the possessed are an abomination."

"She says it will help. It's the only option we have, Fern. I trust Jinny. She says I saved her life. She certainly saved mine."

A moment more of indecision. "Alright. Then please do it. I feel him dying. Whatever it takes, please help him."

Entwhistle nodded again and smiled reassuringly. In truth he was frightened at the prospect of losing control of his body, of himself. But Jinny had practically given her own life to save him and if that did not earn trust, what did?

"Okay, Jinny. Let's do it. I'm ready."

Almost before he was finished speaking he could feel her in his mind. She felt enormous, pushing him aside, compressing him, forcing him into a space so small he feared he would break. He was overwhelmed; like a drowning man his instincts kicked in and he tried to push her out.

Philip, you must allow.

It was the first time she had ever used his name. Up until then she had only ever called him Little Man, as if he was no different from all the others she had known. Hearing his name disarmed him and he forced himself to stop resisting. He accepted his inner banishment. He could still think, but he was disconnected, an observer in his own body. His hands raised in front of him, and the fingers flexed, but it was not his command. His body took a hesitant step forward, then, as if gaining in confidence and control, it took another step to the side of the bed.

Entwhistle watched himself reach out and pick up Arnulf's withered hand, surprised to discover he could still feel. The old man's flesh was dry and felt like coarse parchment. It was the hand of an old man, not strong and hard like someone used to working outside in all weathers.

The djinn pushed forth her mind. Entwhistle could sense her hold on his body was weaker, and he had to calm himself, resist the instinct to force her out. Suddenly he saw with her eyes as well as his own. And as the djinn's strength flowed throughout his body, he could see things, disjointed images. A house, fields, the stumps of trees and a mound. He knew it for a haug although he did not know how he knew.

He saw Arnulf digging on the mound, pulling something from it. He saw him carry it to his truck and douse it with water, cleaning it with a white handkerchief. He saw words, strange letters, and he felt astonishment and tremendous fear in Jinny's mind.

This cannot be. It was lost. The seal was destroyed in the war. It has been gone since the schism.

Entwhistle could not help it. He pushed, forcing out the alien presence of the djinn. And as his mind flooded back he recovered control of his body. But not soon enough to stop himself from falling.

Your fate's already sealed
8

"Seek not to avoid your destiny. You do what must be done."
—*Pontius Pilate, The secret epistles*

Farrell returned to his office, head full of ideas. That the torc was special was an understatement. According to Selvig, nothing else existed of its kind. He poured himself a coffee from the thermos flask his wife had prepared for him that morning, then continued with Bjorn's saga. He read avidly, unconsciously sipping his coffee, scanning the pages like a hawk searching for prey.

Finishing, he put the book down. It was certainly a good read. Very exciting, full of the sort of heroic banditry that Vikings were known for. Although, to be fair, it did appear as if Bjorn was slightly more reasonable than most of his contemporaries. Allowing the towns to keep half their wealth if they surrendered to him without a fight was quite enlightened for a Viking. Even if he was masquerading as a Byzantine, he still had the same basic Viking nature. Take what you can, fight when you can win and deal fairly when you cannot.

Unusually, however, it portrayed Bjorn's death as ignoble. Even Njal had died with more dignity, burned in his house. *He* had even managed to dispatch a few of his enemies in the process. Poor Bjorn had died in the mud from an illness that the narrator strongly hinted as being of a supernatural nature. A curse, or the evil eye.

Of course, the pagan peoples of north Europe were always seeing the supernatural. You could not have a pool of water without a naiad or spirit. Same with the mountains and trees. So for Egill Thrandsson to suspect some kind of malignant force or supernatural agency would be in keeping with their mind-set. However, something in the description of Bjorn's frailty, how he had 'become old overnight' was chillingly like what was happening to Arnulf Aasheim right now.

Even the most skeptical person, and as a scientist Roger Farrell considered himself to be a skeptic of the highest order, would have to admit something remarkably coincidental in the two events. One recounted by a Viking returning from Constantinople a thousand years ago, and what he had seen with his own eyes only the day before.

He had a sudden desire to see the words of the saga as they were originally written. He sat forward in his chair and reached for the computer mouse, opening a web browser. He typed a search phrase and in a few clicks the screen displayed the pictures.

Inscribed on vellum, the edges frayed, and even slightly burned in one area, the saga had been written in a neat hand, the black ink still perfectly legible except where a few stains obscured a word here and there.

Farrell could not read the Old Norse but he examined the first page curiously, focusing on the opening line. He knew what it said in the English translation. But this was too far removed from English for him to understand more than the occasional word.

Það var maður að nafni Björn, sonur Rolf og Svanhild dóttur Eiríks vándr. Björn var maður svo mikill og sterkur að ekkert gæti passa hann, og hann gaf þjónustu í Miklagarðr.

The text ran over six sides of parchment and he clicked through the images without really knowing what he was looking for. Coming to the last page he was about to close his browser when he froze. There, on the image of the original text of the Saga of Bjorn the mighty, he saw something very similar to the writing on the lead tablet. There were only a few symbols but they showed the same characteristic wedge-like shapes and patterns. He frowned. Now how was *that* for a coincidence?

Worried that he might have missed something important, he picked up his copy of *Sagas of the Norse,* and turned the pages back to the start of Bjorn's saga.

There was a man named Bjorn, son of Rolf and Svanhild, daughter of Eirik the Wicked.

He read the entire tale again, but this time his coffee sat untouched on his desk, forgotten as he was pulled into another world.

Jotunheim Valley
Thrandsson homestead

Egill's family farm lay close to a large body of water known as the Kaldfjord. In spite of its name it was really a lake. However, the water truly was cold, even in summer. Egill had grown up on its shores and had first learned to swim in its chill embrace. It lay in a relatively flat valley, the central area of which was perforated by a series of smaller lakes running roughly north-west to south-east. In the distance, the towering form of Jotunheim, one of the great mountains and home of the giants loomed massive, casting its shadow far.

Egill turned and motioned down the valley. "This is it. Home."

Asgeir had been there many times. He had grown up further along the valley and was as familiar with it as Egill was. But the brothers from Bjørkedalen had never been there before. Nor, of course, had Mannuki. The little man looked down on the valley and grunted, whether in appreciation or disparagement Egill could not say.

One of the brothers, Sigurd, smiled weakly, exhaustion writ plain on his face. "They got beds down there?"

Egill chuckled. "Yes, they have beds. And beer and a warm bath too."

At the mention of beer Asgeir's eyes lit up. "Your foster mother brewed good beer, Egill. I remember it well."

Mannuki grunted again. What it meant Egill could not fathom. "Come on," said the Northlander. "We're almost there."

It had been two days since they had left the priest of the White Christ and almost as long since they had last eaten. It was hard going over the mountains, and the night had settled a chill into his bones that their meager fire could not dispel. But coming down into the valley with the lake below and the small homestead belonging to his family visible, Egill knew it had been worth it.

Five years he had been away and he could see that nothing had changed. That was how it should be. The family fished and worked the fields. The thralls helped, watching the sheep and the swine. They were as much a part of the farm as Egill's own kin. He could see, even from this distance, activity far below denoting a working farm. Smoke rose in wispy spirals from the hall, sheep were racing from some unexpected fright, and in chase he could just make out the small form of a boy, trying to coerce them back into the pasture.

They followed the track zig-zagging down the mountainside. Mindful where he placed his feet on the narrow pathway, he kept an eye on the farm below, watching, waiting. Yes, there!

Two figures emerged from the hall and appeared to be staring in his direction. Good, they had been seen. Soon armed men would come to greet them. Strangers from over the mountains were a rare event, either a chance to provide hospitality for honored guests, or the potential for bloodshed. Even in the quiet times there was always the possibility that some long-harbored grudge could turn to feud.

But he was family. There would be no bloodshed this day. He cast a sidelong glance at Mannuki. There were indeed strangers, however.

Four horsemen set out from the farm. He recognized his cousin's ungainly style of riding; all flapping elbows. And that man with the gleam of bronze on his helm would be his uncle Harald. The others he could not recognize from this distance.

It did not take long for the riders to meet them. Before they reached the bottom of the winding path the four mounted men were there. Egill could see his uncle recognized him. Or, more likely, Asgeir, whose hair made him easy to pick out. He kept his face neutral, not wanting his kinfolk to think him a woman, overcome with joy.

He passed the reins of his horse to Mannuki, then strode forward to meet the welcoming party. Before he could speak, his uncle raised a hand.

"Are you a ghost, boy?"

Egill was no specter, returning to haunt his family. But he could not resist a little joke.

"Aye, I'm hungry enough."

His young cousin was grinning from ear to ear but Egill kept his face calm, thrusting out his chin in challenge. His uncle smiled a little too.

"Best not keep you from your food then."

Harald slipped down from his saddle, a little more stiffly and with more grunting than Egill remembered, then strode forward and embraced his nephew in a bear hug. Egill smiled and returned the embrace, patting him on the back.

"It's good to be back."

"It's good to have you back, boy."

They stepped away from each other. Harald moved off to greet his kinsman, Asgeir, son of his wife's brother. Egill examined his cousin. Sigmund was still grinning. Egill found the young man's smile infectious and his own began to grow. He looked up, taking in Sigmund's bigger chest and strong arms. His cousin had become a man since he left.

"Sigmund, you look all grown. You wet your dick yet or are you still a girl?"

Sigmund chuckled. "Married now. Just going on a year."

"Oh? What poor girl did you kidnap? Or did you finally give in to temptation with that sow of yours?"

His cousin had reared a pig when he was younger. When it had come time to slaughter it, he had cried and taken a knife to defend it. They had laughed all winter over that. Even now Sigmund's face became red at the memory. But he did not lose his smile. That was something that Egill loved about him. He was a good man, with a good heart and never held a grudge.

"We ate her. I cut her throat myself. It got pretty bad here, the winter after you left. We lost a couple of the thralls to the hunger."

This was a serious thing and Egill made no further comment about his cousin's pig. He strode forward and they clasped arms.

"Welcome back, Egill."

"It's good to be back, Sigmund."

Harald cleared his throat, then his stentorian bellow echoed out over the valley. "My brother's son has returned! And tonight we feast!"

Tired as the returning travelers were, the walk down was filled with good natured talk and laughter. Harald was clearly happy to see him again, and Egill was equally happy to finally be back. If anyone cast a sidelong glance at the little desert man, they did not say anything.

Fern gaped as the man she loved changed into something she did not understand. One second he was her lover and friend, Philip Entwhistle, a history lecturer. In the next she could sense the presence of the otherworld creature within him, while the essential part of Philip was . . . gone.

The thing that was Philip lifted its hands in front of his face, flexing his fingers, making fists. Then his body stepped forward and stopped, then stepped again. It was like watching a puppet manipulated by an inexpert user. But he made it to the bed and picked up her father's hand. Fern was scared, more than she had ever been in her life. She was putting her faith into the hands of a powerful entity that she knew nothing about and certainly did not trust.

Fern looked to her mother, but she was staring at the bed, not registering what was happening. Without knowing why, Fern began to summon her power, the words of a charm forming on her lips. A glance from Philip . . . the djinn, quelled her though, and she forced herself to relax. She loved Philip, and he trusted the elemental. She would just have to do the same.

Even so, she remained keyed up, prepared. If the djinn attempted to leave the room still in possession of Philip's body, she would kill it, even if it meant killing the man she loved. Such a thing could not be allowed. It was forbidden to allow possession outside the circle, if at all.

Philip's eyes blazed bright as he looked down on her father. His lips moved as if talking, but Fern could not hear what he said. After a moment he was done. He placed the dry, withered hand down on the bed and staggered back, unsteady on his feet. For a moment there was a flash of anger on his face, then it was gone. His legs went, and he started to fall. Fern rushed to support him, holding him by the arm, steadying him.

"Philip, are you okay?"

Entwhistle took a deep breath and his eyes changed, becoming less intense, returning to their normal blue. As if that was normal, she thought. Just something else she would have to accept.

"What did you see?" she demanded.

He did not hear. She shook his arm. "Philip, what did you see?"

Finally, he turned his head. "Everything. I saw him on the hill. He was digging. He found something. A metal plate covered with strange writing. Somehow he could read it and it harmed him. It had a defensive spell. This will sound crazy, but I think it didn't want to be read."

"What about my father. Can the djinn remove the curse?"

"No. At least, not without the plate and maybe not even then. There will be a word to undo the curse. But we could only see one side of the plate in Arnulf's memory. There must be something else on the other side." He paused then, his head to one side as if listening to someone speaking. "But she says she can help him. Give him enough strength to survive a day, possibly two. But we need to get that plate."

She nodded, stepping back. Entwhistle turned, froze for a moment, then twitched slightly. Fern watched it happen again, putting her back on guard. He—no, the djinn—took Arnulf's hand. Now, in much the same way that she had managed to infuse her father with some of her own energy, the djinn did the same. But the difference was like a flood compared to a drop of water. Her father gasped, eyes opening wide. His face filled out, his color returned, and once more she saw Arnulf before her, the father she knew and loved. But she could still sense the presence of a pervading evil.

Entwhistle tottered slightly, regained his balance and turned to her. "This is all she can do, for now," he said, laying her father's hand back on the bed. Fern cried out in joy throwing her arms around him, squeezing him hard. Her mother rushed to Arnulf's side. She grabbed her husband's hand, kissing it. Arnulf looked around, slowly blinking. He sat up, then scowled when he realized he was in a hospital bed.

"What the hell happened?" he said.

"You got sick, papa," said Fern. "Don't worry, We're going to make sure you get better."

"It's true, dear," Fern's mother said. "You were almost gone. The doctor's didn't have a clue. Fern's boyfriend saved you."

At this, Arnulf looked suspiciously at Philip. "So, you're a witch too are you?"

Fern smiled in delight at this, her arm linking through Philip's. "No, papa. He's a history professor."

At that moment Jens returned. He stared open mouthed at the tableau, then turned to Entwhistle but did not seem able to speak.

"We need to get that plate," Philip said. "Where is it?"

"I don't know," Fern replied. "I don't know anything about it. Perhaps Jens knows something?" she said, looking to her brother.

"The plate? The thing that papa dug up? That man from the university took it. Farrell."

Fern felt her heart swell with pride and gratitude to see how Philip took charge of the situation.

"Okay, Jens, is it?" Entwhistle said. "I need his telephone number. I also need to know exactly where he is."

Jens reached for his phone, passing it over. "He's in Oslo."

"Where in Oslo and how long will it take to get there?"

"He'll be at the university. It's a small city, so where he is won't make much difference."

"It's two hours on the train," said Fern.

"Too long," replied Entwhistle. He glanced at Arnulf who appeared to be a picture of health. He leaned in close to Fern and whispered. "Your father has a day or two at most. We need to move fast."

He took a phone and a business card from his pocket and

punched in a number. It was answered immediately.

"Hello. This is Dr. Entwhistle. You dropped me off at the hospital. Yes . . . Yes, thanks. Listen, I need to get to Oslo. Can you do it?" He listened briefly, then hung up the phone. "Come on," Entwhistle said, pulling Fern by her hand towards the door. "Our ride will be here soon."

The pilot grinned as he welcomed them aboard. Entwhistle and Fern climbed into the passenger compartment and put on the heavy, noise cancelling headphones. They could still hear, not to mention feel, the engine, but it was considerably muted. They could also hear each other.

"Excuse me," said Entwhistle to the pilot once they were airborne. "How long to the university?"

"Just under an hour. Which campus do you need?"

Entwhistle groaned. He had not considered the possibility of different locations. He looked at Fern and she shrugged.

"I have absolutely no idea," he said.

"Well," said the pilot, "which department do you need?"

"Archaeology," replied Philip.

"Hang on." The pilot flipped a switch on the control panel. They could see he was talking but not hear him. After a moment, he flipped the switch again.

"I just checked with my dispatcher. There are three locations for the Department of Archaeology in Oslo: Niels Treschows building, Blindern Veien Eleven and Frederiks Gate Three."

"Can you ask them where Professor Farrell is located?"

The pilot nodded and flipped the switch again. A moment later, he had the answer.

"Okay, it's the Niels Treschows building. That's good news. There's a field I can land in. The office is just getting permission from the university. In case anyone asks, you're both visiting professors."

Both Entwhistle and Fern nodded. Then, realizing the

pilot could not see them, Entwhistle replied. "Yes, fine. Actually, I am a visiting professor."

The pilot laughed and said something Entwhistle did not understand and Fern replied.

"I was just telling him that you really *are* a professor. He thought you were pulling his leg."

Under different circumstances, Entwhistle mused, they both might have enjoyed the swift, scenic flight. Soon they were coming to earth in a grassy field next to a huge parabolic antenna and a weather station.

As the helicopter left, the pilot gave them a cheery wave, which Entwhistle returned. He was about to ask Fern where they should go when a police car came racing into sight, lights flashing. It bumped across the field and came to a skidding halt.

Two uniformed officers, a man and a woman, leapt from the car, all business. The man spoke into his radio while the woman held her hand out in warning. She said something Entwhistle did not understand. He looked to Fern for an explanation but she just shook her head, obviously thrown. Of course, he thought. I didn't mention the police.

The officers spun Entwhistle and Fern around, pulled their arms behind and handcuffed them. Entwhistle could not contain himself.

"What the hell do you think you are doing? We had permission to land."

"Just get in the car please. You'll get an explanation at the station."

Fern and Entwhistle were politely but briskly installed in the back seat. The male officer sat behind the wheel and turned the car around, heading out of the university campus.

"Are we being arrested? What for?" Entwhistle demanded.

The female officer, a young woman in her twenties with blonde hair and blue eyes turned and stared at him for a moment before answering.

"You fit the description we received from Interpol. Suspicion of arson."

Entwhistle was about to protest but Fern shook her head, closed her eyes and began to mouth something under her breath. A few phrases and the car filled with a smell Entwhistle recognized immediately. Ozone.

"Drive us back to the university," she said, her voice strangely flat, yet commanding. "We have urgent business there."

To Entwhistle's astonishment the driver of the cruiser did a U-turn. More muttering from Fern and his handcuffs grew suddenly warm. There was a click. Experimentally, he tried to pull his arms apart. The cuffs opened and he was free. He glanced at Fern and she raised an eyebrow in response, a smile playing on her lips. He was not the only one who could draw on resources, it seemed.

He slipped the cuffs into his jacket pocket, gaping at his lover in admiration. She smiled shyly, then impulsively pulled him to her and kissed him hard. The vehicle slowed to a stop outside the Archaeology department. The female officer got out and opened the passenger door and Fern, then Entwhistle climbed out.

"Thanks," said Fern. "You must be hungry. Go and get something to eat. You have a couple of hours before you need to call in."

The police left without a backward glance.

"How did you do that?"

"A simple enough charm. I only needed to give them a nudge. Since we arrived by helicopter I suggested we were VIPs in a hurry and it was their job to get us to our destination. I just made that a stronger mental image than their real memories."

"Handy."

"It won't last long though. They might come back."

"I have to wonder why they were here at all. Who knew

I was going to be here?"

"They mentioned arson. How do they know about the Sandwell thing?"

Entwhistle shrugged. "She said Interpol. Looks like Hanlon finally found something she thinks will stick and alerted everyone to be on the watch for me."

"That doesn't explain how they were waiting for us though."

"No, it doesn't."

"What are you going to do?"

"I don't know. One thing at a time. Let's worry about me later. Right now, we have to save your father."

Entwhistle and Fern ran, stopping twice to get directions. A couple of minutes later they burst into Farrell's office.

Deep in the mountain fastness of Jotunheim, the scarred overlord silenced his council with a savage gesture.

"You have all served the true purpose well. But those who oppose us are strong. The threat is grave and they are not without resources."

An angry murmur rose from the group and Mannuki let them voice their outrage. It was good to have them passionate. Passion, not logic, drove personal sacrifice.

"Long ago, I hid the seal in the grave of a great warrior, expecting a monument to mark the place. But no stone was raised and its location was lost in the chaos of centuries. Now it has been found, and worse, removed. I will have it back. It grows close to the time when I must use it to restore the ancient ones."

Mannuki watched with a sneer as Eikenes, the leader of their little police force, preened. It was his daughter who had discovered not only the fact the seal had been removed before the dig began but also where it had been taken. She would replace her father when the time came. It was tradition for the first-born to take the mantle to serve in the council. So it had been for over thirty generations. But service for its own sake was never enough for the little men. He would have to give Eikenes the praise he craved. It would make the others jealous, but that too served a purpose.

"We now know where it is, thanks to one of our council. You have done well, Svein, and your daughter. Know that you have our thanks."

Eikenes, feigning solemn indifference, swelled with pride. Such predictable, stupid animals, so easily led, thought Mannuki. He moved amongst the council, mingling with them. Some of them reached out to touch him. He allowed it.

"It is vital that we recover the seal. Without it the gods will not be able to return and the old ways will be lost forever."

There was a renewed outbreak of outraged muttering from the men and women around him. He knew exactly what to say, exactly what to do.

"They have tried to stop us before. For a thousand years Christian contamination has dominated the land of our gods. But our roots are deep, the true path strong. We will prevail."

Svein looked up, pulling back his hood so everyone could see him.

"I will bring it to you!"

"No, that is not required. Already those who serve are seeking it. They are in Oslo now and will soon have it. I give you another task. I would punish those that have opposed us. The farmer will be dead soon, but that family has caused more trouble than only one death can repay. Let the sins of the father be paid for by the blood of his children!"

Farrell was working at his computer, so absorbed in his reading that he did not notice Entwhistle and Fern's entry. They were breathing hard; Entwhistle needed a moment to catch his breath.

"Wait," she said. "Talk to him," she whispered. "Persuade him. Don't bully. He will be stubborn, I think."

He trusted Fern. In the short time they had been together he had learned some people were not easy to charm. Seemingly Farrell was one so they would just have to do it the old-fashioned way.

"Good afternoon, Dr. Farrell. Sorry to intrude. My name is Entwhistle. My associate, Fern Aasheim. You know her family, I believe."

Farrell looked up, startled, only now realizing he was not alone.

"Oh, what? Hello? Who are you again?"

Entwhistle smiled and extended his hand. "Dr. Philip Entwhistle. History Department, University of Southern England. This is Fern Aasheim. Her family owns the farm where the Viking burial was found."

"Oh. Yes, of course. What can I do for you? And how do you do, Fern, was it? Please, come in, make yourselves comfortable."

A polite gesture. Papers and books on both the guest chairs made it difficult to take the offer seriously.

"I don't wish to be rude, but we are in a hurry. And I don't exaggerate when I say it is a matter of life and death. It literally is. We've come for the plate, Dr. Farrell. The lead plate with the inscriptions found with Arnulf Aasheim. We believe it's a defixio, a very powerful curse tablet."

Entwhistle had expected Farrell to scoff, but to his surprise the older academic simply nodded. "A defixio, you say. I had begun to suspect it myself, actually."

He turned to Fern, showing his sympathy. "Your father was taken ill. I saw him briefly when I went to the hospital to retrieve the torc. He was . . . hit hard by something. I suspect now that it was the lead tablet."

Fern nodded. "We have just come from there. My father doesn't have much time. There's a curse on him and it's very powerful."

"Indeed, I suppose it must be, to have lasted all that time in the ground. And I believe that it's not the first time it has struck."

Entwhistle's ears pricked up. "What do you mean, not the first time?"

"Just that. I was reading the Saga of Bjorn the Mighty and found a very clear reference to both a sorcerer and a curse. Bjorn may have died as a result of exposure to this tablet. Quite frankly, I'm worried about my colleagues in the Linguistics Department. Whatever happened to Bjorn and Arnulf Aasheim may well be happening to them right now."

Fern shook her head. "I don't think so. There hasn't been enough time."

The two men looked at her.

"A defixio needs to charge. It draws energy from around it. It will probably be years before it is dangerous again."

"How do you know that?" Farrell asked, voice sharp with suspicion.

"Don't ask, doctor," Entwhistle replied. "Right now we have more pressing things to worry about."

The archeologist paused, seemed to be thinking, and made a decision.

"Alright. You don't see what I see in my line of work without learning that not everything is dry bones and clay pots," Farrell replied. "You had better come with me."

They followed Farrell through turn after turn, took lifts and climbed and descended staircases but finally came to a dark door marked by an ancient brass plaque saying *Langues Anciennes* in copperplate script.

"Here we are," said Farrell. "The plate's here. The language chaps will be all over it, mark my words." An almost ghostly quiet reigned inside but a short man on the heavy side of stocky appeared. In a herringbone tweed jacket with a striped bow tie and thick, pebble glasses he stared at them myopically, blinking like a startled vole.

"Can I help you?" he said, drawing himself up to his full five feet and blocking their passage.

Farrell, the tallest of the group, stepped forward. He towered over the linguist. "I do hope so. I'm Farrell."

"Oh, the archeologist? Well now, do come in." The little man stepped aside, and waved them on.

"Where's the plate?" Entwhistle asked brusquely. "The lead plate from the Aasheim farm?"

The little man bristled. "That? In the language lab of course." He hesitated, looking at his visitors closely. "The crypto-analysts are taking a swing at it. They have a computational model they think will crack it."

"Fascinating," said Entwhistle, trying to tone down his impatience. "But we need to see it at once. Where is the lab?"

The little man glared. "Well, I don't know that you can. The research is at a critical stage. We can't just go barging in, disturbing them."

Fern laid her hand on Entwhistle's arm and he bit off his words. She stepped forward wearing her most charming smile.

"It would mean so much to me if I could just take a peek," she said.

The linguistics professor blushed and nodded. "Yes, very well. This way, this way."

"Well done," Entwhistle whispered. "A charm?"

"No," she replied. "I smiled and asked nicely."

The lab, such as it was, consisted of a room with a long bench running along one side holding electronic microscopes, handheld scanners and other expensive gadgets. Two men were reviewing a screen on which a cuneiform text had been broken down into segments of three or four characters. They were busy discussing possible word clusters as the little man and his trio of interlopers marched in. Entwhistle knew enough to guess they were trying to isolate signs, or groups of signs, looking for repetition. The first step in breaking a code.

One of the analysts looked up. "Hello Dr. Nielsen. What's going on?"

"These folks wanted to have a look at the Aasheim plate."

Both men glanced at the gray plate lying on a scanner. Entwhistle strode over to it.

"Don't touch it," warned Fern, alarmed. "Just in case."

"Have you got anywhere?" Entwhistle asked.

"Deciphering it? I'll say!" said the younger of the two analysts. "We're not dealing with another Voynich, I can tell you that much."

At the blank look from Entwhistle and Fern he continued. "The Voynich manuscript is completely indecipherable. Although I live in hope. It has no characters in common with any other writing system and it has so far resisted all attempts to decipher it. What we have here," and he turned back to his computer screen, "is something else altogether."

The older man broke in. "Indeed. As you can see, it is clearly a Proto-Elamite *type* of cuneiform, which interesting, since it is almost certainly not Elamite. However, it has some characters in common. What I believe we are looking at is an even older form of writing. Perhaps much older."

"Now Henrik, please don't bore them with your crazy theories," said the younger man. At this, Henrik's face turned bright red.

"It's not so crazy."

"What do you think it might be?" asked Entwhistle,

genuinely interested.

Henrik blinked as he realized everyone was looking at him. He cleared his throat. "Well, there's no real proof yet, you understand. It's just a theory."

"Go on," said Entwhistle.

"Well, I think it may be the earliest known writing ever discovered. I think it pre-dates Sumerian."

"Why is that so crazy?" asked Fern.

"Well," Henrik said, "it is generally supposed that writing developed in the land between the rivers; Mesopotamia." He turned and pointed to the screen. "And if this is earlier, then the question has to be, who made it? And where did it come from? What civilization existed that could produce writing of that sophistication, *before* the Sumerians?"

The younger researcher tapped the screen and spoke with a certainty born of ignorance and arrogance. "It's Proto-Elamite, I'm telling you. There are clearly common features."

Entwhistle was no expert but he was not convinced by the man's dogmatic certainty. In spite of the urgency of their mission he could not quell his curiosity.

"What makes you so sure?" he asked.

"Well," the younger man continued, "it's a cuneiform style. No one can read the Elamite script, unfortunately. The tablet has striking similarities with the earliest known Elamite writings but it's much more complex. Where early Elamite appears to be lists and basic accounting this tablet has the hallmarks of a narrative. It's not broken down into discrete and unrelated sections the way the early clay tablets are. All in all, I believe that we have a previously unknown writing system based on the Elamite script, or developed in parallel with it."

Henrik jumped in. "Or," and he paused for dramatic effect, "it's the original writing system from which all the other systems were derived."

"If only we knew more about where it came from," said the younger of the analysts.

"It was found with another artifact," said Farrell. "This artifact has been analyzed. It is a gold alloy that might have originated in Africa."

"You're saying this is African?" The young man looked incredulous.

"No, just that it was found with something that is believed to have come from North Africa."

"Okay, this is all fascinating," said Philip. "But it's not why we're here." He removed the lead plate from the scanner. He only hesitated a second before snatching it up. All the talk of it being a curse tablet had made him slightly nervous. But he put his faith in Jinny. She would not let him be harmed. Now that he had it in his hands, he stared at it in fascination. It was covered in tiny, dense cuneiform in neat rows over the entire surface of the plate. He had never seen anything like it. But one thing was for sure, it was not a defixio. Fern leaned in, peering closely at the object they were convinced was killing her father. At first, Philip thought Fern had spoken. He looked at her, but she was staring in rapt attention at the plate.

There it was again, a whisper in his mind. He tugged the chain around his neck, pulling the talisman out. He held it in his left hand, and the defixio in his right. Immediately his connection with Jinny was amplified. Her presence stronger now, he could hear her thoughts clearly.

Man, you do not know what you have. This is a thing that cannot be.

It's not a defixio, thought Philip. He stood, staring down at the plate, with its ordered rows of strange markings.

No. It has been cursed, but that is not its purpose. This is the seal.

The seal for what? He could sense agitation. Even . . . *fear* from the djinn. What was she afraid of? The plate?

It is forbidden, Man.

Okay, thought Philip, trying to direct his thoughts to the djinn. Then can you at least tell me if this is the thing that has cursed Fern's father?

Yes, there is a geas on it.

How do we remove it?

It is a simple matter. You must find the key.

This isn't the key?

No. This is the seal. The key is a word. Say the word, and he will recover.

What word, Jinny?

There was a pause. Philip could still feel the djinn, but there was something new. Something strange. With a shock, he realized he was feeling Jinny's emotions. *Her shame.* This discovery rocked Philip. He had never really imagined she would have feelings like a person. Unconsciously, he had imagined she would be like a robot. Logic and intellect only. When he realized where his thoughts had taken him, it was Philip's turn to be ashamed.

Jinny, what is the word?

I know not.

Philip's heart sank and his shoulders slumped in resignation and defeat. Fern watched him closely, her eyes never leaving his, as if she were trying to see into his head, to follow the conversation she knew was going on.

Philip turned away, putting his back to her. There was a word that could save Fern's father, but no one knew it, and no one could even read the script on the tablet. How was he ever going to be able to find the word? Jinny supplied the answer.

You must read the seal.

I can't. I don't understand the damned script.

Philip waved the lead plate in frustration, face anguished. But at Jinny's next words, his eyes opened wide, blazing blue as a subtle transformation overcame him. He stood taller, head held high and a slight smile pulled at his lips.

Yes, you can.

Dream your dreams, oh mortal

9

Whether 'tis nobler in the mind to suffer
The slings and arrows of outrageous fortune,
Or to take arms against a sea of troubles,
And by opposing end them.
—*Shakespeare, Hamlet act III, scene I*

Jens Aasheim stood by his father's bed, his gaze on an old man he hardly recognized anymore. In spite of the ventilator Arnulf's breath labored, a weak rasp. Jens was angry. He felt like a fool. He had been tricked. Tricked into hoping that his father would be okay; that he would live. Fern's boyfriend had impressed him. Arriving by helicopter, his take charge attitude. And then, incredible as it seemed, Philip had done *something* and his father had recovered. Or at least, seemed to. Now he was unconscious again, skin gray, face lined like an old man's. Exactly the same as before. It looked like whatever the Englishman had done had not worked after all. Jens felt a surge of resentment and rage welling up. He resisted smashing his fist into the wall, but his hands clenched tight, straining muscles, as if crushing pain and frustration in their grip.

The plastic sheeting was back in place. Regardless of what Fern said, the hospital staff were not in the business of curing curses. They were treating it like a virus, at least until they knew better. And that, Jens knew, would only be after the autopsy.

Hearing that his father had been digging in an old grave

had convinced the staff they were dealing with some kind of pathogen. Never mind that their tests all came back negative.

Jens was a big man, strong like his father. He was not used to being useless and he paced about the small room like a caged animal. He thrust his hands into his pockets to stop their involuntary clenching. The door opened and he spun around to see his mother carrying two Styrofoam cups. He sighed, disappointed.

"I thought it might be them."

"They couldn't possibly get back so soon, Jens."

"I know. Still . . ."

Liv was dressed in jeans and a sweater, as was he. At least now they were not required to wear protective garments over their clothes.

"Here," she said. "It's awful, but it's hot."

She passed him a coffee. He noted that her eyes, though red and puffy, were now resigned. She was preparing herself to let him go. His lips pursed in anger at the thought but he did not reply, taking the proffered cup. He took a sip; black coffee, with sugar. Exactly how he didn't like it.

"It's all the machine could do," Liv said with a shrug, placing her own cup down on the small bedside table.

"Thanks," he said, and meant it. She did not seem to hear him as she looked down at his father. "Thank you, Mama."

She turned to him, eyes glistening, hands grasping at each other. For the first time, he noticed how red they were, as if she had been scrubbing them with a coarse brush.

"Oh, Jens. What are we going to do?"

"I don't know."

"Do you . . . do you think that Fern and, and . . ."

"Philip," he supplied.

"Do you think they can save him?"

"Of course, Mama. Fern's a witch, right? They have all sorts of magic powers." It was a lie. He knew it. She knew it. Fern may well call herself a witch, but she had done next to nothing to save his father, and while Philip seemed to have actually helped, for a while, that help was gone and so was he. Jens resigned himself to the fact that his father was slipping away, and there was nothing anyone could do about it.

He took out his phone. Fern should know that it didn't look good. He should let her know that it was time she came back. To say goodbye.

Every eye in the room was on Entwhistle. He became acutely aware of the attention and reddened slightly. They had all been watching him have a silent conversation and all but Fern were looking at him as if he were slightly mad.

Only Fern understood. There was a time when he would have smiled sheepishly and apologized, but that time was past. He lifted his head and returned their collective gaze.

"It's a curse and it can be broken."

Fern's face lit up. She had kept her distance while he was communicating with the djinn, but now she rushed to his side.

"How?" she asked, her face full of hope.

"That's the problem. Jinny doesn't know. All she could say is that we can reverse the curse if we know the right word. Just say the word and it will end."

Farrell looked at his colleagues and back to Entwhistle. "I say, what on earth are you talking about?"

Entwhistle and Fern walked back to the group. He held the lead plate in his hand. Involuntarily Farrell stepped back, eyes darting between the plate and Philip's face.

"I'm not going to explain how I know, but I can tell you that this plate does not tell a story. Not exactly. In fact, I am going to have to take it with me. It is something else altogether, and it needs to be safeguarded by someone who knows what they are doing."

At this both linguists shot to their feet, the younger

MJ Kobernus

man's chair tipping over with a clatter. Henrik's face was red.

"And what makes you such a damned expert?" he demanded.

"Because I can read it," Entwhistle replied with equanimity.

No one spoke. Henrik closed his mouth, which had fallen open in rank surprise.

"You can *read* it?" he spluttered. Then, as if logic had suddenly clicked into gear, he frowned. "I highly doubt it. This language has never been seen before, and you claim to have deciphered it?"

Entwhistle shrugged. "Yes. If you like. I know how to read this inscription. The knowledge was given to me."

At this Henrik could not help himself. He laughed. "What? An angel descended upon you from on high, did it? See many burning bushes on the way here, did you?"

Entwhistle chuckled. It was close enough to the truth to be funny. But he did not answer. Instead he looked at the plate, quickly scanning the surface. And then, to their collective amazement, he stroked one edge. There was a distinct click, and the plate opened like a book. Entwhistle spread open the metal pages, reading. It took only minutes, but he could have stood there hours and no one would have moved. He closed the ancient book and it clicked again, obviously locking itself.

Henrik looked around in confusion. He turned to Nielsen. "Did you know it could do that?"

The little man shook his head and removed his thick glasses, wiping them with a handkerchief. "I had absolutely no idea."

Fern pointed to the lead plate. "Is it there? The word to undo the curse?"

Entwhistle shook his head. "I don't think so, no. This relates to something else altogether. A treaty between mankind and . . . another party." He had almost said the

Djinn Nation, but caught himself. He tried again.

"It's a treaty, between two nations. It specifies the rules of . . . commerce, exchange. It is not what we are looking for. It's important, but there must be something else. More texts somewhere that display this writing. Maybe on the other artifacts?"

Farrell was staring at the floor, brows furrowed. "Hang on," he said, head snapping up, eyes fixing firmly on Entwhistle's. "Are you saying that Arnulf Aasheim was cursed by this tablet," pointing at the lead plate in Entwhistle's hand, "and that there is a word that can uncurse him, but you don't know what it is? And you can read the script written there? Is that correct?"

"Yes, to all three," replied Entwhistle.

"So, you want to know if anything else has this same script written on it?"

"Correct."

"Well, in that case, maybe this is your lucky day!"

Farrell went and sat down at a computer. He clicked open a browser, typed a search phrase and in seconds was flipping through images. He selected one and zoomed in on a section of it until it was visible to everyone in the room.

"I was reading this saga earlier, before you two arrived. On a whim, I wanted to see how it looked in the original. Then I saw something odd. You want more examples of the script? How about that then?" He sat back and pointing to the monitor, which was displaying what was clearly a close up image of the strange writing from the plate. But this was not carved into lead. This was written in ink on vellum.

"Yes," said Entwhistle. "That's it, exactly." He moved closer, peering at the angular characters. Fern too stepped forward for a better view, her hand resting on Philip's back.

"Is this the answer, Philip?"

"If it's not, we have no other options."

"But what does it say?"

"A name, I think. Mannuki." He turned to Farrell and

smiled his thanks, but he had edged away from Entwhistle. Or, more accurately, from the plate. Entwhistle did not blame him. Now they knew it was capable of killing a man, it deserved to be treated with caution. He opened his satchel and put it inside where it rested against the towel wrapped around Jinny's meta-anchor.

"What exactly is this document?" he asked, pointing to the screen, and the fragment of ancient parchment displayed on it.

"That," said Farrell, obviously relieved now that the lead plate was out of sight, "is the final page of the original copy of the Saga of Bjorn the Mighty. It was written at the end of the tenth century, and is one of the earliest narratives of its type. Apparently the marks in the margins have always been thought nonsense."

All of the ancient language researchers were staring with astonishment at the screen. Henrik, in particular, seemed to be the hardest hit.

"How is that possible?" he said, his voice almost outraged.

Farrell shrugged. "No one knows who wrote it. But apparently the marks were made in the same ink as was used to write the saga itself, so obviously it's contemporary."

"But," said Henrik. "That means that whoever wrote *that* was here in Norway a thousand years ago. That doesn't make any sense. How could that script still be in use in almost our own time?"

"Hah!" said his young partner. "That sinks your theory about it being older than Elamite then."

"Actually," Entwhistle interjected. "Henrik was quite right. It is older. You would not believe how much older." He turned to Farrell. "Where is the manuscript now?"

"The National Library, in Copenhagen."

"What? Why not here in Norway?"

The Norwegians in the room were suddenly vocal, all

speaking at once. Dr. Nielsen seemed particularly outraged, a vein on his temple throbbing alarmingly. Entwhistle and Farrell both stared in surprise at the outburst. Fern shushed the linguists.

"It's complicated," she said. "I can tell you about it later. Do you need the manuscript to use the word?"

"I don't think so. I can clearly see what it says. Jinny said that I just needed to say the word." He looked at Farrell. "Is there nothing else? No other examples on other documents, or objects? No other writing in the margins on this manuscript?"

"No. At least, nothing I know of."

"Okay. Then thank you, Dr. Farrell. And thank you too, gentlemen," Entwhistle said, addressing the linguists. Then he grabbed Fern's hand and looked into her eyes. "This is our only hope then. If this doesn't work . . ."

She nodded and took a deep breath. "But what about the torc? The armband?"

Entwhistle turned to look at Farrell and the archeologist looked away, not wanting to meet his gaze.

"Well, Dr. Farrell? Where is it?"

Farrell sighed, resigned. "The metallurgists have it. I'll show you the way."

"Good. And on the way, maybe I could borrow your copy of the saga? I think it might be a good idea to read it."

Farrell nodded. "Okay. It probably is a good idea. There are some things in it that are . . . puzzling. Maybe you can make sense of them."

They headed for the door just as Fern's phone rang. She pulled it from her back pocket as she trailed after Farrell and Entwhistle.

"Oh, no," she said. "We're coming back immediately, Jens. We might have the answer."

Eriksen smiled at his crew, in spite of the cold drizzle that seeped into his bones and in spite of the sliver of fear that knotted his stomach. He had not kept his side of the bargain, and now he would have to tell the girl. He frowned as he glanced at the iron gray sky.

A constant mist enveloped them in its chill embrace. Everyone was wrapped in fleeces and overcoats, hugging themselves and stamping feet to stay warm. Yet there was a sense of achievement, felt by all. More than that. They had made some remarkable finds in a very short time.

Eriksen was very satisfied. The artifacts from the dig so far had been labeled and sealed in plastic containers. The haug had been covered for the night. The team was tired, muddy, yet grinning.

Except Silvi. She had maintained a dour expression throughout, and even now, as they were wrapping things up for the day, she continued to look disappointed.

"I want to say thank you for a job well done," Eriksen said to his assembled troops. "We don't have much time and this has been a very fast survey but we achieved a major objective. Thanks to your efforts, we now know that this was a burial site for a Viking warrior. We even have a suspicion as to who it might be, and I don't need to tell you just how rare that is."

The men and women before him nodded. Silvi gave every appearance of being bored. She turned to stare in the direction of the Aasheim farmhouse, and her face turned almost predatory.

"So, that's it for today," he said, focusing on the other members of the dig. "I'll take the remaining items to the office, and I'll be back here mid-morning tomorrow. The rest of you should be here no later than ten tomorrow to finalize things and start wrapping up."

There was a good deal of back-slapping and hand shaking. The words, 'drink' and 'bar' were loud on many lips.

"Any questions, before you all leave?"

Silvi snapped her head around to stare at him. "Yes.

Why did you send the metal plate to Oslo?"

Eriksen swallowed. "The plate? I didn't even see it. Dr. Farrell from the University of Oslo removed it. They are trying to decipher it, I understand."

That answered his suspicion. The plate was the item that his mysterious caller wanted. Silvi snorted, as if in derision.

"Decipherment? By who?"

Eriksen resisted the temptation to correct her grammar. By whom, he thought. But you won't score any points with that one.

"The linguistics department has it. One Professor Nielsen, I believe."

She turned and walked away without another word. Strange fish, that one, thought Eriksen. He watched as Silvi pulled out her phone and made a call. She glanced in his direction and the look of naked contempt on her face shocked him. She nodded her head curtly, as if receiving instructions, then put the phone away, marching off towards the parked cars.

Definitely a strange fish, he thought. Thank God he would not have to see her again, after tomorrow. He had the distinct impression that the girl wanted to gut him like a fish, and, even more worrying, that she would smile while she did it.

It was a short walk to the train station. Entwhistle and Fern bought tickets at a machine inside, then went out and waited impatiently on the platform. Entwhistle paced up and down. He was partly nervous, partly just cold. It was already late in the afternoon, the evening dark was fast approaching and he had only his tweed jacket over a thin shirt.

"How long will it take to get back?"

"Two hours," she said. "If we take a taxi to the hospital."

"Okay." He had tried calling Rappaport, his attorney and lately Mr. Fixit, but the urbane gentleman told him the helicopter rides were over. Rappaport had discovered that there was a warrant for his arrest in Britain, and that Interpol had been alerted, as he was now considered a flight risk. Trying to hire a helicopter would likely put him behind bars. The anonymity of the train was the best way to get back to Fern's family.

They did not have long to wait. The train roared into the station; very modern, and it certainly looked quick. They found their seats and collapsed into them, Fern facing Entwhistle across a small table. Both heaved a sigh of relief, grateful for a couple of hours rest. At least now they had a plan. With the plate, the torc and the word from the manuscript they were equipped as well as they could have hoped. It would be enough. It had to be.

As the train accelerated Entwhistle examined Fern's face. She was pale, drained of all color, except for dark circles under her eyes. Faced with the enforced inactivity of two hours on a train he feared that the awkwardness of the last days would surface again. But she reached across the table and squeezed his hand.

"Thank you."

Entwhistle smiled in return. "For what?"

"For coming. For helping."

"Of course. I would do anything for you Fern."

"I know."

She looked down at their hands, resting on the table. She seemed agitated. "I really thought I could help him," she said. "Seeing him lying there in the bed, with those tubes coming out of him, I was so sure I could save him. And then they would see that I was not just a silly girl, chasing dreams and fairy tales. I tried. I tried so hard, but I was not strong enough."

Her eyes glistened with incipient tears. He squeezed her hand, not knowing what to say. She pulled it away, as if not deserving even so slight a comfort.

"And do you know what I thought? What I felt? I wasn't

sad because my failure probably meant his death. No, that's not true. I *was* sad for that reason. But there was something else. I was sad for myself too, because now no one would give me the respect I wanted. Philip, I'm so ashamed. I wanted to be the hero. I wanted my family to finally be proud of me. I wanted to show them that I could make a difference."

Entwhistle nodded. He understood. That was something he could relate to. He had wanted to do the right thing once, to be the hero. He too had failed.

"I'm sure they are proud of you, Fern. How could they not be? I've been there, darling. Just the same. When I became guardian to the djinn, I had no idea what I was getting myself into. I made a promise, and didn't doubt I had what it took to see it through. So when Sandwell took the meta-anchor, I was determined to get it back, save the day."

"You did save the day. Sandwell is dead."

He nodded. "Yes, true. But you don't know everything. Jinny brought me to Sandwell. She was preparing to kill the djinn, Fern. I could not stand by and do nothing. I tried to talk Sandwell round, but she laughed. She had a knife at my throat, and I thought that I could somehow persuade her. I didn't. She used it . . . the knife. On me. She cut my throat, Fern."

This last was said with nervous trepidation. Fern's breath caught as the impact of his words became clear. She gripped his hand tightly.

"Instead of Jinny being sacrificed, it was me. But the spell needed the djinn's energy not mine. My blood spilled over her pentacle and made it fail. *That* killed Sandwell, not me. All I did was manage to get my throat cut and bleed out all over her attic floor. It was Jinny who saved me, not the other way round. She used her own life-force to bring me back. Every day since then I have lived with the knowledge that I had failed to protect the djinn. It was blind luck that

Sandwell was killed and I survived. I nearly cost the life of an elemental. Every day I lived with the shame and every night since I've felt the knife open my throat."

He took a deep, ragged breath, then another. "I wanted to be the hero too. But I'm not. Maybe none of us are. We just do the best we can." He stared down at the table.

She nodded, and reached out to him. He took her hand and the tension between them melted away.

"But at least you helped my father. You saved him, Philip."

He shook his head, watching her closely. How would she react to his next statement? "We haven't done that, yet, but at least we have a chance. But it won't really be me, will it?"

Fern sighed, and looked up to meet his eyes. "It's true. And I'm sorry." She tugged Philip's hand, pulling him closer. Both leaned over the table, putting their heads together. Not quite able to hug, they kissed, then sat back, hands intertwined. The fact that she seemed, in some way, to be now accepting Jinny filled him with hope and he smiled. Everything felt right again.

"I was wrong not to tell you before," he said. "I'm sorry I kept her a secret."

"No, I understand. It's not the easiest thing to bring up in a new relationship, is it?"

Philip laughed. "It really isn't!"

Fern's mouth curled up into a decidedly mischievous smile.

"Do you think that I could talk to it . . . her?"

"I don't know. When Mr. Francis was still alive, I talked to her. But then, she was already in the process of bonding herself to me."

Fern shook her head. In wonder or denial, Entwhistle could not tell. He put his free hand on the talisman hanging from his neck. Instantly, he could feel Jinny's presence. She was amused. He could sense her emotions almost as clearly as his own. Deliberately, he took Fern's hand and pressed it to the metal of the Abalak cross. Fern's eyes opened in surprise.

"Fern. I would like you to meet Jinny."

"Oh my . . . I had no idea!"

You chose well, little Man. She is worthy of you.

Philip laughed. "I rather think she chose me, Jinny."

Fern blushed, then looked at him almost shyly.

"She mostly does her own thing," Philip explained. "She can talk to me directly, if she wants. And I can do the same. It's not all that different from living with someone. If you need your own space, you can have it. If you want company, it's there."

Fern pursed her lips slightly, her scar whitening. "That is pretty much what I thought. And what bothered me."

"That it would be like living with another woman?"

"Yes."

"Except she's not a woman. Not human. Not even female. I say *she* only because, well, it seems silly but she – –it—manifested as a female cat. Mr. Francis started it. Jinny would not care. And I can tell you this. For the best part of a century James Francis thought of only one woman. Tajeddigt was murdered only months after they met, and he never forgot her."

"Really? Is that true?"

"Oh yes. The garden is a shrine to his only love."

Fern gazed out the window into the night. Finally, she nodded.

"Okay."

"Okay?"

"Yes. Okay."

Entwhistle grinned. He tucked the talisman beneath his shirt, then kissed her hard. And then again for good measure. Fern smiled, happy, amused.

"A cat, you said?"

"A black cat."

Fern laughed. "That's too rich. A cat? How wonderful. And how utterly appropriate for a house with a witch, don't you think?"

Entwhistle chuckled. "Yes. It really is."

"Thank you, little man," Fern said, "my little man."

Entwhistle laughed. "I'm already regretting introducing you both."

Fern rewarded him with a smile and a touch of his hand that made his stomach flip. He grinned, giving her a hungry look of need and desire.

Fern laughed. "Read your book, Philip. It's a long ride."

Entwhistle chuckled, then pulled the book of sagas from his satchel and began to read.

The Saga of Bjorn the Mighty

There was a man named Bjorn, son of Rolf and Svanhild, daughter of Eirik the Wicked. Bjorn was a man so tall and strong that none could match him, and he gave service in Miklagard. In fellowship with him was one Egill Thrandsson, a man renowned for strength and daring. Bjorn and he shared everything and were as brothers.

Egill was captain in the Varangian guard, charged with the protection of the only brother to the Empress of the World. The prince was a man beloved by the Norsemen, for his drinking and fighting and bravery. It happened that while on a journey they came across a caravan beset by raiders. The defenders were massacred, all but one man, who stood before the great carriage in which the merchant and his daughter cowered.

Bjorn alone stood, wielding a great war axe, bright with blood, shining with glory. Egill and the Prince and the few men with them rode hard, seeking to drive off the bandits. With the last of his companions fallen, Bjorn raised his shield and axe in salute, ready to fight and die. He was outnumbered, yet still he roared his challenge, defending his oath to the last.

Ten raiders moved against him, but Bjorn the Cunning had positioned himself so that they must come at him in ones and twos. And so it was they met their slaughter. He wreaked red ruin upon them. But the prince was loathe to allow one man all the glory and he led the charge against the rear of the caravan, where more raiders plundered. And so it was the merchant was saved. The prince was determined to meet the great man who slew so many, and Egill brought Bjorn before him. He was red with the glory of his conquests but laughed and drank in good cheer.

The merchant was escorted through the wilds back to Miklagard and the prince swore Bjorn as his own man. Egill and Bjorn from that day did not part and were together in all things.

At that time, pirates plagued the Greek Sea and many ships were lost. The Prince took command and sent his best men to sea, under the guise of merchants. Bjorn and Egill took sail on a boat transporting fine cloths and things of value. But the hold did not contain such, filled as it was with men of the guard, Norsemen, sworn to the Prince. They were taken by pirates, but the men of the North fought them man to man and prevailed. The pirates were taken and beheaded, every one. The ships were taken as booty, and the Norsemen who lived were given much gold as reward.

Bjorn and Egill commanded a company of men. They were sent again and again, and in time the pirates learned that the slow moving merchant vessels did not always contain valuable goods of trade, but the deadly blades of the men from Miklagard.

When the pirates were vanquished, the prince was given much praise. He was not a man slow in the handing out of rings and he rewarded his sworn men well. Bjorn was raised up to captain and had his own host. He was commanded to Tunis, what was once the land of Carthage.

There, a rebellion against the empire had caused many to lose their lives. Bjorn and Egill and a century of men travelled by boat, and made landfall in a fishing village of no account. They took horses and travelled overland to the city that was brazen in their treachery. They fought a great battle, and many men died on both sides. But the Varangians prevailed. Bjorn took the heads of all those that defied him, but any that surrendered were shown mercy and allowed to flee with half their goods. The men of the North took the city, and left trusted men to hold it. Then Bjorn and Egill went to the other cities that had defied the Empress of the World and made bloody slaughter.

At the gates of one, they announced the decree of the Empress. Let any man surrender and he live. Let him bear arms against the Empire and death shall be his lot. When the town's people heard this, they grew angry, but Bjorn strode forward, within arrow shot of the walls. He told them his name, and that he would honor the decree. They need only open their gates and only those who were known to be rebels need die.

The people in the town heard this, and they knew of his reputation. They fought each other. A great battle took place inside the walls, while Bjorn stood outside. He grew impatient and the host of Varangians struck their swords on their shields and let loose their battle cries. The gates opened and the people brought forth, bound and bloody, those that had defied the Empress.

Bjorn had them all beheaded, except one who was only a boy. He declared that the child could not be guilty. He was not the man in his house. And he set the boy free with gold of his own and a promise of safe conduct, should he wish to leave.

Bjorn showed great compassion and was cheered by the people of the town. They brought half their goods, and a fortune it was. Bjorn picked what he wanted, and what the Empress might wish, then the men took their share. But his compassion was his undoing. The boy spoke with Bjorn, to thank him. And Bjorn shared bread with the boy. And the boy told him a tale of a great sorcerer in the desert, who demanded tribute from the towns around. He was evil, and of great skill in sorcery. And so it was that Bjorn was led to the desert, and Egill with him. Many of the host remained in the town. But a small group of men, those sworn to both Bjorn and Egill, travelled many days and met and defeated the sorcerer. He was a glorious enemy, and a fiend in battle, but the men of the North were strong and brave and defeated the creature. It was Bjorn who delivered the fatal blow to the Trollman. They hacked him to bits and buried him in a dozen graves and took from him both slaves and gold.

They returned to Miklagard and received much reward. But Bjorn declared that it was time for him to return to the North, and the prince, for the love he bore him, released him from his oath. Egill Thrandsson also went north, and with them their closest men. They took also a slave from the desert who had served the sorcerer and who now served them. They travelled long, by boat and overland by horse, until they came to the land of the Danes. There they found dragonships, and bought passage. In time, they came to Norway's shores, and sailed up the great fjord to the meadows of the gods. For horses they gave gold and silver and so travelled north, following the water and the path to the mountains.

But it was in Norway that Bjorn, who had braved a thousand swords and ten thousand arrows, became sick, as to death. Egill led the party then, desiring only to allow Bjorn to return to the land of his family. But he was cursed by evil, for his death came fast. Bjorn, the most mighty of men, became old in but a day.

And so it came to be that Egill Thrandsson buried his friend and brother in the ground. They performed the rites as best they knew, and Bjorn was buried with the golden dragon, the cunningly wrought armband that was booty from the sorcerer in the land of the Blámenn. And Bjorn the Mighty was sent to Valhalla with such treasures as they had. And Egill declared that his life had been great, and his deeds many, so that his death, not in battle, but by a slinking thief that wasted him to nothing, mattered not.

Egill Thrandsson and his companions continued their journey, but Bjorn, the man who had lived through a hundred battles, and had never felt the edge of steel in his flesh, died with his sword in his hand, but no enemy to slay.

The train ride passed quickly, for all that it took two hours. A short taxi ride and they were striding side by side, following the red line towards Arnulf's bed. Coming down the last corridor they made out Liv, standing stock still, one hand to her mouth, eyes on the floor as if lost in thought. At the sound of their footsteps she looked up.

"Fern!" She hurried to them. She was haggard, her once cheerful features a ruin of despair. Without a word, Fern pulled her close, wrapping her in a tight embrace.

"Don't worry Mama, it'll be okay."

Entwhistle stood to one side, one hand protectively on his old leather satchel. He had not even let go of the bag on the train, gripping it on his lap all the way.

"Let's get this done," he said, and Fern nodded. She pulled away from her mother who looked at them with red-rimmed eyes.

"What are you going to do?"

"Save Papa," said Fern, simply. Liv nodded, as if she had not expected anything else.

Arnulf was alone, looking like a man dying of sheer old age, still hooked into the instruments humming and beeping, marking each moment of his fading life.

"Where's Jens?" Fern asked.

"He had to go back to the farm," Liv replied. "It won't look after itself. There's always something needs doing."

Fern nodded. "Of course. There's a lot to do. And we'll help too, won't we Philip. Whatever you need."

Entwhistle nodded. He came from a small town but had never worked on a farm. That did not matter. If they could use him, he would be there to help.

"Yes, of course. No question."

Liv looked at them both, gratitude mixed with her grief. She wiped away a tear and turned to Entwhistle. For the first time he felt her really take his measure. She nodded.

"Thank you. Thank you both."

Now that he had committed himself to helping out on their farm, he wondered if this meant burning his last bridge with the university. This was starting to look like those shenanigans Sam Evans had warned him about. Well, too bad. He would stay with the Aasheims as long as they needed him. If he had to resign his position, so be it.

He took a deep breath, mindful of the task he had set himself: save a man's life, and remove an ancient curse. No problem. Except he had no idea how. He approached the bed slowly. With both Fern and her mother staring at him he felt faintly ridiculous. He motioned to Fern to come closer to the bed.

"What should I do?"

"I don't know. Ask . . . you know."

He nodded and gripped the talisman in his hand. After a moment, he let it go. "She isn't sure. She says to just say the word."

"Do it," Fern said.

She was trying hard to be strong, not to break down. For her mother's sake, Entwhistle realized. He nodded.

"Alright. I suppose I just say the word that was written on the parchment and that is that."

She nodded and gave him a tight smile. Philip faced Arnulf. He resisted the urge to be dramatic, and said simply, "Mannuki." Nothing happened. Arnulf looked exactly the same, still sucking one rasping breath after another. Entwhistle dragged off the plastic sheet and grasped the husk of skin and bone that was Arnulf's hand. "Mannuki."

Again, nothing. He turned to Fern whose eyes threatened tears. Liv was openly sobbing now, her arms around her middle, hugging herself. Clearly Entwhistle could not save him after all. He felt a surge of anger and shame. Another failure. He still held Arnulf's hand, but he reached up for his talisman to talk to Jinny.

"Jinny, it doesn't work. I said the word."

I am sorry, little Man. That was the only hope.

At that moment the heart rate monitor began beeping faster, then raced. The old man in the bed trembled and as he stilled the beeping turned into a constant tone; flat-lined.

"Papa!" screamed Fern.

Liv gave a sob but gathered her daughter into her arms.

Entwhistle stared in dismay. First at the husk of a man in the bed, then the two women crying in each other's arms. He still held Arnulf's withered hand in his own. He shook his head, eyes closed and groaned.

Goddamn! Goddamn it all to hell. He had tried. He had done everything he could and it was not enough. It was never enough. He felt like a fraud. A useless, lying, feeble idiot. He couldn't do it. He couldn't save one man, even with the help of a powerful djinn at his side.

He could feel Jinny react to his rage, shrinking away from him. Instantly he felt remorse.

"I'm sorry, Jinny. It's not your fault. I just feel so useless. Who the hell was this Mannuki anyway?"

I know not. Mannuki is . . .

Suddenly Arnulf reacted. At the moment Jinny said the name in his mind, Fern's father arched his back as if electrified, a gasp escaping his lips. The heart rate monitor beeped furiously, then settled down into a regular rhythm as Arnulf collapsed onto the bed.

"Papa!" Fern cried out. She lunged forward grabbing her

father's hand from Philip. Arnulf's eyes opened, wide with fear. He seemed to be choking. Fern quickly pulled the respirator free of his face as her father coughed and spluttered. Then he gasped, drawing in a deep lungful of air.

"Fy Fa . . ." he began, cutting short the swear word.

Liv rushed forward, going to the other side of the bed. Philip stepped back, watching as mother and daughter threw themselves onto the old man. No, not so old. Even as Philip watched, the color came back into Arnulf's cheeks, and his flesh grew visibly younger. Within the minute, he was his old self.

A nurse burst into the room pushing the crash cart, another nurse on her heels, then a doctor. Seeing Arnulf they stopped in their tracks, dumbfounded as the two women, crying over the hale and healthy Arnulf Aasheim, ignored the patient's waving arms as he tried to push them off. Entwhistle stepped aside to let the doctor examine Fern's father.

Oddly, though the doctor spoke Norwegian, Entwhistle found he could understand him. They did their best to run their tests, taking his blood pressure, trying to take a blood sample, but Arnulf kept fending them off, barking at them to leave him alone.

Entwhistle went over the sequence of events. Clearly the curse was broken, but only when Jinny had said the name, speaking to him while he held Arnulf's hand. Did that mean something? Was it the djinn, connected through him, that saved Fern's father?

Jinny's voice in his head was faint, but he heard it clearly nonetheless.

It means the geas could only be removed by one of my kind.

Philip could sense consternation, and something else. Was Jinny afraid?

One of your kind? What does that mean?

It means that a djinn cursed the seal. One of the ancient ones from before the schism, I believe.

Arnulf was sitting up now. Liv and Fern were still crying, but now for joy. They could not stop hugging the bed-bound Arnulf who reluctantly allowed it. The medics left, pushing their cart before them. The doctor was speaking, shaking his head in wonder, but Entwhistle ignored him.

Okay, thought Entwhistle. What exactly is an ancient one?

The ancient ones were all lost in the schism. So was the seal. Yet the one known as Mannuki was in this land recently. He is probably still here.

Another djinn then?

Yes.

A premonition like a dark shadow flitted across Entwhistle's consciousness. A djinn who placed a curse like that, alive and nearby. This was bad news.

You talked about the Schism before. A time in prehistory. Something happened?

For a moment there was not reply. Then, *Yes.*

What happened, Jinny?

There was a time when humanity and djinn lived in harmony. We could pass into your plane with ease and many of us lived amongst your kind. At that time, there were those who offered themselves to us. It was a joining. In time, some djinn came to believe they had a right to possess their host. This ultimately led to the schism, and the war.

Philip moved to the window, watching Fern in its reflection.

War? How could there be a war between man and djinn?

Not the djinn. Angels.

Philip frowned as he tried to absorb what he was hearing. A war with the angels? It seemed too incredible. But then, what was there about any of this that was normal?

How could mankind fight the angels?

You did not, it was my kind who fought.

So what did we do?

Jinny did not reply. Philip pressed her, forcing his will upon her. He could feel her reluctance.

What did mankind do in this war, Jinny?

You died.

Fern ended the exchange, dragging herself from her father, throwing her arms around Entwhistle and kissing him boisterously. When her mother joined in, holding his head in her hand and planting a solid kiss on his lips he turned scarlet, but smiled.

"Thank you Philip," Fern said, eyes wet with tears. "Thank you." A momentary pause and then, almost shyly, "Thank you Jinny."

Arnulf broke in. "What the hell are all these tubes?"

Liv stayed with Arnulf at the hospital. She could not be persuaded to let him out of her sight. Although she would not say it, she feared a relapse. Philip assured her that it was not possible but she would not relent. The doctors were baffled but remained cautious, insisting that Arnulf remain with them, at least overnight. Liv forced her husband to agree. He was all for returning home immediately, claiming he felt twenty years younger. Entwhistle thought that an understatement. Fern's father looked fifty years younger.

Since Arnulf was clearly no longer in critical condition, nor did he appear to be contagious, he was moved out of the infectious diseases ward. His doctors finally conceded that it was not bubonic plague or anything of the kind. He was put in a private room, with a television, radio and a comfortable chair. Liv was grateful for the latter. She intended to stay by his side until he was released.

Entwhistle and Fern finally left. It was getting late, so they took a taxi back to the farmhouse rather than call Jens to come get them.

Entwhistle leaned back into the leather seating, his head tilting onto Fern's. They used each other as a pillow, far less romantic than it sounded since every pothole banged their heads together painfully. But on smooth stretches of road, the ride almost lulled them to sleep.

Jens was waiting for them as they pulled into the yard. He had heard the car coming, forewarned by his mother. Entwhistle and Fern climbed out, stretching stiffly.

Jens stepped forward, grabbed Entwhistle's hand and pulled him into a bear hug. He did not speak; he did not have to.

Fern joined the hug fest. "Oh, my boys," she said, laughing.

Inside Jens headed straight for the drinks cabinet, pulling out a bottle on the side of which the word Akevitt and a stylized eagle were prominently displayed.

"We should have a drink, yes? In honor of papa."

Fern sighed in resignation, giving Entwhistle a look that asked him to be patient.

"Sure," he said with a grin. He could use a drink. It had been a very long day.

Jens distributed small shot glasses filled to the brim. Fern shook her head, one hand raised in denial. Jens and Entwhistle raised their glasses and threw them back, downing the contents in a single swallow. Entwhistle coughed and spluttered, losing half the fiery liquid. Jens laughed uproariously and pounded him on the back.

"Here, have another. It gets easier the more you drink."

He poured two more shots, and once again the men drank. Entwhistle hardly felt it the second time. A warm glow radiated from his stomach. He felt released, not drunk, content, happy.

A third shot, and Jens proposed a toast. "To papa, may he live forever! And to Philip, for making sure he does."

The third shot went down like water, proving Jens' point. Evidently three shots were enough. He put the bottle back in the cabinet.

"Mama says papa is fine," Jens began. "That he'll be back in the morning."

"Yes. Back to his normal self. Completely recovered," Fern replied.

"She also said that it was Philip who saved him. That he did . . . something."

Neither Fern nor Philip answered, but Jens did not require confirmation.

"Is it real then? Magic?"

Fern gestured to the dark window, and the world beyond. "You remember the tree house, Jens? When we were children, playing in the forest, did you think the world was magic?"

He nodded, a faint smile tugging at his mouth. "Yeah, sure."

"So what changed?"

"I grew up?"

"So did I," she responded. "And yet I still believe. The world is what you make it."

"No. The world is not the way I would make it," he replied hotly. "Crime, poverty, disease."

"But it *is,*" Fern insisted. "In the way you perceive it."

"So that's all there is to it then? If you believe, it's true? Magic is real?"

Fern shrugged. "The world is a place of magic, whether we believe it or not. But we can choose if we want to see it. And once you see the world for how it really is, then you can start to interact with it. Influence it."

Jens laughed. "Since when did you turn into a philosopher?"

Fern laughed too. Entwhistle smiled, resisting the urge to comment. He had been a skeptic in the very recent past, but had been forced to accept the reality that magic was a very real part of the world.

"I'd like to see something. Show me some magic, Fern."

"Witches don't do requests," she replied. "Or parlor tricks. Come on, Philip," she said, grabbing his hand. "Let's go to bed."

Jens shrugged, then poured himself another shot. He waved them off with a smile. Fern led Entwhistle up a series of creaky wooden steps into a small bathroom. She turned on the shower and began undressing. She gave Entwhistle a look, half invitation, half challenge and then the same smile that had set his heart racing on the train. He shrugged off his jacket, grinning as he tugged at the buttons on his shirt.

Then search for what is lost

10

The Fallen Ones were on the earth in those days, when the
sons of God came to the daughters of men, and they bore
children unto them. Those were the mighty men of old,
men of renown.

Genesis 6-4

At sixty-two degrees north, the morning sun is a feeble
thing in late fall, but it did its best to shine through the
small windows in the Norwegian farmhouse. The light
drew Philip towards consciousness and he awoke with a
yawn, stretching in the narrow bed, his feet knocking
against the bottom while his head pushed against the top.
He smiled as he considered that this was where Fern had
slept most of her life. The smile grew wider as he felt the
sweet ache in his muscles from the night before. Fern's
passion had been a revelation and for the first time he
understood why so many people made a big deal of make-
up sex.

A very good night. For the second time in a month he
had not dreamed about Sandwell and he felt renewed. He
wanted to tell Fern but she was gone.

Jens was in the kitchen, pouring coffee from a glass
carafe. He put the jug back on the warming plate as
Entwhistle entered the kitchen, yawning. Philip had dressed
in a hurry and the buttons on his shirt were misaligned, so

he pushed aside the strap on his satchel and fixed them. The satchel, with its precious cargo of Jinny's meta-anchor, the torc and the mysterious lead plate would go everywhere he did, for the time being at least.

"Good morning, Jens. Where's Fern?" Entwhistle asked.

"G'morn. She went out to collect eggs. Nothing better than fresh eggs for breakfast."

Entwhistle grabbed a mug and helped himself to coffee. One of the perils of travel; you could not get tea when you needed it. He should have brought some with him. Then he smiled to think that stopping to ferret out a few tea bags could have cost him his freedom.

Entwhistle sipped his coffee, trying not to grimace. Jens' eyes flitted up to the clock on the wall and he turned to stare out the kitchen window.

"Fern's taking a long time," he said. "I don't know what could be keeping her." He got up, opened the back door and leaned out, looking around.

"I'm just going to go find her. I'm starving."

"I'll come with you. I could use some fresh air."

Entwhistle hurried after Jens past various plank-built outbuildings, all painted red, one housing a tractor, another hay bales. Then, in a small barn with a work-bench and a quad bike, the chicken coop.

They took in the mesh door hanging open, hens wandering around amongst the tools and machinery. Jens muttered something under his breath, scooped up a hen, and placed it inside its cage.

"Not like Fern to let the chickens out," Jen said, frowning. "And where has she got to?" They both shepherded the birds back into the coop, then Jens fastened the door.

"She was obviously here," he stated, pointing at a basket containing half a dozen eggs on the ground. "This is strange. Why would she wander off?"

Entwhistle looked around uneasily, a tightening knot in

his stomach. Where was she? She was obviously not in the barn. He stepped outside and noticed something odd, just visible behind the open shed door—a syringe lying on the ground. He stooped to pick it up, hand reaching down, when he heard Jens behind him.

"Stop!"

He straightened while Jens pick up the syringe, holding it carefully by the plastic tube, needle pointing away from them.

"You know what this is?" Entwhistle asked.

"No, " answered Jens, his voice quiet. "I don't."

"It's got a little yellow liquid still in it."

Jens sniffed the needle between his fingers.

"Ketamine. Shit!"

Entwhistle looked at him blankly.

"A horse tranquilizer."

"I didn't know you had horses."

"We don't," he replied, almost whispering.

Jens spotted something. He took a couple of steps and squatted, pointing. "Look at those two lines. And the footprints, with the heels dug in. Someone was dragging something. A body."

They looked at each other, stunned. Jens spoke. "Someone's taken Fern."

Fern's head banged against something hard. With a groan, she opened her eyes. Black. Everything was black. For a moment she thought her eyes were covered. She blinked rapidly. Still dark. Another bump, another bang on the head. Her legs were cramped. She tried to straighten but couldn't. Then it came to her. She was in the trunk of a car, hands held tightly behind her by cords, or plastic, biting into her skin. The car lurched and her head banged again. She yelled and began kicking at the side of the car.

After a couple of panicked minutes, conscious of nothing but terror, Fern began to regain her self-control.

She slowed her breathing, focused on taking stock of the situation. How long had she been there? Who would do this? And why?

There was a hot, sore spot on the right side of her neck. Someone had come from behind and stuck a needle in her neck. She remembered the shock and pain. She had a sense that she had not been out for that long, an hour, maybe less. Her head was sore where it kept hitting the wheel arch so she had been in the car for a while, at least.

She flexed her fingers and tried to move her hands but no matter how she pulled or pushed, the bindings would not give. Unlike a mechanical lock, a good knot wouldn't spring open just because you asked it to.

Turning her head to one side she spotted a sliver of daylight coming from around the taillight.

She was no expert on cars but knew that taillights were fragile. She pulled her legs up to her chest and kicked out as hard as she could, feeling the assembly give slightly. She kicked again, and again. On the fourth or fifth kick the plastic housing snapped off, flooding the trunk with light. Now, if she could smash the bulb, maybe the car would get pulled over? It was the slimmest of hopes, but anything was better than nothing.

She tried a couple more kicks but her foot could scarcely reach the light through the gap. Just then the car changed direction. Now they were driving over loose rock and gravel. Wherever they were going, it was off the main road. The car started to climb, the engine working harder. It was no use now. The police did not patrol the mountain roads.

Her slim hope fading to nothing, **Fern fought against despair.** She forced herself to relax. Better to save her energy for whatever was to come. Even with hands bound, she could cast a defensive spell, or a charm. A curse too, if it came to that. She hoped it would not; the law of three was not to be taken lightly. But if she was left with no choice . . .

A wild idea came to her. She would try to *connect* with Philip. Maybe it would work? A mind could reach out and touch another mind, if it was familiar, if there was a closeness. There were those in the coven that could do this, but they had been in contact with their partner for years. Decades in one case. She and Philip had known each other for only a month. Hardly the length of time it took to really understand someone, to get inside their head. But it was her only hope and she had to try.

She had never done it before, but there was always a first time. If she could connect with Philip and let him know where she was, he would come for her. Philip was the most determined man she had ever known. If there was a way, he would find it. She just had to try.

In the semi-darkness, Fern closed her eyes, willing herself into a calm state. She began a low chant. A motif to focus her mind, to reach the state they called *drifting*.

Entwhistle and Jens returned to the house, all thought of breakfast forgotten.

Jens put the syringe down carefully on the table. Both men sat opposite each other, staring at the needle as if it could provide them with the answers they desperately wanted.

Jens looked up at Entwhistle and fixed him in a narrow-eyed, accusatory stare.

"Okay. What's going on?"

"What?"

"Come on. I'm not stupid. You arrive in a helicopter. You and Fern race around doing heaven knows what. The police pick you up in Oslo and somehow you get away. And now someone's taken Fern. Don't tell me you don't know why."

"I don't. God, I wish I did. The thing with the police has nothing to do with it."

"Yeah, sure."

"No. Really." He looked at Jens and dismissed the idea of telling him a story.

"Okay, here it is. I am what they call 'a subject of interest' in an arson investigation in England. The police there have issued a warrant. They alerted Interpol after I left yesterday?"

"Fy faen!"

"I'm innocent, Jens. Well, sort of. But I promise you, if I hadn't needed to get to Arnulf I wouldn't have run in the first place. They can't convict me. I'm not worried about being arrested."

Jens nodded thoughtfully. "Sort of innocent? What does that mean?"

Entwhistle sighed. "The fire was an accident. I burned down a house when I knocked over a candle. But it belonged to a woman who had just done her best to kill me, so I figure fair's fair."

"Great. So you're a fugitive from the law and my sister has been kidnapped, for reasons unknown. What were you doing in Oslo yesterday?"

"I went to get the lead tablet that your father found."

"Why? What's so important about it?"

"I thought it might help with his condition. He was cursed after he touched it. I believed that it would contain some remedy, or clue as to how to undo the curse."

"Did it?"

Entwhistle shook his head. "No, not exactly. But it led us to something that did."

"I still don't believe in this curse."

Entwhistle shrugged and gave a wry smile. "It's not important that you believe. You just need to accept that your father was near death and now he's not."

Jens nodded, grudgingly. "My mother swears you saved him. So the lead plate is worthless then?"

"Far from it. It's extremely valuable. What is written there is volatile, to say the least."

Entwhistle took the plate from his satchel and laid it on the table. They both stared at it. A small, square slab of gray metal. Without the tiny dense writing inscribed in its surface, it would go entirely unnoticed.

"You can read it?" Jens asked, incredulously.

"Yes, it appears that I can."

Jens was impressed, though he tried not show it. Entwhistle scratched the day's stubble on his chin thoughtfully. "We're wasting time," he declared. "We have to call the police."

Jens looked at him as if he were an idiot. "And then what? You'll get arrested and I'll probably be charged with harboring a fugitive. And even if that doesn't happen, they're not going to know more than we do. And we know nothing."

Entwhistle could feel himself growing angry. He took a deep breath, trying to control a sudden surge of rage.

Using Fern's method he slowed his breathing and heart rate; the anger began to dissipate. There would be a time for it, but now he needed a clear head. He closed his eyes and for just a moment there was something else; a tickling in his mind, like when Jinny talked to him. It was formless, without words but it was familiar. Fern! She was calling out to him.

His eyes snapped open and for a moment they flashed before returning to their normal blue. Where was she? Fern! He stood and walked to the sink, looking out towards the mountains. Some instinct told him she was there. He could almost feel her.

Maybe he should ask Jinny. Of course! How in hell had he been so stupid? The djinn could surely help. Entwhistle grasped the talisman and instantly Jinny was there. Before he could even ask, she replied.

It is not possible. I do not know why, but I cannot sense her energy. I fear that the djinn Mannuki is able to block me from seeing her, just as it blocks me from seeing it.

So there is nothing we can do?

You can search.

Philip sighed his disappointment. He turned to Jens.

"Okay, here's what we know," and he began to count each point on his fingers. "First, the mound is found. Second, a dig is immediately authorized. Third your father is cursed."

It was clear that Jens was having a hard time accepting that word, but he managed to nod in agreement.

"Yes," he said. "Then you show up. You delay the . . . curse."

He also stood and began pacing, his face screwed up in concentration as he tried to put the pieces together.

"You go to Oslo, get arrested and *somehow* escape."

He turned to look at Philip, examining him as if for the first time.

Entwhistle ignored the implied question. It was not something he really wanted to get into. Convincing Fern's brother that there was a conspiracy was one thing. Convincing him about the reality of magic was quite another.

"They must have known we were coming. They were waiting for us. We were arrested as soon as we landed."

Jens frowned. "Then that rules out Interpol," he said. "There is no way they could have known where you would be going. Someone predicted your movements. How, I don't know, but someone tipped off the police so they would be waiting for you. Then you escaped, got the lead plate and returned. And the next day, Fern is taken. I'm not really sure how all the pieces fit together, but my guess is we're going to get an offer to trade. The plate for Fern."

Entwhistle nodded. He was not convinced but could not think of another scenario that made more sense.

"We'll have to handle this ourselves," Jens said.

"Handle it how?"

"I don't know yet"

Jens' phone rang. He snatched it up from the table.

"Yes? Who is this?"

He fell silent as the caller spoke. "Sorry, I thought it was about something else." He looked at Entwhistle and mouthed the word 'Farrell.' The voice continued speaking, not loud enough for Entwhistle to hear. Jens swore in Norwegian, then muttered thanks and hung up. He looked at Entwhistle, shook his head.

"There was a break-in at the university. Both the ancient languages and the chemistry departments. Someone was looking for something and they trashed the place."

Both men stared down at the lead plate. Whoever had raided the university was after the plate and the torc. Philip had both. Evidently, whoever had masterminded the break-ins were not aware of the fact.

Entwhistle frowned. Did they take Fern because they could not find the plate? Or was her abduction already planned?

"Look, everything revolves around the dig and the things that were found. If permission was given in record speed to excavate, then maybe whoever pushed that through knows something? Who was in charge?"

"Eriksen."

"Can we talk to him?"

"Sure. His office is not all that far away," Jens replied. "We can go now."

"Isn't it a bit early?" Philip asked. It was barely seven-thirty.

"No. People often start work early here. But first I want to know what you did for my father."

Something in his voice told Entwhistle that Jens was not going to be brushed off so easily a second time. He stared at the younger man, then with a sigh, nodded.

"What I'm going to tell you will sound like rubbish. Your instinct will be to assume that I am either crazy or a conman. Believe me, I am neither. Nevertheless, you will convince yourself that I am in some way deluded and you were tricked."

Jens sat back in his chair, arms folded over his chest. "I'll try to keep an open mind," he said sarcastically.

Entwhistle smiled ruefully. That would not be enough. But he should try, at least.

"Magic is real," he said. "It works."

Jens laughed. "I knew it. You've bought into the nonsense Pernilla . . . Fern, believes."

"Actually no. I came to believe in magic rather through an unfortunate incident with another witch. One not quite as nice as your sister. Let me get one thing straight, Jens. The world does not care if you believe in magic or not. It exists. People use it."

"You know that I'm going to ask you to prove it, right?" Jens said, his chin jutting.

"Yes. I expect you will."

"Well, go on then."

Entwhistle stood, went to the counter by the sink. He picked up a knife and stared at it. It was long and very sharp. He shuddered at the memory of Sandwell's blade at his throat. His stomach was a ball of tension. It would hurt. He almost could not do it. But the thought of someone hurting Fern made any pain he might feel insignificant. Slowly, deliberately, he drew the knife across his palm. The flesh parted easily, blood instantly welling up to drip onto the floor. It stung, more than he expected. Pale, he looked away, feeling sick.

"What the hell are you doing?" Jens shot up from the table, eyes open wide and staring.

Entwhistle held out his hand towards Jens. With eyes closed he said under his breath, "Jinny, please?"

He opened his eyes at the first warmth. There was a slight shimmering over his hand, like a heatwave over hot tarmac. The cut closed, the bleeding stopped.

Jens looked at him with obvious suspicion. "It's a trick.

I've seen that done on television. You've got a capsule with blood in it, or something."

Entwhistle knew he would say that and he was ready with his response. Before Jens even knew what he was doing Entwhistle slashed the blade across the back of the other man's hand. The cut was minor but it hurt.

"What the hell?" Jens shouted, stepping back as if Entwhistle was a madman. He cradled his hand, trying to cover the wound. Blood dripped from the shallow gash.

"Was that a trick?" Entwhistle asked, nodding at Jens' hand.

"No. What the hell were you thinking?"

"Jinny?"

Almost instantly the cut on Jens' hand closed and the bleeding stopped. Jens stared at his hand in stunned disbelief. Entwhistle heard the faint voice in his head, a hint of amusement.

Don't do that again, little man. I need all my energy. I am still weak.

Jens sat again, almost collapsing into his chair.

"It's . . . real?" He looked almost horrified.

"Yes. Very real, I'm afraid. There are good and bad people in the world, and some of them are able to . . . do things."

"You and Fern, you can both do magic?"

"Well, no. Fern can. I don't really know what, to be honest. But I cannot."

"But you healed yourself. And me!" Jens objected vehemently.

"Actually no. It was not me that healed your hand, or my own."

"Then who?"

"More of a matter of what, actually. But I don't think we should get into that. You just have to accept that magic is real, there are some people that can do it, and some of them use it to their advantage. Now, I suggest we pay a visit to your Mr. Eriksen and see if he can tell us anything."

Jens nodded slowly, all the while rubbing the spot on his hand where he had been cut.

"I'll get my keys," he said. "We should stop at the neighbor's too. Maybe Frederik saw something this morning." He went for his coat, still shaking his head in amazement.

Fern's attempts to contact Philip through drifting had failed. No matter how deep a trance she put herself in she could not connect. Although, for the briefest moment she thought she had caught a sense of him. An image of the kitchen at the farmhouse came to her, then it was gone. So she was on her own and that was all there was to it.

Fern made herself as comfortable as possible, trying to relax for the rest of the ride. There was no point wasting energy on things she could not control. The sound of the engine changed. The car was slowing, braking, coming to a stop. Fern hoped the journey was finally over. She strained to hear, to get a clue of any sort that would help her understand where she was.

The driver's door opened and she heard muffled voices. A man and a woman were speaking, but too quietly for Fern to make out what they were saying. The car door slammed and the voices moved away, boots crunching on loose rock.

They had left her in the trunk. Well, they believed she couldn't get out, so why not? Save them the bother of putting her back again, she thought. Of course, she probably could get out, if she willed it. The trunk had a mechanical lock. It would be as easy as the handcuffs to open.

She focused her mind, preparing to cast the spell, when a nagging doubt made her pause. Clearly her family were being targeted. The curse against her father had almost taken his life, and now her kidnapping showed their troubles were not over. Someone wanted to do them harm. If she escaped, she would not know any more than she did already, and she needed to know who was responsible. With a sigh, she let the spell slip from her mind.

Whoever the enemy was they would be more likely to let their guard down if she appeared helpless. A grim smile formed on her lips. She was Fern Aasheim, the hunter. They didn't know who there were dealing with. But before this was all over, Goddess willing, they were going to find out.

Jens pushed his car to speeds that Entwhistle considered beyond reckless. He scrambled to plug in his seatbelt as they fishtailed out of another bend and straightened out, accelerating fast. The roads were narrow, with areas slick with mud where tractors had crossed between paddocks. Jens fought one skid after another, cursing furiously in Norwegian.

Luckily, there were few other cars on the road. Still, Entwhistle clutched the arm rest and braced himself every time Jens took a blind corner.

"Don't worry. I've had high speed driver training. And I'll see cars coming from their headlights."

At barely eight in the morning they saw no heavy traffic until they reached the main road to the city. Jens merged with the traffic seamlessly and soon they were taking an exit for Lillehammer North.

Jens' neighbor, a taciturn farmer named Frederik, had told them of a car earlier in the morning on their shared road. A blue Ford, he thought. He could not say who was driving, only that it was travelling fast, almost hitting one of his geese.

It was something, but not much. An unknown blue car, possibly a Ford, on the farm at the right time. If they got nothing useful from Eriksen, Jens thought the sudden disappearance, the syringe and the car would be enough to get the police moving.

Entwhistle's thoughts returned to Fern. Once again, he felt a surge of anger that someone might harm her and to his immense surprise, tiny blue sparks danced on his fingertips. He pushed his hands under his legs to hide them. Since Jinny had taken his body, Philip had felt subtly different. More aware, somehow. It seemed there were other differences too.

He tried to control his feelings. Rage did not help him now. Jens was angry enough for them both and at least one of them needed to keep a level head. He calmed himself, taking deep breaths, focusing on slowing his heart rate. It worked. Fern was right. Meditating and yoga every day for the last month actually had helped.

The municipal archaeology and surveyor's offices was on the edge of the city, and they arrived after barely thirty minutes of Formula One driving. Jens parked, flung open the door and was out of the car before Entwhistle managed to undo his seatbelt. He chased after the younger man, satchel held firmly against his torso with one hand.

They burst into the building's foyer and no one stopped or challenged them. No one even glanced in their direction. Jens punched Eriksen's name into small computer terminal next to the elevator. It told them his floor and office and extension number.

Inside the mirrored lift Entwhistle could see himself all too clearly. He looked rough, his eyes haunted. Jens worked his jaw, teeth grinding audibly. Fern's brother was on the verge of losing control.

"Jens, I think you should let me do the talking."

Jens shot him a glance, then looked away, but nodded. The door pinged and they exited into an open plan office. Jens nodded towards the other end of the large, mostly empty room, where a middle-aged man was examining a map spread open on his desk.

"That's Eriksen."

Entwhistle headed for him. Jens made to follow, then stopped, pulling out his mobile phone to check a message he had just received. The archeologist looked up as Entwhistle approached. Jens hurried to catch up.

Eriksen recognized Jens immediately and smiled, holding out his hand.

"Ah, Jens Aasheim. What can I do for you?"

Jens shook Eriksen's hand and smiled tightly in return.

"We need to ask you some questions."

"Oh? Well, certainly, certainly. Why are we speaking English?"

"That would be my fault," said Entwhistle. "My name is Entwhistle. We need answers right away Dr. Eriksen."

"Answers to what?" Eriksen asked, raising his bushy eyebrows.

"We need to know about the dig," said Entwhistle. "I understand that it was approved very quickly."

Eriksen looked slightly alarmed. He glanced about, eyes darting. Was he looking for a way out? He looked warily at Entwhistle.

"Yes, it was. But with the weather changing for the worse, and the fact that several people knew where it was and that gold artifacts had been recovered, it was deemed best to do a rapid examination of the site. In the end, we recovered weapons consistent with a tenth century Viking warrior as well as several other things."

He turned and walked to a corner of the room where a table stood. On it were the items taken from the haug.

"Come, see for yourself. I've just put this out on display."

Jens and Entwhistle followed him to a big white table. Bits of iron, a round, hemispherical dome that looked like it might be part of a shield and a remarkably well-preserved sword. Eriksen unlocked a drawer under the table and removed a plastic container. He opened it and placed the object it contained on the table. A gold ring. Startled,

Entwhistle saw immediately see that it matched the torc he now carried in his satchel.

Entwhistle nodded. "Very interesting. However, I am curious about something else. Did you know everyone working on the dig, Dr. Eriksen?"

At this, Eriksen looked down, shuffling his feet as he formulated his reply. "Well, some of them, but not all. Not exactly."

"Please explain, doctor. I'm a historian myself, so I don't really know much about archeology."

"Well, the antiquities department provides the personnel. But I . . . uh, was asked if I could include someone else on the team."

Entwhistle and Jens exchanged a look. It might be nothing, but still.

"Who?" Jens demanded.

"A young woman. Not terribly pleasant. Her name was Silvi. I don't know her last name."

In his mind, Entwhistle felt Jinny's presence. She seemed agitated.

This one lies. He knows more than he says.

Entwhistle examined Eriksen closely. The archeologist seemed to be very interested in a spot on the floor. Entwhistle's instincts agreed with the djinn. Eriksen was lying about something.

"I can see you know more than you want to say, Mr. Eriksen," Entwhistle said. He moved towards the older man, who stepped back, again casting his gaze about. At that, Jens tensed, as if preparing to stop Eriksen should he attempt to flee. Instead, the older man deflated.

"Yes," he said. "I do."

He showed them a website on his computer. It was an article from a Norwegian online newspaper. There was a face of a serious looking young woman. The caption read, *Silvi Eikenes, mottar prestisjetunge forskningsstipend.*

Jens was astounded. "Eikenes? Faen!"

"Who is she?" Entwhistle demanded.

"Only the bloody district police chief's daughter," Jens replied.

Eriksen nodded hopelessly. "Now you see. I was left with no real choice. He is not a man you want to cross."

"She was on the dig?" Jens said.

"Yes. She actually worked quite well, but I got the impression she wasn't interested in what we were doing. She kept asking about the lead plate. The one Farrell took to Oslo."

Entwhistle's hand automatically went to the satchel. He could feel the plate inside, a hard edge against his thigh.

"I think I saw her one morning," Jens said, his voice flat.

"What does she drive?" Entwhistle held his breath.

Eriksen thought for a moment. "A Ford. A blue Ford, I think."

Entwhistle and Jens looked at each other, both immediately thinking the same thing. Forget the police. They were on their own. But now they had a who. They just needed a where.

Entwhistle could sense agitation from Jinny. She was hovering around his mind. He could feel her energy, sometimes moving through him, causing him to tingle. Again he could feel a charge, like static, as tiny blue sparks danced across his fingers. He clenched his fist.

Hearken, Man. The ring on the table. Take it.

Entwhistle glanced at the table, then back at Eriksen. They had the information they needed. Almost.

"Do you have an address for Silvi, Dr. Eriksen?" Entwhistle asked, as he casually walked back to the display table.

"No, sorry."

"Okay," Entwhistle continued. "We can see you were in a bit of a bind. But as a result, someone's life has been put in jeopardy. You owe it to us to help."

Eriksen's eyes widened in surprise. To his credit, he did

not dismiss the statement.

"Of course. Whatever I can do."

"Good. Because I'm going to take the ring."

Eriksen was aghast. "You can't take it. That's a national treasure. You could be arrested for that!"

Entwhistle nodded, but smiled wryly. "They can get in line then."

Entwhistle went to the table and when it looked like Eriksen was going to try to stop him, Jens stepped forward with a look on his face that clearly signaled, *Don't. Just don't.*

Eriksen froze in place. Entwhistle put the ring in the side pocket that contained the handcuffs he had kept from the day before. When he looked back at the archeologist, he felt a wave of sympathy for the man and his situation.

"Don't worry. When this business is over, I'll return the ring and the torc."

Eriksen blanched. "What? You have the torc too?"

"Yes. I believe I may have need of it."

Entwhistle gave Jens a nod and they left the confused archeologist behind them and headed for the elevator.

"I just got a text message," said Jens. "My father is out of the hospital. They're on the way back to the farm." The elevator pinged and the doors opened. They went inside and Entwhistle punched the button for the ground floor. Jens looked at him miserably.

"How am I going to tell them that Fern is gone?"

Jens pulled the car into the farm just seconds behind a city taxi with his mother and father inside. It stopped by the front of the farmhouse and Liv got out. Jens parked at the side of the house and followed Entwhistle, trailing behind, dragging his feet.

Entwhistle had only seen Liv at the hospital. She looked a lot younger now, livelier, as if years had been taken off her too. Her eyes glittered and she could not stop smiling.

She leaned over and reached into the back of the taxi but stepped back abruptly when Arnulf fended her off.

"I don't need help," he said.

He clearly did not. He was healthy and strong as if two days hovering at death's door had never happened.

"I'm not an invalid, Liv!" Arnulf exclaimed. "Please stop treating me like one."

"Well you've just been ill. Maybe you need to take it easy?"

"And the farm? Will it take it easy?"

"You're more important than the farm, Arnulf."

Liv would not be gainsaid. She took his arm and walked with him towards the house. "Jens dear, pay the taxi would you?"

Jens nodded and walked over to the taxi. He looked almost grateful. Entwhistle stood patiently, outwardly calm but his heart beat like a trip hammer.

Fern's parents strode towards him. Arnulf glanced down, not meeting his eyes. Entwhistle was puzzled. Was he nervous? Arnulf was a full head taller than Entwhistle, and immensely bigger, yet he seemed hesitant.

Arnulf's head came up and the steel grey of his eyes met Entwhistle's blue. "I believe that I have you to thank for my recovery." He held out his hand and Entwhistle shook it solemnly. Arnulf shrugged, gave a half smile, then pulled Entwhistle into a bear hug.

"Looks like you are better now, Arnulf," Entwhistle said, as he was released.

"Yes, looks like. I don't seem to be able to remember anything of the last few days though. Liv says I was very ill; close to death. And then you did something magical and I got better." He winked as he said that last, like it was a joke only they understood.

The difference, compared to the man Entwhistle had seen in the hospital, was profound. Even his hand felt different. No longer frail and weak, it was the hand of a strong man, with a calloused grip.

Entwhistle shook his head. "Think nothing of it. I didn't do anything, really."

Arnulf laughed and again pulled Entwhistle to him, slapping him on the back. When he pulled away, Liv moved in and repeated the process, this time adding a kiss to both his cheeks, making Entwhistle blush.

The taxi left, its tires scrabbling in the gravel driveway, and Jens marched back to them. He stared down at this shoes, kicking at a stone, looking a lot younger than his twenty-eight years. Immediately his mother saw something was wrong. She looked at Jens levelly and her tone brooked no argument.

"What happened?"

Jens hesitated. He could scarcely bring himself to say the words. "Fern's been abducted. She's missing. We found a syringe with ketamine. And we know who did it. You're not going to like that part."

At once Arnulf turned and marched into the house. Liv and Jens exchanged worried glances and hurried after him. Entwhistle followed. Inside, they found Arnulf taking down an antique shotgun from over the fireplace. He cracked it open and fed two shells into the barrels, then snapped it shut with a flick of his powerful wrist. He turned to face them.

"Tell me everything," he said, his voice grim.

And if you're willing to give it all

11

Fear not those that kill the body,
but are not able to kill the soul:
but rather fear him who is able to
destroy both body and soul.
—Matthew 10:28

Entwhistle joined the Aasheims in what was starting to feel like a war council. They stood in a small circle by the fireplace, facing each other. Then all eyes turned to him, waiting for him to talk.

He took a deep breath. He could explain what he believed to be the case, from things he had picked up, from what Jinny had told him. The only question in his mind was, how far should he go? How much of the truth would they accept? Convincing them would be like building a house of cards. You could go a long way, then everything collapses.

"Well," Entwhistle said, "this is what I know. Arnulf, after you found the plate, you were cursed. There was some kind of defensive spell on the thing. It would have killed you, but Fern and I discovered the . . . the key to undo it. It was a name. We believe it was the name of the uh . . . person who made the curse."

Arnulf looked at him, brows raised. He glanced to Liv, then Jens, seeking confirmation. Jens shrugged and nodded.

"It's true, papa. I . . . I believe it's true. Everything he says."

"Well I never. Sorry, Philip. Please go on."

Entwhistle sighed. It was crazy, no question. But that did not stop it being any less true. "It seems there was a time when certain elemental creatures lived amongst men. That was a very long time ago. Before something called the schism."

At this, Arnulf looked thoughtful. Entwhistle paused, waiting to see if he wanted to speak, but Arnulf indicated he should continue.

"Well, something happened, and the dj . . . creatures left the earth. Except not all of them. Some stayed behind. Either they refused to leave, or were unable to. One such hid something, here in Norway. It's called the seal. I don't know what it is exactly, but it's powerful and scares the dickens out of . . . a certain individual I know."

"Are you saying," Arnulf said, carefully, "that you know one of these creatures, these elementals?"

"I didn't say that."

Jens' eyes widened. "But you do, don't you?" He pointed at Entwhistle. "That's how you fixed my hand!"

"What's this?" Liv said. "What about your hand?"

Jens eyed Entwhistle for a moment, then continued. "I cut my hand. Philip did something to heal it, or so I thought. Either way, my hand was fixed. It would have needed at least eight stitches, but you'd never know I'd been cut at all." He looked straight at Entwhistle. "If you didn't do it, then it was one of these elementals you mentioned."

Entwhistle said nothing. All eyes were on him. In the end, he was simply too tired to lie. "Yes."

Jens looked almost disappointed. He shrugged. "So, what are they, these elementals?"

"People. Just like us. Only . . . not. To be a bit more technical, pan-dimensional entities."

Liv cleared her throat. "The Aasheims have always been a bit fae, especially on the women's side. Arnulf's grandmother was rumored to have been a volva or spaekona. That is, a wise woman, but in those days no one talked about it. I suppose that's where Fern gets it from. As for these . . . creatures, sounds to me like you're talking about guardian angels."

"Exactly," said Arnulf, triumphantly. "I was thinking the same thing. You remember, in the Bible, it talks about the Nephilim?"

Liv nodded. "The Sons of God. The Nephilim were angels, here on earth, before the flood." She cocked her head to one side as she looked at Entwhistle. "Is that what your schism was? The flood?"

"What? I don't know. I . . ." Before Entwhistle could say anymore, Jinny was there, her voice filling his mind.

The mother of your mate is correct. The schism is remembered by your people as the flood. It was much more than that. But the war ravaged the earth and your people died, nigh unto extinction. After it was over, most djinn left, forbidden to return. I, too was forced out of this realm. When we saw that mankind survived, we watched, we waited. We guarded your kind from the Seraphim. In this, your mate's mother is wrong. The Nephilim were not angels. They were djinn.

"Philip! I said, can your angel find Fern?" Liv's voice, tinged with impatience filtered through to him. The whole time Jinny had been talking, Entwhistle had shut off, not hearing the others speak.

"Sorry, what? My angel?"

Liv sighed, then tried again. "You have a guardian angel, do you not?"

"No. Good god, no."

Liv looked puzzled. "Then what are we talking about? You said it was an elemental that healed Jens' hand. What else are we talking about?"

"Angels are no friend to man. It was Jinny that healed Jens' hand. She has powers, but she can't find Fern. Something is blocking her. Most likely the other elemental. It's still here, in Norway, and probably close."

Arnulf shook his head in confusion. "But if they're not angels, what are they?"

Entwhistle sighed. Did it matter if he told them? Would the world end? Would they suddenly discover a previously unknown desire to possess a djinn? Of course not. Decision made, he looked them each in the eye for a moment.

"The elementals are djinn. The Nephilim were djinn. My guardian angel is actually a djinn. Called Jinny."

"But that's a genie," Arnulf exclaimed.

"No, apparently it's not," Entwhistle replied. "Look, we're getting off track. This is not helping us find Fern."

Reluctantly, the others nodded agreement. Arnulf regarded him shrewdly. "Okay, leaving aside everything else, what you are telling us is that some kind of ancient djinn cursed the stuff in the haug, and now Fern has been taken? In my place?"

"Most likely to negotiate a trade for the artifacts," said Jens, leaning forward, resting elbows on his knees. He looked morose. He clearly blamed himself for the disappearance of his sister.

Entwhistle did not quite buy the theory that Fern was taken in order to effect a trade for the plate. There was still no contact with the kidnappers, even though it had been almost four hours. And if they wanted all the artifacts from the haug, why had no one tried to steal the ring from Eriksen. And why not just come into the Aasheim's house, armed, and take it? Why go to the trouble of kidnapping anyone? He had begun to suspect a rather more chilling purpose for Fern's abduction, but he refrained from mentioning it aloud. He could barely even contemplate it himself. The lead plate was the key.

Jens continued with describing what they believed had

happened. The ketamine, the car, Silvi.

"It sounds like a crazy conspiracy," said Arnulf. "Like one of those detective shows they put on at Easter." He looked at Jens, almost accusingly. "And you think there are police involved in this?"

Jens looked a little uncomfortable. He shifted in his chair, the look on his face one of doubt. "There were rumors," he began.

Entwhistle looked hard at him. "What rumors?"

"About the police chief, Eikenes. I've heard it, on more than one occasion that if you wanted to get ahead in the force, you needed to be a pagan. Worship the old gods."

Entwhistle shrugged. "Okay. That's a little strange, maybe. But why would that relate to our situation?"

"I'm not sure. But this was a pagan burial. The objects found are significant. And he is in the position of being able to do pretty much anything he wants."

Arnulf's eyes widened in surprise. "You really think Eikenes could be involved? I knew the man. He was always a bit crazy, even in school. He was obsessed with the old religion."

Jens made a wry face, twisting his mouth, then let out a sigh. "I don't know. But the police in Oslo were very quick to pick up Philip and Fern when they went to get the plate. And then we hear that his daughter was on the dig, and her car was seen leaving the farm this morning. It's starting to add up."

Arnulf looked at Entwhistle. "You're supposed to be a smart man. What do you make of this?"

Entwhistle looked Arnulf in the eye. "I think that everything Jens said was correct, except I don't believe that whoever took Fern wants an exchange."

"What are you saying?" Arnulf asked, alarmed. "Do you think they'll try to hurt her?"

"I think we had better find her, and quick," he replied.

Liv's hand lanced out, gripping Arnulf's arm. "Then find

her, Arnulf. Find out who took Fern"—she looked to the shotgun, propped against the wall before turning her gaze back on her husband—"and bring her home."

Jotunheim Valley
Thrandsson homestead

The longhouse was smoky, warm and full of the comfortable and familiar smells of home. Egill Thrandsson sat on a low stool near the fire-pit, staring at the straw covered floor. Funny how the place seemed so small now. When he had left, it had been hard to imagine a grander building than this. He was soon disabused of that notion. After what he had seen on his travels, his family's farm now felt entirely too much like peasants scrabbling in the mud. But he would change that. The gold he had brought back would ensure they had the best of everything. During his time in the guard, he had come to the realization that farming would not be in his future. A man's grasp was as long as his arm, so they say. And he could reach very far indeed.

His homecoming had been everything he had hoped for during the long journey. Although cousins, he thought of the girls he grew up with as his sisters. They were older, some of them hand-fasted. There were more children underfoot than at any time he could remember. Perhaps it was not so bad a life, being a farmer. He could take a wife and whelp some of his own little ones.

Egill fingered the strange blade he had taken from the trollman in the desert. Usually it was only swords that had names, but this dagger demanded one. *Soul Eater.* He smiled grimly, pleased with the name he had chosen. The knife was more dangerous than any sword, so it needed a worthy name.

The blade was black and very smooth. There was a slight wave in the reflected light from its surface. If you looked very closely, you could see that the cutting edge had been created by chipping with a stone, like the flint weapons from the time before time that were sometimes found in the ground. Egill had seen these curious things in the bazaar in Miklagard, but they were crude and clumsy compared to this weapon. It was sharper than steel and more beautiful than even the patterned blades of Damascus. Egill had never seen anything like it before, and he doubted he would find anything like it again.

He peered closely into its black depths. He could see himself easily in its polished surface. And something else. He turned: Mannuki.

The smaller man stood seemingly at ease, hands hanging loosely by his sides, but from his stance, Egill surmised that Mannuki was ready to fight. Standing suddenly, Egill took a step back, knocking over the stool in his haste.

It would be foolish to underestimate the desert man. Mannuki had fought the trollman like a crazed berserker. His attack had distracted the creature allowing Egill to wrest the blade from his hand. Without Mannuki's help, he doubted that they could have bested the trollman.

But now Mannuki was unarmed and Egill held Soul Eater, the weapon of a powerful sorcerer.

Mannuki made no threatening move and Egill slipped the blade into the leather sheath at his belt. It was a strange companion to his sword, but he had a feeling that if it came down to it, Soul Eater was the weapon that mattered.

"What is it Mannuki? Do you need something?"

"I must leave now. I shall go into the mountains."

Egill was surprised, but he did not show it. There was nothing in the mountains. Certainly no way a man could live there. But then that nagging thought. Mannuki was no ordinary man. On a hunch, he spoke.

"Why? Are we not far enough from your homeland that you are yet safe from your enemies?"

It was just a guess, but Egill could clearly see he had

struck a nerve. Mannuki's eyes narrowed, regarding the Norseman shrewdly.

"Why do you say that? I go where I please."

"Yes, I suppose you do. But you cannot go back to the desert, can you." It was a statement, not a question. Mannuki eyed him balefully.

"No. I cannot. There are those that seek me there, that would prevent me in my task. I must go to the mountains and prepare the way."

Now Egill was curious. "Prepare the way for what?"

Mannuki laughed. "You would not understand, little man."

Egill felt his anger rise. Mannuki looked eager, then he seemed to relax.

"I must have the knife you took from my captor. Return it to me now."

"No. It is mine."

"You fool," Mannuki spat the words, his eyes full of hate. "You would have died there, but for me."

That was enough for Egill. His anger erupted.

"You dare insult me in my own hall? You are a guest here Mannuki, but no longer. You must leave. Now."

Mannuki laughed at his outrage. "I shall leave. But I will take that."

He pointed to the knife at Egill's belt. Egill shook his head. "No. Soul Eater is mine."

The desert man cocked his head to one side and regarded the bigger man in surprise. "Soul Eater? Yes, that is fitting. I want it."

He took a step towards the Northman. Egill laughed in scorn.

"I took it from the trollman. You were not his equal and were made slave, but Bjorn and I killed him. Do you think you can take it from me? It is mine by right of conquest."

"Yours because you killed for it? Very well."

Mannuki advanced on Egill, his hands tracing a curious

pattern in the air. Before Egill knew what was happening he felt the breath crushed from his body, as if a pair of very strong arms were wrapped around him, squeezing tighter and tighter. Egill struggled to move, but was held fast. He spat a curse. Mannuki merely smiled.

Just then the door swung open and Red Asgeir entered. He took in the scene, and froze, open mouthed with shock. Egill could not breathe. It felt like his head was going to explode from the pressure and he stumbled.

Asgeir pulled his sword, and with a yell lunged at Mannuki. The smaller man dodged aside, but it broke his focus, and Egill was free of whatever force had held him.

"Trollman," he rasped, pointing to Mannuki.

"Why am I not surprised," Asgeir replied. He swung again with his sword, but Mannuki leapt back. Just within reach of Egill. Quick as a striking snake, Egill pulled the small black blade from his belt and lunged. He grabbed Mannuki's shoulder, spinning him around, but the blow to the belly was blocked, and Egill was pushed back. He fell to his knees, still winded from the spell the desert man had cast upon him. Asgeir advanced on Mannuki. The little man eyed him warily backing away slightly, coming closer to Egill, who struck again, his hand flashing out with the deadly little knife. It found its mark high in Mannuki's thigh.

The desert man howled, looking in stunned disbelief at the blade protruding from his flesh. Asgeir swung again, intent on taking his head, but Mannuki still had the presence of mind to duck. He pulled the blade out and tried to run, but the damage and the pain of his injury slowed him. Asgeir swung again. The blade flashed down, the edge cutting Mannuki's face from temple to chin.

The desert man spoke quickly, his blue eyes flaring, and Asgeir was pushed back by a blow to his gut. Then to their incredulous eyes, the savage cut on the trollman's face began to close, healing itself.

Asgeir cursed, and advanced again, his blade making short arcs before him, dancing like a deadly snake. Mannuki laughed, then made a gesture, fingers moving rapidly to describe a pattern in the air. Then with a grunt, he pointed, and a bolt of blue erupted from his hand.

Red Asgeir looked down and stared wide-eyed at the ruin of his stomach. Tendrils of smoke drifted up from the cauterized flesh around the hole that went clean through his body. He fell sideways, a last pleading look to Egill.

Mannuki sneered. "There is nothing you can do to stop us, little man. We do as we will."

He limped to the door. Although his face was now hale, the wound from Soul Eater still pulsed blood.

Egill Thrandsson stood, pulling his sword free of its scabbard, but Mannuki had what he wanted and darted through the still open door. Egill ran to Asgeir, but though the eyes were open, his kinsman's soul had fled. He went on one knee, his face stern with pride for his cousin.

"You did well, Asgeir the Red. You died with a sword in your hand and your enemy's blood dripping from it. You will be hailed in Odin's hall."

Egill climbed to his feet. He was in a killing mood and was more than ready to meet Odin himself. Outside the hall, a woman screamed; one of the thralls. Egill set off in pursuit of the viper he had allowed into his family's home.

He rushed outside, expecting to see Mannuki but there was only a woman lying face down in the dirt.

"Which way did he go?" he roared, his voice hoarse with rage.

"He ran there, my lord," said the woman as she sat up, pointing to the path that led to the high pastures. Egill followed her direction.

Egill had good eyes, but he could not find any sight or spoor of the trollman. He raised his head, and there, far distant already, he could just make out Mannuki running. No, hobbling, but at a greater speed than any man could run. Soul Eater had hurt the trollman badly, but it did not seem that it would kill him. Egill's lips curled back in frustration and he growled. There was no chance to catch him. At least, not now. But the creature would surely freeze up there, trollman or not. Egill eyed the great mountains uneasily. At least, he hoped so.

In the cramped darkness of the car's trunk, Fern could hear footsteps approaching. Two people. Her abductor and an accomplice. Her? Why was she so sure it was a woman? Fern listened hard, then realized that one of them stepped with a heavy crunch, the other lightly. So one was bigger than the other. The crunch of boots on loose rock ended directly by her head. There was a fumble of keys in the trunk lock and Fern was blinded by sudden light. She blinked rapidly, trying to regain her vision as quickly as possible.

Hands reached in, grabbing her. All she could see of her kidnappers was their blurry silhouettes. They pulled her roughly, forcing her to stand. Though stiff, she had not suffered debilitating cramps in her legs thanks to constant flexing and relaxing of the muscles. She stood straight and tall, unwilling to give her captors the satisfaction of thinking she was beaten.

"Who are you?" Fern demanded, still blind as her eyes adjusted to the bright mountain light.

They ignored the question. Now she could see she was right about the pair. One was a woman, the other a much heavier man. They grabbed an arm each and marched her to a nearby cabin. But not before she could have a good look around. Even though she could not say precisely where she was, Fern could clearly see the great jagged peak of Jotunheim, home to the legendary giants of Norse lore. There were no other cabins in sight, but that was not unusual. Norwegians liked their solitude. This cabin stood alone at the base of the great mountain. It was built with dressed logs, laid end on end in the traditional style, with the grass turf roof so beloved by tourists. There would be no fishing here and not much to attract people to the area, so other family cabins would be unlikely. No one to help her, in other words.

Her captors pushed Fern through the open door into the main room. There were tapestries and oil lamps hanging on the walls. In every respect it was a typical cabin, only frozen in time from the last century. No electrical appliances or modern conveniences of any sort were visible.

"Make it sit down." The woman spoke, her voice emotionless. Fern winced. Not a good sign. They were treating her as a thing. She had seen enough movies to know what that meant. It would make it easier for them to kill her. Well, she was not planning on making things easy for her captors. She would force them to see her as a person.

"Why thank you. Yes, that would be nice. It was quite the bumpy ride, I can tell you."

"Shut up." The same emotionless voice.

"No need to be rude. We're all here together, so why don't we try to get along."

"Just sit down, will you?" This time the voice was slightly softened.

"Of course. Do you think it would be okay if I had something to drink?"

Fern sat in a hard backed chair, her bound hands pressing into her back. She smiled at her captors, who studiously ignored her. But the man left the room, returning quickly with a glass of water. He offered it to her, then frowned as he saw that she could not take it. With a sigh, he tilted it slightly so she could drink.

Fern was careful to maintain eye contact with the man. As she drank, she drew him deeper into her gaze, in her mind the words of an incantation, her fingers performing the simple actions necessary to establish the charm. In seconds it was done. He would not be aware of his new role until it became necessary. For now, he would continue to act and behave as if he had not been completely subverted to the will of a powerful witch.

"Alright," said the woman. "If you are done, find some rope and tie her to the chair."

The man nodded. This did not conflict with his new subliminal instructions and he went outside. Sounds of rummaging came dimly through the open door. The woman sat on a small couch and looked at Fern with contempt.

It would not be possible to charm this woman. Even though she was young, younger even than Fern, she was strong minded, very focused and . . . something more. Something dark. There was an evil presence within her. This one could hurt her and enjoy doing it.

Fern smiled, then asked, "Why am I here?"

The woman snorted, but did not reply.

Fern tried again.

"What's your name? Surely that can't hurt?"

This time the woman looked at her. "I wonder if I should cut out your tongue?"

Fern was stunned, as much by the comment as the casual way the woman had said it. She could sense a darkness before her. The woman was evil. A psychopath. The words were not said to frighten. Fern knew that if she said too much, or annoyed her, this woman would take a razor, or a pair of shears, and slice off her tongue, simply to deal with an inconvenience. Time to play at being powerless. No more bravado.

"That's not necessary. I am not a threat. I am in your power. You have complete control over me. What harm can there be in answering my questions?"

If this mollified the woman, it was not easy to see. She turned her head away from Fern to stare at the wall. The cabin door slammed shut behind the man as he entered, a length of thick, hessian rope in his hands. He wound it around Fern's body and chair, looping it, then pulling it tight. Not too tight. He was not consciously aware, but he would not actively do anything to hurt her. He made sure they were slightly loose. He tied the rope off behind the chair.

"See? Now I am totally in your power. Why not tell me why I'm here?"

This time the woman turned her head. She stared at Fern and a slow, malicious smile spread over her face. "Someone wants to meet you. It is a very great honor."

The engine roared as Jens pushed his car to the limits of its ability. Heading northwards, the mountains gradually grew larger with each passing minute. Already huge from a distance, they now towered high above.

Arnulf rode in the front, the shotgun laying across his lap. Entwhistle sat in the back, wedged into the corner, feet braced as they hurtled through bends and over bumps and potholes.

Memories came to him. People, dark hair and skin, clothes cut from woven cloth, or dressed skins. They sat in a circle, laughing, telling stories. A fire burned, as the day turned slowly into night. One man, with ritual scars on his cheeks and startling blue eyes stood and spoke. His words contained clicks, which sounded jarringly strange to Entwhistle, but almost immediately their meaning became clear.

"This day, we welcome a new member to our family."

The talking stopped, and all eyes turned to him. He beckoned, and a young girl stood and came forward. She looked down at her feet. She was bare breasted, around her throat a necklace of small shells. She fingered one as a murmur of approval was voiced by the others present.

"J'wera has been chosen. She comes to us willingly, and willingly takes up the duties of the chosen."

More voices, some offering congratulations. J'wera smiled shyly. At the urging of the scar faced man she came to the center of the circle, close enough to feel the heat of the fire on her back.

"J'wera, are you sure that you want to live a life of sacrifice and service?"

The girl lifted her head, and this time there was no shy uncertainty in her gaze. She nodded, and spoke. "I do. It is my right. I have been chosen, and I choose to serve."

The man nodded. He too had been chosen as a child. He too had become a host for a djinn, living a life dedicated to the care of his family.

"Then come, J'wera. Know your fate."

As he spoke the words, the girl, J'wera, closed her eyes and sank to her knees. She held still for a moment, then she lifted her head, opening her eyes: they were bright blue, just like the older man's.

The mark of the djinn was upon her. Instantly there was clapping and cheering from her family. They surged forward and embraced her, lifting her to her feet.

Their leader spoke again, his smile and bright blue eyes standing out in the encroaching darkness of night. "Tell us your name, child."

The girl, who had been known for her first thirteen years as J'wera, lifted her hands in front of her face turning them over, flexing the fingers, almost as if she had never seen such things before. She smiled broadly. "I am J'wekrin."

Her name. The name of the host and her djinn combined. They were one entity now. One person, both of them embracing a life together, dedicated to helping the family.

The leader nodded. "It is good. Soon it will be time for me to pass on, and the family go forward with a new chosen. Welcome J'wekrin."

The vision or memory ended as quickly as it had begun. Philip frowned. The language was utterly unlike anything he had ever heard. How old was this memory?

For thousands of your lifetimes, man and djinn were as one. We guided your people. Helped, protected.

Philip could feel Jinny in his mind. Her presence was almost familiar now, comforting.

So, our two species had a symbiotic relationship? He knew as he asked the question that it was wrong.

No. It was a relationship built on trust, not mutual survival. We do not need your species, as you do not need us. The schism has proven this. We watched you, encouraged you. We have long known your kind. Long, even as we measure time. As your species developed, many of us chose to live amongst you. In time, we shared ourselves with your kind. Until the schism.

That word again. Always that word. What did it mean? Philip pushed the thought to the djinn, and she answered with another vision. This time, Philip's body went rigid in shock as Jinny's memories of mankind's ancient past flooded his mind.

The man's name was Torsen. The woman was Silvi Eikenes. With his partner out of the cabin, Torsen had proven to be considerably more loquacious, freely admitting their names. He would not say why she had been taken but Fern could tell he was struggling with the compulsion to protect her, and with the knowledge of why she was there. From the struggle going on in his subconscious, it was clear to Fern that they intended to kill her. But so long as her charm continued to work, Torsen would not allow that to happen. She had been alone with the man for well over an hour, and with Silvi out of the cabin, now was the time to persuade Torsen to let her go.

"You don't really want to hurt me, do you?"

Torsen looked at her with unspoken misery writ heavily in his face. He shook his head.

"Why don't you untie me. These ropes are very uncomfortable."

"I can't do that. You're needed. The Master wants you."

Shame. She would need more time. His fear was greater than her ability to bind him. Still, if he would not let her go, then at least she could get more information. Who was this mysterious master? She had to be quick, before his partner returned.

"Who is he? Why does he want me?"

"He is the one who will restore the world. You should feel honored." He did not look like he believed his own words. He grimaced as he spoke. "You're going to be part of something wonderful."

"What do you mean, restore the world? How?"

"I can't say. It's a secret. I'm not really supposed to know, but the others talk. The nine are not as clever as they think. We know."

Nine. Interesting. It was a sacred number. There was a significance there. Nine was a number that had meaning in a great many cultures. But this was Norway. In the pagan times it was believed that there were nine worlds. Nine was the number of nights Odin spent on the Tree of Life. It was also the number of gods that survived Ragnarok.

"The nine. Tell me about them."

"They think they're so special. Just because they get to do the rites. But we're the ones who do all the work."

Fern might have laughed. If he was part of a cult of some kind, perhaps an offshoot of the old religion, it appeared that there was a degree of dissatisfaction amongst the ranks. A sudden thought occurred. If it *was* the old religion, a cult of Odin for instance, that could only mean one thing. *Sacrifice.*

"You don't want me to go to them, do you? You know what they will do to me."

He swallowed visibly, a haunted look in his eyes. "I obey. We all do. It's for the best. Really."

Before Fern had a chance to find out more about her fate, the cabin door opened and Silvi entered. She looked at them, her eyes narrowing, shrewdly assessing captive and captor alike. Fern tried to look confused and worried. It was not so hard.

"Okay," Silvi said. "It's time. Let's go."

Torsen approached Fern, pulling a folding knife from his pocket. Fern's heart raced and she eyed the blade warily. She almost sighed with relief when he sawed through the rope binding her to the chair.

"Get up. We have to go."

"Where? Where are we going?"

Silvi laughed, but neither would answer. Torsen gently gripped Fern's arm, pulling her to her feet. A push, and she was guided to the door. The sky was dark, the last of the pale afternoon light quickly disappearing. She stepped outside the cabin.

With hands still bound behind her back, running would not be an option. She was going to have to go with them. At least then she would get some answers. A small part of her wondered if it might be best not to know. From what she had deduced already, she was beginning to suspect things were much worse than she had feared.

"If you don't do everything we say," said the woman to Fern, "then I shall hurt you. No one said you had to be healthy, just alive. So let's go. We have a lot of walking to do."

She marched off, leaving Torsen to propel Fern forward. They started to make their way along a path created by the passage of many feet. Wherever they were going, it had been a popular destination. Maybe it still was?

No, not likely. Fern looked about herself, taking in the wilds of the mountain. It was a desolate location. No one in their right mind would put a cabin here. Not unless they wanted total isolation. She frowned and shook her head as she finally understood. Of course, that is exactly what they would want, a cult doing Goddess knows what.

She dug a finger into her back pocket and fished out one

of the charms she had made on the train, dropping it on the ground. Torsen did not notice. They walked ten more meters and she dropped another.

Fern dragged her feet, buying time. This made Silvi angry and Fern did not dare risk making her too mad. She sped up.

After fifteen or twenty minutes they came across a few parked cars on a natural flat area at the end of a gravel road. Something told her they did not belong to tourists and that the armed police officer was not there to give directions. Whatever Silvi and her chums were doing, they were clearly deeply entrenched with the establishment.

The policeman nodded to Silvi as they passed and continued the climb. Fern counted ten cars. Nine, plus the policeman's. Torsen's Nine.

Both her captors glanced from time to time to the mountain looming over them. They seemed to be looking for something. Fern scanned the slope and thought she caught a glimmer of light. Someone was up there.

They continued to climb, Torsen steadying Fern by the arm. When she stumbled, he strained to hold her. Good. The charm was still in effect. He did not want her to hurt herself. The corners of her mouth twitched in a slight smile. That would prove useful, and soon, if she did not miss her guess.

Of course, she wished Philip was with her. Not the most physical man, but he would throw himself in front of a train for her without a second thought. She tried once again to send her mind out, allowing herself to fall into a near trance state. But no matter how hard she strained to reach him, all she felt was a void. Nothing for it then, she thought. I'll have to get myself out of this mess.

The car continued to rocket forward at highly illegal speeds. They swerved, taking a corner fast enough that the back end started to drift but Jens compensated almost casually.

Entwhistle lay on the back seat with closed eyes, paralyzed by the violence of the images in his mind. At some abstract level he was aware of Arnulf talking to Jens in rapid Norwegian. He could hear instructions, directions. But his mind teemed with destruction and death. In the same way that Jinny had once given him Sir James' memories, now it was her own that flooded his mind.

It was overwhelming. Clearly it had all happened long ago. Nothing was familiar. He could not guess which continent, what people. There were round houses, with thatched roofs, dark-skinned people, in simple clothes. And there was death.

He saw a mud slide thundering down a mountain washing away village after village. In another a fire raged, sweeping through an inhabited forest. Everywhere people fled, only to meet their deaths. Death en masse, an unimaginable holocaust. Entwhistle moaned in horror, his hand clutching the arm rest as if to save himself.

Another memory formed. A large, heavily wooded valley, seen from far above, as if he were flying over it. Was this how Jinny saw the world? A string of villages lined a river meandering through a green valley. It was a lovely place. Hundreds of the round houses, many people, visible even from his great height. Then a noise like thunder, the snapping of thousands of trees and a wall of water engulfed the entire valley, rising ever higher. The water hit the first village, and it was gone, then the next, and the next. Within what seemed mere seconds he was looking down on a flood, thickly strewn with wreckage and bodies as far as the eye could see.

But when he was shown an electrical storm, the black, roiling clouds seemed wrong to him, like nothing in nature.

Nor the lightning that struck with thousands of deadly fingers, arcing between ground and the seething dark mass of cloud. Were they Jinny's feelings or his own? He could not be sure. But he could sense that the clouds contained a malevolence. There was something evil in them. Something that wanted to kill and kill and kill.

The images continued. A city leveled by an earthquake, a fleet of ships dashed to pieces. An unending parade of death and destruction.

And then a mountaintop. A small band of survivors. Men and women, their eyes blue. Fierce energies erupting from their hands, aimed at other men and women whose eyes were the same. The djinn were fighting each other.

You should know nothing of this.

Jinny's voice, reluctant, afraid.

None of your kind have known the truth since it happened. Our shame is eternal. We will not allow it to happen again.

What did it? Entwhistle thought. What happened?

There were those who were impatient to know your kind, to be one with you. Only a few were ever selected. I was one such. It was a great honor.

For a moment Entwhistle could see people dressed in flowing robes, date palms and tents. Intuitively he knew it was northern Africa.

There was one djinn who led them. This djinn was never known. But he had nine supporters and together they were strong enough to resist us, those who were chosen. We could not persuade, we could not compel.

These djinn did not want to be chosen, they wanted to possess, conquer. We would not allow it. When we fought the rebel djinn, the focus of my people was taken from our true enemy. The seraphim nearly destroyed us. We barely survived. For a very long time, we did not believe that any of your kind lived. Since then, my people have been vigilant against the angels. But it came at a cost. There are very few djinn that still continue the old ways. But I fear that there is, at least, one of these rebel djinn still alive. If it can once again open the barrier between our worlds, it would allow others to take hosts. If this happens there will be another war. And if the angels came again we would not be able to stop them.

What do I need to do?

There is nothing you can do. There are only certain periods when the seal can function, but one such time is close. If Mannuki gains the seal, it will allow others to enter this realm. I am doubtful that I am strong enough to stop Mannuki, yet we must try. You will need to give yourself to me. Otherwise, there is no hope.

Entwhistle considered what this meant. To be taken by the djinn: possessed. He did not like it. The experience in the hospital was entirely unnerving and the thought of doing it again was almost too much. Fear rose in his throat at the thought of being inside his own head, looking out, but unable to act, to move.

Before he could react to Jinny's proposition, Arnulf turned around to face Entwhistle.

"We're almost at Eikenes' cabin. I came here once, years ago. I remember the layout. They're gonna see us coming. Nothing we can do about that. So we come in fast. When the car stops, get out and . . . well, see what happens, I guess. Just don't stand still. Don't make yourself a target."

Entwhistle nodded, his stomach turning over. He had not considered that anyone might try to shoot him. But why not? If Fern really had been taken by Eikenes, maybe he was there. And according to Arnulf he was a crack shot with a pistol. Entwhistle's hand automatically reached for the talisman under his shirt, pulling it free. If ever there was a time he was grateful for Jinny, now was it.

He sensed amusement from the djinn? Almost shocked, Entwhistle directed a question to her.

Oh, so my getting shot is funny to you?

No, little man. But you cannot be harmed. Use the torq and the ring. They will protect you. They are wards. There were made to protect and they will stop almost any physical attack.

Entwhistle blinked in surprise. An enchanted ring? He almost laughed at the absurdity of it. But to hell with doubt. If Jinny said the items were magical, who was he to argue? He opened the satchel, pulling free the torc. It was heavy and beautiful. Looking at it, he could almost imagine it *was* magic. He slipped it on his arm, where it hung loosely, threatening to simply fall off. The ring was in his jacket pocket along with the handcuffs. He took the ring out, pushing it onto the middle finger of his right hand. Instantly there was a strange sensation on his wrist. The armband had tightened. Entwhistle pulled back his sleeve, shaking his hand. The great golden dragon would not move, even when he tugged at it.

The saga he had read on the train did not make any mention of this. Entwhistle stared at it in wonder. Would these things really protect him?

Whatever the case, Entwhistle had to admit that he suddenly felt a good deal bigger, stronger and more dangerous than he had before. The armband and ring were like a drug. He suddenly felt invincible.

He leaned forward, between the two front seats. In perfect Norwegian, he said. "When we get there, you two will stay behind me. I will deal with whatever we find."

Arnulf looked back in surprise, even Jens risked a glance. Neither man spoke. Whatever they saw in Entwhistle's face brooked no argument.

They did not have time to discuss it further. The car had been steadily working its way up a gravel road, and finally they could see a wooden cabin in the half-light of dusk. Jens drove towards it, and the blue Ford parked nearby.

As the car skidded to a halt, Entwhistle flung the door open and stepped out. He strode towards the cabin. He was aware of both Arnulf and Jens behind him. One hand raised itself. He could feel Jinny's will, commanding, directing. Energy erupted from the hand, instantly obliterating the wooden door. A few fragments of wood remained, hanging from the hinges.

Entwhistle crossed the threshold, hands held before him. He was ready for anything. But no attack came. The cabin was empty.

For a moment he was bemused. He was so sure that Fern would be here. He could sense her presence. He could *smell* her. There was a chair, and rope on the floor. So, she had been here, and very recently.

Jens and Arnulf barreled through the entrance. If either of them were surprised at how he had taken out the heavy wooden door, they did not say it.

Both the Norwegians were disappointed. This was the one place they knew of that Eikenes might use. Apart from this cabin, they had no other ideas. The blue car clearly indicated that this was the right place.

"Where is she?" Arnulf demanded, as he searched in the kitchen and a nearby bedroom.

Entwhistle shook his head. "I don't know." He grasped the talisman. It was no longer necessary to amplify his connection to the djinn, but it was his habit.

Can you feel her, Jinny?

No. Not her. But there are others. There is a place, not far with many conveyances.

Entwhistle was momentarily confused. Conveyances? Of course, she meant cars. It was their one remaining hope. He hurried through the door. Then he saw it on the ground, not too far away. A button, with a sprig of something green tied to it. Immediately he knew. *Fern.*

It had taken well over an hour of pushing and shoving to get Fern near their ultimate destination. The path was very dangerous in places, and good balance and nerves of steel were required, especially as it was almost dark now. Several times Torsen had stopped her from falling, as she was unable to use her arms for balance. But the more he touched her, the more his desire to protect her grew.

Fern had long ago dropped the last of the charms. Made for good luck and health, she hoped that by seeding them as he had, they would do her some good.

Silvi glanced back at her. She seemed to think Fern was up to something, but here, precariously edging along a strip of rock barely the width of her hand, there was nothing she would do, even if she could. Even so, the younger woman did not miss a chance to threaten.

"You cause any trouble, and maybe I'll give you a little nudge. The Master won't have to know. We've lost people before that way."

The drop was almost sheer at this point. Even with the sub-conscious orders in Torsen's mind, if Silvi decided to push her, there was nothing he could do to stop her from falling.

"I won't cause any trouble. I'm doing the best I can." The latter, at least, was true. Silvi seemed mollified. She enjoyed exercising power over the helpless woman. It was the only thing to raise a slight smile on her rather pinched lips.

Fern could now plainly make out a light, not too far above. They were almost there. All too soon they stood on a ledge, looking down over the valley. On one side was the mouth of a cave, the source of light she had seen. There were candles everywhere, illuminating the almost tunnel like entrance. Fern gasped. There was a palpable sense of evil to the place. Under normal circumstances she would never have gone near it, much less entered. The place reeked of death.

She looked over the ledge. Far below were the unmistakable outlines of the parked cars. She thought she could see people there. Some of the guests were late. Well, they wouldn't be getting up here any time soon. It was getting dark, and the path would be infinitely more dangerous.

Silvi gestured with her head for Fern to enter the cave. Torsen gave her a gentle push. She walked in, ducking slightly to avoid banging her head on the low entrance. Inside it was much bigger, the ceiling hidden in darkness. The candles provided enough light for Fern to see a series of wooden boxes, filled with street clothes, beside which stood many pairs of shoes. She counted them; nine pairs. They were all here all already. Then who were the late arrivals below?

Without another word, Torsen cut the rope binding her hands. She rubbed her wrists, raw from the chafing. At once Torsen pulled at her sweater, lifting it above her head.

"You gotta strip," he said. There was no hint of emotion in his voice. Silvi watched from the cave entrance, smirking.

"I'll do it," Fern said, pushing Torsen's hands away. She was not embarrassed in the least to be naked in front of strangers, and as long as they didn't touch her she would go along with it. She pulled her clothes off without a word. Now naked, they were about to lead her further into the cave when Silvi grabbed Fern's hand, lifting it chest high.

"You bitch," she said with venom, roughly ripping a ring from her finger. It was not a valuable thing, made of stainless steel. But Fern knew all too well that it was enough to disrupt a spell. The fact that Silvi also knew this said a great deal. Silvi tossed the ring aside, and it pinged off a rock before spinning away into darkness. She turned on her partner.

"No metal. Are you stupid, Torsen?"

For once the young woman's hate was directed at someone other than Fern. Torsen seemed to whither under Silvi's glare.

"Sorry. I didn't see it."

Fern bowed her head, allowing her shoulders to slump, looking for all the world like a woman who was beaten, who accepted her fate. It was enough to calm Silvi, who now seemed to be waiting for something. Fern wondered what. Minutes later, she knew. The sound of voices chanting strange words echoed from within. She froze as she recognized the language. It was the same her father had spoken under the curse.

Now she began to shiver, openly, from fear. She realized exactly what they wanted of her, and it scared her to her soul. Silvi saw the transformation and laughed, delighted that the slender, beautiful woman who had been so calm was now terrified. The chanting continued, getting louder. It seemed to be building to a crescendo. Fern understood only too well that when it finished, most likely so was she.

She reached out with her senses. Under the general reek of evil, of great malevolence and great magic, there was something more. Something not human.

Then you may bear the cost
12

Amongst the righteous were those that were not;
we were divided in our ways.
— *sūrat l-jin, Qur'an*

They ran fast, pounding along the rough path, Philip leading. Jens and Arnulf struggled as the Englishman kept up a punishing pace. They were not as sure footed in the murky twilight, as the ground was a uniform gray, comprised of loose stone and shale and they could not see well in the near dark.

It was not long before they came to a number of parked cars arrayed randomly on an open flat space. One of them was a police cruiser. Jens nodded to it, his face florid as he caught his breath.

"I see it," Entwhistle said. "It's not just Silvi Eikenes acting alone, that's for sure."

"Yeah. Makes no difference," Jens replied, breathing hard.

They made their way towards the vehicles. Immediately a figure emerged from the shadows.

"You can't be here. This is private land. I'm going to have to ask you to move on."

A police officer, dark blue uniform and leather jacket strode towards them, hand hovering over a holstered pistol.

"Hey, I know you," said Jens. "You were a year ahead of me at the Academy. "Lunde, right? Roland Lunde?"

The officer smiled briefly in response, then his eyes

narrowed, fingers twitching nervously. "Yeah, that's right. I've seen you around. What's your name?" Then his eyes widened in recognition. He took a step back, hand scrabbling for his weapon.

Entwhistle stepped forward, one hand raised. Instantly, the officer froze, gasping for air, mouth opening and closing like a fish out of water.

If Entwhistle had not thought about it before, now he did. The will was Jinny's, the power hers too. And yet it seemed as if they acted in concert. He was not a passenger in his own mind. They had, for a moment, become one.

He closed in on the hapless officer. "Where is she?"

If the man could breathe, perhaps he would speak. Entwhistle relaxed his hold and the man sagged to the ground. He glared up at them with hate filled eyes.

"Dead. She'll be dead by now. So fuck you."

Behind him Arnulf moaned, but Entwhistle was not convinced. She was close enough that he could feel her energy and she was very much alive.

"I don't think so. Where did Silvi take her?"

The man's eyes darted up towards the mountain. It was just a momentary lapse but it was not missed. Entwhistle turned and examined the great peak. Was that a light?

The policeman realized he had given something away; he went for his gun. There was an ear splitting bang and the man was flung back, a gaping hole in his chest from a shotgun blast. Entwhistle looked away.

Arnulf cracked opened the breech, removed the two spent shells, pocketed them and reloaded. He looked up at the mountain to the same place where Entwhistle had seen a light.

"We better get started. That's going to be one hell of a climb."

Both he and Jens started towards the trail that was just visible in the half-light.

"No. It will take too long. If Fern is up there, we can't

waste time with climbing. I'm sorry, Jens, Arnulf. I cannot take you with me."

Entwhistle closed his eyes.

We need to go there, to the light, Jinny. We need to go now.

The chanting stopped, the final echoes fading away. Silvi tensed, as if fearing Fern might try to make a run for it. But there was nowhere to go. Her only hope was Torsen. Fern carefully held his gaze, her will reinforcing the command to protect her. She only had a moment more to bind him.

Two men emerged from the depths of the cave, wearing robes and sandals. Fern almost laughed. Did they think they were in the Hellfire Club? Dilettantes, playing with Devil worship?

Her obvious contempt for the men confused them. One of them stopped in consternation, but the other, a forty-something man with blond hair grabbed her arm roughly, giving her a shake.

"So, you think we're a joke, do you?"

"Yes. As a matter of fact, I do." She smiled as she looked him in the eye.

"Well, you're not going to like the punch-line," he replied, leering at her naked form.

She ignored his gaze as it traversed her body. "It doesn't matter what you imagine you're doing, you're wrong. Your master's a fraud."

Now the blond man laughed. "Oh no. Whatever you might think you know, I promise, you don't. The Master is very much the real deal."

"Papa, I think she might be a witch," Silvi said.

"Is that so?" he replied. "Well, well, well. The Master will be pleased."

The other man grabbed her by the arm, effectively penning her in between them. The blond man turned to Silvi. "You did well. Now both of you get back down the mountain. We have work to do."

Silvi's face fell, but with a glance at her father she stiffened and nodded. Then she turned to Fern and looked her up and down, grinning almost lasciviously. "Bye bye sweetie pie, time to kiss your ass goodbye." And with a peal of laughter she was gone.

Torsen looked confused and stood looking from the cave entrance to Fern. The two men propelled her into a passage. At one point it was so narrow they had to release her, pushing her forward then quickly catching up and grabbing an arm each. She sensed their desire to be seen presenting their prize. Finally they entered another, bigger cavern. Much bigger. She tried to maintain her calm but was overcome by a terrible sense of dread. Death was far from the worst thing that could happen to her here. Corporeal death was not the end of life. Just its transformation. So she had always believed. But here and now, there was no question in her mind that the creature they called the Master would do far more than merely kill her. She gathered her will. If she was going to die, she would do her best to return the favor.

There were shadowed figures in the cavern. The many candles did little to dispel the dark. It seemed concentrated here, the essence of darkness.

A man turned. Was this the Master? He was smaller than she expected. Dark-skinned and short, he was clearly not a native of Norway.

He smiled at her, raking her with his eyes. It was not her nudity that pleased him. She knew he could sense power in her, far more easily than she could in him. He would relish killing her, taking her essence. Her soul.

"So, you are the djinn."

He blinked in surprise. Then his mouth opened in a wide, leering smile. "You know more than you should, little woman." He slowly turned his head to one side, regarding her, reading her. Then he licked his lips.

"Bring the witch."

She was pushed forward. Two more people, one a woman, stepped from the shadows, positioning themselves by her.

Behind the small man with the scarred face was a great slab of ice. It reeked of evil, as did the djinn. Awful things had happened here. Abominable things. And now they were going to happen to her. Fern's heart beat harder, faster. She willed herself to calm.

Rough hands pulled her swiftly to the ice, forcing her onto her back. Her arms were pulled straight, legs forced open. For a moment she thought they intended to rape her. She took a deep breath. The brutal attack did not come, but the sting of the ice on her naked skin burned and she writhed, trying to free herself. There was no escape.

Mannuki raised his hands above her. Men and women emerged from the shadows, silent observers to the rite of sacrifice. She knew now, full well, what was intended. But she was not defenseless. Not yet.

"Here is the scion of those that oppose us. Here is one whose family has caused us harm. But we avenge ourselves. We will taste her blood and rejoice. When our enemies are gone, we will recover the seal, then we will be triumphant and the gods will be with us again."

A glittering knife appeared in his hand and he moved purposely towards Fern.

"Torsen!" Her voice was a shriek. A command. Obey. A moment of confusion amongst her captors, then the figure of her former guard cannoned into the djinn, knocking him to the ground. There was a gasp from the others and hands reached out to stop him. Two men leapt forward to help.

Mannuki sprang to his feet, a snarl on his lips.

"No," he ordered. "Leave him to me."

Torsen lay sprawled on the floor. He looked confused. Then, as if by invisible strings, he was pulled to his feet. He struggled, trying to move. Mannuki reached out a hand and slashed at the air. Torsten's throat opened, blood erupting in a great, pulsing arc. The djinn had not touched him.

Torsen collapsed to the floor. "Not worthy," Mannuki said. He turned back to Fern where she was still held on the altar of ice. "You obviously have some understanding, little one. But it will not be enough to save you."

He had dropped the blade, but now it flew to his hand, a glint of dark light reflecting from it. He turned it slowly, showing Fern death in its shiny surface.

"This is Soul Eater. For a millennium it has consumed those we sacrificed to Odin. Now it will consume you too."

He stepped forward, the blade poised above her throat. "We offer this life . . ." His head snapped up, eyes opening wide. Fern turned her head in time to see what was causing the men and women in the dark robes to scream and yell. Philip.

Entwhistle felt a rush of power course through his veins. Jinny's strength was incredible. He felt like a god! Either Jinny was infusing him or she was unlocking his body's resources. He wanted to run, to jump. He quivered with energy, with anticipation. His fingers twitched and once again he felt sparks darting from them.

He felt as if he could fly up the mountainside. Arnulf and Jens watched him closely. Arnulf's mouth was moving. He was speaking but Entwhistle did not hear. He centered on himself, internalized his mind to a degree that the outside world was now little more than a shadow.

I can feel Mannuki. He is close.

Can you take me to him?

You are strong now, stronger than any man living. And yet you are nothing to him. The wards you wear will not protect you for long.

Fern is there?

Yes.

Is she . . . is she alive?

I can feel her life force. She yet lives.

Then take me to her.

I believe it will mean your death, little man. And mine too.

Entwhistle could have wept with frustration. He stared up at the mountain. It was too far to climb. It would take far too long. There had to be another way. He focused on the faint light, high on the mountain, willing himself to be there. He felt a momentary surge of panic from Jinny, then with a sudden lurch he was standing on a ledge, looking down on the valley.

Entwhistle staggered, disoriented. He reached out a hand and grasped cold rock, steadying himself. He took a deep breath. He had moved by thought alone. How was that possible? Jinny's power. He had not considered that it could be his to wield. His eyes widened as he understood the implications. They were a team! They were equal. This was shocking. But there was no time to consider all that it meant.

Entwhistle turned and strode into the cavern, past many candles. There on the floor, Fern's sweater. He bent to pick it up, hardly noticing when it flew to his hand before he could reach it. Anger and fear poured from him, waves of energy. They would be his sword and his shield.

In the back of his mind was the memory of the helpless rage that had encompassed Sir James when Tajeddigt was killed. He had been only a little older than Entwhistle when his young wife was taken from him. Entwhistle had experienced his memories, tasting the bitter vitriol of his mentor's emotions. It had left him in a killing rage at the time, but that was nothing to how he felt now. He would tear the world apart before he let anyone harm Fern.

Suddenly Fern's voice rang out from somewhere in the cave, "Torsen!" Ahead of him a shadow moved as a man raced into a narrow passage. Entwhistle dropped the sweater and followed.

He traversed the narrow passage and entered a large cavern. He registered people in dark robes, but his eyes went straight to Fern. She was naked, held down by four hooded figures on a block of ice that glowed with a blue light. He snarled, his rage visceral, coming from a place more primitive than intellect. Torsen ran at a smaller figure, bowling him over. The djinn! He could sense the creature, feel its vast power. He watched as the djinn ripped open Torsen's throat with a motion of his fingers. Then the scar-faced man with bright blue eyes turned to Fern, something black and glittering in his hand. The djinn was speaking, but Entwhistle did not hear. He simply moved, allowing Jinny to guide him.

Time seemed to slow as Entwhistle weaved through the acolytes. Once before he had felt Jinny's influence in a conflict, and once again he became analytical, emotions completely suppressed. All that was left was logic and the objective. Free Fern and escape.

Without conscious volition, he kicked out a foot, catching one man on the side of the knee. The hooded figure collapsed, falling forward, a cry escaping his throat. Entwhistle moved past him, turning, one arm lashing out to catch another man in the face, fist crushing bone and cartilage. Like a scythe, he moved amongst the robed figures, cutting them down like so much wheat, getting closer to Fern. And Mannuki.

The djinn moved too, faster than the others. Entwhistle launched himself forward, lunging for the hand that held the blade. Fern's eyes opened wide as she saw him. Entwhistle could sense resolution in her and an unbending will.

He had become one with Jinny. She gave him speed and strength that seemed preternatural, inhuman. His hand reached out and grasped the arm that held the knife. Mannuki fought him, but Entwhistle pushed the arm back. He would not let the blade touch Fern. No matter what happened, he would save her. He would not fail again.

The four acolytes holding Fern wavered in indecision. He could see the question in their minds. Obey their master, or move against the intruder?

Free will accounts for most human decisions. One of the men holding Fern's arm pulled back, letting her go. He reached for Entwhistle. Mistake. Fern's hand instantly described an intricate pattern in the air as she formed a charm, the arcane shapes spun by her nimble fingers triggering the intent in her mind. Flames erupted on the four acolytes, witch-fire, burning their robes, blackening their skin. Instantly they became living torches, as the light from their writhing bodies blazed bright. Hidden corners of the cavern were revealed and a stack of grinning skulls stared back at Entwhistle in wide eyed horror, made more macabre by shadows from the dancing flames.

The acolytes screamed as they ran into others, setting them alight too. The fire seemed a living thing, leaping from one to another. One woman, hair burning, ran shrieking towards the mouth of the cave. Her voice trailed off, growing fainter; she had gone straight over the edge.

Entwhistle watched the djinn with deadly intent, but from the corner of his eye he could see Fern roll off the altar of ice, falling to the ground in a crouch. She looked up at the djinn and her eyes opened wide, the pupils huge, black. Her fingers extended like claws as she reached towards the creature with hand and will.

Entwhistle moved closer to Mannuki, wary of his strength and speed. He could hear Fern breathing, sense her life force. She was strong, powerful. She would help him. Together they were strong enough.

Jinny's influence gave him startling powers of perception. He could sense things so completely, it was overwhelming. He could feel Fern absorbing energy from the air, the rocks, from the universe itself. She placed one hand on the slab of ice, and sigils that till now had been hidden blazed into view, glowing brightly as she drew from their stored energy.

Fern pointed and blue sparks spat from her fingers and a ball of energy formed on her palm. Mannuki's face went almost comically slack in surprise. Entwhistle took the opportunity. He lunged, reaching for the knife in the creature's hand.

But that was his undoing. Mannuki turned, unbelievably fast, pulling Entwhistle before him, using him as a shield. Fern cursed, then moved, creeping closer to the djinn, trailing one hand along the slab of ice, until she reached its end. She pointed and the ball of blue lightning flew. Entwhistle pulled away, but Mannuki dodged and the deadly energy missed. He pushed Entwhistle sprawling to the floor. Then the djinn turned, running from the cave with a curious gait, favoring his right leg.

Fern unleashed the energy she had pulled from the slab of ice, pouring it from her hand, directing it at the fleeing creature. One of the acolytes, a blond man, robes now only smoldering, stepped inadvertently into its path. He was obliterated, his body coming apart, blasted by the intense release of energy.

Philip staggered up, then grabbed her, pulling her off her feet in a bear hug.

"I've got you," he said. "I've got you."

There was a mad scramble as the remaining acolytes fled the cave. Entwhistle smiled at Fern and kissed her fiercely on the lips. The killing rage was gone. He had her. He had won. He pulled her tight until she began to struggle.

"I can't breathe, Philip."

"Oh, sorry." He released her, letting her down, but still holding an arm protectively around her. He could feel everything she felt. He could feel her fear, her anger. Her love. It almost made him weep. He marveled at the sensation of her emotions. But he could sense something else too. An instinct, a need. There was still a job to do.

"It's not over," she said. "I have to stop him."

Entwhistle shook his head. "No. This is not your task."

She looked like she wanted to argue, then she nodded. Without another word, he turned and ran towards the cave entrance.

Mannuki ran from the cave, scrambling up a narrow path leading higher up the mountain. His limp did not seem to slow him. Entwhistle followed, struggling to keep up, trying to keep him in sight in the near dark, but the smaller man scaled the steep path with incredible speed. Fit as he was, Entwhistle's muscles screamed in protest. He was falling behind.

Then a surge of adrenaline flooded his body and he felt renewed, stronger than ever in his life. He pushed himself, running faster, effortlessly. In his mind, he flashed a question at Jinny.

Did you do this?

It is your body. You have resources. I released them.

With the knowledge came an understanding that he would pay for having used them. But that would be later. Right now he had to stop the djinn escaping.

Mannuki disappeared above him, scrambling up the mountainside like one intimately familiar with it. Moments later, Entwhistle climbed up onto a wide ledge. Mannuki was waiting, a sneer on his dark face. There was an almost sheer drop below them, at least a hundred and fifty feet to jagged rock. High above, a steep valley ended in a wall of snow, hanging in defiance of gravity, held in place by weight and cold.

Entwhistle sucked in air, chest heaving. He forced himself to inhale deeply, mentally willing his heart to slow its furious pounding. All those times Fern had tried to teach him how to meditate, how to control his own body, suddenly made sense to him. His heart rate returned to normal.

"It's over!" Entwhistle shouted above the wind. "You don't have the right. There is no place for you here."

The sneer turned to a broad smile and Mannuki laughed.

"You amuse me, little man." He marched on Entwhistle, coming to a stop mere inches from him. He leaned in close, his deeply blue eyes boring into Entwhistle's.

"I am the first and the last of my kind. I am the Omega. I will be supreme and my vision will prevail. You are nothing to me. An insect. Your kind are fit only to be used. And to die."

He stepped back and raised a hand. An intense heat punched Entwhistle in the chest. It centered on the talisman hanging around his neck, hidden under his shirt. Once again, Sir James' gift saved him from a curse, the talisman becoming cold, channeling malignant energy, dispersing it. Mannuki lowered his arm, face thoughtful.

"You are more resourceful than I had expected, little man. But you cannot stop me. I have other safe holds and others to do my bidding. When the time comes, I will break the seal and the nine shall return."

He turned to flee. In desperation, Entwhistle flung himself at the djinn, grabbing him around the chest, locking his fingers together. Mannuki flung his head back, smashing Entwhistle in the face then shrugged him off as if he were not there. Entwhistle staggered back, eyes watering. The djinn was stronger, he was faster. There was nothing he could do. If Mannuki wished, he could toss Entwhistle off the mountain ledge and that would be that.

Entwhistle shook his head, wiping his eyes to clear his vision. Undeterred, his hand slipped into his jacket pocket and he advanced again. Mannuki gave him a look that seemed to hold a fleeting admiration. Then the djinn's fist lanced towards Entwhistle's face. But Entwhistle moved his head slightly and the fist that would have pulverized bone went past his ear. At the same time, he pivoted, grabbing Mannuki's arm. His hands slid down to the djinn's wrist, and in seconds he had snapped on the handcuffs. Before Mannuki could react, he had shackled himself to the smaller man.

Mannuki laughed in surprise. "You wish to stop me? You bind me with iron?" Then his smile turned predatory. "All you have done is made it easier for me to kill you." And with that the djinn possessed human launched a series of blows at Entwhistle, striking him in the chest, the stomach, the ribs. The sound of cracking bones could be heard over Entwhistle's moans.

Jinny desperately tried to heal him, the shimmer of her energy flowing over Entwhistle's body, but Mannuki kept attacking until Entwhistle was driven to his knees, blood flowing from nose and ears, his breathing ragged and lips flecked with foamy blood from ruptured lungs.

"You are dying. Give me the key to these bindings and I will let you die in peace."

Jinny continued to heal Entwhistle, using her strength to repair his damaged flesh. Entwhistle could feel his body becoming hale. He staggered to his feet, one hand gripping the djinn's arm for support.

"No. It ends now. You have to be stopped."

Mannuki laughed again. "Very well. Let us see if you can stop this!"

The creature turned to face the wall of snow high above them. He opened his mouth and an inhuman shriek emerged. It rose to a howling crescendo, higher and louder, the sound of a thousand souls crying out for release. The pain in Entwhistle's head was beyond bearing, the sound seemed to go through him, shredding him. He clapped his hands over his ears, almost doubling over, dragging Mannuki's arm with him.

Then it stopped.

Mannuki turned to Entwhistle, a triumphant sneer on his face. Entwhistle returned his gaze without flinching and for the first time looked deep into his enemy's eyes. Was there something there, something in the deep blue? Philip had a distinct impression that someone else was looking back at him. Realization hit. A man, some poor wretch Mannuki had taken and subdued. He was still there, or at least a part of him was. A silent witness to millennia after millennia of atrocities. Entwhistle was resolved. It could not be allowed.

"It ends now, djinn."

"We do not end, human."

"No. You are wrong. This body you are wearing. It is very old. It wants to die. And I am going to make sure it does. You are not welcome in my world, djinn. And without your vessel, you will be nothing."

A sudden rumble alerted Entwhistle and he turned to see the wall of snow high up on the mountain slip. As if in slow motion, it began to move, slowly collapsing, sliding. And with a noise like a thousand thunders the avalanche began, flowing down the narrow valley towards them.

Mannuki looked gleeful. "We have perhaps thirty seconds to reach safety. Release me of this iron and we can both live. If you do not, then you will die in this place."

Entwhistle did not move. He watched the wall of moving snow advance, a huge white boiling cloud. He pulled the djinn closer.

Suddenly alarmed, Mannuki pulled back, but the handcuffs held him fast. "Do you not understand? We will die if we remain. We can live, if we run. Separate us and we live!"

"I understand," said Entwhistle, his voice level. "I don't think you do."

Mannuki struggled. He pummeled at Entwhistle with fists like stone. Entwhistle defended himself by crowding in closer, hugging his attacker. The wards, the ring and armband seemed to absorb some of the energy of the djinn's ferocious attack, but not all, and once again Entwhistle felt bones crack and break. Mannuki's face was wild with rage, then terror. He produced the same black blade that he had attempted to use on Fern. Entwhistle understood intuitively. The djinn would cut his way free. Desperately, Entwhistle held onto the knife hand, trying to stop it from plunging into his flesh. They struggled, but the djinn's strength was greater, and he forced the Englishman to turn, to face the thundering wall of white. Already a wave of light snow was flowing around their ankles. It thickened and swelled, sweeping them off their feet to the very edge of the precipice. Mannuki wrenched his arm free of Entwhistle's grasp and raised it, ready to stab. At that instant his eyes changed, losing their fierce blue, becoming brown. For just a moment Entwhistle could see someone else; a man determined to help end his living nightmare.

Then the roiling cloud of white enveloped them and they were gone.

The council of Odin had scattered. Only three made it to the base of the mountain. As Fern dressed and hastily pulled on her boots she could just make them out, fleeing like panicked sheep. As she watched, one shoved past another, pushing him off balance. Hands flailing in the air, he tottered briefly on the brink of the narrow path, over-balanced and plunged hundreds of meters to his death. Even in the fading light she could see another body far below. Her lips pursed in contempt, the scar blanching. She turned away.

Now she closed her eyes, reaching out with her mind, visualizing the mountain, the valley, snow and ice. An impression came to her. Philip was this way. She turned to the northeast and began the laborious climb up the mountainside.

He was fighting, she could sense his pain. She cried out in frustrated anguish, trying to go faster, desperate to reach him, to help.

Then she heard it, the unmistakable low frequency rumble felt in the gut as much as heard. Native born, at home in mountains and snow, she knew the meaning of thunder in a cloudless sky. She hurled herself down the slope, sliding and rolling to the safety of the ledge, reaching the cave mouth seconds before a wall of snow flowed past, entombing her. Then, as quickly as it had begun, it was over.

Immediately she went to work, frantically tearing at the white wall. It was almost translucent, glowing blue-white, which told her it was not too deep. In only moments, she saw the early evening sky. Evidently the avalanche was almost spent by the time it had reached the cave. But what about above?

Fern emerged, wriggling through the hole she had dug, hands red and raw from the sharp crystal ice. She climbed to her feet and looked around. Everything was different. The crags and crevices were now smooth, a continuous snow slope. It shone in the light of the pale moon, hanging low on the horizon, a glittering expanse of pristine white, snow dust still settling like powdered sugar on a great confection. Fern turned slowly, trying to get a sense of Philip.

Minutes before, she had felt his struggle as he fought with the djinn. Now there was nothing. She tried to suppress the lurch in her heart, a foreboding of unbearable loss. Not yet, she thought. Find him.

Somewhere above. She started to climb, plunging up to her knees with every step. She knew he did not have long. If he had been buried, she had only minutes to locate him and dig him out. She pumped her legs, an exhausting high stepping progress through the deep snow.

Philip was up there, alive. She could feel him. But it was taking too long! She came to a place where the snow was almost level. A gentle slope led away, upwards, always upwards. She spread her hands, her fingers divining rods, seeking the essence of the man she loved. She spoke the words of a spell and the familiar smell of ozone enveloped her briefly. It drifted west and she followed it, slowly marching across the gray-white landscape.

The helicopter announced its presence long before she could see it, powerful search beams probing the ground. One of the council members must have called for help. She wondered why. Of course, trying to save their master. She did not know or care. They were here and they could help her now.

The helicopter came straight towards her. She ignored it, putting her energy into finding Philip. It did not risk landing, hovering a few feet above the ground, disgorging four red-suited figures who leapt from its side. Then the craft flew away and Fern put it out of her mind.

The SARs team spread out, probing the snow with long poles. One headed for Fern but she continued to stride across the field of white, reaching out with her senses.

There! She could feel him. He was close, and, impossibly it seemed, still alive. Or was it merely a remnant of his departed life force? No! No! She knelt in the snow, hands pressed down against the surface. There was something here. She started to dig, scrabbling desperately, the tiny sharp crystals wearing her fingers bloody. Now the snow was streaked with pink but she pressed on, already arm deep, thrusting her hands into the cold expanse, heaving aside armfuls of snow. How long had he been buried? At least twenty minutes. Too long for a man to live. But still, she dug.

The red-suited SARs team member finally caught up with her and immediately set to work with a small shovel.

"Someone here?" he asked, breathing hard.

"I don't know. Yes."

"How can you be sure?"

"Just dig," she cried. "Dig!"

The SARs man worked with her, digging at a rate that would have astonished her had she not been so worried. She stopped. They both saw it at the same time. A shoe.

The man turned and shouted and another came running, a woman, ploughing her way through the deep snow in an ungainly but effective gait. She dropped a box with a red cross on its side and she joined them, the three working furiously. Soon they were tugging at the legs. There was no movement, no indication of life. In a few minutes more, they had the body on the surface. He was ice cold, face alabaster. It was Philip, in his hand Mannuki's obsidian dagger.

Fern suppressed an urge to scream. She stared at his face, his blue lips. Within seconds the woman had a respirator mask on Entwhistle's face. She squeezed the pump, forcing air into his lungs. Then her partner pounded his chest, focusing his body weight on overlapping hands. He pumped ten times and stopped for another burst from the respirator. Again and again they went through the cycle.

Entwhistle did not react. He did not gasp and sit up the way they do in the movies.

"Don't you dare, Philip. Don't you dare leave me." She punched him. On the arm, the thigh, tears forming in her eyes. "You cannot leave me like this. Not like this . . . please."

The two SARS team members stood back, helpless. They would leave her to her grief. The brief survival window was closed. If there were others they would turn up in the spring. This year, or maybe next year. Or in a thousand years. There was no telling.

Fern moaned, then turned her face up to the sky, eyes wide. "GODDESS!"

She said words that were forbidden. Words that would invoke, invite possession. She was not strong enough to save him on her own.

She chanted the invocation, but nothing happened. In desperation she clawed at her face, nails digging deep. The wounds did not bleed, she was too cold. But her hands left bloody streaks on her face and her tongue tasted harsh copper. Then there was a smell like lightning on a summer's eve and she went rigid, back arched, hands turned to claws, as if a million volts poured through her.

The two SARs team members stepped back, unsure what was happening, a little frightened. Fern rose to her feet, ascending, as if pulled from above. Black super-dilated eyes regarded the man and woman in red. She stared at them for a moment before dismissing them, turning back to the body. The volunteers looked at each other and took off down the slope.

Kneeling, Fern placed one hand on Entwhistle's chest and the other on his head. A pulse of energy surged through her and his body bowed from head to heel, then collapsed, motionless.

Fern's eyes cleared, returning to their normal gray-blue and she fell onto Entwhistle's body, exhausted, unable to move.

She lay there for a moment, gasping, eyes screwed tight. What she had done could have killed her. But there was no future if he was not in it. She dared not look. As long as she lay there, eyes closed, he was neither alive nor dead and she could put off the dreadful moment of truth. Then she felt a hand stroke her head, gently caressing and she sat up. Philip was looking at her, a crooked smile on his blue tinged lips. The emotions that filled her then totally overwhelmed her. Gratitude, joy, relief and anger. She slapped him hard across the face. He blinked in surprise, then blinked again as his eyes watered. Instantly she felt a world of remorse and flung herself upon him.

"I thought you'd left me. I couldn't bear it."

Philip's chest heaved as he breathed deeply. "I'm okay."

Fern kissed him then, long and hard. He wrapped his arms around her. She noticed the handcuff, dangling from his arm, the deadly blade still in his hand.

"What's this?"

"Ah, well. I had to stop our friend escaping."

"He got away?"

"No. I caught him. He was buried with me. We . . . we died together."

"Are you sure? Where is his body?"

"Gone, I think. It was old. Really old. I think it fell apart when the djinn was forced out."

"Good."

"Yes, it is. There was still someone in there. The poor soul whose body Mannuki took. He helped me. Just for a moment he regained control. The avalanche knocked us off our feet and as we fell . . . well, I stabbed him. Both our hands held the blade. He wanted to die. The body broke down. It was the djinn holding it together. Thousands of years catching up in an instant. The poor man."

Fern climbed to her feet, and helped Philip stand.

"I think when the body evaporated, it left me a little air pocket," he said.

The man and woman from Search and Rescue returned with survival blankets. They approached cautiously, as if afraid of Fern. Philip waved to them cheerfully, and they hurried over. They wrapped him in a blanket, all the while eying Fern as if she were a dangerous and unpredictable animal.

One of the rescue team nodded to her. "How long was he under?"

She shook her head, uncertain. "I'm not sure. Thirty minutes, maybe more?"

"It's amazing," he said, addressing Entwhistle. "By rights, you should be dead."

Entwhistle smiled grimly, then coughed. "Yes, I believe I was, just for a moment. Now I know what people mean when they say they feel like death warmed over."

The SARS man spoke into a handheld radio, and a moment later the helicopter could be heard returning.

Philip stumbled. He reached out a hand, and Fern put his arm around her shoulder, turning to press her body against his. He looked into her eyes and Fern gazed back. This time she did not mind that they were blue.

A few days later, and Entwhistle was finding the train to Oslo oddly like déjà vu. He half expected to see the same passengers. Once again he and Fern sat opposite each other across a small table, but this time there was no tension. Entwhistle doubted Fern would ever come to embrace Jinny but she seemed willing to tolerate the djinn and that was as much as he had hoped for.

The fight on the mountain had exhausted Jinny almost as much as the last time she had saved Entwhistle, and now she was quiet, not intruding at all. This might have been from necessity, or that Jinny was simply being circumspect, but either way, her absence came at an opportune moment, giving Fern and Philip the time to reconnect.

Philip looked across the aisle. A man, holding a newspaper caught his attention. The headline on the paper was similar to those he had seen for the last several days. MURDER CULT stood out, in bold black letters. Arnulf had captured Silvi Eikenes and two members of the council of Odin as they attempted to get to their cars. He was being touted as a national hero. Apparently there were many more people involved at various levels, and the trio he and Jens had apprehended were revealing a long history of murder, intimidation and worse.

The Aasheims had managed to keep Philip's role out of the official story and he had hidden at the farmhouse while Jens and Arnulf were interviewed by the police. Fern claimed to remember nothing of the entire incident, and she escaped close scrutiny. It was easy to believe she had been traumatized by the events. And after all, the cave was more than evidence enough. Already several bodies had been discovered and identified as missing tourists and there was evidence that something had been going on for hundreds of years.

Philip shook his head in wonder. Mannuki wanted to break down the barriers between the dimensions and allow other djinn to possess human hosts. The nine of the inner council would have become the first victims, but there would have been more. Many more. What this would have meant for humanity did not bear thinking about. But according to Jinny, another civil war amongst the djinn would destroy them.

An hour on the train and they were at the airport. They had not pre-booked a flight as there was every chance that Philip would be on a no fly list, and the last thing he wanted was another visit from the Norwegian Police. So with some trepidation he approached the ticket sales desk. The attendant clucked and gave every indication that late tickets were, if not impossible to get, then at least supremely unlikely. Entwhistle was impressed that even sitting, the attendant still somehow managed to look down her nose at him.

"Sorry. There's nothing until tomorrow evening. We have two on the last flight to Heathrow. They're not together, but at least you'd be on the same flight. Shall I book them?"

"Really? Nothing else?"

The attendant sniffed. "Unless you want first class of course. We have a flight leaving in an hour with seats available in first class."

"That will be fine," Philip said hurriedly, afraid they would go if they delayed another second.

"They're very expensive," she replied. Her tone left no doubt that the disheveled pair in front of her were not suited for first class travel. Entwhistle noticed Fern's eyes narrowing, saw the tension in her shoulders. Having now seen what she was capable of when angered, he hastily produced a credit card.

"Whatever it costs will be fine, thanks." He passed over a black card with silver lettering. The airline attendant's eyes widened slightly as she took the card, holding it carefully as if it were precious. She clearly recognized that it offered the cardholder almost unlimited credit as her immediate response was positively servile, her lips curling into an unaccustomed smile.

"Thank you sir. My apologies for the delay, this will just take a moment. I'll need both your passports too, please."

She passed Fern's passport under a scanner, then Philip's. A beep made her glance down, then she looked up at Philip, a far less genuine smile on her face. "I'll just need to check with my supervisor that we can accept this," she said, brandishing the credit card.

Fern leaned over the counter, her eyes boring into the check-in woman's. "It's fine. The passports are fine. Please issue the tickets."

Was that a hint of ozone in the air? Entwhistle could not be sure, but whatever nervousness had suddenly plagued the woman instantly disappeared and she processed their purchase quickly.

"Please, make yourselves comfortable in our Golden Elite lounge. I will have your boarding passes brought to you."

"What was that?" Entwhistle asked as they walked towards the lounge.

"I think she was about to alert the authorities," Fern replied. "We can't have that."

"No. What did you do?"

"Nothing much. I just gave her the impression that everything was in order. Simple, really."

They approached security and were waved in together. Entwhistle had left Mannuki's evil black blade with Jens. Neither he nor Fern wanted it. Somehow they sensed that it belonged to him, more than any other, and he agreed to safeguard it. But as they were going through security, the X-ray machine that scanned their luggage picked up the lead plate, raising a momentary stir of interest. Entwhistle launched into a long and complicated explanation on the history of language and how the plate might possibly fit into the language tree.

"In fact," he continued, "the comparison with Elamite script suggests . . ."

"Yeah, right, thanks very much," interrupted the guard. "Next."

"Wow," said Fern, as they passed through. "You have a new superpower."

Entwhistle grinned. "What? Boring people to death?"

Laughing, she linked her arm through his as they strolled along the moving walkway to their gate.

"No, not boring. Never that."

Entwhistle would gladly have paid anything to ensure that Fern or her family were safe, but now the danger was over he was shocked and mildly ashamed at how much he had spent in the last few days. Rappaport had emailed him a breakdown of the expenses. It came to just over twice his yearly salary.

Almost as shameful though was the fact that the income from Sir James' estate would cover those costs in only three months. Entwhistle was not sure what was worse. That he had spent so much so quickly, or that it did not appear to matter. He consoled himself with the thought that since he had been the djinn's guardian he had been murdered by a witch, then suffocated on a mountain, so perhaps it was not completely excessive.

On the plane, a flight attendant showed them to their seats and handed them an embossed menu of food and refreshments that would not have been out of place in a Sloane Square restaurant. Entwhistle smiled, and Fern laughed like a schoolgirl as she settled into the expanse of the leather seat.

"I feel like we're on our honeymoon," she said.

Entwhistle did not reply but he squeezed her hand. As always the satchel with Jinny's meta-anchor was slung over one shoulder, and he moved it onto his lap.

"I'll never be able to thank you enough for saving my father's life."

He shook his head. "There's no need. You would have done the same for me."

"Yes, I would. But you did something that no one else in the world could have done, and I am grateful. We all are."

Jens had gotten more than a little drunk the night before they left and in between declarations of eternal friendship, he had admitted how terrified he was at the prospect of losing his father, not least because it would have meant the end of his own dreams.

"They approve of you," Fern said.

"Your parents?"

"Yes. And Jens. They think you're a good influence and will straighten me out."

Entwhistle could not help laughing at that. If there was anyone being influenced in the relationship, it was him.

"Well, I'm glad they like me. They're wonderful people, and I'm happy to know them. In fact," he looked at her levelly, "I want to be part of your family Fern. Do you think that is possible?"

"You know you are! Even if I wasn't . . ." She stopped in mid-sentence.

"Champagne, sir? Madam?"

The stewardess had returned, with two glasses on a tray. Entwhistle smiled and reached for them.

"Yes, thank you."

He passed one to Fern, but she shook her head.

"Not for me." She looked down at her lap, a slight blush coloring her cheeks.

Entwhistle was not used to seeing her embarrassed. Then his stomach lurched at what he sensed was coming. "Wait, what were you saying? Even if you weren't what?"

She looked at him, biting her bottom lip. "Pregnant."

Jens Eriksen came out of the elevator and approached the front desk. The receptionist stared at him blankly.

"I got a message. Something about a parcel?" he said.

"Oh, yes. Special delivery," the receptionist replied, nodding to a man dressed in tight fitting thermal clothing, wearing a baseball cap that read 24/7.

"Are you Jens Eriksen?" asked the courier.

"Yes."

"Sign here." The courier proffered a small pad and pen, and Jens dutifully signed his name. He gave back the pen, receiving a small square box in its place. It was heavy. He had not been expecting anything.

"What is it?"

The courier shook his head. "I don't know. Have a good day."

Jens turned back to the receptionist. "Do you have a pair of scissors, or something, there? Anything sharp."

She passed a pair of scissors to the archeologist and he used them to slit open the box, cutting neatly through the tape. He opened the box carefully. It was full of little white Styrofoam peanuts. He slid his hand in, grasped something and pulled.

The exquisite arm band Arnulf Aasheim had found came into view. Eriksen marveled at the intricate detail. A snake, or dragon, biting its own tail. He smiled.

"Oh my. Just as I remember." He fished again in the box and found the ring. It was the first time he had seen them together. They seemed to glow in the muted light of the ground floor reception area.

"Pretty," said the receptionist. "For your wife?"

Eriksen laughed in delight. "No, I don't think so. These are a little too valuable for any one person."

With a shake of his head in silent admonishment at Entwhistle for entrusting the precious artifacts with a courier, Eriksen made his way back to his office. But at least the dapper Englishman had kept his word. He had promised to return them.

Jens peered at them closely as he rode the elevator. No signs of any damage or scratches. Now they would have to be assessed and valued. Aasheim would need to be compensated. And the national museum was about to get an extraordinary new exhibit. It was a good day! Then he remembered the lead plate. Where was the plate? He would have to email Entwhistle. He hoped it had not been lost.

The plane landed fifteen minutes ahead of schedule. The flight had been relaxing and Fern and Philip were in the best of spirits. Philip could not stop smiling, or touching Fern, holding her hand, stealing a kiss. When the doors finally opened, he grabbed Fern's small backpack and the pair left the plane, thanking the stewards on the way out. They strolled, arms linked, riding innumerable moving walkways until they finally emerged at baggage claim. Since they had no baggage to wait for and nothing to declare, they headed straight for the green zone.

Halfway there they were intercepted by two men. At first, Entwhistle assumed they were customs officers. He made to walk by but was stopped by an upraised hand. Suddenly a knot of tension gripped his stomach.

"Excuse, me sir, but if you could come this way please. You too miss."

The men each grabbed one of Entwhistle's arms and propelled him through an open door into a nearby office.

"What on earth . . ." Entwhistle began. His protestations died in his throat. Standing in the office were a man and woman entirely too familiar.

"Philip Entwhistle," Detective Hanlon began, "I must caution you that you do not have to say anything but anything you do say may be used in evidence against you."

"Really? Are we going to do this again?" Entwhistle said in exasperation.

Detective Hanlon unsuccessfully tried to suppress a

smile as she produced a pair of handcuffs.

"Yes, Mr. Entwhistle. We are."

Detective Topley spun him around, pulling the strap of his satchel over his head, and then, far more gently than Entwhistle would have given him credit for, pulled Entwhistle's hands behind his back. Hanlon snapped the cuffs on.

"I apologize for the handcuffs," she said, "but you are a proven flight risk."

Fern caught his eye. She raised an eyebrow, glancing down at the cuffs. Entwhistle shook his head. No, it would not be doing him any favors to escape from the police a second time. He had already pushed his luck as far as it would go. Better to let the lawyers handle things now.

"Fern?"

"Yes, Philip?"

"Be so good as to call Rappaport. I suspect this is the sort of thing he enjoys dealing with."

She nodded, then looked at the overweight detective gripping Entwhistle's arm with one hand, his satchel in the other.

"Am I under arrest too?"

Topley shook his head. "Uh, no miss. Just your, uh, that is, . . . just Mr. Entwhistle."

"Then I shall need a ride home. You can arrange that, I hope?"

Topley looked at Hanlon. She shrugged. "Well, to be fair, we're about to raid the place, so I suppose I can have a squad car take you. So long as you wait outside while we search the premises."

Philip blinked in surprise. "Search my house? Why?"

Hanlon smiled broadly, showing perfect teeth, then her eyes narrowed and the smile dropped. "Because we have reason to believe that you are in possession of an artifact relevant to our investigations. A clay bowl?" She eyed him carefully. "Ring any bells."

Entwhistle sighed. "No need to go to the trouble of a raid, for goodness sake. It's there."

He nodded to the satchel in Topley's ham of a fist. The detective opened the bag, and rummaged. He pulled out the bowl and held it up triumphantly, its cracked and weathered surface revealed.

"Well, well. What do we have here then?" the large man said, chuckling.

Philip's heart leapt. If he should drop it! "Please be careful with that, Detective. It is incredibly old and valuable."

"Don't worry," said Hanlon. "We don't want anything to happen to it either." She smirked, as if at a private joke.

Topley passed Hanlon the bowl. She pulled a plastic evidence bag out of her pocket and carefully slipped the bowl inside.

"Do you mind if I have our hand luggage back?" Fern said, pointing to the satchel the large detective still held. He looked to Hanlon, waiting for a decision. She glanced up and shrugged.

"Sure. Why not? Give her the bag, Topley."

Fern took the satchel and pulled the strap over her head. With both hands now free, Topley pushed Entwhistle towards the exit. They went through, following a windowless corridor, Fern and Hanlon following. They exited through another door into a secluded part of the airport, away from the crowds.

"We have a car waiting for you," Topley said. "To take you to your new accommodation as a guest of her Majesty."

"What?" Entwhistle said. "Where are we going?"

Hanlon broke in, openly laughing. "You're going to prison, Mr. Entwhistle. You're under arrest for the murder of Elizabeth Sandwell!"

ABOUT THE AUTHOR

MJ Kobernus is an Anglo/American living and working in Norway. He is the founder of Nordland Publishing. He loves his work as an editor and publisher and hopes to continue doing that for many years. He also works in the Environmental arena, doing unspeakable things to bits and bytes.

MJ drives a vintage motorcycle, plays a vintage guitar and has a love of 70s rock music. You can find out more about him on his personal blog, Metaphysical Geometry.

http://metaphysicalgeometry.blogspot.no/

Blood in the Snow is his second novel of the Guardian series. Look out for the next book, Blood in the Fire.

NORDLAND PUBLISHING

Follow the North Road.

nordlandpublishing.com
facebook.com/nordlandpublishing
nordlandpublishing.tumblr.com

NORDLAND
www.nordlandpublishing.com

www.ingramcontent.com/pod-product-compliance
Lightning Source LLC
Chambersburg PA
CBHW031547240626
47153CB00002B/418